The Gingerbread House

R.M. Whitaker

Paper Elephant Publishing, LLC
Oregon

Published by Paper Elephant Publishing, LLC
paperelephantpublishing.com

Copy edits by Will Tyler.

For Patrick, my eternal love story.
And for Bonnie, our darling miracle.

Prologue
The Snow Ball

December 2004

I WORE GLITTER IN my hair that night, gold with little white flecks. It almost looked like snowflakes when I turned my head just right—an exciting illusion in Roanoke, Oregon, where it almost never snowed.

"You're going to make the best memories," my older sister Tiffany said with bobby pins pinched between her lips.

I eyed the picture taped to her bedroom mirror from a disposable camera, of Tiffany and her friends laughing as they danced with fold-up chairs at the 2002 Roanoke Snow Ball. Girls had outnumbered boys two to one that year, the story went, and Tiffany had refused to be a wallflower. She'd swept a chair onto the dance floor, and her friends still talked about how funny it was to watch her dance with such confidence.

"Just don't take anything too seriously," Tiffany said, "and you'll have a blast."

"I'm not nervous," I assured her. After years of watching through the stair banisters while my older siblings took pictures in the entryway before leaving for their respective Snow Balls, I was beyond ready for this night. Finally, it was my turn.

I'd spent months scouring every thrift store from Portland to Lincoln City in search of the perfect vintage formal dress. Vintage, because that was my thing back then. I'd finally found the perfect one—a fifties number in ice blue that would have made Audrey Hepburn proud—but it had been too tight around what Tiffany called my "womanly bosoms."

Is anything more embarrassing than being fourteen years old with a C-cup?

I bought the dress anyway. A few alterations and a fresh overlay of sparkly transparent fabric later, and I was wearing the dress of my dreams, the ice-blue color complimenting the red in my brown hair. I felt like an old-time Hollywood princess.

My heart gave an anxious flutter as I wondered what Benson Miller would think when he saw me tonight.

"What are you smiling about?" Tiffany pinched my arm playfully. "A boy?"

Busted. Heat rose to my cheeks as I giggled and squirmed away from her prying fingers. "I'm just so happy you're here," I said, evading the question.

It wasn't a lie. Tiffany had surprised us all by coming home a week early from Corvallis, where she was attending Oregon State University. It was a relief to have her do my hair and give me a ride to the dance instead of Mom. Not that Mom was embarrassing or anything, but Tiffany was cool, and she knew how to make my baby-fine brown hair look like it had some serious volume. Somehow, she'd transformed my shoulder-length locks into a complicated updo of twists and curls that added several inches of height to my short stature.

"Uh-huh," said Tiffany, unconvinced. "Sure. Who is he? Do I know him?"

I pursed my lips, avoiding her eyes in the mirror.

"Come on," Tiffany coaxed, nudging me with her elbow. "Richie Jones?"

I snorted. "Richie's a Backstreet Boy wannabe. *So* not my type."

"You don't still have a thing for Fran Miller's little brother, do you? Benny-Bun?"

I grimaced at the old nickname for Benson. "No one calls him that anymore."

"Ah, so it *is* Benson."

In the mirror, I saw my cheeks go red.

"Aw," Tiffany sighed. "That's sweet. He's a cutie-pie. Fran always said Benson had the hots for you." She waggled her eyebrows at my reflection.

My stomach did a little flip, but I looked down at my French-tipped nails in my lap. Benson and I had liked each other since we were kids, but we'd always been too shy to get close. And he wasn't that chubby kid who Tiffany remembered anymore. Over the last year, he'd shot up and thinned out. Other girls were noticing him now, and I feared he was going to notice them, too. Tonight was my chance to find out if he still liked me or if he'd moved on.

"I hope he asks me to dance" was all I said.

"If he doesn't, it's his loss. Cover your eyes."

I didn't register Tiffany's warning until she'd already begun showering me with hairspray. Coughing, I threw my hands over my face.

Tiffany completed my look with a thick swab of frosty lip gloss, and we headed out to the entryway, where my parents were waiting to see my transformation.

My mom snapped pictures like the paparazzi as I made my way down the stairs. I tried to ignore the sinking feeling in the pit of my stomach from the idea of Benson not asking me to dance. This was the night I'd been waiting for my whole life. Finally, I wasn't watching from the upstairs banisters. I was the one posing in the entryway for pictures.

Dad said I looked like Elizabeth Taylor. Mom handed me a silver clutch that matched the silver heels of my clear plastic shoes. She let me borrow Great-Grandma Dale's white fur coat with my word that I would take good care of it.

Even my brother, Luke, paused on his way from the kitchen back to his den with an armful of snacks to whistle and say, "Don't twist your ankle," before disappearing again.

Tiffany was still in her sweats and an oversized T-shirt, hair in a messy bun, when she grabbed the car keys and said, "Let's get you to the ball, Cinderella!" She slipped on a pair of Dad's big sandals over her fluffy socks and dashed to the car without a coat.

She was so cool.

I burrowed farther into the warmth of Great-Grandma's fur coat as I followed her, careful to avoid any icy patches on the driveway.

Christmas music played on the radio as we drove to the old Morley Mansion in the woods. I tried to imagine what it would be like to dance with Benson in the Victorian-era ballroom. Should I try to sit by him during dinner? Would he try to sit by me?

In the more heavily wooded part of Roanoke, where the houses were older and more spread out, all the streets were named after various composers and their most beloved compositions. A thrill went through me when we reached the Tchaikovsky streets, passing Sleeping Beauty Lane and Swan Lake Drive, before finally turning onto Nutcracker Circle.

As we pulled up the long, horseshoe driveway, the sight of the Morley Mansion nearly took my breath away. It was missing some shingles on the turret, and its butter yellow paint was peeling, but with the abundance of Christmas decor, it looked like it belonged inside a snow globe. The windows glowed with cozy, soft light from inside. White fluff lined the roofline like snow, filtering the twinkle of golden string lights. An aged banner draped over the entryway read *Roanoke Snow Ball* in silver sequins, with a golden *2004* banner just below. The sight of it sent a thrill of nervous excitement through me.

"I swear, they've been using the same banner since the 1950s," Tiffany said from the driver's seat. "Same decorations, too." She leaned over the steering wheel to take in the old nativity set on the lawn before shifting into Park to give my hair a final once-over.

"Everything feel solid?" she asked.

I touched my hair. The curls were crispy with hairspray. "I think so."

"You sure? Give it a good shake. Trust me, you're gonna wanna dance once you get in there."

I shook my head from side to side.

Tiffany blew raspberries. "What was that? *Grandma* dances with more enthusiasm. I said you're gonna wanna *dance!*" She turned up the radio and started head-banging to Mariah Carey's "All I Want for Christmas Is You."

Laughing, I shimmied my shoulders along with her.

It wasn't enough. Tiffany grabbed my hand and used my fist as a microphone as she belted off-key, "Oooh, bay-bay!"

Her bun fell apart as she continued her wild dancing. "Come on, AJ," she screamed into my microphone hand, "show me your moves!"

I gave in. Glitter rained onto my ice-blue dress as I followed my sister's head-banging example and sang along with her.

"That's more like it," Tiffany laughed. Mariah Carey's voice faded into John Erickson announcing "Portland's nonstop Christmas station, K103," and headlights flashed as another car pulled up behind us for a drop-off.

One curl slid loose from my updo. "See?" Tiffany said as she resecured it with a bobby pin. "I knew there was a weak one in there. Now you're all set. Go knock 'em dead, kid." She gave me a cheesy wink with a thumbs-up.

I shook my head, still laughing, as I opened my car door. "Thanks for doing my hair, Tiff."

"My pleasure. Have fun, okay? Pick you up at ten?"

"Okay." I closed the door.

As I turned and made my way up the porch steps, I heard Tiffany roll down the passenger side window. "You look hot, AJ Banner!" she yelled before driving away.

Hopefully Benson would think so. With an audible gulp, I climbed the stairs and stepped into the foyer.

Music welcomed me in the entryway. Warmth brushed my cheeks. Paper snowflakes and glistening Christmas trees adorned the front hall.

My two best friends were already there at the ticket table receiving their dinner cards. Christy Weineggar looked like a vintage punk fairy princess in a knee-length poufy dress of black-and-white lace with black fishnet tights and her signature black Converse sneakers all marked up with Sharpie checkers and stars. Her dyed black hair was in a classic romantic updo that somehow complemented the spiked choker around her neck in a way that only Christy could pull off. Beside her, Aisha Tan was a stark contrast in a floor-length lavender sheath dress with spaghetti straps and slits on either side that went above her knees. Her black hair was down and crimped with tiny jewels throughout. Aisha waved excitedly when she saw me, and my nerves evaporated into thin air.

"No way," Aisha gushed as she looked me up and down. "That dress is fetching perfect for you!"

Christy spun around to see and her jaw dropped dramatically. "Dang, AJ! It fits you like a fetchin' glove! Benson is gonna poop his pants when he sees you."

"Shh!" I flapped my hands to silence her, looking over my shoulder to make sure no one heard. I loved Christy for being so outspoken, but sometimes it was mortifying.

"Oh, he can't hear me," Christy snorted, jerking a thumb toward the entryway to the ballroom behind her. "He's already inside."

"He's here?" My heart gave a nervous pitter-patter.

"He was in front of us in line," said Aisha. "You should have just ridden with us."

I tried to ignore the sudden pang of disappointment. The night was young. There would be other opportunities. I exchanged my ticket for a dinner card with instructions to place it on the table once I'd chosen a seat for dinner. My hands fumbled with sudden urgency as I accepted the card. Benson was in there right now choosing his seat.

"Where should we sit?" I asked Christy and Aisha as we handed our coats to another volunteer at the coat closet and received ticket stubs in return.

"Sky said he'd save us some seats," said Aisha.

Christy groaned. "Oh great, are we gonna have to watch you two making googly eyes at each other all through dinner?"

Aisha and Skylar Townsend were a new thing, but the three of us had been friends with Sky for a long time before that.

"Oh please," Aisha retorted. "We do *not* make googly eyes at each other."

"You totally do," I said absently, pulling at my dress as we neared the ballroom.

I actually thought Sky and Aisha were cute together. They weren't all over each other like some couples. But it was still more fun to be grossed out by them.

"This is AJ's first dance," Christy said. "You don't want to make her sick right from the start."

I ignored the twisting sensation in my chest at Christy's reminder that I was the newbie here. She and Aisha were both a year and a half older than me. It had been painful hearing them talk about the Snow Ball the last two years when I couldn't go with them. But that didn't matter now. I was here, and Benson was here, and we needed to get in there before all the dinner seats were taken.

As we crossed the threshold into the ballroom, fake snow drifted to the floor from a silver arbor, landed in our hair, and stuck to the sparkles on my dress. I blinked as my eyes adjusted to the low light. Sheer white drapes lined the walls, with twinkly lights shining through them. Sparkling snowflakes hung from the ceiling at various heights. They caught the light from old-fashioned lampposts and lanterns scattered throughout the room. Beside the open dance floor, a silver sleigh stood piled high with fake presents wrapped in white, gold, and silver paper. My gaze swept beyond the dance floor to the cluster of dinner tables in search of Benson.

It wasn't hard to spot him. Five years of puppy love had trained my eyes to pick him out in a crowd. I knew his thick brown hair and the way his head bowed to avoid attention, the quiet sound of his laugh, the deepening tone of his voice. He was already sitting at a table. Our eyes met across the room for a split second before we both looked away quickly with the familiar pretense of just casually looking around.

He'd been waiting for me. Tingles spread from my toes up to the crown of my head.

"Hey, earth to AJ!"

I blinked as Christy waved a hand in front of my face. "What?"

"Want me to invite him to sit with us?"

"Who?"

Christy raised her eyebrows in her *Are you serious?* way.

A flashback of Christy yelling "AJ loves you, Benson!" across the parking lot after school last year filled me with dread. "No!" I sputtered, throwing out a hand to stop her. "No, please don't!"

"Why not?" Christy asked.

"You'll embarrass him."

"I will not!"

"Sky could do it," Aisha offered quickly.

As if on cue, a familiar voice spoke up behind me. "I could do what?"

I spun and found myself facing a lavender tie that matched Aisha's dress perfectly. Skylar Townsend shook fake snow from his spiked sandy hair. He wore a white collar shirt with the sleeves rolled up to the elbows. I'd complimented his forearms once, and it had definitely gone to his head.

"Make Benson sit with us," Christy commanded.

"No, don't," I said just as quickly.

Sky looked back over his shoulder toward the tables. "I don't know. He looks pretty happy to be with his friends."

"He is," I agreed. The realization struck me that Benson probably wouldn't feel comfortable sitting with us. He was my age, a freshman. Christy and Aisha were both juniors, and Sky and his friends were seniors. I still felt weird around them sometimes myself. Not around Sky—he was too much like a brother to feel intimidating. But Benson's older brother Daniel hung out with Sky's friends, and to them, Benson might just be that chubby little "Benny-Bun" that Tiffany thought of.

"Whatever," said Christy. "You and Benson are too shy for your own good."

She didn't understand, I thought as we sat at our own table. Christy didn't know Benson like I did. He was old-fashioned, like me, and ours was a slow-burn romance. Over Christy's shoulder, I could see where Benson sat with his friends. Occasionally, his eyes wandered to me and then away again quickly. I pursed my lips to keep from smiling. What we had was pure and innocent—nothing like Christy's thrill-seeking flings.

Dinner was turkey and mashed potatoes with gravy and cranberry sauce. Tommy Pippin, one of Sky's friends, said it was probably leftovers from the Thanksgiving meal for the homeless that the local church had served a few weeks ago. I laughed with the others but refused to let his snarky comments ruin the magic of this night for me. I enjoyed my fancy formal dinner, with Benson and me sneaking peeks at each other across the room when we thought the other wasn't looking.

When the dance music started, I was the first one out of my seat. Christy grabbed my hand, and we jumped onto the dance floor to sing along with the All-American Rejects' "Swing, Swing."

Aisha tried to get Sky to join us, but he waved her off with a laugh and leaned back in his chair to watch as she jumped along with Christy and me.

I glanced back at Benson. He was still sitting at his table, talking with his friends. He stayed there for the next two songs as well, but I could feel his eyes on me as I laughed and tried different dance moves with Christy and Aisha.

Then a slow song came on. "The Lady in Red" brought Sky onto the floor to ask Aisha to dance. Christy, as usual, was snatched up quickly by some guy who'd probably had his eye on her from the moment she walked in.

I moved toward the wall, where some other girls in my year stood together awkwardly.

"I like your dress, AJ," said Andrea Rodriguez. She wore a plain skirt and tank top herself.

Beside her, I felt a little embarrassed for having fussed so much over my dress. "Thanks," I said. "You look pretty, too." I leaned my back against the wall and looked out at the dancing couples. Benson was still sitting with his friends. I turned to face Andrea and the other girls. "Is it weird that we're just standing here?"

"I don't know!" a girl named Jessica gushed, as if I'd just read her mind. "What are we supposed to do? Like, I wanna dance, but it's a slow song, and the guys are all just sitting there like ducks." There was laughter in her voice, but she shrank as she spoke, as if fearing that her words might be treasonous in such a setting.

The other girls giggled in agreement. "I mean, I guess we could just, like, do an interpretive-style dance," said one girl I didn't know well. She waved her arms in a dramatic demonstration.

"I got a better idea," I said with a smile. Excitement rose in my stomach as I grabbed one of the fold-up chairs from along the wall, folded it shut, fluffed the tulle bow that decorated it, and then led it to the dance floor in a dramatic sweep.

Behind me, the other girls snickered. At just the right moment, I whipped my head back to face them, pressing my face against the cool metal of the chair as I sang along with Chris de Burgh about dancing cheek to cheek.

The girls burst out laughing. Two of them grabbed chairs of their own. Soon there were five of us swaying on the dance floor with our chairs, laughing and twirling. When the song ended, we put the chairs back and jumped into "The Middle" by Jimmy Eat World.

"That was some fancy dancing there, AJ," Aisha laughed.

"You are so funny!" said another girl I didn't even know.

I'd hardly finished saying thank you before a junior guy pointed at me with both hands and said, "Chair Girl, you rock!"

My cheeks were sore from smiling. Was this how Tiffany felt all the time?

I looked back to see if Benson was watching. He was.

Please, I thought. *Please ask me to dance next time.* That was the only thing that could make tonight more perfect than it already was.

When the next slow song came on and the other girls and I found ourselves standing along the wall again, we took up our chairs gladly, with every intention of dancing the night away. Most of us did, anyway. Andrea said she needed to catch her breath. She leaned against the wall to watch us and laughed at our fancy moves.

This time, some boys interrupted our performance by asking the other girls to dance. One by one, the girls around me set their chairs aside and joined the other swaying couples on the floor. Before I knew it, I was the only one left dancing with my chair.

Then I saw him.

Benson rose from his table. With his head bowed in that adorable shy way of his, feet shuffling, he made his way toward me.

I held my breath.

My hands gripped the sides of the chair. My heart beat so loudly I thought my ears would burst. I spun with my chair so he wouldn't know that I'd seen him coming.

Coming. Benson. Coming for *me*. What would he say? What would I say? I'd imagined this moment so many times, yet I felt so unprepared. I knew it was silly. We'd known each other since we were little, but we'd never been alone before, just the two of us talking, holding hands, swaying to music.

Come on, AJ, I told myself. *Breathe! Get it together.*

From the corner of my eye, I saw the shape of him getting closer, sidestepping other dancers. With my heart in my throat, ears ringing, palms sweating, I bit my lip to keep my smile from splitting my face in two. This was it. I had my back to him, chair hugged against my chest. He cleared his throat. I waited on bated breath for the tap of his finger on my shoulder.

But then he passed me, so close that our arms almost brushed. He didn't stop or look at me. He kept right on going.

Had he lost his nerve?

My steps faltered for a moment as I watched him walk to the edge of the dance floor, right to where Andrea stood leaning against the wall. He said something to her. She smiled. They turned together, walked onto the floor, and began dancing.

My mouth went dry. I looked away.

The ringing in my ears continued, now sounding less like bells and more like a teakettle that someone had forgotten to take off the stove. I hugged my chair more tightly and continued to twirl. Because I was having fun, wasn't I? This was fun, dancing with a chair, making people laugh. I forced a smile and bent back dramatically as if the chair partner were dipping me. I wanted to dance with a chair, I told myself. I didn't care if anyone asked me to dance ever. I was here to have a good time. This was the dance I'd been looking forward to my whole life.

"May I cut in?"

I sprang up from my dip and found Sky standing there with a friendly lopsided grin, his hand outstretched.

My chest went tight. If I danced with him, it would look like he had saved me, like I'd only been dancing with a chair because I was desperate, because no one else wanted to dance with me. That wasn't why I was dancing with a chair, I told myself. It was because I *wanted* to, gosh darn it. This was my dream.

"No, no," I laughed, my voice higher than normal. "Go dance with Aisha! We're having a grand ol' time, Harvey and me." I hugged the chair against my face to make my cheek smoosh.

Sky chuckled, but didn't withdraw his hand. "Come on, AJ. I think Harvey's had you to himself long enough."

"No, really, we're having fun! Look, Aisha's waiting for you."

"Aisha said she doesn't want to dance right now. I'm sure she'd love to keep Harvey company—"

He moved to take the chair.

In a moment of panic, I twirled out of his reach. "Don't take Harvey away!"

Sky's hands went up in surrender. The humor faltered in his eyes, replaced by the last look I wanted to see—pity.

I wished I could disappear. Why did he have to do this? He was making me look pathetic. Why couldn't he just let me be the funny girl?

Skylar recovered more quickly than I. His lopsided grin returned. "You really gonna turn me down like that? That's cold, woman. Losing to a chair—how will I ever live that down?"

He was offering me a way out, making himself the one to be pitied instead of me. I felt sick with embarrassment, but I surrendered. "Well," I said, "I guess it does sound pretty bad when you put it that way..."

Sky reached for the chair again. This time, I let him take it.

"Thanks, Harvey," Sky said as he shook the chair open and left it sitting alone. "I'll bring her back in one piece." He winked as he took my hand. He spun me once and then placed his other hand on my waist, and we began dancing.

It was my first time dancing with a boy like this. I'd always thought my first time would be with Benson.

"Hey," Sky said, as if reading my thoughts, "he's a chump. Don't waste your time on him."

My throat felt thick. "You don't know him."

"I think I know him better than you do."

I rolled my eyes. "Being friends with his older brother doesn't make you an expert on him. He's sweet. He probably saw that Andrea was all alone. I'm glad he asked her to dance."

Sky pursed his lips as if he wanted to say something, but decided against it.

"What?" I asked.

He shook his head. "Nothing. Hey, this is your first dance, isn't it? You having a good time?"

My shoulders relaxed with the change of subject. "It's amazing! They really go all out on this thing. I still can't believe that snow machine when you walk in."

He laughed. "I'm glad someone liked it. Christy's been complaining all night about how the fake snowflakes won't come out of her hair." He lowered his voice. "Don't tell her it was my idea."

"The snow was your idea?"

"Well, I can't take all the credit. You know, my mom's been helping with this thing for years. They used to have a bubble machine at the door, but I kind of—uh—mighta dropped it when I was helping them set up."

I laughed at his guilty grimace. "Oh, snap."

"Yeah. If you look at the floor near the entryway, you'll see it's a lot cleaner than the rest of the room. Soapy water *everywhere*. It was like, Bubble Armageddon, I'm telling you."

My laughter went from a polite snicker to a full-bellied gush. Sky's eyes danced the way they always did when he made people laugh. "What did you do?" I asked.

"You mean after I turned the floor into a skating rink? I got the mop from the janitor's closet—"

"No, I mean about the machine! Was it broken?"

"Oh, that. Yeah, it was busted pretty good. The thing was old anyway. I said I'd replace it, but then Bea Carston said I should see if I could find something better. The snow machine was my idea, but my dad helped me design it."

"Wait." I pulled back to see if he was serious. "You *built* that thing?"

He scrunched his nose and waved it off. "It's not as impressive as it sounds. When you look closely, you can see how simple the design is. It could use some improvements. But it gets the job done."

The song changed then to "Mr. Roboto" by Styx. We stepped away from each other as, all around us, people seemed to transform into dancing robots.

"Thanks for the dance." Sky motioned toward the lone chair we'd left standing near the edge of the floor. "Shall I...return you to Harvey?"

My stomach gave an uncomfortable churn as my embarrassment a few minutes ago came flooding back. "I wasn't trying to beg for a dance, you know," I explained. "I really was just having fun."

"I know." Sky smiled reassuringly. "And I really did just want to snag a dance."

Behind Sky, I caught sight of Benson. Andrea was thanking him for the dance. He nodded and his eyes flickered for the briefest moment in my direction before he turned and went back to sit with his friends.

Sky looked over his shoulder, following my gaze.

I avoided his eyes when they returned to my face, desperate to avoid another pitying glance. Andrea was coming over anyway. I moved to meet her.

"AJ," Sky said.

I looked back at him.

"You look great tonight. That dress is—" He pantomimed perfection with pursed lips and a pinched okay sign. "Have fun, okay? This is your night."

I managed a smile. "Thanks, Sky."

He nodded, smiled, and went back to Aisha.

I picked up the lone chair on the dance floor and returned it to its place along the wall, where Andrea stood fanning herself.

"Hey," I said, "I saw Benson ask you to dance. That's awesome."

"Yeah." She smiled but didn't quite meet my eye. "Yeah, it was nice."

I was itching to press her for more, but I'd made a fool of myself enough for one night already. Swallowing back the questions that burned on my tongue, I turned to rejoin Christy and Aisha.

"It's weird," Andrea said, drawing me back. She was looking down at her shoes. "I thought he was coming over to ask *you* to dance."

I swallowed, forced a laugh. "Really?"

She nodded. Her eyes came up to meet mine. "I mean, haven't you guys kind of liked each other, like, forever?"

Heat tickled my ears. "Well...yeah, I guess... But, I mean, he probably saw I was already dancing." I waved a hand in the chair's direction.

I expected her to laugh with me about that. After all, hadn't she been dancing with a chair, too?

Instead, she looked away, into the crowd of robo-dancers. "Yeah, he saw that." Something about the way she said it made me feel uneasy.

"Did he"—I paused—"think it was funny?"

Her eyes flitted to my face and then away again. She shifted her weight. "He said it seemed like a pretty pathetic way to get a guy to ask you to dance."

For a moment, the words didn't sink in. I stared, frozen in place. "He said that?"

Andrea nodded.

Suddenly, I felt dizzy.

A kid attempting to moonwalk like a robot bumped into me, and I teetered on my plastic heels.

"Oh dang, I'm sorry," he said.

"It's fine," I stumbled away to rejoin my friends.

"Ugh, I hate this song!" Christy yelled at me over the music. "Want to see if there's any leftover dessert in the kitchen?"

I shook my head. "My feet hurt."

"What?" she leaned in for me to speak louder.

"I said my feet hurt! I'm going to sit down." I staggered out of the ballroom.

My stomach turned as I emerged into the entryway, which was crowded with teenagers escaping the heat of the ballroom. One group argued with a chaperone who stood guard at the foot of the arched staircase to make sure no one went exploring.

"Come on, man," a kid with shaggy red hair said, "we just want to see what it looks like up there—"

"Where's the bathroom?" I interrupted him.

The chaperone pointed over his shoulder. "Down the hall to the left."

I passed them all in a daze, found a free chaise in the dark parlor, and took off my shoes. My feet were sweaty from the clear plastic and there were blisters forming in long thin lines where the straps had been chafing.

Andrea's words replayed through my head again and again.

He said it was a pretty pathetic way to get a guy to ask you to dance...

Had Benson really said that about me? The thought made me feel sick.

With sudden urgency, I left my shoes on the parlor floor and stumbled down the hall to the bathroom. The bathroom door was locked. Of course. Old house, old bathroom. There wouldn't be a row of stalls inside, just a single toilet. I leaned my head against the wall as I waited my turn, a sharp pain cramping my stomach.

A pretty pathetic way to get a guy to ask you to dance...

The sound of a toilet flushing followed by a rush of water from an old faucet made me straighten up. I paced in place until the door finally opened. A junior girl emerged with a groan, clutching her stomach. "Sorry," she said. "I don't think that turkey agreed with me."

At the word "turkey," I retched, pushed my way past the girl into the bathroom, and doubled over the toilet.

He said it seemed like a pretty pathetic way to get a guy to ask you to dance.

I vomited.

Sky's friend must have been right about the turkey being left over from Thanksgiving, because we all got food poisoning that night.

Once I got home, I slept on the bathroom floor. Each time I woke to expel the poisonous contents from my gut in bouts of twisting, painful agony, Andrea's words repeated in my skull like an alarm that won't turn off when you're half asleep.

A pretty pathetic way...

Pretty pathetic...

Pathetic...

1

Twelve Years Later

December 2016

"ON TO BIGGER THINGS, eh, Banner?"

On my hands and knees, I look up from the Hobs and Sanderson office floor to see my coworker Lucy leaning back in her desk chair to peer around the cubicle wall at me. A green sprinkle rests on her cheek from the Christmas cookies I brought to work as a farewell gesture.

"I guess so," I reply as I unplug my laptop charger from the socket under my desk. Standing, I wrap the cord into a coil before adding it to "the box."

My box is sadly bare compared to ones I've seen other employees carry out on their last day of work—employees who'd been working at Hobs and Sanderson for years. I've only been with the company for ten months, so my accumulation of personal items only includes a framed picture of my family, a potted succulent plant, and an assortment of Hobs and Sanderson merch I received in lieu of a Christmas bonus—miniature plush kitchen appliances and pens with the company logo and tagline, MAKING LIFE EASY SINCE 1946.

Staying here long term was never the plan. Hobs and Sanderson was the stepping stone I'd needed to get me to New York, even if it was just a marketing assistant position with a high turnover rate. High because lots of writers use Hobs and Sanderson as a stepping stone before moving on to jobs they actually want. There are still pushpins in the cubicle wall from the person who worked at this desk before me, and I suspect the supply of staplers, pens, paperclips, cough drops, and keychains in the desk drawer are a collection of left-behinds from others who came before them. I briefly wonder if leaving a knickknack behind is a good luck charm that will ensure I'll never come back.

"I'll be looking for your article in next month's edition," Lucy says as she waves the November issue of *Verité* magazine at me. The cover features Margot Robbie, bare-faced and bare-skinned from the shoulders up in the usual *Verité* format, with bold pink letters declaring, "Behind the Glam: Margot Robbie Unfiltered."

I straighten with a laugh, box on my hip. "If *Verité* is publishing articles from their junior editors in the New Year's edition, then their journalists must enjoy one long holiday vacation."

Lucy purses her lips and nods. "Right. I won't waste my money, then."

Ahmed speaks up from the other side of the cubicle wall, "Don't lie, Luce. We all know you've got a subscription."

Lucy's mouth pulls down to a guilty pout as she adds the magazine to her not-so-secret stash in her bottom desk drawer.

"I won't be starting with them until January, anyway," I say.

Ahmed stands up, his unshaven face visible over the wall. "What's your hurry, then? Stay another four weeks."

"I'm going home for the holidays."

He gives me his signature deadpan face. "For a month?"

"It's been a couple of years since I've been able to," I say, feeling the need to explain. "And who knows if I'll get much vacation time once

I'm at *Verité*? Thought it might be nice to spend some time with my family."

"They're in Idaho, right?" Lucy squints an eye, trying to remember.

"Oregon."

"That's a long flight," says Ahmed.

"Six hours nonstop."

"Gross," says Lucy. Then she sighs. "We'll miss you. Who's going to laugh at Ahmed's jokes when you're gone?"

"You laugh at my jokes," Ahmed says to her.

"No, that's just my cough. I get dry when the heater kicks on."

Ahmed rolls his eyes at Lucy before telling me, "When you get tired of all the fashion world drama, we'll have a place for you here."

A wave of nausea sweeps through me.

Lucy must have noticed, because she waves Ahmed's words aside. "Ah, I'm sure all that magazine drama is only in the movies. It's just a job. Don't make it a big thing."

I appreciate Lucy's encouragement, but the drama isn't what I'm afraid of. Ahmed has just voiced my worst fear: that things with the magazine won't pan out and I'll have to return to this desk with my tail between my legs.

Verité isn't just a job for me. It's my dream. It's why I moved all the way across the country. It's my reward for all the sleepless nights I spent trying to prove myself as a journalist. It's the ability to keep my apartment when the rent goes up next year.

Little colorful spots appear in my vision, and I force myself to take a breath. *It's okay*, I remind myself. *I don't need to worry about that until January.*

"Thanks, guys," I say to Lucy and Ahmed. "I'll keep in touch."

Before leaving the cubicle, I do a final scan to make sure I didn't miss anything. My eye lands on the drawer of left-behinds. I remove a tin of breath mints from my box and place it there before giving my cubicle neighbors a wave that feels like a strange salute. "Merry Christmas."

As I make my way down the rows of cubicles, bidding farewell to my other coworkers, I'm a little sad that I don't feel any sense of nostalgia over leaving this place. The people are great, and I'll miss Lucy and Ahmed's banter, but I haven't allowed myself to grow any roots here. Now, as I take the elevator to the first floor, the anticipation of leaving it all behind feels thrilling in the way that skipping school probably would have felt as a teenager, if I'd been that kind of teenager. Cold air hits my cheeks as I pass through the glass doors for the last time. Snowflakes land on my eyelashes. They drift over the contents of my box and melt into my deep purple scarf.

My Christmas vacation has officially begun.

I start toward the subway station on Lexington and Fifty-Third. It usually takes about twenty-five minutes to get to my apartment in Bushwick if I dodge the more touristy parts of the city, and I still have some last-minute packing to do before my early flight home in the morning. But as I wait at the crosswalk on Fifty-Second Street, I realize that this is the last time I'll make this commute.

White lights twinkle in the twiggy branches of the trees along the street. When the Walk sign lights up on my left, I make a split-second decision and cross Lexington, heading toward Fifth Avenue instead.

Snow compacts with a soft crunch under every footstep. Taking the scenic route home will add at least another fifteen minutes to my commute, but I don't care. Suddenly I want to soak in the sights and sounds of New York at Christmastime without thoughts of job applications and work projects.

Busy professionals weave around one another on the crowded side-walk. I'm still learning how to move in that confident, intentional way that seems to come so naturally to seasoned New Yorkers. With the box in my arms, I have to keep moving at a steady pace to avoid making myself a nuisance in this flow, but I still take in the sparkling holiday displays in the upscale shops around me as I go. I don't stop until I reach the Rockefeller Center with its giant lit tree.

Two years of working in Manhattan, and I still feel like I'm living in a movie sometimes. It's not as crowded here tonight as it will be in another week or so, when the swarms of holiday tourists come to feel like *they* have stepped into the movies.

My sister Tiffany wanted to come visit me last Christmas, and I prepared a tour for her, but then she felt guilty leaving her kids and her husband so close to Christmas, and they couldn't afford to bring everyone. I should have just taken the tour myself after that. Instead, I spent the week wallowing alone in my apartment feeling more home-sick than ever.

Now, standing in the glow of holiday lights, I watch skaters glide on the ice below and wonder why I still haven't gotten around to skating here myself.

There are so many things I haven't gotten around to doing here yet. I've been so busy trying to secure a job, it was easy to keep putting off the fun stuff.

What if this is my last Christmas in New York?

The thought comes unbidden and unwelcome. I try to shake it off, but the anxious itch I've been feeling below my skin for the past few weeks flares up all the more. Determined to shake the feeling, I find a free bench in the Channel Gardens across the street and dig a pen and notepad from my box. With the notepad propped on my knee and my pen at the ready, I take a deep breath and observe.

A white wire angel towers over me, glowing with golden lights. Other angels just like her line the garden, all blowing bronze trumpets toward the Rockefeller Center's holiday display. I hear the rush of water from the fountain behind me, smell the fragrant cinnamon and sugar on toasted nuts in paper cones carried by a family passing by, hear the live string quartet playing "Silent Night" above the ever-present drone of traffic and feet and voices and competing speakers blasting music or advertisements. I go to write these observations down, but the moment my pen touches paper, my mind goes blank.

What was that word I just used to describe the angels? That twiggy white stuff...?

It doesn't matter! Angels. There are angels.

I write the word, then stare at it. Pressure builds in my ears, muting all the surrounding sounds. My chest tightens. Spots freckle my vision.

With a gasp, I shoot to my feet, startling an old woman passing by, who clutches her purse as she scuttles away.

The tightness in my chest lingers, but I know it will subside once I get moving, so I toss my pen and notepad back into the box and keep walking toward Herald Square.

What is wrong with me? I've had writer's block before, but this is something different. This crippling anxiety that freezes my thoughts and takes my breath away is unlike anything I've ever experienced. It first came on after I got the offer letter from *Verité*, and it's steadily gotten worse.

On the subway, I watch the city go by in a blur. Some Christmas trees are visible in the windows of high-rise apartments, like little glowing tiles in a cityscape mosaic. I want to belong here—to be part of this. It's what I've worked for since graduating from the University of Colorado four years ago.

What if I can't get over this block before starting my job at *Verité*?

There's no draft on the subway, but I shiver.

By the time I make it back to my apartment, I'm cold and wet.

My roommate Jody and her boyfriend Devón break apart as I enter. I can tell from her tangled magenta hair and flushed face they were really going at it a second ago.

"Hey," I say into my box, head low to avoid eye contact as I sneak into my room.

My tiny room is just barely big enough to fit a bed and a desk, with all my clothes stored in fabric bins from IKEA under the bed. A desk was prioritized over a dresser because, well, that's why I'm in New York: to be a writer. But as I plop my damp box onto it and squeeze past, I can't bring myself to look at the desk. We haven't been on the best of terms lately, that slab of particle board and I. The waste basket underneath is packed to the brim with crumpled papers from failed attempts at "morning pages" and journal sessions that experts swear are supposed to help writers work their way out of a slump.

The walls around my bed are bare, aside from a calendar I got from Hobs and Sanderson when I was first hired. It's still on September, showing an autumn scene from a New England coastal town. I take it down and sit on my bed, flipping through the next few pages to look at the pictures I missed: pumpkins on an old porch in Salem, Massachusetts, for October and a mountainside of flaming orange and red trees for November.

September and October are only a blur in my memory of caffeinated nights and an aching back from all the hours I spent crouched over my computer during the rigorous application process for *Verité*. The euphoria from receiving my initial "congratulations" email from Evelyn Marx in November is quickly wearing off as I accept that the hardest part of securing my dream job is yet to come.

What if I don't have what it takes to make it through the trial period? What if I have to return to Hobs and Sanderson with my box of succulents and company merch?

I flip to the last page of the calendar. It's the very scene I just left: the Channel Garden angels blowing their trumpets toward the glowing tree in front of the Rockefeller Center. The sinking feeling in my stomach plummets even lower. What if I don't have what it takes to make this calendar-worthy place my home?

The sound of the front door scraping on its crooked hinges signals Devón leaving. A moment later, Jody comes to lean on my doorframe. "Last night, huh? It's gonna be so weird without you here for a whole month."

I give her a teasing side glance. "I think you'll find a way to deal with the loneliness."

She laughs through her nose. "Yeah, but how am I gonna get him outta here when I want my alone time?" She glances into the box on my desk and pulls out a plush refrigerator. "Can I have this?"

"Sure." I set the calendar aside, heave my half-packed suitcase onto my bed, and start throwing things into it haphazardly.

Jody squeezes the little fridge like a stress ball as she watches me. "It's weird," she says. "I feel like you're moving out. Leaving me for someone else."

"It's only four weeks," I say. "I'll be back in time for New Year's Eve." But I know what she means. It's surprising how empty my room looks once I've finished packing. My determination not to get too settled at Hobs and Sanderson must have extended to my living situation, because I haven't accumulated much of anything since I arrived in New York two years ago. I make a mental note to change that when I come back. Get a rug for the room or something like that.

I zip my suitcase closed and plop beside it onto my bed, facing Jody. "I've got some food in the fridge. Think you could finish that for me before it goes bad?"

"I'll see if Devón wants it."

I quirk a smile. Jody eats like a child. Of course she wouldn't want my "nasty" mixed greens and almond milk. "I'm pretty sure I've got a sleeve of Oreos in the cupboard."

"I ate those last week," Jody admits, not even peevish about it. She tosses the plush fridge and catches it. "What are you going to do in Oregon for a whole month?"

"Uh, spend time with my family."

She makes a face. "For a *month*?"

"Yeah?"

Jody stares at me suspiciously. "Is this because of Adam?"

Leave it to Jody to cut to the chase.

"No." I manage an exasperated laugh. "It has nothing to do with Adam."

"Really? Because it kinda seems like you're running away."

"Yeah, well, I'm not. So..."

"There's a lot of other fish in the sea. Best way to stick it to Adam would be to move on and enjoy your life."

"I'm not—" I take a breath, look her in the eyes, try to show her how serious I am. "I actually *like* spending time with my family. I'd spend this time with them even if Adam were still...you know...in the picture."

She swears. "Ten bucks says you go stir-crazy after three days."

I laugh. "You don't know my sisters! They're both going to be there with their families, and my brother. There's never a dull moment with those three."

When Jody still doesn't look convinced, I sigh. "Okay, yeah, maybe I would've planned a shorter vacation if Adam and I were still together. I kind of hoped that this year..." I shake my head. Jody already knows I had hopes of bringing him home with me, and I don't want to hear myself admit to it now. "Whatever. The thing is, I could really use some time with my family. People who know me and make me feel good about myself. My sisters—they're like my battery recharge stations. I could use that boost before I start my new job at *Verité.*"

Jody considers my words, then shrugs. "Must be a big-family thing."

I almost ask if being an only child is really so bad, but then I remember that Jody's parents split when she was in high school. "When's the last time you spent the holidays with one of your parents?" I ask instead.

"Been a few years," she admits. "I used to spend Thanksgiving with one, Christmas with the other, and switch it off every year. But now"—she tosses the plush fridge and catches it again—"it's like, what's the point? It was awkward when it was just me, but now they're both in new relationships, and we're all adults now, you know? Might as well do our own thing."

Her words make me uncomfortable. The uncomfortable you get when you first hear someone say Santa's not real and you know it's true, but you don't want to know it yet. "I'm sorry," is what comes out of my mouth.

"Pshh." She waves it off. "Pretty sure I got over my childhood expectations a long time ago. You'll be back for New Year's, though, right? Not that I've got anything sentimental planned or anything, but just so I know how much junk food to get."

I haven't even gone home yet, and Jody's already talking about when I get back. A sudden wave of premature after-Christmas blues washes over me. It's too soon to be thinking about that, but I manage a smile for her. "Count me in."

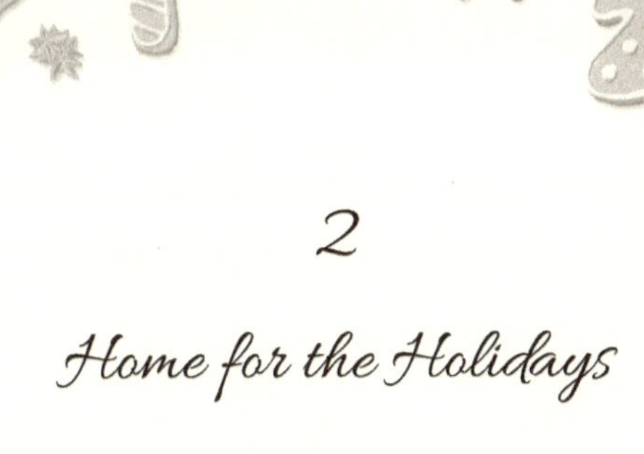

2

Home for the Holidays

I SNAP A PICTURE of my feet against the green carpet with the crisscrossing pattern of blue, red, and yellow specks at Portland International Airport. It's no yellow brick road, but my rain boots are red, so I caption the photo No place like home #homefortheholidays #PDX before posting it on Facebook.

The airport hasn't changed much in the two years since I last saw it, except that they've added a Gustav's restaurant, I note with approval. Best German food in town! My mouth waters at the prospect of visiting all of my favorite restaurants while I'm here. For all the hype around food in NYC, nothing compares to the familiar flavors of home.

A river of people winds from baggage claim toward the MAX departure. I wonder if that's new or if I just never noticed it before because I'd never used public transportation before leaving home. New York must have changed the way I travel, because I catch myself following the tide in that direction before stopping to change course. The MAX line doesn't go to Roanoke.

I'm glad my mom prefers to make the drive through Portland to pick me up. It's a one-hour commute without traffic, but at least we'll have each other to talk to on the way home.

Icy wind blasts my face, blowing my hair back over my shoulders as I push through the rotating glass doors and out to the pickup zone. I check my phone for any new messages from my mom.

Nothing.

She must still be driving.

I text her.

I'm at passenger pickup.

Outside door…

I check behind me for the door number, but hear my name before I find it.

"AJ!"

My eyes dart to the source of the sound, and I spot Mom's blue Subaru Forester with the passenger window down, pulling up behind a Volkswagen. Leaning over the center console, Mom waves wildly to get my attention. There's a little jumping sensation in my chest at the sight of her.

Mommy.

My suitcase bounces on its wheels behind me with a *clunk, clunk* over every seam in the pavement.

Mom jumps out of the car and runs around the front to throw her arms around me. "Welcome home, sweetheart!"

"Thanks, Mom." I get my short stature and curvy figure from her, but her strawberry blond hair and blue eyes were no match for my dad's dominant brown-eyed, dark-haired genes. My siblings and I are all brunettes. I like to think that some of that sassy red from my mom's thick, bouncy locks made it into my hair, though. As I embrace her, she feels much smaller than before. I know she's been losing weight, even seen pictures of her on Facebook, but it's so different seeing her in person.

I barely register this thought before she pulls free from the embrace with a "Brr, it's freezing out here! Let's get you home." She takes my messenger bag from me, and I follow her to the back of the car with my roller suitcase. We throw everything into the trunk, and I sigh with relief once we're in the heated seats of Mom's car.

"Mom, you're tiny!" I say as we begin the drive home.

She waves my words off with a smile. "Ohh, stop it some more."

I laugh. "I guess I won't be able to steal your clothes anymore."

"Are you kidding me? I'm looking forward to stealing *yours*, you fancy New York woman! I almost mistook you for some highfalutin magazine editor when I saw you standing there. Oh, wait—" She drops her jaw, as if she's only just realized that's what I am.

"It's the coat," I say with mock seriousness. "All the highfaluters are wearing them in the magazine industry these days. They have to be black or gray, though. No bright colors. That's what makes it official."

It feels good to hear my mom laugh. Even better to see the pride in her eyes when she looks at me the way she used to look whenever she talked about my older siblings and their accomplishments to her friends. It comes with being the baby of the family, I suppose, looking forward to the day when I'd measure up to my older siblings.

Thinking of my siblings brings on another wave of excitement. My whole body tingles with such energy at being home, I have to sit on my hands to keep them still. I can practically hear my sister Tara's tinkling laughter now, can almost taste Tiffany's famous hot cocoa concoctions.

"So, when are Tiffany and Brett coming up?" I ask.

"Tiffany's coming on the fifteenth with the kids. Brett has to work, but he'll come up the twenty-first and stay through the weekend.

Tara and Mike fly in on the nineteenth, and your brother"—she shrugs—"he'll surprise us, I'm sure."

Luke never was one to tie himself down to a schedule. "I don't know how Kesha puts up with him," I say. But even this annoying trait of my brother warms my heart with its familiar reliability. It's comforting to know my brother is still the same old free-spirited Luke, even if he is an AV technician now who hit the jackpot in his career field.

Mom pats my knee as if she's thinking the same thing. "Looks like it's just going to be you, me, and your dad at the Malans' party tonight."

"No way, that's tonight?" I check the clock on the dashboard. Almost five thirty. The Malan family Christmas party has been a tradition for as long as I can remember. They always put it on during the first week of December to avoid clashing with other Christmas festivities—a brilliant scheme that fills their house year after year. But because I've only been able to spare a week at most for Christmas vacation time in recent years, I haven't been able to attend the Malans' party since before I started college.

"Everyone's so excited to see you!" Mom gushes. "They're always asking about how you're doing in New York, how your writing is coming along."

Cold dread seizes my chest. I glance guiltily at my mom, but she seems completely oblivious to the effect her words have had on me. I swallow, thinking I should tell her. Maybe she can help. Instead, what comes out of my mouth is "Wow. I'm surprised they still remember who I am after all this time."

Mom swats my knee with a laugh. "Oh please! You're like one of their own kids. They all see your Facebook posts, you know. You're not as private as you think you are."

I imagine facing all my parents' friends, all my friends' parents, and hearing their questions about New York and my writing. A nervous pang forms in the pit of my stomach. The last thing I wrote was an ad for a stainless-steel refrigerator at the beginning of November.

I clear my throat. "You know I've only been hired as a junior editor at the magazine, right? I probably won't even get to write anything for a while…"

Mom waves this off. "Oh, potato, potahto. No one cares about that. It's just exciting to know someone in the magazine business. Gives people something to brag about."

One thing I love about my family, and my hometown, is the way everyone makes me feel like I can do no wrong. I thought a good solid month of this kind of talk would surely help me get over my imposter syndrome. Only now, sitting in the car with my mom, does it occur to me I'm in danger of the opposite.

It's already dark out when we pass the familiar old sign welcoming us to Roanoke: HOME OF THE OAKS. Twinkling Christmas lights wink at us as we go by, wrapped up and down the trunks of trees and glowing from the snowless rooftops of my hometown.

It feels like I've gone back in time, but to some kind of strange, alternate universe. There's the same taco wagon on the corner by the Shell gas station, but the old library's been torn down and replaced by a new police station that stands out like a bad nose job among all the old houses and crumbling buildings of my childhood. A funny ache forms in my chest the closer we get to my house. I'm eager to see it but also kind of dreading all the ways it might be different.

Dad's old inflatable nativity set glows on the front lawn of my parents' home as we pull into the driveway. The sight of it makes Mom shake her head—she's been trying to get him to throw that old thing out and get a newer, nicer one for years—but I feel my shoulders relax at the sight of it. I need that dose of familiarity to ease the blow of the front door, which is no longer brown with peeling paint but a new robin-egg blue. The potted trees on either side of it twinkle with gold lights.

"You painted the door," I say.

"I know!" Mom claps her hands, scrunching her nose with childlike delight. "Just wait until you see the kitchen. We *finally* knocked out those horrendous fluorescents."

"Aw, no more horror light show?" I draw my bottom lip down in a pout.

"Thank goodness," laughs Mom. She throws open her car door just as Dad bursts onto the front porch with Char, the family dog, following close behind.

Dad's a big guy. Six foot three with Hulk-like shoulders, and hands so thick they can still swallow mine whole. When I was a kid, I was used to my friends asking if his first name was Bruce every time they met him. My dad's answers were always playfully cryptic, as if he really were the Marvel superhero just trying to live a normal life in quiet old Roanoke. Like Mom, he's lost some weight since the last time I saw him, but his belly looks like it's there to stay.

Char doesn't bark, because he's a good boy that way. But he gives me his most intense boxer stare—the one that says, *You mess with my people, you got me to deal with.* I fumble in my haste to get out and wipe that serious look off his adorable mug with the sound of my voice.

"Charleston," I call, opening my arms to him. "Charly Boy! Where my Char at?"

The recognition touches his stubby tail first, travels up his spine in a hesitant wiggle, and by the time it hits his face, he's running toward me with his tongue flapping out the side of his mouth.

"Oh, I see how it is," Dad teases from the porch as I let Char slobber all over my face. "Say hi to the dog first!"

There's a click behind me when Mom opens the trunk to get my things. I straighten to help her, wiping the dog drool from my cheek. "Hi, Daddy!"

Dad meets me in a hug. We both take a bag from Mom's hands and let her close the trunk as we head inside.

The house smells different. I don't know if it's just because I've been away so long that I'm no longer used to our family smell or if Mom's started using a different plug-in scent.

"I hear Mom's been putting you to work." Following my dad into the living room, I can already see how the lighting from the kitchen has changed. There's no subtle flicker like there used to be. It's warmer and brighter at the same time.

Dad chuckles. "Yeah, she's been crackin' the whip all right." I get my husky laugh from him. It's comforting to hear it in this unfamiliar lighting.

The family room has changed some, too. "New couches?"

Mom snorts. "I wish. That's the next thing on my list! These are just covers for now, to hide all the grandkid stains."

I can feel that she's about to tell me to come see the kitchen. Dad must see it coming, too, because he's quick to check his watch, which reminds Mom of the time. "I know, I know." She waves a hand at him as if she were already thinking the same thing. "Party starts in fifteen minutes. You want to change, AJ? Freshen up before we go?"

"Yeah," I say, relieved to put off facing the destruction of my childhood kitchen memories. "I'll be quick!" I take my roller suitcase from my dad and head up the stairs to my old bedroom.

I'm grateful to see that here, at least, things look the way I left them. That's the benefit of being the only unmarried sibling—my room is still my room, no matter how much time passes between uses.

I consider taking a quick shower but decide against it in favor of spending more time on my hair and makeup. As a kid, the Malans' Christmas party was always a chance to see my friends and boys my age. Even though I know everyone my age is away now doing their own things, I guess I still feel that nervous excitement to look my best. Especially if Mom's been talking me up to be some big shot New York career woman. The thought makes me smile, despite my anxieties.

I go for a festive look in a classy red blouse and black slacks, with red lips to match. The silk flower clips and headbands I wore as a teenager still form an arc around my bedroom vanity like a Kentucky Derby garland. I used to wear sprigs of holly with berries in my hair at Christmas parties. Now I feel like maybe I've outgrown that kind of thing, but a part of me feels strangely naked without it as I leave my room.

"Va-va-voom," Mom says when she sees me. "Are you a journalist or a model?"

I strike a goofy pose.

Dad laughs.

They're both decked out in classic Banner family Christmas gear, Dad wearing reindeer antlers with blinking lights and a Frosty the Snowman sweater. Mom is her classy self, but with jingle bell earrings and bracelets, and a Christmas tree brooch in her red scarf. I consider going back to see if I can find my old stash of holiday hair decor in my room somewhere, but we're already late enough as it is.

The Malans live only a few streets away, but we drive to the party as always, because it's cold out and we're lazy people. Though their house isn't huge, it stands tall with impressive gabled roofs draped with icicle lights. I always thought it looked like a mansion when I was a kid. Now it seems smaller than I remember but every bit as charming. A warm, inviting glow shines through the windows, where I can already see the Christmas tree in the front room and people milling about with plates of food and drinks in their hands.

Jeff Malan welcomes us in his classic boisterous, booming voice. "Come on in, Banners! Late as usual, eh Todd?" He elbows Dad at the same time as he winks at Mom. When his eyes land on me, his smile grows even bigger. "Hey, you've still got kids, after all!"

He probably can't tell which one I am. It's a common occurrence when you grow up with two sisters who look just like you. But Mrs. Malan saves him from himself by flying into the entryway with her arms wide, hands flapping as if they could pull me into a hug any sooner that way. "AJ," she cheers. "Oh, welcome home, sweetheart!"

I smell vanilla and nutmeg as I'm enveloped into her soft, plump embrace. "Thanks, Peggy."

Mom and Dad look on with pride, making me feel like I've won first place at some kind of science fair just for being home.

Peggy grips my shoulders as she pulls out of her hug to look at my face. "We hear you're a big-time writer now for *Verité*. I can't wait to show you off at the beauty parlor. We always have that magazine sitting out."

"Well, it's a junior editor position, actually—"

"Lucile!" Peggy is already shouting over her shoulder. "Did you see that AJ's home?"

Another one of Mom's friends waves from the cookie table and swallows her mouthful of mulled cider before replying, "We bought a subscription to *Verité* as soon as we heard the news! Congratulations, AJ."

For the next several minutes, I'm the center of attention as all my parents' friends shower me with congratulations and welcome-homes. My older siblings used to get this kind of attention whenever they came home for the holidays; it feels strange to be the recipient of it myself, especially when I've done nothing to deserve it yet. I don't have a vast collection of gorgeous ceramic art pieces like Tara or a stunning portfolio of highly sought-after graphic designs like Tiffany or stories of meeting celebrities at lavish parties like Luke.

"It's just a junior editor position," I keep saying. Or "I probably won't even be doing any of the writing for a while." "I'll be more like a glorified receptionist, really," I tell one person. "More of the coffee runner than anything else," I tell another.

I scan the room for a glimpse of anyone else my age, but it's mostly older adults and younger kids in this part of the house. There are voices and footsteps coming from upstairs, where my friends and I used to play video games in the Malans' game room when I was little. I wonder if that's still a tradition at these parties now that the Malan kids are all grown up and gone. I'll sneak up and see what's going on there in a bit, but first, cookies.

One of the best parts about the Malan Christmas party is the food. Peggy could have been a master chef. Everything she touches turns to gold in the kitchen. There's an entire table of just drinks—eggnog and hot mulled cider, wassail and hot cocoa with a multitude of toppings. Cookies of every kind imaginable form a pyramid of holiday magic at the center of five tables arranged in a circle, displaying charcu-terie boards, cheese balls with crackers, meatballs with crispy potato wedges, pigs in a blanket, and quiche tarts. My stomach grumbles at the aroma of a warm ham garnished with oranges and cloves. I haven't eaten since breakfast.

My plate is full within seconds as I make my way around the dining room. Peggy's collection of nutcrackers looks on from their various posts with teeth clenched, as if warning me I'm going to make myself sick from eating so much. I ignore them and cram an entire quiche tart into my mouth.

"AJ, is that you?"

Mouth stuffed with buttery, flaky quiche crust, I turn and my tongue goes dry. There, looking at me with the same dark brown eyes that melted my heart for years, tall and slender with a manly jaw and shoulders, stands Benson Miller.

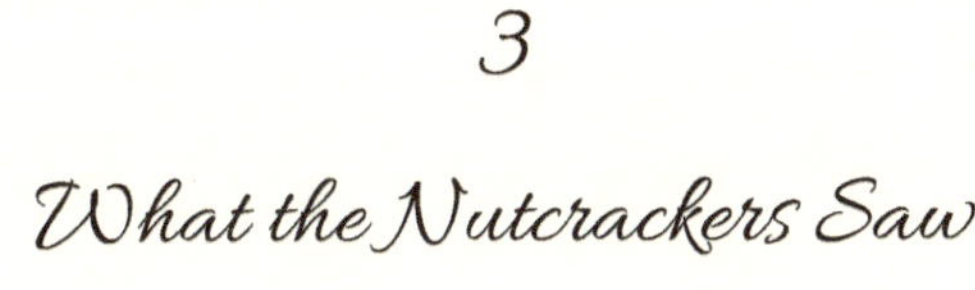

3

What the Nutcrackers Saw

IT'S HARD TO BELIEVE he was ever that shy, chubby boy whose quiet humor and subtle attention captured my heart. The sudden interest in fitness that gripped Benson as a young teenager wasn't merely a passing phase. Now he looks like a movie star. Thick dark hair, dark eyebrows, dark eyes, fair skin, subtle smile. He's standing closer to me than I think we've ever been, facing me head-on for the first time, the way I always used to imagine he would when we were younger.

I realize my mouth is still full of food and try to swallow it all at once. I cough. My mouth is too dry. "Sorry," I cough again, taking a step back and beating my chest with my free hand. As if that will somehow help.

"Sorry," he says at the same time. "I didn't mean to jump out at you like that."

My eyes water as I swallow the last of the quiche tart. I wave my hand in a way that I realize too late looks rather frantic. "It's okay! It's okay! I just—haven't eaten all day and—you know, long flight, cramming the food down too fast." *Oh my gosh, please make the words stop. Shut up, AJ!*

"You flew in from New York, right?" he asks.

Grateful for the subject change, I nod. "Yeah. And you're...in medical school, right?" I furrow my brow as if I'm not sure, but it's total

BS. I saw on Facebook that he graduated last year. He's a full-fledged doctor now. I try not to imagine how good he must look in a lab coat.

"Nah, I finished school a while back," he says modestly. "I'm doing my residency in Portland, actually, at Doernbecher Children's Hospital."

He saves children for a living. Of course he does. How am I supposed to hold anything against a guy like that?

"Portland," I say, "that's a long commute from Roanoke."

"I have a place downtown. I'm just here for the weekend to help my dad finish some stuff around the house before Christmas. You know, putting up the lights and stuff."

I nod and say something stale and automatic, like "Oh, that's nice," and the awkwardly polite conversation rolls on from there.

No, his siblings won't be coming home for Christmas this year. Yes, mine will be here next week, and so on.

I can't get over how strange it feels to be talking to him. Did we ever speak one-on-one, face-to-face like this when we were kids? Most of the communication I can remember was indirect or via online chats. Is he thinking about this, too? Does he feel as weird as I do? Why did he approach me? I'm suddenly aware of how high I stacked the food on my plate. *What am I, some kind of ogre?*

"What do you do in New York?" he asks.

"I'm a writer." Then I amend, "Well, that is, I *was* a writer—then I started working as a sales assistant for this refrigerator company. I wrote promotional things and sales contracts and...basically any boring document you can think of that a refrigerator company would need." I laugh at my own joke and simultaneously want to bury myself. For someone who worked in sales, I'm sure not selling myself very well. Clearing my throat, I try to shake off this strange childhood insecurity which seems to have come over me. "But I'm not doing that anymore.

I actually just got a new job doing something else. Not writing yet, but hopefully I'll be able to work my way up to that."

I can see in his eyes that he's unsure whether to congratulate or console me, and I try to backtrack. "That...didn't come out right. I haven't been demoted or anything like that. This new job is actually a really good opportunity. I'm excited about it."

He gives an understanding smile and nods. "Ah. Well, in that case, congratulations." He points over his shoulder with both thumbs. "I actually need to head out, but, hey, it was good to see you." He touches my shoulder lightly—an action that would have sent my teenage self into a happy coma for days—before eyeing my loaded plate of holiday heart attacks. "I'll let you enjoy your dinner. You going to be in town for a while?"

"For the month," I nod.

"Nice. Maybe we'll run into each other again."

"Yeah... Yeah..." Nothing else comes to me.

He gives me a two-fingered wave and wishes me happy holidays before making his way out of the dining room.

I stand there like a stunned marmot staring after him. The stench of my word vomit curdles my stomach as I relive the conversation. Seriously, how hard is it to say, "I'm a writer. I just got hired on as a junior editor for *Verité* magazine. I start in January. How's your family?"

I can see him in the entryway shrugging into a black peacoat. He's talking to someone who's obscured from my view by the garland on the staircase railing. He laughs as he wraps a green-and-blue scarf around his neck. Whoever he's talking to gives him a hearty shoulder grip—the kind men give to each other instead of a hug—and for a split second I glimpse messy light brown hair.

Benson leaves, and the man he was talking to steps out from behind the stair railing and into the dining room. A small cry of surprise escapes me as I recognize Skylar Townsend.

The last time I saw him must have been over six years ago, before his mom died. He's taller now, more filled out, with some stubble on his chin that makes him look like a lumberjack just rolled out of bed, but when he sees me, his easygoing grin sends me back in time.

"Sky!" I practically sing.

He points at the plate of food in my hand without missing a beat and asks, "That for me?"

My anxieties from a moment before subside as I laugh incredulously and open my arms to him. He's still the same old Skylar I knew back in high school. "Sky, what are you doing here? I thought you were off in Africa somewhere?"

He squeezes me tight before stealing a cookie from my plate. "I got home last month," he replies, taking a bite. "What about you? Benson says you're living in New York now." He waggles his eyebrows as he reaches around me and grabs a cookie to replace the one he took from my plate. I don't know if the eyebrow waggle was regarding my living in New York or that Benson was talking about me.

I take a bite from the cookie he just set on my plate. It must be New York he's referring to. My little-girl crush on Benson was so long ago, I doubt Sky would remember something like that. Still, the words that come out of my mouth seem to have gotten on the wrong train. "When did Benson tell you that?"

"Just now." Sky nudges his head toward the entryway. "I was giving him a hard time about leaving right when I arrived, and he said you were here." Sky wipes imaginary sweat from his forehead. "Glad I'm not the only one our age at this party."

Our age. Funny how adulthood levels out our definition of age categories. Back in high school, there was a world of difference between being a freshman and being a senior. Now, as long as we're within the same decade of life, we're the same age. "We're it, huh?" I ask.

"You just get here, too?"

I nod. "I thought I heard people in the game room upstairs…"

"Grandkids," Sky says. "Benson tried going up there earlier."

"Dang," I say. "Think they'd let us play Mario Kart with them if we begged?"

"Or bribed." Sky takes another cookie from the table and holds it up like he's seriously considering it.

"Worth a try."

He nods. "Let's do it. Put more cookies on that plate!" For a second, I think he's actually going to stack more cookies onto my already-full plate, but then he notices the slice of ham and the savory hors d'oeuvres there. "Is this your dinner?" he asks.

"I'm fresh off the plane," I admit.

Sky rubs his chin thoughtfully. "On second thought, I'll prepare the bribe. You eat. You'll need your strength if we're gonna beat a bunch of kids at Mario Kart."

I consider sitting down to finish my food, but one glance at all my parents' friends on the sofas makes me change my mind. That's social quicksand over there. Instead, I follow Sky along the tables while he gathers tempting treats.

"So, Africa," I venture cautiously. "Where? Why?"

I have a feeling the why has a lot to do with his mom's passing, and I'm prepared for him to grow sober and admit to this, but he chuckles instead. He's probably been asked these same questions a million times already. I can't be the only one who wonders what he's been doing since he disappeared after his humanitarian trip five years ago.

"I was in Ethiopia," Sky explains, "just outside of Addis Ababa." He looks up at me through his lashes. I can see on his face that he's just waiting for whatever "same old" question people always ask next.

I purse my lips and nod, trying to come up with something that might be more original. "Ethiopia. Okay."

He spares me the questions game. "I went for a humanitarian internship with Oregon State to get some experience in infrastructure. It was only supposed to be three months, but, you know"—he shrugs—"I fell in love with the place. Got involved with some friends there who were trying to start a school, came home for a month, felt pretty useless, and went back to help."

"Wow," I say. It sounds weak after what he just told me. "Sky," I try again, "that's awesome! That's what you've been doing for the past five years? Building schools in Ethiopia?"

He smiles wryly. "Well, not really. That does sound pretty romantic, though, doesn't it?" He winks. "Actually, I ended up working with some NGOs as an infrastructure volunteer, then worked my way into a leadership role, and...things just kind of took off from there. I helped with the schools a little at first, but mostly I did projects in sustainable housing and clean-water initiatives."

I want to ask more about his experiences there, but he's quick to change the subject.

"What about you? What have you been doing in New York?"

Now it's my turn to make a face.

Sky reads my mind. "No, wait." He holds up a hand. "Don't tell me! Let me guess." He takes a bite of his cookie, chewing thoughtfully as he studies my face. "You're running a small retail shop online for vintage women's wear."

I tilt my head and squint an eye. "That...would be pretty cool. But, no. I don't really do the whole vintage thing anymore." Apparently, he's missed the lack of pin curls that were my trademark when we were teenagers.

"No? Dang, you wore that stuff so well." He takes in my clothes for the first time, and for a moment, I feel a twinge of nerves. They vanish at the admiration in his eyes. "Nice coat." He snaps his fingers. "That's it! You're the executive assistant to the CEO of a large fashion magazine who sends you on crazy errands to complete impossible tasks to prove yourself."

I laugh. "You watched *The Devil Wears Prada*."

"Aisha made me do it," he says. "We all saw it together. In the theater, remember?"

"We did?" I tilt my head, trying to remember. "I thought I saw that for the first time at a sleepover..."

"No, remember, we put M&M's and Milk Duds in the popcorn? Christy sneaked a bunch of food in her bag?"

"Christy *always* sneaked a bunch of junk food into the theater."

"But that time Christy sneaked in hot takeout and it made the whole theater smell like pad Thai."

That sounds familiar.

"You were terrified of getting kicked out." Sky laughs as he imitates me, shrinking. "You sank down so low in your seat."

The light bulb comes on. "Oh yeah! We got popcorn and candy just so we could say we paid for something!"

"And it was my idea to put the candy in the popcorn."

"Yeah!" I laugh as the memories come spilling back. "Oh my gosh, I remember being so embarrassed about the smell but also being kind of jealous that everyone else was eating the pad Thai without me." My brow furrows. "We saw *The Devil Wears Prada* that night? I don't remember the movie at all."

"You were so preoccupied with not getting caught."

"Sounds like me," I admit.

Sky's eyes are warm as he smiles at me, and the fondness of our childhood memories passes between us.

My heart swells.

He shakes his head, clears his throat, and straightens his shoulders. "Alright, so you're not an executive assistant. Must be a writer, then."

A funny-sounding squeak pops up my throat, something between a laugh and a surprised hiccup.

"For a big-time magazine," Sky adds as an afterthought.

"Who told you?" I accuse.

He feigns an innocent shrug. "What? I'm a good guesser. To be fair, there are only so many cliché New York businesswoman jobs to choose from."

"Ha ha," I say sarcastically. "Benson told you, didn't he?"

Sky rolls his eyes. "Oh, come on. I was in *Africa* for five years, not on Mars."

I'm not sure what he means by that for a second. That's all it takes for him to catch the blank look in my eyes.

"Facebook," he says.

Now I feel a little guilty, because I haven't seen a single thing about him on Facebook in years. "I didn't think you had Facebook anymore," I admit.

He allows this with a guilty grimace and a tilt of the head that serves as a kind of nod. "Yeah, I haven't really been active on there for a while. But it's the best way to keep in touch with my friends in Ethiopia, so I hop on now and then." He holds up the plate of cookies he's prepared. "Shall we?"

I realize I've hardly touched the food on my plate and quickly shovel in a few more bites before we head upstairs.

Benson was right—the game room that once served as the teenage hangout at this Christmas party is now a zoo of grandkids. Star Wars and Matrix movie posters are still there in all their fading glory, but they're barely visible behind brightly colored plastic slides, dollhouses, and a foamy floor mat that looks like it's made of giant puzzle pieces. The younger kids literally bounce off the walls—which are covered with thick padding specifically for this purpose—while the older ones congregate around the TV playing with a Wii. The oldest kid can't be over ten.

"Hey, hey, hey," Sky calls out by way of greeting. "Looks like we found where all the fun is happening!"

Some kids stop to stare at us. Others are too busy running and squealing. The older kids' eyes are glued to the TV screen. I imagine cartoonish swirls whirling around in their pupils.

"What are you playing?" I ask the oldest kid. He's the spitting image of the Malans' oldest son, Aaron, so he must be in charge here. It kills me a little to realize that he must be that chubby baby we all cooed over the last time I came to one of these parties. What was his name? Michael? Micah?

"*Tropical Freeze*," the kid intones without breaking screen-eye contact.

"Looks like Donkey Kong," I say.

"It *is* Donkey Kong," says Sky. He waits until the end of the current level before offering our bribe. "Give you this plate of cookies if you let us play a round with you."

Now all the kids look at us. "Do you know how?" a girl asks. She must be five or six, with her black hair twisted into thick spirals. This must be Florence Leffler's daughter.

"I think we can figure it out," Sky says, "if you give us a quick rundown."

Aaron Malan's son shows us how to operate the Wii controls sideways—which looks way less complicated than the PlayStation controllers we used to play with in this room—and we begin.

Sky picks up on the game a lot more quickly than I do, but we laugh as we watch our cartoonish characters bumbling around the screen, accidentally picking each other up, and walking off cliffs.

By the time we finish, all the cookies we brought up are gone, except for two gingerbread men. "Figures," Skylar sighs as he retrieves the plate. "I hated these things when I was a kid."

We head for the stairs. "I love gingerbread," I say, taking one cookie and biting off a leg.

"I like them *now*," says Sky. "But that's because I'm a wise old man."

"Funny how your taste changes when you get older, isn't it?"

"Yeah, it is."

The way he looks at me when he says it feels surprisingly tender.

"AJ, hon, you up there?" My mom's voice echoes softly off the tall windows from the entryway below.

I break away from Sky's gaze. "Yeah, we're—I'm on my way down."

Sky motions for me to go ahead of him, and I lead the way down the stairs. Mom and Dad are already putting their coats on. There's a cold draft from the open front door where others are leaving.

Mom smiles warmly at Sky. "Hello, Skylar. Welcome home!"

Sky nods. "Thanks, Mrs. Banner."

"How is your father doing?" Her voice is thick with sympathy.

"He's alright. I tried to get him to come tonight, but, you know, I think it's still hard for him to come to these things without..." He nods to fill in the obvious blank.

My mom nods, too, to show that she understands. "Let him know he was missed," she says, and squeezes Sky's arm. "Will you be home for long?"

"Yeah." Sky sucks in a big breath. "Indefinitely, by the looks of it. I'm, uh, taking over the business for him." His eyes dart to my face and then away again just as quickly.

"Really?" I ask.

"That's wonderful," Mom says at the same time.

Sky nods.

I wonder why he didn't tell me that before. Why didn't I ask?

"Yeah, well, I know the drill after working for him before."

He's still the same upbeat Skylar, but I recognize something else in his voice now. It's the same way he used to talk when we were teenagers and something was wrong, but he didn't want to upset anyone. I want to reach out to him, to ask what it is, to let him know I'm here for him. But Mom is saying how great it must be for Doug to have him home with him and giving Sky a tight embrace. When she steps back, she looks at me with that *ready to go* expression.

"It's really good to see you, Sky," I say.

"You too." Sky opens the door for us. "Maybe we can get together sometime while you're in town."

"Yeah, I'd like that." Cold air nips my cheeks as I follow my parents outside.

When I turn back before getting into the car, Sky is still there watching from the open doorway.

He waves.

I wave back.

Then we drive home.

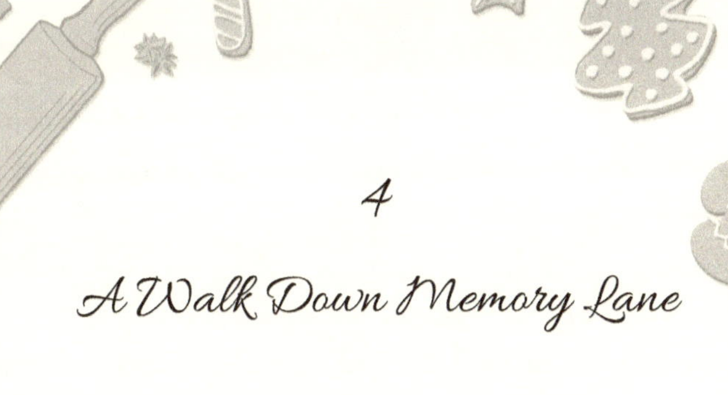

4

A Walk Down Memory Lane

I T'S STRANGE, BEING IN my old room again. Maybe it's the run-in with Benson, but I almost feel like I'm back to being an insecure teenager as I pull back my pink vintage-inspired comforter and climb into bed. Deco collages I made from Norman Rockwell paintings and old Hollywood movie posters still plaster the walls. Fred Astaire and Ginger Rogers smile at me cheek to cheek from one of the decorative pillows. I made that one. Behind it, a bigger throw displays a checkerboard of old-time heartthrobs like James Dean, Gordon MacRae, and Cary Grant. Christy made that one for my Sweet Sixteen.

I sink farther down into bed. It still smells like Victoria's Secret Love Spell in here. Or is that just an olfactory trick being played on me by the memories oozing from every corner of this room?

The bookshelf beside my bed still holds some of my old journals. For half a second I contemplate pulling them out, but the sensation that I am slipping backward in time sends a weird shudder through me. I've got to shake this off. I throw off my covers, retrieve my laptop, and bring it back to bed with me. Sitting up against the wooden headboard, I check my email for any word from *Verité*.

Ping!

A notification appears in the upper right corner of my screen from Facebook: Benson Miller liked a photo of you.

My heart skips a beat. Talk about a throwback. In defiance of my inner fourteen-year-old self, I resist the urge to click on the notification before it disappears.

My finger hovers over the mouse pad. I blink, trying to remember what I was about to do before the interruption.

Screw it. I open up Facebook. The picture in question is one Mom posted of herself, Dad, and me all decked out before going to the party tonight. The caption reads, It is so fun to have our AJ girl home for the holidays! Benson's name stands out like a beacon under the photo beside the Like button.

Does he like that I'm home for the holidays?

Maybe we'll run into each other again, he said at the party. Does that mean he hopes we do? Should I let him know I'd like that, too?

Would I like that?

Before I know my answer, I click on his name and look at his profile picture. I don't know why I expected it to be of him in a lab coat, looking like a *Grey's Anatomy* dreamboat. Instead, he's wearing a regular T-shirt, smiling with Haystack Rock in the background on Cannon Beach. *He's just a normal guy*, I remind myself.

After he snubbed me at the 2004 Roanoke Snow Ball, I avoided him, watching him grow taller and more fit and handsome by the year. We had some of the same friends in common, but somehow, we never really hung out. The shyness of our childhood became an unspoken distance as we got older. I'm surprised he approached me tonight, as if that distance had never existed—as if we were old friends who just hadn't seen each other in several years.

Was the awkward distance between us all that time just a figment of my teenage imagination?

I think of our conversation at the party tonight, and how he seemed so...human. Handsome, yes, but not untouchable in the way I painted him in my mind for so many years. It occurs to me, perhaps for the first time, that maybe the Benson I thought I knew was more imagined than real.

Still, there's this lingering itch in the back of my mind as I look at his profile picture. He's wearing a Beatles T-shirt.

In high school, I didn't listen to popular music like most kids my age. I listened to 97.1 KISN FM, the oldies station, and to CD collections of the best hits of the fifties, sixties and seventies that my dad bought from TV infomercials. I used to think that Benson and I had some kind of connection because he liked the Beatles, like I did. That was before I realized that everyone and their dog liked the Beatles.

I can laugh now at my naivete, but that itch under my skin won't go away.

Maybe it would be good to see him again, to really talk to him and get to know him, to set my assumptions and curiosities to rest once and for all. To find closure.

Could that be what I need to get over this crippling insecurity that has a hold of me?

Benson's most recent post really is of him in a lab coat, but instead of looking like a romantic hospital drama promo poster, he's got an N95 mask strapped under his chin, and he's holding a big *Happy Birthday, Dr. Miller* card signed by children at Doernbecher Children's Hospital.

I click the Like button under the photo and promptly slam my laptop shut before I can undo it.

My heart pounds like I've just done something illegal. Being in this old bedroom is weirding me out. All I'm missing now are the braces and pin curls to make my time warp complete.

I tap my fingers against the lid of my laptop as I try to remember what I was about to do before the blast from my past.

Verité. Right. The major magazine that I'll be working for a month from now. *I'm an adult with a grown-up job,* I remind myself. *I'm confident and mature, and I bought these silky Julianna Rae pajamas that I'm wearing with my own money.* Clearing my throat, I straighten my shoulders before opening my laptop again and going to my email.

Nothing new from *Verité.*

Why would there be? It's the holiday season, and I haven't officially started working for them yet.

Even though I practically have it memorized, I click open the last email I got from Evelyn Marx, the senior editor, and my eyes immediately go to the second paragraph:

Your first three months with Verité will be a probationary period. During this time, you and a few other new hires will showcase your skills, creativity, and dedication to our editorial vision.

I'm to compete with other writers for this spot. I imagine myself in a leather cuirass and greaves, fighting for my life in an arena of skilled gladiators while bloodthirsty crowds jeer from the stands.

This period will assess how well each candidate aligns with our magazine's standards and values.

Who's got what it takes to survive?

At the end of this trial, we will select one or two individuals to join the team permanently.

It'll be a fight to the death. Winner takes all.

I curl my legs up under me and bite my thumb. I think of all my mom's friends with their *Verité* magazine subscriptions, and I feel sick.

Ping! Skylar sent me a message on Facebook. I click the notification banner without hesitation.

Skylar: You still up?

Relieved for a distraction from my anxieties, I lean back into my pillows and angle my laptop more comfortably on my knees.

AJ: Yeah. It's so weird to be back in my old room.

Skylar: Tell me about it.

I glance at the framed picture of me, Aisha, and Christy on the vanity and shake my head at the brace-faced teenager smiling back at me.

AJ: I feel like I've time-traveled. My parents left everything untouched in here.

Skylar: Dang. That must be crazy.

I immediately regret my thoughtlessness. He's the one who left home and didn't come back for five years after his mom died. What did his dad do with his room during all that time? Has it been converted to a storage closet, or is it even more of a time capsule than mine?

AJ: Are you back in your old room?

Skylar: Sorta.

I want to ask him what he means by that, but he's faster.

Skylar: It was good to see you tonight. Did you get enough to eat? I feel bad I interrupted your dinner.

AJ: You did no such thing.

I hesitate.

> AJ: What's it like for you? Being home?

The three little dots that indicate he is typing appear, disappear, and reappear again. Maybe this isn't the best medium for talking about his mom, I realize. We used to talk about everything over AIM, back in the day. Then over MySpace Messenger. Now Facebook.

> Skylar: Could you go for some Norma's right now?

A half laugh escapes me. Norma's is the old diner where we all used to hang out after events because it was open all night long.

> AJ: Jeez, I haven't been to Norma's in years. Is that place still open?

> Skylar: I think so. I saw it on my way home tonight.

> Skylar: We can go another time if you're not hungry. I know it's getting late.

My eyes flit to the email tab on my screen. The imagined sounds of clashing swords and bloodthirsty jeers echo briefly in my mind, but I turn my attention back to Skylar's message.

> AJ: Honestly, Norma's eggs Benedict sounds amazing right now.

> Skylar: Pick you up in 5?

> AJ: Perfect.

I slip on the red blouse and slacks I wore to the Christmas party. Back in the day, I would have just thrown on some warm boots and a coat over my pj's, but I'm not a teenager anymore. I can't go traipsing around in my pajamas the way I used to.

Sky's old blue Chevy pulls up in front of my parent's house within five minutes, and I shoot a quick text to my mom to let her know I'm going out with friends before slipping through the front door.

Sky is halfway up the walk when I step outside. He looks surprised for a second when he sees me on the porch, then waves while he waits for me to meet him. "Your folks asleep?" he asks as we walk to his truck together.

"Not sure," I admit. "I just didn't want to disturb them."

Sky opens my door for me. He's always been a gentleman like that.

"Wow," I say as Sky takes his place in the driver's seat, "I can't believe this old truck is still kickin'."

"Right?" Sky laughs. The engine roars to life with a familiar chugging sound that brings me back to the days of cramming into the cab with Aisha and Christy on our way to the movies or Norma's for a late-night milkshake run. "It pretty much just sat in the garage gathering dust the whole time I was gone, so I had to do a little work on it. I actually told my dad to sell it a long time ago, but"—he shrugs—"might as well drive it until it falls apart."

His 2005 high school graduation tassel still hangs from the rearview mirror. It swings as we bounce over speed bumps leaving my neighborhood. I run a finger through the green and gold strings. "I'm surprised you didn't replace this with your Oregon State tassel."

He blows raspberries. "Nah, I...actually never finished school."

"You didn't? Oh," I say, remembering with a grimace. "That's when your mom..."

"Yeah."

From what I remember, Sky got into Berkeley but wasn't there for long before his mom got sick and he transferred to Oregon State University in Corvallis to be closer to her. I heard he used to come home to take care of her on the weekends while he was in college, but by then I was in Boulder at the University of Colorado. There are so many things I want to ask him. Was it hard to focus on school? Or was school a welcome distraction from the cancer? But every question sounds so hollow now, with how much time has passed. These are questions I should have asked him years ago, when he was going through it all.

"That must have been so hard," I say. It sounds weak. "I'm sorry I wasn't here for you, Sky."

His reply is quick. "Don't be. Everyone was away at school. You were where you needed to be."

He's mostly just a silhouette in the dark, barely illuminated by multicolored Christmas lights as we drive past glowing houses. His voice is light, easy. But Sky never was one to make things heavy if he could help it. I wonder if he's allowed himself to grieve, or if the last five years in Ethiopia were his means of escape from dealing with his mother's death.

"So, how are you doing?" I ask. "Being home and all."

He considers for a few moments before answering. "You know...I'm good. I admit, I was kinda nervous about coming home. It's hard. I can't lie about that. It's hard to see how much is the same, and how much is different..." He rubs the back of his neck. "Ethiopia was good for me. But my dad...I don't think I should have left him alone for so long."

I remember the concern in my mom's voice tonight when she asked about Sky's dad. "Is he okay?"

The blinker ticks for a few moments and Sky looks back over his shoulder for longer than he needs to before turning. "He's getting old, AJ. I don't think you'd recognize him if you saw him in the dairy aisle."

I didn't exactly hang out at Sky's house a lot growing up, but I went over a time or two with Aisha, and Mr. Townsend was always cracking dad jokes that made us laugh. It must have been a shock for Skylar to come home after five years and find his dad almost unrecognizable. "He must love having you home."

He gives me a sideways look and blows out a rush of air. "Hey, I didn't drag you out here to talk about me the whole time. How's life in the Big Apple?"

I want to know more about him, but I can see in his face that he needs a break, so I lean back in my seat. "New York is great. It took some time to get used to it. The first year was rough, but now I love it."

"Rough why?"

"Oh, you know...different from home. It's so busy and noisy, and I thought the people were mean at first. I didn't expect it to be such a culture shock, but it was."

"But now you love it."

"I do."

"What do you love about it?"

I pause for a moment to consider. "Lots of things. I love the diversity. There are so many people with unique stories all crammed together. You can hear ten different languages in just a few minutes walking down the street. I love that it feels like there's always something going on. Sometimes they block off a street to film a movie and you get to see all these camera crews and actors just right there in real life, looking surprisingly small in person, and it just...makes you feel connected to the world somehow. Like everyone is just a person living their life, doing their job, whether they're famous or not."

Sky furrows his brow thoughtfully. "Huh, I never would have thought of it in that way."

"How did it feel being in Ethiopia?"

"Kind of the opposite of that, I guess. But also, exactly like that. Not the diversity or the famous people, but the connectedness. I've never felt more connected to the Earth or to the human family..."

I hold my breath as a faraway look crosses Sky's face, waiting for him to tell me more about his experiences in Africa. But he quickly returns to the present and knocks the ball back in my court before I have a chance to ask him any questions.

"So, you moved to New York for this magazine job?"

"Indirectly. I've always loved the magazine, but I never in my wildest dreams thought I'd actually land a job there. I was still working remotely for this indie magazine in Boulder when I first moved to New York. Then I worked for a home appliance company, and when I saw *Verité* was hiring, I applied. But I didn't think I'd actually get the job; I thought I'd just see what the application process was like so I could prepare for another chance in the future. I still can't believe I made the cut."

"*Verité*...isn't that the one with the naked people?"

I choke back a laugh. "They're only naked from the shoulders up. It's an authenticity thing, not a...nudity thing."

The familiar sound of tires on gravel rolls through the truck as we pull into the parking lot of Norma's diner.

5

Order Up!

NORMA'S DINER LOOKS EXACTLY the same as I remember it, with a few letters from the blue neon NORMA'S sign flickering inconsistently over the faded red metal roof. A string of white-and-red holiday lights snakes around the aluminum stair railing out front. Vinyl booths and counter seating are visible through the windows that line the front face of the building. There's an old couple seated at one booth and a small cluster of teenagers in another, but otherwise, the place looks empty.

A bell dings overhead when Sky opens the door for me. Inside, the air smells perpetually of coffee, bacon, and homemade pie. Alvin and the Chipmunks croon "Christmas Don't Be Late" from an old speaker over the pass-through window, competing with the hiss and sizzle of bacon as a casually dressed cook tosses raw meat onto the grill.

"Two?" the hostess asks from behind the pie counter, already reaching for the menus.

Sky nods and we follow her past the quiet old couple and the rambunctious teens to the end booth.

"Talk about a time warp," Sky laughs as he pulls a menu toward himself. "I don't think they've updated this menu in a decade."

I don't need to look at it. I already know I'm ordering the eggs Benedict, like I always do. I watch Sky as he flips through the plastic-covered pages, struck by how the years have chiseled his features and filled out his shoulders. A five o'clock shadow tints his jawline. The time he spent in Africa left his skin tan and weathered like a cowboy's. The way he's slouched over his menu, there's a tiredness about him that makes me ache a little, but just as I think this, he sits taller.

"Are you admiring my rugged good looks?" he asks without looking up, a smile playing at the corner of his mouth.

I laugh. There's the boy I knew. "You look good," I admit. "I like your hair like this."

He runs a hand through the sandy waves. "I need to cut it." He pushes away the menu and looks up. I resist the urge to fix my hair as his eyes take me in. "You look good, too," he says. "Like a real New York woman."

I scrunch my nose. "You think so?"

He nods. "Oh, definitely. You've got that polished, high-end thing going on."

Why does that make me sad? "It's really competitive in my field," I say, feeling the need to explain.

"Are you nervous?" he asks.

For a moment, I think he's teasing me about the funny tickle in my stomach that I feel under his gaze, but then I realize he means about my new job. "A little," I say. Then, surrendering the truth, "A lot."

"Yeah?" he leans in.

The sincere interest in his eyes disarms me completely, and I break down. "I don't actually have the job yet. Not really. I have to make it through this ninety-day fight to the death with a bunch of other candidates first. If I don't make the cut, I'll have to find something else. Maybe look for a cheaper apartment."

Sky raises his eyebrows. "Fight to the death? That sounds serious."

"They hired I don't know how many of us, and only one or two will get to stay on permanently after the probationary period."

"Yikes."

A knot forms in my neck just thinking about it. I knead it absent-mindedly. "The application process was a real beast."

"That's why you took the month off between jobs."

I nod. "Honestly, I hoped that coming home would boost my confidence before I start at *Verité*. But so far, it seems to be doing the opposite."

Sky smirks. "I'm not surprised."

Our waitress comes then and introduces herself as Janessa. She's middle-aged, with hair dyed fire-engine red and nails painted like mermaid scales. She places a basket of chips with salsa on the table and fills our waters. As we order our food, I wonder what Sky meant by his cryptic comment. He orders his old-time usual—house fries with a chocolate mint milkshake—and I almost forget it's 2016, not 2005.

As soon as Janessa leaves, I pounce on what he said before. "What do you mean, you're not surprised?"

"Roanoke's a time trap." Sky helps himself to a chip with salsa. "You moved away, grew up, and now you're back where people only knew you as kid AJ." He pops the chip into his mouth.

"Well, yeah." I take a chip. "But shouldn't that highlight how much I've grown? Don't you feel more grown up now than you did when you left?"

He shakes his head. "Did you see that truck I'm driving? Sometimes it feels like Ethiopia was just a dream and I never actually left."

That's different, I think. I'm on the verge of launching my dream career, and Sky is living with his dad, falling back into the same work he was doing before college. I consider my next words carefully. "Are you really going to take over your dad's business?"

Sky stares through the chip in his hand, poking it around the salsa bowl without scooping anything. "That's the plan."

I try to read his face, but there's no expression there. "Is that what you want?"

He sighs. "I think it's what I need to do for now. Just until I can get my dad to a better place." In a quick move, he finishes his chip and leans back in his seat. "It's not good to wallow in the past. I think you'll feel better once the holidays are over and you get back to New York. Sounds like you've just got a case of the holiday blues."

I pull in my chin. "I don't feel blue. I love being home. I've been looking forward to coming back for weeks."

"But now that you're here, you're doubting yourself."

"Yeah, but...I don't think that's got anything to do with Roanoke. If anything, it was running into Benson at the Malans' party. I think that just stirred up some of my old insecurities."

Sky frowns, confused. "Benson? Why? Did you guys date or something?"

I give him a pointed look, waiting for him to remember, but he shakes his head, lost.

"Remember the Snow Ball?"

He rubs his chin, squinting over my head as he tries to jog his memory.

I suddenly feel embarrassed for bringing it up. Sky doesn't remember because it wasn't a big deal. Some boy I never even dated didn't ask me to dance. Big whoop. Why have I let this affect me for so long?

Then recognition dawns in Sky's eyes. "When you were dancing with the chair?"

Grimacing, I nod.

I expect Sky to ask why I haven't gotten over that yet, but he shakes his head. "Weird what resurfaces when you come back to your old stomping grounds."

But that isn't it. The worst part isn't that I suddenly remember the incident, it's that I've never forgotten it. I'm starting to fear this is one childhood hurt that's interfered with all of my relationships since. My love life is like a skipping record, where I bend over backward to be enough, and just when I think I'm going to make it to the next line of the song, I'm back to being single. I think of Adam and how things ended with him. How they always seem to end: with me wondering what I did wrong.

"So, I'm curious"—Sky pulls me from my thoughts—"you said writing for *Verity* has always been a dream of yours—"

"It's *Verité*," I correct with feigned primness.

"Oh, *Verité*." He emphasizes the accent in his most posh voice and bows with a flourish of his arm. "A pox upon me, fair lady. So *Verité*"—he sobers—"what makes this the job of your dreams?"

"Have you ever read it?"

He hesitates, perhaps trying to come up with another way to make me laugh, but then settles for a polite shake of his head, which is good, because he just opened the floodgates of my passion.

"It isn't like any other fashion magazine out there—it's a movement."

"A movement?" A corner of his lip goes up, as if he's not sure if I'm joking or not.

I take a breath. "Imagine you're a teenage girl. Millions of dollars are spent every year on advertisements and products that tell you you're not good enough on your own—that you're not pretty enough, that your stomach isn't flat enough, or your butt isn't the right shape, or your hair is too thin or too frizzy or too dull. Then you see a picture of your favorite celebrity without makeup on the cover of a magazine with every freckle and imperfection visible under bright studio lighting. And then you read about a different standard of beauty: a healthy lifestyle, a healthy mindset. And it's all presented with stunning photography that takes a more wholistic approach to beauty and fashion." I lean forward with almost giddy excitement. "*Verité* magazines are accessible to the same readers as any other fashion magazine, but their content feels like journalism that matters. There was this article they published last summer about textile artists whose techniques were being used without credit by major designers. It had beautiful photography, but more than that, it was investigative journalism that actually led to policy changes."

Granted, that one article was exceptional among the typically featured stories about celebrity skincare and fitness routines, but it seems to get Sky's attention. I plow on, encouraged by the genuine interest in his eyes. "What I like about *Verité* is that they celebrate authenticity. That's why their covers always feature people without makeup or adornment. It's all about the raw beauty of imperfection. They're proving that fashion journalism can have substance and integrity while still celebrating creativity and beauty. I want to be a part of that. Those are the kinds of stories I want to tell."

Janessa the waitress returns then with our food.

I sit on my hands to stop them from waving around, suddenly feeling bashful for my passion.

But there's no judgment in Sky's eyes. Only admiration. He thanks Janessa for the food, then waits for her to leave before he blows out a soft laugh. "Well, now I feel like a jerk. That sounds genuinely awesome. Naked covers and all."

"It is awesome."

"So, what do you need to do to beat out your competition for this job?"

I puff. "Work my tail off."

"Anne Hathaway style?"

"Anne Hathaway style." Golden yolk oozes from the poached egg on my plate as I dig in. "I've got a week and a half before my sister Tiffany comes into town, so I'm going to spend the time studying while my parents are at work during the day. And...probably eating way too many Christmas cookies."

"Solid plan." Sky pushes his fries to the center of the table, within sharing distance.

I take a fry and push my plate closer to the center so he can try my eggs Benedict.

He points his fork at my plate. "That's good."

"Yours too."

He offers me a sip of his milkshake, and I take it without a second thought.

"Do you know what everyone else is up to?" he asks. "I kinda lost track of people who don't leave a digital trail on social media."

"Not even Aisha?"

"I know she's living in New Jersey. She sent my dad a Christmas card from her family. Cute kids. Do you stay in touch?"

"A little. We've been meaning to get together for lunch sometime because she's just across the river from me, but...I guess it's easier to put off stuff like that when you live close enough to make it happen whenever you want but far enough to make it inconvenient."

"Sad."

"Yeah, it's kind of messed up now that I think about it. I should call her when I get back."

"How about Christy?"

"Christy," I smile, "is in the Marines."

"Seriously?"

I nod. "Dead serious. She's been in for two years now. Got another three to go."

He laughs. "Wow. Now, that I didn't see coming. Where's she stationed?"

"Dubai, last I heard. But I think she's being moved to Hawaii in January."

"The Marines." Sky leans back in wonder. "Dang. Good for her."

We spend the next several minutes catching up on the whereabouts of any old friends we can think of as we share our late-night feast. When we're done eating, Sky insists on paying for us both.

As we walk back to his truck, I venture, "So, if taking over your dad's business isn't what you want to do, why do it? Because he wants you to?"

Sky opens my car door for me and doesn't answer until he's settled in his seat. He hesitates before turning the key in the ignition. "I don't know what else to do. My dad's business has been suffering since we lost my mom. It's been...not great." He shakes his head.

"It's not your fault. It's no one's fault, Sky."

"I shouldn't have abandoned him. If I'd come home sooner..." He glances at me out of the corner of his eye and shakes his head again. "We don't need to talk about this. The point is—I'm going to stick around Roanoke for a while. Help my dad."

"What's the dream that you're putting on hold in the meantime?"

Again, he doesn't answer right away. I can't tell if it's because he needs to think about it or because he has to get up the courage to allow himself to think about it. Finally, he says, "I want to build things."

"Isn't that what you do with your dad?"

"Not really." He steers one-handed, arm straight. "We do finish work—countertops and cabinetry, that kind of stuff. Lately, business has been slow, so it's mostly just been warranty runs and repair work."

"What do you want to build?"

A smile creeps up one corner of his mouth. When he looks at me, half his face is illuminated by colored lights twinkling through the branches of the trees that line the road. "I'd like to do something similar to what I did in Ethiopia, but here in the US. Sustainable structures. Affordable housing. I like building communities."

"That sounds cool. You'd do that around here or...?"

"Wherever it's needed. I like the idea of traveling, but"—he shrugs—"this is all just hypothetical, anyway. I'd have to finish my structural engineering degree and all that first."

We turn onto my parents' street. "Have you considered going back to school now?"

He's thoughtful for a moment, then says with a heavy sigh. "I've thought about it, but...I just don't know if I can handle that *and* catching up on all the TV shows I missed while I was in Ethiopia."

There's the humor I remember. I nudge his arm playfully as he pulls up in front of my parents' house. "Well, that *is* an overwhelming task."

"I might have to pull a few all-nighters to get it done."

"Right." I roll my eyes, because from what I remember, Sky barely has the patience to sit through one movie from start to finish before he's got to move around and find something to do with his hands. It used to drive Aisha nuts. "If you make it to the third episode of *Stranger Things* in under a week, I'll be impressed."

Sky's laugh is deep and warm. It feels like home in a way that stepping into my parents' house earlier today didn't. Something locks into place deep inside me, like a puzzle piece that was lost between couch cushions for years and has finally been found. I lean my cheek against the headrest as I take in the shape of him in the dark: the broad shoulders, the hair that looks more like a tumultuous sea now than like rows of frosted spikes, the way it once did. I have to resist the urge to reach out and touch it. "It's really good to see you, Sky Guy."

"You too, Jay-Jay." He's facing me, mirroring my posture with his cheek against the headrest. His truck engine purrs contentedly in Park.

"It's weird," I say. "Some friends, it takes a while to get back into the groove after being apart for a few months. I haven't seen you in six years, and somehow it's like we never stopped talking."

"I was thinking that, too. Remember that time Aisha and I both came home for the holidays and we spent all our time hanging out, the three of us?"

"I remember. I felt bad taking up your alone time."

"That's the thing, though. We tried to have some alone time at first, and it was too awkward. Things only felt normal once you were there."

"No. Really? Well, no wonder your relationship didn't last."

"No kidding."

I used to look up to Skylar because he was older than I. There was always an untouchable quality to him, no matter how many late-night chat sessions transpired between us on AIM or MySpace as we gave one another dating advice and encouragement. It wasn't just that he was my best friend's boyfriend. It was that he drove a car when I had to ask my mom for rides. He was a senior when I was a freshman. He was in college when I was in high school. Only now, sitting across from him in his old truck, do I see him differently. Maybe it's because we're both adults now. Maybe it's that we're still single when most of our friends are married with kids. Maybe it's that we're home for the holidays and feeling strange about life. Whatever the reason, as I look at Skylar Townsend now, I see an equal.

"So, are you going to give Benson Miller another chance?"

His words are so jarring they pull me from my thoughts. "What? Benson? What makes you say that?"

He tilts his head in a kind of shrug. "I don't know. You two were talking at the party. He's single. You're single. You *are* single, right?"

I roll my eyes. "Is it that obvious?"

"I totally made a rude assumption, didn't I? I guess I figured if you were dating someone, you would have told me by this point." He nods to the clock on his dashboard, which shows nearly one in the morning.

"No, no, you were right. I'm single. Newly single, actually."

"I'm sorry."

"Don't be. It's for the best, I guess."

"How recent?"

"Two weeks."

"Dang."

"Yeah."

"You okay?"

I nod. "Yeah. It sucks, but I guess it always does when something ends."

"How long were you with him?"

"Six months." I shake my head. "Pretty consistent with every other past relationship."

He raises his eyebrows. "Really? You haven't dated anyone for longer than that?"

"Nope."

I can see in his face that he wants to ask, but he's too polite.

"It's me," I answer. "I don't know why, but it's me. There's something about me that puts guys off after six months."

"What?" His voice is thick with doubt.

"No, it's true! I seem to have what some guys want, but then once they get close enough to me, they realize that they like what I've got, but they don't like *me*."

"Is there a difference?"

"It's like…" I exhale. "Do you remember how Benson and I kind of had a thing for years?"

"I vaguely remember that you liked him, and then he hurt you."

I allow this comment with a noncommittal rocking of my head. "Did you ever notice that all the girls he dated after that were kind of like me?"

"Uh…"

"Vintage clothes? Red lipstick? Oldies music? The first one even kind of *looked* like me."

Sky shakes his head. "I can't say I ever noticed that, no. To be honest, I don't remember any of the girls Benson dated."

Of course he wouldn't remember. Sky had already graduated high school and moved on with his life by the time Benson was dating. "Trust me—he had a pretty specific type.

"What's your point?"

"For years, I never understood why he didn't date me when I was so obviously his type. What did those other girls have that I didn't? Now, after a few failed relationships, I think I've realized that it isn't about what I have or don't have. It's about me. Who I am. That's what guys don't like."

"Why is it about what guys want? What about what *you* want?"

Once again, his words catch me off guard. "Well," I say, recovering, "if a guy doesn't want me, then it doesn't really matter what I want, does it? I wanted Benson back when I was a kid, but he didn't want me, so that was that."

"Did you still want him after he turned out to be a jerk?"

I don't remember. "No. I guess not."

"So it sounds like it was mutual, then. He didn't want to be seen as predictable by everyone who expected him to ask you out, and you didn't want to be with someone so shallow and insecure. The two of you were incompatible. That's why relationships don't work out. Incompatibility."

For some reason, I feel miffed by his oversimplification of the problem that has plagued me for years. "Oh really?" I say. "So that's what happened with you and Aisha, then? It was mutual? The two of you were just incompatible?"

"Yeah."

I shake my head. "That's not what you said back then. You said you wanted to make it work and she didn't. So, if she'd wanted to, the two of you could have been good together."

"That's what I thought at the time, but it doesn't work that way. We weren't compatible. She just recognized that before I did. It took me a few years to realize she was right."

"Oh, and now that's made you an expert on dating, has it?" The fire in my voice surprises me.

Sky holds up his hands, "No, I didn't mean it like that."

I back down, but there's a thickness in my throat now and a pressure on my chest. "You haven't been in my life for six years, Sky. You don't know the guys I've dated or how my relationships ended."

"You're right. I'm sorry. I shouldn't have—" He shakes his head, blows out a heavy breath. "Man, I must have sounded like a jerk. I'm sorry. Forget I said anything."

"Okay."

My heart thumps hot in my ears as I look out the car window at my parents' house, embarrassed for my reaction. *What is wrong with me?* Maybe this is what Adam meant when he said I was too intense.

I know I should go inside now, but I don't want to leave on this awkward note. Not after the good time we've had together.

Sky breaks the silence. "It's just that I hate for you to believe that you're some kind of broken. You're this smart, beautiful, funny girl with a lot going for you. I don't know what your life has been like over the last six years, but if tonight is any indication, you're still the girl I enjoy being around. If a guy can't see you for who you are, there's nothing wrong with you. I hate to see you play the victim. You deserve better, and I think you deserve to believe better about yourself."

Suddenly it feels like I'm back on the dance floor in 2004, my ice-blue vintage dress tight around my waist as Skylar pries a cold metal chair from my hands. I feel the same desperation to cling to that chair, to that protection from the reality I'm not ready to face. I'm mad at him now, the way I was mad at him then, for taking it away from me.

"I know you mean well," I say. "And I'm thankful that you care." I force myself to look at him. "But I didn't ask for your help, Sky. You can't force me to take it."

There's confusion in his eyes. What's worse, there's disappointment. I can imagine what he's thinking: that AJ hasn't grown up as much as he thought she had. That she's still that same, insecure little girl who puts boys on a pedestal and sets herself up for heartbreak. It stings because I know that it's true. But I don't want to hear it from him. Not tonight.

"I better go," I say. "My mom's probably sleeping with one eye open until she hears me come back." I open my door with a pop of the handle and cold air nips at my hand.

"AJ." Sky reaches out, catching my wrist lightly.

I look back at him. "I had a really nice time tonight, Sky. It's good to see you."

"I don't want to end it like this," he says. "Do you?"

"No," I admit. But I can see in his face that he doesn't get why I'm upset, and I don't really understand it myself, and I just need some time to think through all these crazy feelings.

Thankfully, Sky doesn't pry. Instead, he unbuckles his seat belt. "Come here," he says, opening his arms to me.

I release the door handle and accept his embrace, nestling into the warm comfort of his chest. He smells like woodwork and Old Spice and gingerbread cookies. He rests his chin on the top of my head as he rubs my back. "It's really good to see you, AJ," he murmurs. "I'm sorry I upset you."

"I'm sorry for getting upset," I reply into his chest.

He kisses the top of my head.

Warmth floods my body. My head buzzes with tingly static.

His hands stop rubbing my back for the briefest of moments. Did he feel what I felt?

If I turn my face upward, his lips would be right there. Would he kiss me? I imagine the feeling of his lips on mine and immediately pull from his embrace. My face feels so hot, I wonder if he can see the red in the dark. "I better go," I say again. Cold air washes over us both as I push my door open.

Sky faces forward in his seat, looking as rigid as I feel. "Yep," his voice cracks. He clears his throat. "Yeah, don't want to keep your mom waiting."

The curb is icy. I nearly slip but catch myself on the truck door. "I'll see you later, then?"

"Definitely, yeah."

"Goodnight, Sky."

"Goodnight, AJ."

I close the door. Sky waits until I'm safely inside before I hear his truck drive away.

I'm still hot and tingly all over minutes later as I climb into bed. With my head on the pillow, I feel his arms around me again, relive the sound of his kiss on my head. I trace the lines of his face behind my closed lids, the shape of his lips, and I wonder why I never noticed before that his eyes have little flecks of blue in them.

Part of me wonders what would happen if I text him now and ask him to come back and try that again. The idea makes me shiver. I shake my head, burrowing it deeper into the comfort of my pillow. Sky is my friend. I can't ruin that by using him as my rebound therapy. Especially not when he's in a rut himself. He deserves better than that.

And then there's the other thing. The thing about him that terrifies and infuriates me that I can't quite put my finger on. The thing that made me snap at him when we'd been having a perfectly lovely time moments before. What is wrong with me?

It's late. I'm sure I'll laugh at myself in the morning once my head is clear.

6

Silver Bells

A DAM BROUGHT ME FLOWERS the day he broke up with me. Gerbera daisies.

White ones.

I still don't know if they were supposed to be congratulations for getting the job at *Verité* or if they were a peace offering for the end of our relationship. Maybe it was both. But I still feel stupid every time I think of the way I accepted them with such naive enthusiasm.

I genuinely believed he was about to tell me how proud he was of me for all my hard work—that he was sorry he hadn't believed in me—that he knew I'd do great.

There was no hint of regret behind his tortoise-shell glasses in those puppy-dog brown eyes that had won me over months before. He didn't stumble over his words or shuffle uncomfortably as he tried to put things as delicately as possible. He was straightforward, matter-of-fact, unapologetic.

"This is as far as I go." He said it as if our relationship had been little more than a chance encounter on the subway and we'd reached his stop.

I thought he was joking. Even when he said I was too intense for him. It wasn't until he kissed me goodbye and left me standing there in the doorway of my apartment with the gerbera daisies wrapped in pale pink crepe paper that I realized it was over.

I still don't understand what happened to us. We made a good couple; everyone who knew us said so. We had the same sense of humor, the same taste in movies and music, the same favorite restaurants. When we went out to eat, it was like we'd stepped straight out of a rom-com. He knew to give me his tomatoes, and I knew to give him the ice from my drink without having to say anything. I don't understand how we could have gone from that to over.

Why don't I understand? How could I have been so blind to his loss of interest in me? True, I'd been preoccupied with the application process for *Verité*, but Adam always said he liked a woman who went for what she wanted. Maybe that only applied to when he was the thing being wanted.

I toss in bed as the memories smother my dreams.

Before now, I feel like I've done an impressive job of not dwelling on all of this. I moved on like an adult. And with the new position at *Verité* to prepare for, I haven't had time to cry over another failed relationship. But talking to Sky last night seemed to uncover what was still smoldering beneath the surface. His words ring through the empty hallway of my flashback: *The two of you were incompatible. That's why relationships don't work out. Incompatibility.*

Is it really that simple? Were Adam and I just incompatible?

If so, why couldn't I see it?

If Sky is right and all failed relationships simply come down to incompatibility, then why am I always the one who's blindsided? Am I so desperate to be in a relationship that I can't see when someone isn't a good fit for me?

It's easier to believe that I have some freakish flaw that scares guys away once they get close enough to discover it. Flaws can be resolved. If there's something wrong with me, then that means there's something I can fix. What can I do about compatibility blindness? Nothing.

The smell of bacon wafts into my room, stirring me from my heavy thoughts. I'm home now; I shouldn't be fretting over Adam. I came to enjoy my family. And from the smell of it, this morning with my parents is going to be delicious. My mom is the best at spoiling visitors with top-quality breakfasts.

I stretch, ignoring the fact that I just thought of myself as a visitor in this house, and reach to check the time on my phone screen.

There's a text from Skylar.

Heat flushes my face as I remember the way I snapped at him last night, and how confused he looked by it. He couldn't have known he was poking at hot coals with his kind words. Cautiously, I thumb open his message.

> So, when do I get to read something you've written?

Despite the tension that's kept me tossing and turning all night, I can't help but smile.

> When you subscribe to my girly magazine ;)

My thumb hovers over the Send button. Too flirty?

I erase the message and watch the cursor blink expectantly at me for several moments before setting my phone back on the nightstand and rolling onto my back to stare at the ceiling.

Maybe I should wait for my head to clear before I respond. I still feel somewhat feverish from the memory of his lips on the top of my head last night, and clearly, I'm still a mess from my recent breakup. I need to be careful.

But I don't want Sky to think he scared me off with his innocent peck, so I snatch my phone back.

> When I can actually get myself to write something.

His reply is quick.

> Any way I can help?

I hesitate. Sky is sweet and patient and understanding. He's also handsome and available, and everything about him spells "danger" in my current state. It's probably best if I take a step back until I'm feeling more stable.

> That's sweet of you to ask. I'll let you know.

There's a scratch on my door followed by a familiar doggy sigh. It's the last push I need to get out of bed.

Char's stumpy tail goes crazy when I open the door to let him in. He knows not to jump, but his body wriggles with excited energy as I shower him with kisses and back scratches before making my way down the hall.

Dad appears at the foot of the stairs, all dressed for the day in a green flannel shirt with jeans, but the look is rendered less rugged by the addition of a frilly apron. "There's our sleeping beauty," he announces loudly at the sight of me before stepping back into the kitchen.

"Morning, hon," Mom's voice calls.

I follow the sound of sizzling bacon into a kitchen I hardly recognize. "Whoa." I take a step back.

Not only have the boxed fluorescents been replaced by a fancy new light fixture, raising the height of the ceiling by almost a full foot, but the yellowish laminate countertops have also been replaced by glossy granite. The cabinets, once a pale honey oak, are now white. New blue curtains hang from the window over the sink. And an entire row of cupboards that used to be above the buffet counter is gone. Now I can actually see my mom in her red plaid apron standing behind the stove before I've even entered the kitchen. "What do you think?" she sings with a dramatic sweep of her arm in the new space.

"Where am I?" I reply. "This can't be the same kitchen."

Mom claps her hands in delight.

Behind her, Dad stirs a bowl of waffle mix. "Probably could have bought a new house for what it cost."

Mom waves him off. "Oh, hush, it was practically free. Come and feel these countertops!"

I join her at the stove and let her guide my hand along the smooth granite. "Oooh," I say, more to please her than anything else.

"Right? And look!" She points to the sink. For the first time, I notice that it, too, is new. It's bigger now. Deeper. One of those farmhouse styles, with an old-fashioned dark bronze faucet with a head that pulls out like a hose.

"Dang, Mom, you really went all out."

"She always wanted a fancy kitchen," says Dad. "Doug Townsend installed the countertops, but I did everything else."

"It looks amazing." I sit on one of the barstools at the buffet. "When did Doug do the countertops?"

Mom and Dad look at each other, trying to remember. "It's been a while," Mom says. "February? March? Somewhere around there. Why?"

"Just wondering."

If Doug managed to install my parents' countertops earlier this year, maybe it's not such a long shot that he'll be able to get back on his feet now that Skylar's home.

There's a soft sizzle as Dad pours batter onto the hot waffle iron.

Mom tongs the last strips of bacon from the stove before turning off the burner.

I remember my manners. "May I help?"

"There are some strawberries in the fridge," Mom suggests.

I jump in to help chop but quickly realize I don't know where anything is in this new kitchen. Mom has to hand me a knife from the last drawer I would have checked, and Dad pulls a built-in cutting board straight out from the counter. *Yeesh*, I think, but I say, "Fancy-shmancy."

"It's just a pain to clean," Dad grumbles.

Mom humphs. "I like it."

I don't know what unsettles me more: my bedroom staying exactly as I left it, or the unfamiliar upgrades to the rest of the house.

As I slice strawberries, Dad looks at his watch. "We better eat quickly if we want to beat the Saturday rush."

Mom returns to the kitchen. "We'll be fine."

"What rush?" I ask. "Where are you going?"

They both stop to look at me. My dad tucks his chin so he can see me over the top of his glasses as he indicates his outfit. "Silver Bells!"

For the first time, I realize he's not just dressed for a quiet day at home. He's got his tree-hunting shirt on and his hiking boots. Mom is ready to go traipsing through a muddy farm in her work jeans and red flannel, too.

I gasp. "We're getting the tree today?"

"Ding, ding, ding!" Dad chimes like I've just won a game show.

I was so distracted by the changes to the house, I didn't even realize there wasn't a Christmas tree set up in the living room yet. In the past, my family always went to Silver Bells, the local tree farm, on the day after Thanksgiving.

"We wanted to wait and do it with you," Mom says.

I hesitate, thinking of Evelyn Marx's email and the weight of the battle that awaits me in New York. I was going to study today. But one look at the excitement in my parents' eyes and I push these thoughts to the back of my mind. A few hours won't hurt.

"Jingle Bell Rock" plays from stadium speakers overhead as I follow my parents through the candy cane–striped arch into Silver Bells tree farm. There's a gift shop to our left that looks like Santa's workshop, where they sell homemade fudge and Christmas decor from July to January. There's already a line out the door of kids waiting to sit on Santa's lap. I remember the Silver Bells Santa setup being the best I've ever seen, with a real antique sleigh and free hot cocoa for the taking. But Dad charges right past the shop with a crazed urgency that he reserves for this activity alone.

"Alright team," he says, drawing me and Mom into a huddle. "Looks like the competition is fierce today."

I look past him toward the rows of trees, stretching on for acres. From here, I spy maybe three or four other families moseying down the rows.

"Focus, AJ!" Dad pulls me in closer until I look at him, trying not to laugh. "I think we'll improve our odds if we split up."

Mom rolls her eyes. "Oh, come on, Todd. What's the point of coming together if we're going to split up?"

"There aren't that many people," I point out, but he cuts me off.

"We've lost almost two weeks already! The best trees have been picked over. We can't afford to make any more sacrifices. We're Banners. This is how we've brought home the best trees every year since 1981."

Mom and I share a surrendering glance. "Fine," we sigh in unison.

Dad gives us both a shake. "That's my girls! Alright, AJ, you take the north quarter." He points with two fingers toward the far end of the lot, like a football coach describing a play. "Fiona, center field. I'll go south." He hands us each a roll of neon orange flagging tape.

I roll my head back in exasperation. "Dad, seriously?"

Ignoring me, Dad shoves the tape into my hand. "We'll meet back here in an hour and review our findings together."

"An hour?" I protest. "How about fifteen minutes? I can't stay out here all day—"

"I've got book club at two," Mom cuts in. "We've gotta speed this up."

Dad looks injured. "What is this? Have you both gone soft on me?"

"No, I've just grown longer legs," I say. "Let's make it a race. Last one back to the gift shop buys fudge for the other two?"

"I like that," says Mom.

Dad chews on the idea for a second before nodding. "Alright, alright. But don't get sloppy. We're going to have to look at this tree for the rest of the month. And forever after in pictures."

I hold my hand in. "Break on three?"

Mom and Dad place their hands on mine. Mom is already crouching, ready to sprint.

We chant together, "One, two, three, break!"

I dart toward the north end of the lot as my dad charges the other direction, nearly bowling over a family with young kids in his haste. Mom is so fast I don't even see her disappear into the trees.

I never used to understand why my oldest sister Tara complained about getting a real tree instead of opting for a fake one like a lot of our friends had. Now, as I make my way down a row of Douglas firs, I suddenly have memories of shivering under a blanket with Luke and Tiffany while the sky darkened and our dad refused to go home until we found the perfect tree.

The only way we're getting out of here before noon is if I take my job seriously. I need a strategy. I hurry past the Douglas firs without stopping to look at any of them. Dad's a blue spruce man. I recognize the silvery greenery up ahead and round a corner without realizing there's a person behind the tree nearest to me until I nearly knock us both to the ground.

"Oof!"

"Oh, I'm sorry," I gasp as hot chocolate sloshes down the front of my sweater.

The man steadies his paper cup as he takes a step back. "Crap, my bad."

I freeze. It's Benson Miller wearing a red scarf and a black peacoat and looking like he stepped out of a J. Crew catalog.

"AJ," he says.

I stumble back a step. "Benson! What are you doing here?"

He winces at the sight of my wet sweater and moves his hands uselessly, as if trying to figure out how to undo the spill. "I'm so sorry. They really should put lids on these things." He empties the rest of his cup with a toss before searching his pockets for something to help.

"Don't worry about it," I blurt. "It's my fault. I wasn't watching where I was going."

"Uh, here." He hands me a travel-size packet of tissues from his pocket and watches as I dab at my sweater.

"Really, it's fine," I say. "This sweater is old, anyway. It's seen a lot worse than hot chocolate spills, I can tell you that." I regret the words as soon as they tumble from my mouth. A *lot* worse? What? Am I constantly smearing poop and vomit on my sweater?

"Those tissues suck," Benson says as he watches a tissue practically disintegrate in my hand when it meets with the wet fibers. "Here," he unwinds his scarf, and for a second I think he's going to use it as a towel on me.

I step back, "What? No! Don't ruin your nice scarf."

He pauses, then nods at my bare neck. "It can cover the stain. And hopefully keep you from freezing once the cocoa cools."

"Oh." I let him wrap the scarf around my neck. It smells like sandalwood and mulled wine, and it feels like a cloud. Benson is so close to me I have to look up to see his face. He's taller than I realized. Feeling the warmth of his body takes my breath away for a moment. I swallow as he steps back. "Thank you."

He smiles the subtle smile that used to make me weak at the knees as a teenager. "Did you ask what I'm doing here?"

I blink. "Uh..." Seeing the humor in his eyes, I allow myself to laugh. "I guess I did. Stupid things come out of my mouth when I'm surprised."

He laughs, too. I'm amazed by the sound of it—soft and subtle, like his smile. I've never made him laugh before.

"My folks sent me to pick out a tree," he explains. His hands come up in a lost gesture. "Raccoons built a nest in the fake one, and my mom wants to wait for the after-Christmas sales to replace it." He nods at the roll of orange flag tape I'm wearing like a bracelet. "Are you...running a race?"

"Ha, you could say that. Are your parents here with you?" I'm not about to tell him my family's tradition of marking potential trees like a bunch of hoodlums.

He shakes his head. "Nah, this is just a quick run so I can help put it up before I have to head back to work tomorrow. Yours here?"

"Yeah." I wave my hand vaguely toward my parents. "We split up to make sure we don't miss a single twig."

Benson turns to take in the sprawling farm. "A lot of ground to cover," he says.

"Well, I've learned how to cut a few corners over the years. Skip the ones with obvious holes or twiggy necks, go for something sturdy like a Fraser fir or a blue spruce."

He makes an impressed face. "Sounds like you know your trees. What do you think of this one?" he nods to the tree he was coming out from behind when I ran into him.

I scrunch my nose at it. "Eh, that's a Douglas fir. It's got that classic cone shape you want, but it's a glorified bush. If your mom's got heavy ornaments, the branches will droop." I bounce a bough to demonstrate. "See? Floppy."

Benson clicks his tongue in disappointment. "Shoot, I guess I better keep looking. Mind if I join you? Learn your ways?"

My stomach feels like it does a little flip. "Sh-sure! I mean—" I clear my throat, try to be cool. "As long as you understand we're rivals in this arena. My dad will fight you for the best tree in the lot."

He blows a breath. "Guess I'll have to settle for second-best."

Biting back a smile, I nod for him to follow me toward the silvery spruces ahead. Benson falls into step beside me.

"You don't *have* to settle for second-best," I clarify. "There is no objectively perfect tree. You might have a different taste than my family."

Benson considers this. "Hmm, well, I don't want floppy branches."

"Personally, I'm partial to a tree with some character. I like it when the branches angle upward and there's just a little trunk visible."

He grimaces. "No naked trunk for me. We like our trees nice and full at the Miller house."

I offer my hand palm up. "There you go. We're not competitors, after all."

We weave our way through a row of Fraser firs, pausing now and then when Benson points one out. "Too much trunk?" he asks.

I shake my head. "Too much for me."

"How about that one?"

I walk in a circle around the next one he points out and stop to tie a piece of flag tape to a bough. "Just the right amount of trunk. My mom likes Frasers."

"What's with the ribbon?" Benson asks.

I shrink, embarrassed. "Part of the process. Puts it in the running for the Banner Tree of the Year Award."

When Benson laughs, I feel as if I've grown a little taller. That's twice I've made him laugh now. Would he have found me funny if we'd talked more back when we were teenagers? Would things have been different between us?

"Won't it throw the Silver Bells people off?" he asks. "Marking their trees?"

"That's why we have to be fast," I say. "We remove the flags as we go until we find *the* tree."

We weave our way farther into the lot, and I mark a tree occasionally, but it's hard to focus on the trees when Benson's arm brushes mine as we walk or when I catch him looking at me out of the corner of his eye. Suddenly, I find myself back to our old game of stealing glances and looking away again quickly. It's exciting, but also makes me feel slightly sick.

What am I doing? I can't fall into this again. I'm a grown woman! I should have outgrown this little-girl crush and this puppy-dog eagerness to please.

"So," Benson says, stopping in front of a tall, full noble fir. "How does this one measure up to your standards?"

Shaking away my anxious thoughts, I give the tree a once-over, noting the strong branches and deep green needles. "Now *this* is a tree with character. Sturdy, full, good branch structure. A little bushy for my taste, but you like that, right? It'll hold any ornaments you've got."

"Really?" He walks around it, inspecting the tree from all angles. "I think it might be the one, then."

My chest flutters. We found a tree. *Together.* I shift, feeling a little awkward. "Yeah, you're not settling for second-best, after all."

Benson smiles. "I guess not." The way he says it while looking right at me makes my neck burn hot and my ears feel like they'd glow redder than Rudolph's nose in the dark.

He pulls his eyes away from my face and takes in the tree again. "Think you could hold it for me while I cut?"

I shake myself. "Yeah, of course, yes."

As Benson kneels on the ground and begins sawing, I grip the tree's trunk with my face turned to the side to avoid a mouthful of pine needles. With a final crack of wood, the tree comes free.

Benson stands, panting from the exertion. He wipes a bead of sweat from his forehead before taking the tree off my hands. "Thank you."

"Of course." I step back, maybe a little too far, too quickly. Suddenly I don't know what to do with my hands. "That's a good tree. I hope your family likes it."

I expect him to wave goodbye and haul his tree away, but he lingers, looking at me. "I'm glad I ran into you," he says.

There goes my stomach again, doing flips.

"Yeah," I get out. "Me too." Then, remembering his scarf, I start to unwind it from around my neck.

Benson holds up a hand. "Keep it," he says. "You can return it to me next time we see each other. Maybe over coffee?"

I freeze mid–scarf removal, trying to process the words. I blink. "Oh."

"If you want to. No pressure."

"No, yeah, that sounds great." I let the scarf fall back around my neck and shift my weight. "Sure, yeah. Yes, I'd like that. Coffee. Coffee's great."

He laughs again. "Good. It's a date, then. Here, let me"—he hugs his tree with one arm and pats his pockets with the other until he finds his phone—"just get your number."

Benson Miller is asking for my number. I fumble for my phone before I realize I don't need it to give him what he's waiting for. I rattle off my number and watch in a daze as he plugs it into his phone.

"I've got a crazy work schedule this next week," he says as he hits Save with his thumb. Then he slides his phone back into his coat pocket and looks up at me. "But I've got a free morning on the fourteenth, if you're available."

"The fourteenth..." I thumb my phone like I'm checking my calendar, but really, it's just nervous scrolling. I can't see a thing through the haze of my disbelief. "Yeah, that should work for me."

"Great, I'll text you."

"Great. Okay, yeah. Sounds good."

"Good."

"Good."

Benson gives his tree a little shake. "Alright, I better get this guy home. See you next Wednesday."

As I watch him leave, I feel like my head might float away like a balloon.

Did I really just set a date with Benson Miller?

7

Book Club

P EGGY MALAN'S HOUSE SMELLS like cinnamon and stewed apples when my mom and I walk through the front door. A cheer goes up from several women sitting in the parlor as we slide off our shoes in the entryway.

"AJ, sweetheart, so glad you could join us!" Peggy clasps her hands together from her seat in front of the opulently decorated fireplace. Her dining room chairs sit in a circle, filled with familiar faces from my childhood, all beaming back at me.

"Sorry we're late, ladies." My mom hangs her coat. "We're coming straight from Silver Bells."

I follow her into the parlor, but there's only one seat left.

Peggy jumps to her feet. "Oh, here, let me get a chair for our honored guest." She squeezes her way out of the circle and goes to get another chair from the dining room while Aisha's mom, Claire Tan, stands to give me a hug.

"Welcome home, Amelia Jane," she says in that warm, honey-slow Southern accent I've always loved. She's the only person I know who calls me by my full name. I can still remember the first time I went to Aisha's for a tea party and her mother asked what AJ stood for. *Amelia Jane*, she repeated after me, and the name had never sounded dreamier. *What a beautiful name. May I call you Amelia Jane?* I think I would have let her call me anything she wanted. Her embrace feels like being wrapped in a blanket fresh from the dryer, and she smells like a spa.

"Thank you, Mrs. Tan," I say. "Is Aisha coming home for the holidays?"

Claire releases me from her embrace, but her hands stay on my arms and slide down to my elbows so she can hold me while she looks into my face. "Oh, not this year, I'm sorry to say. We had them for Thanksgiving, so Ryan's family gets them for Christmas in Oklahoma."

Peggy returns and slides a chair behind me. My mom and Sharla Marie—a local consignment boutique owner—scoot over to make room.

Claire Tan gives my shoulders a final squeeze before she returns to her seat.

"We're so excited to hear about your big break with *Verité*," says a girl from across the circle. She's the same age as my oldest sister Tara. Her name escapes me for the moment, but I remember her big hipster glasses that look especially large and round because she is so tiny. Her auburn hair is swept up into a messy bun under a maroon beanie that has a hole in the top for the bun. She's got more freckles than anyone I've ever seen, even in the winter. More are visible on her slender arm when her oversized sweater pools around her elbow as she pushes her glasses up the bridge of her pointed nose.

Peggy picks up the latest issue of *Verité* from a basket at her feet and waves it for everyone to see. "Did anyone else order a subscription when they heard?"

My stomach gives an anxious twist as several other women in the circle laugh and say they have. "Will you sign our copies?" Sharla Marie jokes beside me with a playful wink. Her collection of vintage necklaces and bracelets jingle against each other with the sway of her body.

"Oh geez." I force a laugh and squirm under their gazes. Big Glasses Girl's magnified blinking is especially unnerving. Can she see right through me? "You flatter me. What book are you all reading this month?"

Mom pulls her copy out of her purse as Peggy holds up her own for me to see. "Have you read this one?"

I squint to read the title. *Beneath the Oak Tree* by Isabelle Greyson. I don't recognize the name, but the cover looks similar to others in its genre, with a hazy image of an old tree in an idyllic Southern setting, a little blurred around the edges, with a romantic script font.

Peggy takes my hesitation as a no. "This woman inherits her grandmother's farm, and when she goes to restore it, she finds a bunch of old love letters hidden in an oak tree."

"No spoilers, please!" Larissa Miller holds up her hand to stop Peggy. "Some of us are still on chapter eight." Benson gets his fair skin and thick dark hair from her, but her eyes are a striking blue instead of deep brown like his.

I suddenly remember that I'm still wearing her son's scarf around my neck and cross my arms self-consciously. Has she noticed? Would she recognize Benson's scarf? Does she know he asked me out this morning? Did he tell her I helped him pick out their tree?

But Larissa Miller doesn't look at me. Her eyes are still on Peggy.

"She didn't say anything that isn't already in the synopsis," says a woman across from Mrs. Miller. *Shipley*, I think. *Donna Shipley*. I know her mostly as the woman who used to work in the Students Resources Center when I was in high school, but I know she replaced Skylar's mother as president of the Roanoke Neighbors Network after she died. Donna is a stout woman with frizzy, curly hair that's mostly gray with a hint of copper from faded dye. I remember being intimidated by her as a kid because of her no-nonsense tone of voice and serious expression. Even now, her voice seems to command a certain level of respect around the circle.

"I haven't gotten to the part where she finds the letters yet, either," says my mom.

I'm relieved when the conversation moves forward into discussing the book and away from me and *Verité*. It gives me a chance to observe and try to remember people's names as I look around the circle. There are two other women who haven't spoken yet. One with thick red hair about my mom's age I recognize as Matilda Hatch, who always used to help Skylar's mom organize events like the Snow Ball, and a younger blond woman I don't recognize sits beside Big Glasses Girl.

My stomach growls. I hug myself as if it will smother the sound, but everyone in the circle is too polite to look at me. Hunting for a Christmas tree took up our entire morning, and Mom and I skipped lunch to make it to the book club. I can't help but notice that everyone in the circle has a little plate of food they're picking at while they talk and mugs of something warm to drink.

Sharla Marie nudges my arm and holds up her small plate of pastries for me to see before nodding her head toward the window, where a table of tasty things waits to be enjoyed. "Help yourself," she says in a whisper so as not to interrupt the discussion.

Mom nods for me to go for it. Since I have nothing to contribute to the conversation about a book I haven't read, I comply.

The spread is nothing less than what I would expect from Peggy Malan. There are a few leftovers from her Christmas party—cream cheese balls with crackers, succulent ham made into little tea sandwiches, and some cookies. There are also little fruit tarts and flaky Danishes that look like they belong in the window of a French patisserie. No doubt Peggy made it all herself.

"I like your scarf," someone whispers from behind.

I jump and whirl around, fully expecting to see Benson's mother looking disapproving. But it's Big Glasses Girl, come to refill her mug with hot apple cider.

"Oh, thanks," I breathe. Mrs. Miller is still in her seat with her back to me. "It's not mine." I feel the need to explain, just in case Mrs. Miller is listening. "I borrowed it from a friend." The word "friend" tastes strange on my tongue when describing Benson. Is that what we are now?

Big Glasses Girl raises her mug but doesn't take a sip, just holds it there under her chin while the steam fogs the lower half of her lenses. I'm not tall, but I stand a full head above her. "You look so grown up," she says, shaking her head in disbelief. "I remember when you were just a cute little girl playing with sidewalk chalk."

I rack my brain for her name. She wasn't one of Tara's closest friends, but clearly, they hung out enough for her to remember me. "Your kids must be getting big," I say, hoping that hearing about her family will jog my memory.

Her eyes widen, "They're huge! Prue will be sixteen next year, can you believe it? Scott's been helping her prepare to get her learner's permit—" She shakes her head, like the thought is too much for her.

Scott. *Scott Keys!* That's a name that's easy to remember. He was one of Tara's friends in high school. Suddenly everything clicks. Big Glasses Girl is Reagan Keys. I recognize her name mostly from my mom talking about the book club, but I didn't realize who she was until now. She and Scott married right out of high school, if I remember correctly.

Matilda Hatch, who's sitting closest to the table, turns around in her seat to participate in our conversation. Her thin lips purse into an even thinner line when she smiles, but the apples of her cheeks are so prominent, sloping into friendly dimples, that she always looks like she's smiling.

"All you kids have grown up so fast," she says. "We need this next generation to fill the void you left in Roanoke when you all grew up and moved out."

Reagan sips her cider. She never left Roanoke.

Quickly realizing her mistake, Matilda amends, "Except for you, Reagan. You do so much to keep the lifeblood of this little town pumping."

Reagan forces an appreciative smile, but it's clear she's still miffed. "I just want my kids to have what I had. We used to have so many fun things to do around here. Summer fundraiser picnics, pinewood derbies, the Snow Ball..."

Matilda nods her understanding with a sigh. "Kate used to head up a lot of those events. I think when most of you young people moved out and she passed away, we never fully recovered."

The book discussion comes to a halt at the mention of Skylar's mom. Donna Shipley puts her book down. "I don't think that's fair," she says. "The RNN has grown a lot in the last six years. We just host different events to meet the needs of an older neighborhood demographic."

The Roanoke Neighbors Network is a private organization that manages most communication and events in Roanoke.

"Yes," Matilda says, "but the next generation is growing up now. Reagan's kids are teenagers. When's the last time we hosted an event for their age group?"

"We're getting there," Donna replies. "Once we have our own building, it'll be easier to organize things like that."

Now it's my mom who speaks up. "A building is going to take time. Kids grow up fast."

Sharla Marie says, more to herself than anyone else, "Here we go, another RNN meeting." She stands, jewelry tinkling, and joins me at the table to refill her plate.

"Well..." Matilda says, and shares a look with Donna, who nods her consent. "Actually, we hope to have a building within the next few months."

Everyone looks at Donna to explain.

Donna smiles and makes excited fists. "We got approved for government funding to start a community center."

Peggy throws her arms into the air triumphantly.

My mom claps her hands.

The blond girl cheers.

"It's about time," says Reagan.

Donna nods. "Claire has been scoping out a few potential locations. Most of what's available right now is farther away than we'd like, but hopefully something will open up soon."

"What about the Morley Mansion?" Sharla Marie asks. "That's been sitting empty for a while. Maybe you could use the government funding to renovate it."

Donna shakes her head. "The idea came up, but it won't work for us. The board agreed we want something bigger, more modern."

"And ADA accessible," Larissa Miller adds. "Old houses have a lot of stairs and narrow hallways."

"And cramped rooms," says Claire Tan.

Donna nods. "Yes, we want lots of open space. Tennis courts, a basketball court, maybe a swimming pool..."

"Oh yes," says the young blond woman I don't recognize. "*Please,* let's have a swimming pool!"

"Right?" Reagan and the woman exchange a look. "It would be *so* nice not to have to drive all the way to McMinnville to take the kids swimming."

Donna holds her hands up. "I know, I know. Let's not get ahead of ourselves. We need to find a building first. The pool, most likely, will need to wait until we can afford to install one."

"You should put the word out in the newsletter," Larissa Miller says. "I'm sure there are properties people will sell if they know it will go toward something like this."

"Margot is working on it," Donna says.

At the mention of the newsletter, Matilda Hatch turns back to me and grabs my hand. "AJ, you should write something for our little paper while you're in town. It would be so fun to read something of yours."

"Oooh," Sharla Marie says beside me through a bite of cranberry tart. "That might get people to actually read the newsletter."

"I read the newsletter," says my mom.

Matilda Hatch is still holding my hand, waiting for me to reply. I feel the eyes of Mrs. Miller on me and wonder if she's recognized her son's scarf around my neck yet. Does she even remember who I am? "Oh, I don't know about that," I say.

The last thing I need is to draw more attention to myself and my writing. What if things don't work out at *Verité*? Really, I should be home right now preparing for that, not here flaunting my writing abilities.

"You should," my mom says. "You've got time!"

My stomach gives a nervous twist. Why didn't I just tell my mom about the trial period on that long drive from the airport? "I'll think about it," I say.

Larissa Miller looks at her phone and groans before shoving her book into her purse.

Peggy looks at her. "Are you heading out?"

"I'm sorry," Mrs. Miller sighs. "We had a raccoon problem in our attic. Benson says they got to the ornaments, so I've got to go assess the damage."

There's a collective groan of sympathy around the circle.

"We had squirrels chew right through our storage bins last year," says the blond girl I don't know. "I guess there was still some candy in the Easter grass."

After Mrs. Miller ducks out, Peggy brings the conversation back to *Beneath the Oak Tree*, and Sharla Marie returns to her seat.

Before she leaves my side, Reagan leans in and whispers, "I'd love to hear all about New York while you're in town. Some of us just have to live vicariously through you." She gives a half smile on her way back to her seat.

I release a slow breath.

No more putting it off. It's time to get serious about preparing for this new job.

After book club, my mom and I walk home. It's cold out, but the sun breaks through the clouds, making the sidewalk misty as fallen rain evaporates before our eyes. Wet leaves stick to the pavement like a decoupage art project. It smells like pine.

"What do you think?" my mom asks as we walk. "Is the tree ready for decorating, or is your dad still stringing the lights?"

"I think he got halfway through stringing the lights, and then half of them went out, and he's still trying to figure out which bulb is the culprit."

Mom laughs. "That's probably right. We should have him pick up dinner when he goes out to buy a new strand."

After another moment, I breathe in. "Mom? I need to work for a bit when we get home."

"Oh." She tries to think what I'm talking about on her own for a second before asking, "Work on what?"

"The job with *Verité*? It's not really...in the bag yet."

"Oh," she says again.

"Yeah... I mean, they hired me! But then there's this ninety-day trial period—"

"Oh, honey, all jobs have that."

"Yeah, but not all jobs hire multiple candidates for the same position and then only keep one of them after the ninety days end."

"Oh."

"Yeah."

"How many candidates?"

I shake my head. "I don't know. The details are vague. All I know is, they're going to be evaluating my performance against everyone else's for the first three months, and then if I don't make the cut, that's it."

My mom chews on this for a few moments. Finally, she says, "Hmm. That does sound like a challenge."

I drop my face into my hands and groan. "What do I do?"

"Hey!" Mom stops and pulls my hands down, turning me to face her. "I said it sounds like a challenge, not the end of the world. When have you ever let a challenge hold you back from reaching for the stars? Hmm?"

I look into her eyes. They are so earnest, so full of confidence in me, it makes me want to melt into her arms and cry.

"You're my AJ," Mom continues. "My determined girl. You made your own clothes in high school and wore them through the halls like a queen, not a care in the world about what the other girls were wearing."

I almost don't correct her, but can't help myself. "I only made a few things. The rest came from thrift stores."

Mom says, "Pshh! I mean, you had your own style, and you wore it fearlessly. You also worked hard to get into the school you wanted. You moved to New York all by yourself. I am so proud of you."

A lump forms in my throat. "But all these people expect me to have the job," I croak.

"Sweetheart, people in this town would support you if you flipped burgers at a fast-food joint. We only make a big deal about your new job because *you* care about it and we love you. So don't you think for a minute that you're going to let other people down. The only person you can let down is yourself if you don't try your best. So try your best."

My mom. I forgot how wonderful her pep talks can be. I swallow the lump in my throat and shake myself to get rid of the silly doubts that have been pestering me. "You're right," I say. "It's just a challenge. I can face a challenge."

"That's my girl! Now, what's your game plan?"

As we fall into step again toward home, I consider the invitation to write for the RNN newsletter. "I guess a newsletter article could be a good place to start. Normally I'd be able to whip something like that out in an afternoon. But lately I've been...blocked."

My mom nods her understanding. "Writer's block."

It sounds so run-of-the-mill when she says it out loud. I want to tell her that this is different. That I've never felt anything this paralyzing before. But I cringe at how pathetic it would sound.

"You know, Dad and I will be at work during the week," she says. "You'll have the house all to yourself for most hours of the day until the others come. That should give you some quiet time to work through this. What do you think?"

I nod and try to muster up my usual determination. "Yeah, I'm sure that will help."

"But until Monday," my mom says, "your dad and I would love to spend the weekend with you. Would that be alright?"

Feeling relieved that everything is out in the open, I manage a smile and nod. "Yeah, that sounds wonderful."

"Alright, let's go decorate this tree!"

As we round the corner onto our street, I want to shake off my worries, but something still nags at me.

My mother still thinks of me as that fearless girl who wore vintage clothes to school without a care in the world. But part of me wonders if that girl still exists. I haven't been able to write a word since Adam left me with that bouquet of gerbera daisies. Would that fearless young AJ have let a breakup break her, the way Adam seems to have broken me?

Maybe she would have...

My hand goes to Benson's scarf around my neck. All this time I've thought it was my breakup with Adam that brought on this writer's block, but this creative paralysis must have roots that go back further than that. Could it be that all of my problems started that night at the Snow Ball when I experienced my first heartbreak? That would explain why running into Benson last night seemed to stir up old insecurities for me, and why I haven't managed to let go of that hurt after all these years.

Maybe this was meant to be. Maybe I need to go on this date with Benson so I can confront him about what happened between us and close the book on that chapter of my life once and for all. Maybe he wants that, too.

I know it might be too much to hope that the solution to all my dating woes and career roadblocks could be this simple. But it's worth a shot.

It's time to let go of the past and look forward to a new future: one where I don't let my childhood insecurities hold me back.

8

Buttons and Beaus

A BELL JINGLES WHEN I enter Sharla Marie's Buttons and Beaus Consignment Boutique. It smells like nutmeg and vanilla. Eartha Kitt sings "Nothin' for Christmas" from a crackling record player in the corner while the floorboards groan loudly beneath my feet. The place looks plucked from a French countryside, with chic white armchairs and pastel pillows around a pedestal and floor-length mirror, and a vintage fireplace mantel tastefully adorned with garlands and candlesticks. Beyond this, racks of clothes stand between me and the counter, but Sharla Marie is nowhere to be found. I seem to be the only one here.

Just as I think this, Sharla Marie's voice calls from the back of the store, "I'll be right with you!"

My parents' old film Nikon hangs from my neck. I familiarize myself with the camera as I peruse the boutique, playing with the aperture ring and the shutter speed knob, snapping a few practice photos to get the exposure settings right.

I spent the morning on my parents' living room floor with the last years' worth of *Verité* magazines laid out in a circle around me and my laptop open on my lap. It's how I spent most of September and October when I was applying for the junior editor position. My roommate Jody had called it my séance circle, claiming I went into a kind of trance and began muttering incoherently under my breath after midnight if she didn't intervene and send me to bed. This time, I didn't stay in the circle for long. I practically have those magazine issues memorized by now. Mostly, I studied the email from Evelyn Marx.

You'll be working on a variety of editorial tasks, including article writing, content editing, and assisting with photo shoots and interviews. We encourage you to bring fresh ideas and your unique perspective to the table. We'll evaluate your performance based on the quality of your work, your ability to meet deadlines, your collaboration with the team, and your initiative to contribute to the magazine's overall goals.

Before moving to New York, the tiny independent magazine I wrote for in Boulder, Colorado, covered topics ranging from restaurant reviews to community events. The position wasn't competitive, and I could select my own topics because the senior editor of the magazine cared more about having something to print each month than he did about *what* was printed. As long as I cranked out so many words per week and came up with snappy titles, I was good enough. Prior to that, I wrote for my school paper at the University of Colorado as a student.

How long will it take before Evelyn Marx realizes I'm a fraud? That I don't have nearly enough experience to compete with the other candidates for this position? Honestly, I don't even know how I made it through the application process with my limited experience.

I snap a picture of the festive mantel at the front of the store. One of the fun challenges with an analog camera is that I can't know for sure how well a picture will come out until the film is developed—which is its own kind of creative freedom. I can take decent photos with my phone with less fuss, and I'm sure I won't be expected to actually take photos during *Verité* photo shoots, but there's something reassuring about the weight of the SLR in my hands that makes me feel like a legit journalist. Or maybe it's just more fun. Either way, it'll be good to brush up on the skills I learned in my college photography classes.

A rack of formal dresses catches my eye toward the back of the shop, because most of them are vintage, and I spent years training my eye to spot vintage formal wear in thrift stores. I'm admiring a sparkly ice-blue gown that reminds me of what I wore to my first Snow Ball when my phone buzzes with a text.

It's from Skylar.

How goes the work, Anne Hathaway?

I can see him in the dim light of his truck, the unruly hair brushed across his forehead, his face close enough to take my breath away.

The moment I realize I'm smiling, I drop my phone into my messenger bag like it's hot. *Nope!* I can't afford that kind of distraction right now.

Sharla Marie appears then behind the counter with a box of merchandise. "Well, if it isn't Miss AJ! Looking for a new treasure or just stopping by to say hello?"

It takes a second to reorient myself. "A little of both, maybe." I replace the sparkly blue dress on its rack as Sharla Marie pulls consigned clothes from her box and begins sorting them on the counter. "Need a hand?"

She smiles suspiciously. "Looking for a job?"

I laugh. "Actually...I'm working on that article for the RNN newsletter. I was wondering if I could pick your brain?"

"Oh?" She pulls a moss-green sweater from the box and gives it a shake before putting it on a hanger. Vintage rings adorn almost every finger on her hands. Her style is an eclectic combination of boho and shabby-chic retro. Today she's wearing a tiered peasant skirt with a 1950s blouse and a long lacy cardigan. Her usual assortment of necklaces and bracelets jingle with her every move. "Well," she smirks, "my opinion might not be what the RNN ladies want to put in their newsletter."

"Sounds juicy," I prod.

She barks a laugh. "There's that niggling journalist. Maybe you should write for *Gossip Girl*."

"I'm not looking for gossip. Just a good conversation. Why do you think your opinion won't be welcome?"

Sharla Marie waves a jangling hand around her shop, as if this should answer my question. "They want to construct some modern monstrosity. Sounds like a lot of money for a new Roanoke eyesore, if you ask me. Have you seen the new police department downtown?"

"It's hard to miss."

"Is that really the face we want for Roanoke's future? A bunch of sterile modern buildings without personality or charm? Once we get a few more government buildings like that, Roanoke won't even be recognizable anymore. That's what I think. But, you know"—she shrugs and goes back to sorting through her box—"I'm just the kooky lady who combs through people's castoffs."

"You find hidden gems and breathe new life into them." Something flickers inside me, the beginnings of an idea. I reach for my field notebook before the light can fizzle out. "So, would you say you'd rather they used an existing building in Roanoke for a community center rather than build a new one?"

"Well, yeah! But the pickings are slim. There's the old granary they talk about tearing down and building back up the way they want it, but that's no different from just building something new. I say, if you're going to breathe new life into something, hold on to its original charm." She inspects a pair of shoes before tossing them into another box on the floor. "Or pass it along."

"How do you decide what's worth keeping and what isn't?"

"That's the trick, isn't it?" Sharla Marie pulls out a blouse and looks it over as she speaks. "Some people come in here thinking they're just unloading their old clothes, but half the time, they don't realize what they've given up. Like this little number. It's got a tear on the hem, but it's silk. A good clean, a few stitches, and it'll look like new. In contrast"—she bends down to retrieve a sweater she's already tossed into a second box on the floor—"sometimes I get items like this that people think I'll be able to save, but it's just not worth my time. There aren't any stains, no tears, but there's too much wear on the fabric all over. It's not going to carry the weight of someone new, no matter what I do." She tosses it back into the box.

"See, that's interesting to me. I think a lot of us struggle to know when something from our past is worth keeping or when it's time to let it go. Clearly"—I indicate the boutique with an arm sweep—"you have a gift for that."

"It's an art," she agrees.

Notebook and pen in hand, I fish around my bag pockets for my field recorder. "Would you mind if I record our conversation?"

Sharla Marie reaches for another hanger under the counter. "Record away, my dear. Whatever you need to do."

I hit Record. "How did you get started with Buttons and Beaus?"

Three days later, my lungs burn with every inhale of cold air as I run the wetlands trail near my parents' neighborhood with Char at my heels, his leash tugging lightly every time our pace gets out of sync.

Running has never been my favorite form of exercise, but today I crave the rush. I want to feel my muscles burn, my lungs scream. I want the prickle of cold air nipping my skin. Anything to wake me up and drown out the heavy thoughts of self-defeat that have been growing heavier by the day.

Lately, I've been alone with Char for eight hours while my parents work. For three days, I've had all the peace and quiet a writer could ask for. In that time, I've been productive in every way but the one that matters. I've cleaned every room from top to bottom, organized every drawer and cabinet, cleared dead bugs and baked-on dust from the inside of every light fixture, and washed all the blinds, but I'm no closer to writing the Roanoke Newsletter article than I was on Monday. Five transcribed interviews take up thirty pages in my document, but I couldn't tell you what a single interviewee said. It's like the sentences fly through my eyes and out the back of my head every time I try to read through them.

After half a mile, I stumble to a stop on the boardwalk trail and brace myself against the wood railing, gasping for air.

What am I doing here? I should have just stayed on at Hobs and Sanderson for another two weeks. At least then I'd have an income and a chance to enjoy the city one last time before...

No. I can't let myself think like that.

The wetlands spread for miles around me in an open vista of waving silvery sage reeds and frosted mud with the occasional icy puddle. A blue heron bobs its head slowly with every cautious step it takes through the marsh. In the summer, these trails are rife with wildlife, but other than this one tall bird, I haven't seen much moving out here this morning. Even the birds and animals have more important things to do.

I don't know why I thought being home for a month would help me prepare for *Verité*. So far, it's only made things worse. Now, not only do I have crippling writer's block, but I have the added pressure of all my mom's friends, the RNN board, and every shopkeeper I interviewed on Monday expecting me to write this article for their newsletter. I came for a confidence boost, but it looks like I'm going to make a fool of myself instead.

One more week until my siblings arrive with their families. At least I can enjoy some quality family time before I have to face the fate that awaits me in New York.

Until then, it's just me with Char, trying to make this trip feel less like a waste of time.

For what must be the dozenth time, I reconsider Sky's offer to help. Maybe it would be good to have someone to bounce ideas off of. Someone to help me get out of my head.

Normally, my roommate Jody is that someone for me when I'm feeling stuck.

Sky's got to be busy helping with his dad's business. I'm sure he only offered his help to be polite.

As I make my way back to the trailhead, I call Jody.

She answers on the second ring. "I knew you'd get bored."

I want to deny it, but I'm already fake-crying. "Why didn't I listen to you?"

"Because you're you. Once you get an idea in your head, there's no changing your mind."

Adam's voice echoes in my head, *You're too intense.*

I groan. "Why am I like this?"

"Beats me." The familiar sound of Jody swishing one of her paint-brushes in a jar of water makes me pine for our little cramped apartment with the smell of her paints and the noise of the city outside. "You owe me ten bucks, by the way."

"Why?"

"I bet you ten bucks you'd get stir-crazy after three days. Remember?"

"I remember you saying it. Don't remember agreeing to it. Anyway, it's day six, not day three."

"Don't tell me you've been tallying the days on your bedroom wall."

Even though she can't see it, I roll my eyes. "I did something stupid."

"If it doesn't involve several rounds of shots and a sexy guy, I don't want to hear about it."

"I agreed to write an article for this neighborhood newsletter—"

"Girl, why are you *working* on your vacation? You should be living it up! Enjoying your freedom before you sell your soul to the fashion magazine industry."

"It wasn't supposed to be a big deal. I should be able to finish it in an hour. I'm just too much in my head. I need you to ground me."

"You're grounded. Go to your room and think about what you've done."

"You know what I mean."

"If you can finish this thing in an hour, then why haven't you finished it yet?"

"I'm too stuck in my head. It's a loud echo chamber in here. My siblings won't be home for another week, and my parents are at work all day, and the silence in their house is suffocating."

"So, get out of the house."

"I'm on a run right now—"

"Yuck, not in nature. I mean, go be with *people*! Get out of your comfort zone. Do something wild for once."

My phone buzzes in my hand. It's probably another text message from one of my sisters on our family thread talking about the supposed snowstorm in the forecast next week.

I force a laugh at Jody's suggestion. "You don't know my hometown. Nothing wild happens in Roanoke. It's supposed to snow sometime next week, and that's got everyone so excited, you'd think the circus was coming to town."

"Then *make* something happen. Or go to Portland, or whatever. If you want to get out of your head, shake things up. Add some color to your world, ya know?"

There's another tinkling swish of a paintbrush in water.

"What are you working on?" I ask.

"I'm not sure yet. Just going where the brush takes me."

"Will the cat be making an appearance?"

"You know it."

I smile. No matter what she paints, Jody always includes a cat somewhere in the piece.

"Look," Jody says seriously, "this writer's block thing you're dealing with came on after Adam dumped you. All I'm saying is, maybe you need to blow off some sexual steam. You know? Have a little holiday fling. See that there are lots of other fish out there. Get over him."

My phone buzzes again. This time I check.

Two messages from Benson Miller. Could it be a sign? I thumb them open.

The second message is a link to a cute little French café.

"I think it would be good for you," Jody continues. "You might be surprised how inspiring a night of irresponsible passion can be."

A disbelieving laugh escapes me. "Actually, Jody…I have a date next week."

"Liar."

"No, really. With this guy I knew in high school. We ran into each other at a party—"

"Yaaas! Get some! That's what I'm talking about!"

"I don't think it's really like that—"

"Nope, I don't want to hear your excuses. Don't ruin this by over-thinking it. You deserve to have fun. Get over your stinkin' ex. Get over your stinkin' writer's block. Bada bing, bada boom, you're back in business. Say, 'Yes, Jody.'"

I groan noncommittally.

"I'll take that as a yes. Gotta go now. You're kind of ruining my flow. This painting looks more uptight than your October cram sessions."

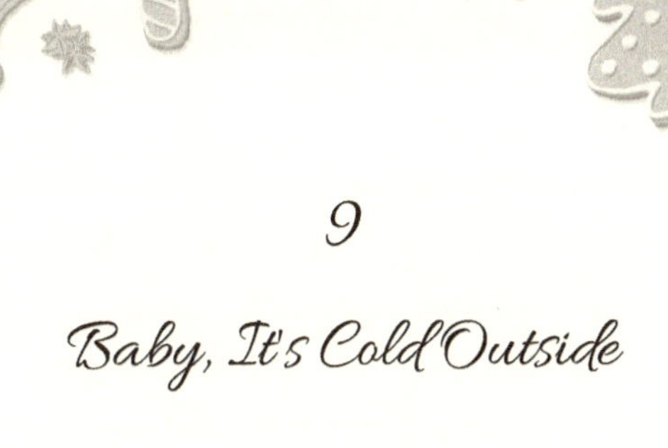

9

Baby, It's Cold Outside

MY BREATH FORMS SILVER clouds in the frosty air as I step from my Uber driver's red Honda in front of a classy little French café adorned with white lights in downtown Tualatin. *Le Petite Poule Rousse* is stenciled on the glass front door in swirling gold script, and a small tree glows inside, illuminating tidy rows of bistro tables.

Although Benson's intention was for us to meet halfway between Portland and Roanoke, the café he chose is definitely closer to Portland. Even leaving before the crack of dawn to beat the workday traffic, it took nearly forty-five minutes to get here. Forty-five minutes of making light conversation with my Uber driver to distract me from the nervous turning sensations in my stomach as I folded and refolded Benson's scarf in my lap.

I check the time on my phone. Five minutes to ten. I'm early.

My driver rolls down his passenger-side window. "You want me to wait until your friend shows up?"

"No, that's alright. Thanks for the ride."

As he drives off down the street and I stand there blowing into my gloved hands and stomping my feet on the sidewalk to keep warm, I regret being left with my thoughts.

What am I doing here? Driving all this way to meet up with the boy who broke my heart years ago, what does that make me? I should have told Benson this was too far away. I should have made him work for it. Standing here in the cold, I feel exposed, pathetic.

I shake the thoughts away. *No*, I tell myself, *you will not be that pathetic, needy girl this time.* I realize I'm hugging Benson's scarf to my chest and immediately hold it at my side instead. I'm going to give it back to him, let him clear his conscience, and then forgive him and move on with my life.

Benson pulls up just as I'm about to walk inside and wait for him.

"AJ." He looks surprised to see me. "I hope you haven't been waiting long. I thought for sure I'd get here first."

"I got an early start to beat the traffic."

As realization dawns, his face falls, and he drops his head with a regretful wince. "Ah, the traffic." He pinches his eyes before looking apologetically up at me through his eyelashes like a penitent child. "You had the longer commute, *and* you had to compete with all the traffic into Portland, didn't you? Gosh, I'm an idiot."

"It's fine" slips from me before I can stop myself. "Really, it's not a big deal."

He rushes to open the café door for me. "No, I wasn't thinking. Seriously, that was a jerk move." He twists to scan the street parking, which is empty aside from his Mazda. "Where's your car?"

"Oh, I, uh, just took an Uber," I mumble quickly as I duck inside, half hoping he won't hear.

"From Roanoke? That must have cost a fortune."

It did, but I try to wave it off. "Ah, it's about the same as taking a taxi from my apartment to Manhattan."

"Is that how you get to work?"

"I did once…" And quickly learned my lesson.

He shakes his head. "I'll take you home."

"You don't have to do that. You've got work—"

He rolls his eyes. "I have work at three. Let me take you home. I insist. This is supposed to be a treat for you, not a pain. I swear, this place is good. All I was thinking was that you've got to try their Monte Cristo."

"It looks great," I assure him as the hostess approaches. "Honestly, I'm sure it's worth the drive."

"One hundred percent," he promises, hands pressed together as if he's praying it will be so. Then to the hostess, "Your best table for two, please."

The hostess looks momentarily dazed by Benson's smile but quickly fumbles for a pair of menus and gushes, "Of...of course!"

As we follow the girl to a table at the front by one of the big windows, I want to chide myself for being so accommodating, but I can't muster up enough anger. Benson clearly feels bad, and I should have said something as soon as I realized how inconvenient it was going to be for me to get here. Then again, I'm not the one who has to work today, so it makes more sense for me to be the one with the longer commute.

The hostess leaves us with our menus.

"Please, order anything you'd like," Benson says.

I scan the menu in my hands, but the words may as well be hieroglyphics, the way my vision glazes over. I can't believe I'm on a date with Benson Miller. I want to play the confident adult who has bigger things to care about than impressing my girlhood crush, but whatever levity I found at the tree farm escapes me now.

Why did he ask me out? Is this really supposed to be a *date* date? Why now? He can't actually be interested in me after all this time. And even if he was, why bother when I'm leaving in a few weeks? He can't be hoping for a one-night stand, or he would have asked me to dinner instead of brunch.

No, the only logical explanation is that he feels bad about how he treated me in the past, and this is his way of making it up to me so he can ease his conscience.

"The Monte Cristo is my favorite," Benson says, "but everything is good. You really can't go wrong here."

I try to see through the fog of my thoughts to find if eggs Benedict is on the menu, but it's no use. I can't pretend ease for another second. I set my menu on the table. "What are we doing?"

Benson blinks. "Uh..."

"You never wanted to hang out with me before. Why now?"

He straightens, surprised, then a laugh escapes, "Well, right to the point, huh?"

The waitress appears then, introduces herself as Saoirse in a clipped Irish accent as she places two waters on the table and asks, "Know what you want to order?"

Benson asks her to give us another minute, and he takes a sip of water. Once she's gone, he smiles in the shy way that used to make me swoon as a teen. "What makes you think I never wanted to hang out with you before now?"

"Because..." Is he really going to make me state the obvious? "You didn't. We had every opportunity to become friends growing up, and you looked the other way."

For reasons I can't fathom, his eyes practically dance with amusement. He leans back in his seat, folding his arms as he takes me in. "Oh yeah?"

"Yeah."

He tilts his head. "Huh. That's interesting. The way I remember it, *you* were always hanging around with the older crowd. I thought you were too mature for the likes of me."

My mouth opens, but nothing comes out. I was not expecting that.

Benson seems pleased with himself for rendering me speechless. "Am I wrong?" he asks.

"Yes," I huff breathlessly. "Yes, you're way wrong! You knew I wanted to be friends."

"Is that right?"

"Yes!"

Benson laughs.

"What is so funny?" I demand, and I want to be furious, but his amusement is annoying and stupidly exciting at the same time.

"Wow," he says. "All this time, I thought I knew my own mind. Thanks for setting me straight."

Now he's awakened the competitor in me. Without hesitation, I lay down my strongest card. "The Snow Ball," I say, "2004. You snubbed me."

That wipes the laughter from his face, but instead of looking caught, Benson only appears confused. He squints, trying to remember.

I wait. My heartbeat pumps faster by the millisecond like the piston of a train hurtling out of control, heat building in my ears as I watch Benson's face for the moment when he'll give up his act and admit he knows what I'm talking about.

But that moment doesn't come. Benson shakes his head, brow furrowed. "I don't... At the Snow Ball?"

My hands tremble. I clasp them in my lap so he won't see as I force a smile and roll my eyes as if it's nothing. "Oh, I was dancing with a chair to be funny, and you told Andrea Rodriguez that I was being pathetic, trying to get you to ask me to dance." I wave it off and duck back into my menu. "It was silly."

But the pounding in my chest and the tremor in my bones remind me I'm far from over it.

Benson grimaces. "Yikes, did I really say that?"

Anger rears its ugly head inside me. I want to call him out for being a terrible liar. I want to tell him to enjoy his breakfast for one and walk confidently out the door. But when I look at his face, there's no denying the truth: He really doesn't remember.

Benson shakes his head, runs a hand through his hair, and scratches the back of his neck as he blows out a heavy breath. "Wow. What a douche."

And suddenly my anger melts into a steaming puddle of defeat. Here I've spent the last decade boo-hooing over a moment that was so insignificant for him he can't even remember it. "Yeah," I say. "You were."

For a few awkward moments, we sit in silence. Benson thumbs his chin as he looks for a way out of this mess I've made. I wonder if I should just go.

"Hey," he says, and waits until I look him in the face again. His eyes are penitent, sincere. "I'm really sorry, AJ. Honestly, it doesn't surprise me to hear I said something so stupid. I kinda went through a phase in my early teens... I was a jerk. I understand if you want to leave me here with my shame. I'm sure I deserve it! But if you let me, I'd really like to make it up to you if I can."

I manage a side smile and wave it off. "Eh, it was a long time ago. We all did stupid things when we were teenagers. So, the Monte Cristo is good, you say?"

He smiles, relieved. "The best."

"Great," I say, just as the waitress returns. "I'll have the eggs Benedict," I tell her.

Benson slaps a hand to his heart with a wounded "Oof!" He smirks at me before ordering the Monte Cristo for himself. "Guess I've got to earn your trust after all. That's fair."

"More than fair." I blow my straw wrapper at him and he dodges it playfully.

Behind me, the hostess calls out from her position by the front door, "Uh-oh, here it comes!"

Benson and I follow her gaze to the large windows. Outside, tiny white flecks drift through the air.

It's snowing!

I clap with excitement.

Benson curses under his breath.

"What?" I ask.

"Sorry." He eyes the falling snow with trepidation. "I didn't think it would actually happen."

In Roanoke, snow in the forecast is almost always wrong. But usually, locals see it as a kind of miracle when it does occur. I've never seen anyone look upset about it before. Then I realize, "What time do you have to be at the hospital?"

"Not until three..." He looks at his watch. "But if it gets worse before then..."

It's barely past ten. "It won't stick," I say. "It never does."

"Yeah, I'm sure you're right." But he pulls out his phone and reviews the weather updates anyway with an apologetic mumble that sounds somewhere between "Just a sec" and "Lemme see."

While Benson thumbs his screen, I take in the peaceful scene outside. The few shoppers on the street all stop to celebrate the white miracle, one doing a jig on the spot while another cheers so loudly we can hear it from inside. There were several inches of snow on the ground when I left New York, but I feel as giddy as a little girl at the prospect of even a meager sheen here in Oregon. It takes all my restraint not to jump up and press my face against the window to see if anything is sticking. Looks like my sisters were right about the snow after all.

A stream of customers slowly trickles into the café for coffee, some sitting down to order brunch.

Benson laughs through his nose at a few snarky posts on social media about the long-promised blizzard being nothing but a few measly snowflakes. "Yeah," he says with what I expect is more hope than confidence as he puts his phone away, "it'll probably let up soon. Sorry for being on my phone. I just want to make sure I'll be able to get to the hospital in time."

"It's alright," I say. "It must be heavy, knowing people's lives might depend on you getting to work on time. I can't imagine."

He almost agrees but then admits, "Well, I mean, there are other doctors there, and they can't leave until I arrive. So, it's more about not letting them down, I guess. But still, I try to be reliable."

"Very important," I agree.

Saoirse returns with our food. "Wow," she says, "it's really coming down out there."

"It's sticking!" the hostess cheers at the same time.

Café employees rush from the kitchen to see. I can't help but laugh. I've missed this unrestrained Oregonian enthusiasm for snow! "In New York, my coworkers wouldn't even look up from their computers."

"Well, yeah, but you guys probably have snow plows to take care of it there." Benson tries to match my lighthearted tone, but the tension in his voice is unmistakable. "We're not equipped for it here." His smile twitches as he places his napkin across his lap.

"That Monte Cristo looks so fancy."

Benson seems to appreciate the change of subject. "Is that a hint of regret I hear?"

"Not a chance," I laugh. "Are you seeing this?" I indicate the eggs Benedict on my plate. They look straight out of a gourmet magazine, with a vibrant dash of paprika sprinkled on the velvety hollandaise. My first bite confirms all of Benson's hype about the restaurant.

"Good?" Benson asks.

I blow a chef's kiss in reply. "Want a bite?"

He hesitates. "That's alright, I'm more of a sweet breakfast kinda guy." It's only a split second, but that's all it takes for me to see it in his face: he's not a food sharer. I guess that makes sense, being a doctor, that he'd be more conscious of germs.

"Oh good," I say quickly. "I'm a savory breakfast girl all the way."

Benson smiles, but his eyes flick to the windows more than once. I can tell he's trying not to check the weather updates on his phone. "So, New York," he says. "Is it everything you imagined?"

"I love it" is as far as I get before the blood drains from Benson's face and I follow his gaze to the front door, where the hostess has just flipped the OPEN sign to CLOSED.

There's a hiss as Benson sucks air through his teeth. He flags down our waitress. "What's going on?" he asks. "You're closing?"

"Don't worry," she says with a wave of her hand. "You can take your time."

"Because of the snow?" I ask.

"Our cook lives out in Forest Grove; we just want to make sure he can get home before it really starts coming down. Nothing to worry about."

By the time she leaves, Benson's face is already glowing blue from his phone screen. "The zoo is closed, too. And Hoyt Arboretum." His thumb scrolls frantically.

I sit taller in my seat to catch a view of the street outside, where the layer of sticking snow is still thin enough to see the lines on the road through it. Benson still has several hours before he needs to be at work. "If things are closing, maybe that means you won't have to worry about traffic," I suggest hopefully. But I regret it almost instantly when I see how hard he's trying to smile through his poorly concealed concern. I switch gears. "We don't have to stay. I'd enjoy this just as much out of a to-go box."

"Are you sure?" His hand moves to flag the waitress again before I answer.

"Yeah, for sure. Better safe than sorry."

"Right. Gosh, I'm so sorry. This is not going the way I meant—hi, can we get some boxes and the check?"

Hopefully, my Uber driver is still in the area. I pull out my phone to check, but Benson stops me.

"I'll get you home."

I object. "Benson, it's too far—"

"AJ, come on, there's no way I'm going to drive off and leave you standing in the snow waiting to pay a fortune for some stranger to drive you home from the worst date of your life. Let *me* drive you home from the worst date of your life."

I almost push back, but I can't help the smile that slips out with a breathy laugh. My eyes roll to the ceiling. "It's not the *worst* date of my life."

"Good," he says. "I can't wait to hear about my competition on the way home." The wink he adds at the end is charming enough to cover a multitude of sins.

We order warm drinks to go and Benson starts his car with a click of a button on his key fob while we wait. "Just warming it up for us," he says.

As we slip into the heated seats of his red Mazda, the new-car smell is unmistakable behind the scent of balsam and pine from an air freshener on the vent. Benson places his coffee in the middle cup holder, but I hold my orange blossom tea under my chin and breathe in the sweet aroma while I melt into the heated seat.

"Ringo, take me to Roanoke," Benson says.

The screen on his dashboard comes to life, showing a map while a robotic man's voice answers, "Sure, Roanoke Home. Arriving in—thirty—minutes."

Fancy. "Did you name your car after Ringo Starr?"

He laughs. "Guilty. You a Beatles fan?"

I purse back a smile and look nonchalantly out my window. "They're alright."

"Whaaat?" he protests. "Ringo, play the *Sgt. Pepper's* album." He makes a point of turning up the volume. "We'll make a believer of you yet, AJ Banner."

I laugh. "I'm kidding! Who doesn't like the Beatles?"

"People with bad taste."

I wouldn't go that far, but singing along to the Beatles with Benson Miller was literally a daily fantasy of mine when I was thirteen, so now all I can think is *Holy crap, it's actually happening!*

And it does. I pinch myself discreetly as our voices belt the lyrics to "Sgt. Pepper's Lonely Hearts Club Band" in unison. Benson drums his steering wheel to the beat.

Then the snowfall thickens, and his hands stop drumming. His singing gets quieter, then stops altogether.

Traffic slows to a standstill. Somewhere up ahead, a car is stalled, another in the gutter.

"No, no, no," Benson groans, slapping his steering wheel with surprising force.

According to the clock on his dashboard, it's still only eleven fifteen, but if the snow keeps up at this rate, and if traffic doesn't improve, we could be stuck here for hours.

"I should have found another way home," I say, apologizing.

"No," he says. "No, it's fine." But he can't hide the edge in his voice. He turns the music down and hisses under his breath, "Man, I hate snow."

We follow a stream of other cars moving slowly around the stalled vehicle. I wonder momentarily if we should see if the person needs help, but one look at the stress in Benson's face keeps my mouth shut. He's going farther and farther in the opposite direction of where he needs to be, with traffic growing worse by the minute.

Guilt weighs down like a bowling ball in my stomach. This was a mistake. I should have insisted on finding my own way home. Music still plays at a low volume, but the car feels painfully quiet compared to several minutes ago. Benson's grip on the steering wheel tightens. "This sucks."

I hand him his coffee. "Well, at least we've got these."

"Thanks." He takes the cup but just holds it on his lap as I sip my tea before putting it back in the cupholder.

It's not my place to be Miss Sunshine in this situation, I know. The stakes aren't as high for me as they are for him. But what am I supposed to do? Be angry about the snow with him? Would that make him feel better?

"Maybe you should just drop me off here," I suggest as we enter Newberg. We're still a good twenty minutes from Roanoke, but Benson's mounting anxiety is so palpable it's unbearable.

"Are you sure?" he asks, already pulling into the nearest grocery store parking lot.

"Yeah, I'll just have my mom pick me up here. No problem. You should head back to Portland before things get worse."

"Thank you for understanding." Benson shakes his head. "Man, I feel like such a jerk leaving you here. Are you sure you'll be okay?" He pulls into a spot and then puts the car into Park. "I'll wait with you until she gets here."

"No, no, that would hardly save you any time."

He nods, and I suspect he already thought of that but offered to be polite. "At least let me stay with you until she's on her way."

"Are you kidding? The roads are getting worse." I step out of the car into a winter wonderland. "I'm in my happy place," I assure him as I turn back to get my boxed food and my tea. "I'll be fine, really. Go save some lives!"

He nods again, his face pained. "AJ, I'm sorry—"

"Go!" I say it playfully and smile so he knows there are no hard feelings, but as I stand in the snow and watch him drive away, I'm relieved to be out of that fancy car with its heated seats and frigid atmosphere.

10

Marshmallow World

F IFTEEN MINUTES LATER, I still can't get ahold of my dad. My mom is stuck in traffic herself, trying to get home from work, and I'm not exactly on her way. At first, I don't mind. It's fun to watch the Fred Meyer parking lot turn into a winter playground, with kids and adults alike throwing snowballs at each other.

I sit in the nearest coffee shop as I try my dad's phone again. It goes straight to voicemail. That man never remembers to charge his phone at night. I make a mental note to gift him a car charger for Christmas this year.

Outside, the snow shows no sign of stopping.

My mom calls. "AJ, hon," she sighs. "I'm so sorry! My car slid into a ditch and I'm getting a ride home with a coworker."

"Don't worry about it," I say. "I'll see if I can catch an Uber."

By this point, I already know there are no Uber drivers on the road for the rest of the day.

Only after all my other options are exhausted do I give in and pull up Sky's number on my phone.

"Sorry for the wait," Sky says as he opens his passenger side door for me. "It's a skating rink out here."

"You're a lifesaver," I reply. "Thank you for coming all this way to get me."

He waves my thanks off before closing the door behind me and dashing around to his side. The heater is on full blast, so hot it actually makes the skin on my face feel tight. As soon as Sky settles into his seat, he turns it off completely. "Cocoa?" He offers me a thermos from the center console.

"Thanks." Since I finished my tea while I waited for him, I take the thermos with both hands. "Still warm!"

"You'll need it. And there's a blanket at your feet," Sky nods to the basket hogging my leg room as we join the jam of cars sliding from the parking lot.

"Dang, Sky," I laugh as I lift the blanket and find an assortment of snacks and car games beneath. "Do you just keep this stocked for work?"

"Pshh, no way. That's just for you. You're getting the five-star ride experience. It's the Townsend Snow Package." He winks.

With the heater off, it's surprising how quickly the cold seeps in through every crack and seam in the cab. "May I?" I ask, reaching for the heater knob.

"Of course."

I turn the knob to the lowest setting, but nothing happens. Another twist, still nothing. "What...?"

Sky says, "That's weird. It was working a minute ago. Did you break my truck?"

My stomach drops. "I didn't do anything. Oh my gosh, did I break it?"

He reaches for the knob and turns it back and forth a few times, his face creased with concern. He's had this truck since he was a teenager. It must be his baby. Did I really just break it? How?

"Sky, I'm so sorry, I don't know what happen—"

Sky cranks up the heat all the way and we're blasted with the same scorching air that filled the truck when I first got in.

A glance at Sky reveals that he's trying not to laugh. "You're messing with me," I say. It comes out sounding like a plea more than an accusation.

He tries to keep it in, but a snicker bursts from his nose, and his shoulders shake.

"Sky!" I slap him playfully. "It was already like that before I got in the car!"

His snickers erupt into full-bellied laughter. "I'm sorry, that was mean."

I want to be annoyed with him for making me feel so bad a second ago, but his laughter is contagious. How did I fall for his trickery? He told me himself this truck was barely running last month. Of course he wouldn't be so surprised—or upset—about a tiny malfunction in the heater. This realization makes me laugh along with him.

"Old truck," Sky sighs as his laughter subsides. "We have two temperatures: arctic ice box or hellfire blast."

"Thus, the blanket and hot cocoa," I say.

"No, those are for funsies. There's a bag of marshmallows down there if you want to add some. I don't know how you like your hot chocolate, so you've got options."

I turn the heater off to eliminate the risk of my hair catching fire as I bend down to pull the basket onto my lap. There's a half-empty bag of mini marshmallows, along with a few broken candy canes and the final rattling corner of a bag of chocolate chips. Somehow, the thought of

Skylar taking the time to scour his cupboards for treats before rushing out the door warms my heart. There's also a bag of pretzels and a jar of peanut butter. "I like the Townsend Snow Package. It's like a party in a basket."

"Oh yeah, can't forget the music." He turns on the radio, and "I Want a Hippopotamus for Christmas" crackles through bursts of static. Eyes on the road, Sky adjusts the tuner with the concentration of a surgeon.

"What's this?" I ask, pointing at what looks like a cassette tape in the player.

"The Carpenters. They've been stuck in there for a while."

When Sky finishes fiddling with the tuner, there's still a hint of crackle from the radio as Bing Crosby croons "White Christmas."

"What were you doing in Newberg?" Sky asks.

I hesitate. "Actually, I was coming from Tualatin."

"Oh," his brow furrows. "Did your car get stuck? I can try towing it out with the truck."

"No, no, I hitched a ride with someone else. They just...could only take me as far as Newberg."

"A work thing?" he guesses.

"Sorta..." But I'm allergic to lying, and I can't stand the itch. "It was a date."

He makes a face and laughs. "A work date?"

"No, just a date." I want to leave it at that, and to his credit, Sky might let me. But we've still got a ways to go, and traffic isn't picking up. Being cryptic won't make the ride more enjoyable for either of us, so maybe it would be better just to get this conversation over with so we can move forward, like ripping off a Band-Aid. "With Benson Miller."

For a beat, there's silence. Then Sky squints his eyes and says, "Huh."

Here it comes. The lecture on letting the past go. I invite him to get it out. "What?"

He shrugs. "Nothin'. Just, huh, that's interesting."

"Oh yeah?"

He nods, then quirks a smile. "No, it's not really that interesting. Hey, could you pass that bag of marshmallows?"

I lean back in disbelief. "What? You don't have an opinion about that?"

He shrugs again. "Not really." He holds out a hand palm up. "Marshmallows?"

I plop the bag of mini mallows into his palm. "Good."

"Good," he agrees.

"Fine."

"Yep." He tosses a handful of mini marshmallows into his mouth, chews, then muffles, "Stale."

"He wanted to take me all the way home." I feel the need to explain. "I was going to get an Uber, but he insisted. Then the traffic just got so bad, and he's got to be at Doernbecher by three..."

Sky eyes the clock on his dash. It's noon. I could have been home by now, and Benson would have been well on his way back to Portland. I wait for Sky to point this out, but all he does is nod with eyebrows raised as if I've just told him a less-than-interesting fact about cheese and says, "Hmm."

"I'm not defending him. I'm just saying..."

"For sure."

"Okay, you know what...?" I grab the bag of marshmallows from him. "What were *you* doing before I took you away with my SOS?"

Now it's his turn to look uncomfortable. "Working. Kinda."

"A date?" I tease, popping a mallow into my mouth. He was right, they're stale.

Sky smirks. "Does an awkward one-on-one with my dad count as a date?"

I try to ignore the twinge of relief I feel to hear that he wasn't on a date. "Awkward how?"

He lifts a shoulder. "It's uncomfortable helping him with his business. Makes me feel like a real punk, coming in and telling him what to do when he ran things fine my whole life." He shakes his head and the movement travels down his body like a dog shaking water from his coat. "Anyway, how about this snow, huh?"

It's striking how quickly Sky can shake off something unpleasant and light up like a little kid as he leans over the steering wheel to take in the view outside. He's illuminated by the snow-reflected light, and I can see the smile lines forming around the corners of his eyes. But the heaviness I sensed in him a moment ago lingers in my gut. "Why do you do that?" I ask.

"Do what?"

"Deflect when I ask about your life."

"Because it's a boring conversation."

"Not to me. I haven't seen you in over six years. I want to know what's going on in your life."

"There's not a lot going on."

"Come on. I told you about my life. Back at the diner, you interrogated me, and I did all the talking. Now it's your turn."

"Oh, is that how it is?"

"Yeah, it is."

He shakes his head, doesn't quite laugh. "Okay, Miss Journalist, interrogate me."

It's equal parts thrilling and nerve-racking to get this kind of permission. It's what I crave, but there's always a danger of digging too deep and hitting a wound that doesn't want to be touched, then the whole interview can go downhill fast, and clearly Sky has some wounds he's been burying for a while.

"Actually, I'm curious about what happened with Berkeley. I remember how excited you were when you got into their engineering program. Did you ever think about going back there after...everything?"

Sky's fingers drum against the steering wheel. For a moment, I think he's going to deflect again, but he just exhales heavily. "For a while, that was the plan. I was going to finish helping my mom through her treatments, then go back. I had it all mapped out—even had the department chair holding my spot. Then things got worse and the plan changed. I figured I'd just finish school at OSU instead."

"But then, after your mom..."

"Died. After my mom died. Yeah. It's okay, you can say it." He takes a breath. "My dad...he just shut down. You remember how my mom was: always involved in everything, life of the party. My dad was used to just going along with whatever she wanted to do. After she was gone, I thought he might step up and..." He releases his breath in a heavy rush, as if he could blow away the weight of these memories. "Anyway, he didn't. After the funeral, he could barely get out of bed. I told myself it would be just one semester to help him adjust. Then another. Then the opportunity to do humanitarian work in Ethiopia came up, and I knew it was the kind of thing my mom would have wanted me to take advantage of, so I took it. And it was good. It felt good to do something for other people instead of being the constant reminder around town that Kate Townsend was gone." He's talking fast now, trying to blow through these memories to get this conversation over with.

I offer him an alternative direction before he burns out, and I lose him. "At Norma's, you said something about feeling close to the Earth when you were in Ethiopia. Close to the human family. What did you mean by that?"

"Oh, you know...being away from all the prying neighbors in Roanoke. Away from the constant access to technology. Living in a mud hut. That kind of thing."

For a moment, I think he's going to leave it at that. But I count to ten before asking more, and my patience pays off. The silence gives Sky a moment to relive his experience, and his shoulders relax as a faraway softness comes to his eyes.

He smiles. "The people there were... I really came to love them. And the work felt good. I've always enjoyed working with my hands. And the simple way of life there...I've never felt more grounded. Sleeping on a dirt floor in a little hut with the sounds of animals at night, and the stars so bright you don't even need a flashlight to see...there's nothing like it. And, AJ, when you wake up in the morning and see this breathtaking landscape of rolling green hills with the sunrise sparkling on the dew"—he shakes his head—"you walk out of the hut, and there are chickens darting past your feet and scratching at the dirt and goats being herded by a boy who smiles at you like you've just climbed out of a storybook. And then Ayana makes sour flatbread for lunch, and you all sit around in a circle and feed each other with your bare hands... Everything felt so real. So tangible."

"It sounds like paradise."

"Oh, no, it was far from that. There's so much pain and hardship and toil there... But no one acts like those things are unfair. It's just part of life. I can't explain it. The reality of life is so present, there are no pretenses or expectations for something other than what *is*. I mean, toilets!" His arms wave as he speaks, as if they might catch the ideas he can't find the words to express. "We are so disconnected from the basic realities of what it means to be alive, we don't even have to deal with our own waste—we just flush it away and forget about it. But there, nothing you do or make just disappears. Everything is so—just—there! In front of you. Saying, 'Deal with me now or I'll start to stink.'"

His passion fills the car, even when he's talking about toilets. But I know he's talking about more than waste.

"Is that why you stayed?" I ask.

He nods. "After my mom, it felt..." He shakes his head, lost for words, then tries a different approach. "In Ethiopia, life and death go hand in hand. Here, we only focus on life, on living. Death is taboo. But there, if you eat meat, you kill the animal yourself—usually an animal you raised from birth. There's this complex and beautiful appreciation for life and acceptance of death that I'd never experienced before. It made death feel so...normal." He glances at me, maybe to see how I'll take this radical idea. When I nod for him to go on, he sighs. "It made me feel like it was okay, what happened with my mom. Like I could move forward and keep living, and I didn't need to be sad forever."

His passion fades in the silence that follows.

Then he continues. "After my initial internship ended, I came home for a few months. Coming back to my life, everything hit me all over again. It felt like everything and everyone wanted me to be sad and heavy, and I felt stuck. Everything felt like a gray shell of what it used to be—the house, the town, my dad—so I went back to Ethiopia. And I felt useful every day. I felt like I woke up every morning with purpose."

"So, why did you leave?" I ask.

He shakes his head. "It wasn't my place to call home. I was an outsider, just there to help. That land, the culture, the victories and struggles, they all belong to the people of Ethiopia, and the longer I was there, the more I realized they didn't need me as much as I needed them. And I knew I had things I needed to finish here."

"With your dad?"

He nods. "With my dad. And my life. So here I am at twenty-nine: I never finished school. I live in my dad's basement. I'm back to working the same construction jobs for him I did throughout high school, and now things are uncomfortable between us because we're grown men living under the same roof with a bunch of unresolved relationship issues." He forces a cold laugh.

"And school is off the table?"

"My scholarship expired a few years ago. And my spot's long gone, so I'd have to apply all over again. To be honest, I'm not sure I even remember calculus anymore."

I gather my thoughts for a moment. We're out on the country roads now, surrounded by winterized vineyards and farms, and there's not a lot of traffic out here, but the few cars ahead of us move slowly, carefully navigating the slick pavement. I shift in my seat so I'm facing Sky, my cheek against the headrest as I take him in. It sounds like he's had to relive the grief of losing his mother all over again by coming home. I feel bad for making him talk about it when he didn't want to.

"So, you're saying I shouldn't take relationship advice from a guy who can't even sort out his relationship with his dad or do basic math?" I tease, hoping to lighten the moment without dismissing his vulnerability.

Sky's laugh is genuine this time. "Fair point."

"For what it's worth," I say, "I think what you're doing is really brave."

He raises an eyebrow. "Living in my dad's basement?"

"No." I shake my head. "Choosing to face the hard stuff instead of running from it. Coming back to finish what you started, even when there was an easier path."

Sky's expression softens. "I wouldn't call it brave. Stubborn, maybe—whoa!"

The truck slides from side to side like a snake as Sky brakes to avoid colliding with the sedan in front of us. The car ahead of them spins out, then recovers and keeps going, but braking to avoid a collision makes the sedan slide off the road and into the shoulder.

Without hesitation, Sky pulls off behind the sedan and leans past me to grab a pair of gloves and some neon nylon straps from his glove compartment. "Hold on," he tells me before jumping from the truck. He doesn't hang back and ask if the people in the sedan need help. He just heads straight for the driver's side window as if this were his job, and I can see him pointing back at his truck as he talks to the driver.

Moments later, Sky climbs back into his seat and checks over his shoulder to make sure the road is clear before turning the truck around. Snow clings to his sandy hair, melting into droplets that trace down his temples.

"Are they alright?" I ask.

"Yeah, just stuck. Hey, somewhere around your feet there's a tow hook and some D-ring shackles," he says.

I lift the basket of snacks and games onto my lap and find what Sky's talking about on the floor. "Are you going to tow them out?"

Sky backs up the truck until we're bumper to bumper with the sedan. "Yeah, they're stuck pretty good. All-season tires—useless in this stuff." He pulls on his gloves.

"Need help?" I ask, already reaching for the door handle.

"Yeah, hop into the driver's seat. I'll let you know when to pull forward. This shouldn't take long."

I watch through the fogging back window as Sky trudges through ankle-deep snow to the back of his truck and crouches down out of sight. A moment later, there's the clanking of metal on metal as he attaches the tow hook to his hitch.

I climb into the driver's seat and turn on the heater to un-fog the windows. Hot air blasts my skin, blowing my hair into my face as I peer out the back window for my cue.

Sky reappears in my field of vision with the bright yellow straps in his hands just long enough to say something to the woman through her window, then he disappears again under the sedan's front. When he emerges moments later, his jeans are soaked to the knees. He instructs the woman on what to do, demonstrating with his hands, then stands well back from both vehicles before giving me the thumbs-up.

I turn off the heater. Suddenly nervous, I tap the gas cautiously. The engine growls as it strains against the weight. In the rearview mirror, I can see Sky motioning for me to step on it.

I push the pedal to the floor. An anxious thrill blooms in my chest as the truck lurches forward with surprising power, roaring like a dragon. I swear I can feel the weight of the sedan breaking free from the shoulder through the steering wheel in my hands. A yelp escapes my throat. It quickly transforms into a giddy laugh as Sky motions for me and the woman to stop, then gives me two thumbs up.

While Sky unhooks everything and waves off the other driver's thanks, I scurry back into the passenger seat. My heart is still thrumming with excitement when Sky climbs back in.

He's breathing hard, cheeks reddened from the cold, but the smile on his face is as bright as the delight in his eyes.

"You've done this before," I say.

"Once or twice." He grins. "Great job." He holds up a hand for a high five.

I laugh as our hands collide. "You were so well prepared."

"You don't have somewhere you need to be, do you?"

I realize then that he didn't just drive out here to rescue me. He came to help anyone he found stuck on the road along the way. "No," I say, "no rush on my account."

As we continue toward Roanoke, the bag of mini marshmallows catches my eye, and an idea strikes. "I think we've earned some pretzel s'mores." I spear some mallows onto the ends of a few pretzel sticks, then turn on the heater. As scalding air blasts our faces, I hold the little marshmallows over the heater vent.

Sky laughs. "Hang on." He rummages one-handed in the middle console before holding up a metal spoon. "Use this to melt—"

"The chocolate!" I practically squeal with him. "Yes!"

We balance the spoon on the dashboard with the bowl directly against the vent and let it warm up while I retrieve what's left of the chocolate chips.

"How long do you think it'll take to melt?" I ask as I place as many chocolate chips as will fit onto the spoon.

"Let's time it," he says.

We're barely a minute into the timer before sweat trickles down my neck.

"It burns," Sky laughs through clenched teeth.

"I'm turning it off," I say, but he catches my hand.

"No! We can take it. It'll be that much sweeter for the sacrifice."

I collapse into a fit of giggles I can't suppress.

Sky sucks air through his teeth and scrunches his face in pain. "It's melting my face, but—ah—it'll be so worth it!" he yells like a warrior charging into battle.

I can't breathe from laughing. "Stop!" I gasp as tears stream down my cheeks. "I can't see!"

"Is it melted yet?"

Wiping the tears from my eyes, I lean forward to check. The chocolate chips have held their shape, but the touch of my finger reveals that they're fully melted. "It's ready!" I cheer.

"Turn it off!" Sky yells.

Our hands collide painfully as we both reach for the heater knob at the same time. Someone's knuckle pops loudly and we burst out laughing again.

"Was that you or me?" he wheezes.

"I think it was you!" I'm crying again from laughter.

Through the blur of tears, I see Skylar shaking out his hand. "You've got knuckles of steel, woman!"

"I'm sorry." I take a few deep breaths to get my laughter under control before dipping a mini marshmallow speared on a pretzel stick into the melted chocolate. "Here," I hand it to Sky, "tell me how it is."

He chews thoughtfully. "Hey, that's not bad. The heater vent gives it a rustic hint of old-truck taste."

"Gross." I snicker before trying one of my own. "You know"—I smack my tongue against the roof of my mouth after swallowing as I try to identify the aftertaste—"I'm not sure if it's the smell of the heater, or if the marshmallows soaked up that *hot* flavor."

"Yeah, hot flavor," he says.

"Weird, right?"

"Yeah, hand me another one."

I prepare a second pretzel s'more for him. "Oooh, should we add peanut butter?"

"Oooh, yeah! Peanut butter. Dooo iiit!"

Cackling like childish fiends, we enjoy our musty, hot-tasting s'more experiments every way we can think of, braving hellish blasts from the heater to melt more chocolate when we run out.

We're just on the outskirts of Roanoke when we reach the end of the chocolate chips. "Uh-oh, last ones," I say as I place the last two onto the spoon. Hand on the heater knob, I look at Sky. "Ready?"

He braces himself straight-armed against the steering wheel with a flinch. "Do it!"

The hot air slaps us like an oven door being opened too quickly.

"Okay," Sky says, "after this, we're jumping into the snow. Deal?"

"Deal!"

Anticipation tickles its way from my feet, up my spine and into my burning face as we leave the open country with sprawling vineyards behind and head into the dense forest surrounding Roanoke. The snowfall has only gotten thicker, and now I hardly recognize the surrounding landscape. Can this really be my hometown under all that white?

"Done!" I announce, cranking off the heat the moment our chocolate is soft.

Sky pulls over before we've even enjoyed our treat. He opens his door and steps out.

"What are you doing?" I ask.

He shivers in the sudden chill, snowflakes landing in his tousled hair. "*We* are jumping in the snow, remember?"

My mouth opens in surprise, but then I bite back a smile.

"You coming?" He closes his door and walks around to my side.

I take a steeling breath before joining him. The snowflakes feel good on my hot face as they melt on contact. But it will only take a few moments for the heat of the car to seep from my skin. We need to make this quick. "Okay, when you say 'jump,'" I say, "do you mean—"

I yelp as Sky takes my hand and leaps into a crisp, even mound of snow, pulling me down with him. A thin layer of ice cracks as we break into the soft white beneath. There's a moment of cooling relief before the cold bites. I yelp again and try to roll to my knees, but Sky squeezes my hand.

"Wait! Five seconds!"

"What? When was that part of the plan?"

"One...two..."

The wet seeps through my shirt. My coat is still in the car, along with my hat and scarf. "Threefourfive!" I yell quickly before fumbling to stand.

Sky helps me up and we dash back to the truck with chattering teeth.

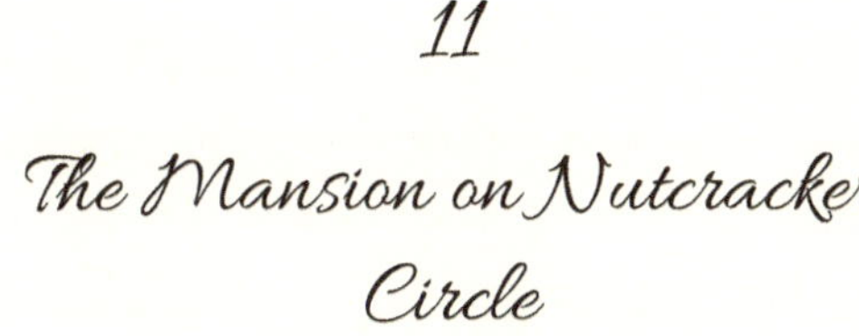

11

The Mansion on Nutcracker Circle

THE CAB IS STILL warm when we climb back into Sky's truck. Our last s'more skewers are waiting for us in all their hot-tasting glory. We take turns dipping them in the peanut butter as our pink fingers thaw before Sky starts the engine and we continue down the road.

"Uh-oh," Sky says. I look up and follow his gaze to where an old white Toyota Corolla is nearly invisible in a ditch up ahead. If it weren't for the headlights glaring against the embankment, I might have missed it entirely.

Sky pulls over again and we both get out to investigate. The Toyota is nose-down in the ditch with its trunk facing us, but I catch movement through the back window. "There's a dog inside."

The driver side door opens, and a plump elderly woman leans out to see us. "Hello?" she calls. A small dog yaps frantically in her lap.

"Miss Carston?" Sky asks.

The woman shushes her dog and sounds relieved as she says, "Oh, thank goodness! You're Kate Townsend's boy, aren't you?"

It takes a moment for me to recognize the owner of the Morley Mansion, Bea Carston, with her white hair in its signature curly crop cut. I'm amazed Sky recognized her so quickly through the falling snow. But then, with all the events his mother used to host, Sky probably saw a lot more of Bea than I did growing up.

Sky braces his arm against her open door as he bends down to talk to her. "That's me. And AJ Banner's here, too. Are you hurt?"

"No," says Bea. "It was a slow slide, but I couldn't stop."

"We've got a trailer hitch. Let's see if we can pull you out."

It warms my heart that Sky includes me, as if I had anything to do with his emergency preparedness.

Bea strokes her little black dog to calm him. "Bless you," she sighs between his yaps as Sky returns to the truck to get the tow hook and straps.

I fold my arms against the chill. "How long have you been here?" I ask.

"Over an hour," says Bea. "I was about to walk home."

It's a good thing we came when we did. We're still a good five minutes' drive from town. I hate to think of her walking all that way in the snow with her little dog.

Sky gets right to work hooking up the two cars. I shiver at the sight of him kneeling in the snow. His jeans are still wet from the last car we towed, and jumping in the snow a few minutes ago didn't help.

He nods at me once everything is ready to go. "Think you can handle the truck again?"

"Yeah." I start for the driver's side, but he takes my arm, stopping me.

"This one might be trickier than the last one was," he says.

"Okay...should I—"

"Do it just like we did before, only this time it might take a little more maneuvering. I'll be at the wheel in Miss Carston's car, so I'll motion to you through the window." He looks back at Bea. "Is that alright with you, if I take the wheel for a minute?"

"Please do!" She throws her hands into the air in surrender.

Sky helps Bea out of her car with as much care as if she were his own grandmother. She pins her little dog to her bosom with one hand and takes Skylar's arm with the other as he walks her around to the passenger side.

I climb back into Sky's truck. This time, we're attached to the back of the car being towed, so Sky will have to put the Toyota in reverse.

On his signal, I punch the gas. Snow and mud spit up from the back tires with a scraping whine from Bea's car, but nothing budges. In the rearview mirror, I see Sky wave for me to stop.

A moment later, he jumps out, jogs over to the truck, and rummages through the bed before lifting out a shovel. After he ducks down out of sight, I hear the scrape of the shovel on ice and snow. A few minutes later, Sky tosses the shovel back into the truck and holds up two fingers to me. *Round two!*

This time, there's less kick up, but Bea's car still doesn't budge. I can hear the tires turning uselessly over the roar of Sky's truck. At a motion from Sky's arm, I stop again and get out of the truck.

He meets me halfway between the two vehicles, holding his chin as he considers what to do next. "We need more traction," he says. "It's getting too icy."

I eye the surrounding forest. "Should we try laying down some branches?"

"Worth a shot."

We spend the next several minutes wedging twigs and greenery under the Toyota's tires, but ultimately, this does no good, either. After our third failed attempt, I watch through the rearview mirror as Sky talks with Bea in her car. When he finally steps out, he doesn't look at me but walks around to Bea's passenger side to help her and her dog out of the car before leading them to the truck.

"We're going to give Miss Carston a ride home," he tells me. "I'll see if my dad can come back with me tomorrow to get the car. We've got some two-by-fours and sandbags in the garage that might help."

"Bless you," Bea says again. "Bless you both!"

I move to the back as Sky goes to remove the tow strap so Bea can take the passenger seat. Her dog—a pug mix with long wiry hair—trembles in her lap, eyeing us warily through bulging eyes, one of which is fogged a milky white. His underbite is made more prominent by the visibility of a snaggle tooth. "What's his name?" I ask.

"Theodore," she replies, caressing the little creature. "He's usually more friendly. Not much more, but a little. He's just scared because I was scared."

"Well, you're safe now," I say.

Sky climbs back into the truck and stuffs the tow straps into the middle consol. "Alright, let's get you home." As we continue down the road, he asks, "What were you doing out here in this weather?"

"Theodore had a veterinary appointment," says Bea. "Or he was supposed to. By the time we got there, the place was closed. They probably left me a message on my machine at home to let me know, but I must have left the house before they called. I left early because of the snow."

"Did you have a way to call anyone?" I ask.

Bea shakes her head. "Guess it's time to get me one of those cellular phones."

It's hard to imagine how helpless she must have felt. I don't know much about Bea Carston, other than that she lives alone and runs the Morley Mansion. But if she has no cell phone, she likely has no kids or grandkids to convince her to get one.

"I can help you set one up if you'd like," Sky says. "It's easier than you might think."

I can't see Bea's face from where I sit, but her hesitation before answering relays her aversion to the idea. "That's sweet of you to offer, honey. I'll manage it when the time comes." She points toward the Tchaikovsky streets, "Right through there."

Sky follows her directions, past Sleeping Beauty Lane and Swan Lake Drive, before turning onto Nutcracker Circle.

The Morley Mansion comes into view, with its horseshoe driveway, romantic wraparound porch, and charming turret. The landscaping clearly hasn't been done in a while: shrubs overtaking the porch like unkempt hair and tall grass bowing under the weight of snow. But even with peeling paint and missing shingles, it looks magnificent. I remember the first time I got to go inside and suddenly I feel like a fourteen-year-old girl again in a sparkly blue dress, eager for my first dance. With actual snow lining the rooftops, and frost blooming across the windows, it looks less like a Victorian dollhouse and more like an elegant gingerbread house.

For a moment, I wonder if Bea actually lives here, but Skylar doesn't stop at the porch steps. We loop around the driveway until we reach a small dirt road I've never noticed before that snakes down the property behind the house.

I vaguely recall someone mentioning the Morley Mansion at my mom's book club, though I can't remember what they said. Something about it sitting empty? "How are things with the mansion?" I ask. "Do you have any fun events coming up?"

Bea sighs. "If getting torn down is fun."

For a beat, I'm not sure if I misheard her. Sky's brow furrows in the rearview mirror. "What do you mean?" he asks.

"Buyer wants to tear it down."

"You're selling it?" I gasp.

"Got to. It's about to be condemned since a pipe burst on the first floor a couple years ago, and I haven't been able to do the repairs." She says it matter-of-factly, but there's an aching strain she can't hide from her voice.

"Is the damage that bad?" Sky asks as we pull up to a small rambler-style home in the trees. He sounds as incredulous as I feel. "Can't you have it repaired?" He puts the truck in Park and turns to face her.

Bea clicks her tongue. "I wish I could. But without the income from event bookings, there's no way to pay for it. We're going on four years now since the last event." Her shoulders rise and fall helplessly. "The development company's been after this property for years." She looks out the window at her home. Antiques clutter the covered porch like a flea market, and a couple of pre–World War II cars collect a fine blanket of snow in the driveway.

"I've lived on this property my entire life. My great-grandfather built the mansion in 1889." Her voice softens with memory. "My mother used to tell us the background of every room in the house, every piece of furniture. Every nail, every floorboard has a story. But as a kid, all I cared about was how many fun places there were to play hide and seek." She chuckles. "My brother and I used to send secret messages to each other through the dumbwaiter. I remember one time we forgot a basket of Easter eggs in there. Boy, did we find it a few weeks later!" She laughs. "You could smell the rotten eggs on every floor. My mother was so angry. 'You kids need to show some respect for your ancestors' legacy!'"

"I don't understand," I say. "Why sell it? Shouldn't insurance cover a burst pipe?"

The way she deflates at my words, I might as well have dropped a sandbag on her shoulders. "Well, that's the irony of insurance, isn't it? You don't need it when you're paying for it, and the moment you stop, an accident happens. I was between policies when the thing happened, and no one will take me on with preexisting damage… It's a long story."

Sky winces empathetically.

"There's got to be a way to raise the money you need for repairs," I say. "Everyone in Roanoke has fond memories here. I'm sure the whole town would help."

Bea looks over her shoulder at me. Her blue eyes soften. "That's sweet of you to say, dear."

"What exactly needs fixing?" Sky asks. I can see the analytical wheels turning in his head. He's probably already mentally rolling up his sleeves to fix this problem for Bea the way he used to fix leaky faucets in our friends' houses when we were teenagers.

"Oh, everything." Bea waves a hand dismissively. "The flooring, the walls, the roof. I haven't had it assessed, but I can tell it's a lot." She looks back at me with an *oh well* kind of expression, then smiles. "Would you like to come in for a bit? I've got cranberry juice and crackers. It's not much, but it's the best I can do to thank you folks for helping me out."

Sky and I look at each other, and I see in his eyes that he's up to it if I am. I'm still reeling from the news that Bea's about to sell the Morley Mansion just like that, and to someone who wants to tear it down! There's no way I can leave now. "That sounds really nice," I say. "Thank you, Mrs. Carston."

"Call me Bea," she says. "I never was a Mrs. Nothing my whole life."

As we follow Bea into the house, the smells of dog, lavender soap, and mashed potatoes mingle with a cozy hint of pine from a pile of chopped wood beside an old wood-burning stove in the corner. The small space is crammed with treasures clearly salvaged from the main house—ornate picture frames, delicate china figurines, and faded photographs of the mansion in its heyday. "Make yourselves at home," Bea says as she shuffles into the kitchen. Theodore's paws tap against the wood floor after her.

It isn't much warmer in here than it is outside. With a shiver, I eye the damp knees of Sky's jeans. "Aren't you cold?" I mouth more than whisper.

He shrugs in response, then nods his chin toward the woodstove.

I shake my head. I don't know how to work that thing.

But Sky does. Why am I not surprised when he goes over and starts loading wood into the stove as casually as making himself a cup of coffee?

I peruse the photographs on the walls. Most of them are black-and-whites, or so faded with age that they appear as dreamy pastels. Aside from some framed ones of Bea's pets, the most recent photo I can find must be from the mid-1980s, showing a younger Bea with a man who I assume is her brother. They have the same hooded blue eyes and narrow noses.

"You know," Bea calls out from the kitchen, "I come from a long line of social butterflies. The Morley Mansion was built for entertaining. But you two are the first guests I've had here in the pool house in...I don't know how long."

"It's a cozy setup you have here," Sky says from the woodstove, where a fire begins to crackle just as he closes the little cast-iron door.

"Cozy, yes." Bea emerges from the kitchen with a little silver dinner tray and sets it on a fold-up TV dinner table beside her couch. "Yes, it's been a cozy life I've lived here..." For just a moment, grief creases her brow. She purses her lips and shakes the expression away. "Hard to imagine living anywhere else. Juice?" She passes us each a crystal glass that seems too fancy for the humble setting.

"But isn't that house your livelihood?" Sky asks. "What will you do without it?"

Bea shakes her head. "The house hasn't been profitable for years. Ever since Katie Towns"—she looks at Sky and her tone softens—"ever since your mother passed away, no one's been planning many events around here. For over a year before the flood damaged the main level, I couldn't book enough events to cover the cost of maintaining the place, anyway."

"So, you're just going to sell it to developers?" I can't keep the surprise from my voice.

Bea's eyes grow misty. "What choice do I have?"

"Maybe renting it out as an events center isn't working anymore, but you could still use it as a bed-and-breakfast or a hotel or—"

She shakes her head again. "I can't keep up with that kind of work. I'm seventy-six years old. Can't even drive myself home in a snowstorm." She looks toward the window, beyond which the dark silhouette of the mansion looms. "I'd rather sell it myself than have it condemned and taken."

Sky frowns. "I'm sure there's no danger of that if you own the house outright. But if you're set on selling it, why not wait for another buyer who'd be interested in keeping the house on the property?"

"Exactly!" I spring. "It has historic value. It's a treasure of a building! I can't believe anyone would want to tear it down."

"They want to build more of those cookie-cutter townhomes," Bea explains. "Five acres in the heart of town. They can make more money off the land that way. It's all about money these days. That's the sad truth."

"But," I say, "couldn't you hold out for another buyer who sees the value of the house?"

Bea hesitates. "I don't know if I can wait that long..."

Because she needs the money. As soon as the realization strikes me, I feel bad for pressing.

Behind her hangs a large framed portrait of a man and a woman in period clothing standing in front of the newly constructed mansion. Bea's great-great-grandparents look down on us with serious faces.

Bea follows my gaze, and her shoulders slump. "It breaks my heart to see the house go. It's all that's left of my family. But it was built for a different time, when the Morleys had money and hosted lavish parties. I've known for a long time that it couldn't last forever. The family fortune dried up before I was even born. All my life, I watched the house lose features my parents couldn't afford to maintain." She turns back to face me and Skylar with a sad smile. "When you get to my age, you learn to accept what you can't change. Cherish what you have while you have it."

The resignation in her voice makes my chest ache. I think of all the community events that mansion has hosted—the Christmas balls, charity auctions, summer concerts. My own memory of standing in that ballroom, feeling like I was in a fairy tale despite the teenage drama. It seems impossible that something so grand, so central to Roanoke's identity, could simply disappear.

Sky fingers the rim of his glass. His voice is soft. "Do we even recognize what we have until it's gone?"

"Oh, I don't know. I'm just an old lady." Bea holds up a plate of golden-brown Ritz crackers arranged in a spiral. "You two are too young to be worrying about this kind of stuff. Crackers?"

"I hate to think of Bea Carston losing that house," Sky says as he drives me home. "That land is all she's ever known."

"It isn't right," I say. "She shouldn't have to. There's got to be something we can do."

"I was thinking that, too, at first, but... I don't know. She sounds like she's let go already."

"Because she doesn't think she has any other option."

The sun is setting now, but in the fading light, I see the corner of Sky's mouth quirk up in a smile.

"What?" I ask.

"Nothing. It's just..." He glances at me, and his smile grows. "It feels good to be with you, that's all."

My guard is down, and his words go straight to my heart. I melt into my seat. "Aw."

Sky rushes to explain himself. "I think we both want to save Bea from this major change in her life because we're feeling weird about the big changes in our own lives. But maybe this is what she needs now."

I'm still warm and swoony from a moment ago, but I force myself to recover quickly. "How could this be what she needs? Losing her home and her family legacy?"

"I don't know," Sky admits. "Either way, it's not really up to us. She's made her decision. But she said something that got me thinking—about accepting what you can't change. When I came home from Ethiopia the first time, I was surprised when everyone seemed to think I should still be drowning in my grief, and I wondered if it made me a bad person that I'd managed to move on when my dad was still struggling. People spend so much time and money on therapy to dig up the past and turn it over and put it under a microscope and view it from every possible angle. But I don't think we grow by going backward and trying to fix what wasn't meant to be fixed. We grow by moving forward, by letting go of the things that don't serve us anymore."

I hesitate, thinking of my date with Benson. Maybe Sky is right, and my attempt to right the past with him is futile, but moving across the country hasn't seemed to help me get over it. And spending five years in Ethiopia didn't resolve Sky's issues at home. "How is that different from running away?"

He sucks in a breath and holds it, lips pursed as he considers. When he releases the breath, it rushes out in a surrendering laugh. "I don't know. Guess I'm just trying to wax philosophical to impress you."

I don't buy it. "I think you're on to something," I say. "But I don't think you *can* move forward without making peace with the past. That's the difference between growing and running away. Don't you think?"

Now it's his turn to hesitate. "Maybe you're right."

We pull up in front of my parents' house then. When Sky parks against the curb, I don't want to leave. It feels natural to be here with him, talking about life while snowflakes continue to fall in the headlights' beams. I smile. "So, you want to impress me, huh?"

He turns in his seat so he's facing me with his back against the door, a lopsided grin sneaking over his face. "Well, yeah, you're an educated woman."

It's a playful dig at himself for not finishing school, but the admiration shining in Sky's eyes is real. Warmth swells in my chest under his gaze. "I was impressed when you towed those cars today." Even I can hear the flirtatious tone in my voice. It's thrilling to be so bold. My heart races as if I've just buckled myself into one of those rides with a sudden drop, and it's too late to back out now.

The corners of his eyes crinkle as Sky chuckles softly. "Yeah? Well, that makes two of us."

"Oh? You were impressed with yourself, too?"

He laughs. "No, I was impressed with you!" He nudges my arm playfully, sending a tickling thrill up my shoulder. "Seeing you rev up the truck and pull that sedan out of the ditch?"

"That was a first for me," I say.

"And you jumped in to do it without hesitation." The playful flirtation fades from his voice into admiration so genuine it catches me off guard. "It's one of the things I've always liked about you—the way you commit to new experiences without reservation. Remember that time you saved the goat?"

"Oh geez," I groan, running a hand down my face. "I hoped everyone forgot about that."

"What? Why?"

At first I think he's teasing me, but the puzzled furrow of his brow is genuine. "You mean the time *you* saved the goat, and I just made everybody late for that concert, and Christy and Aisha were so annoyed with me?"

I remember the incident all too well, because it was one of my first times going out with the older crowd, and I almost blew it. We were on our way to an outdoor concert in St. Paul, and I couldn't believe I got to tag along as Christy and Aisha's friend. Somewhere along the winding country roads, we passed a goat who'd gotten his head stuck through a hole in the fence of his pasture. I still cringe when I remember the way I insisted that Tommy Pippin turn the minivan around so we could help the poor animal.

Sky pulls in his chin. "I didn't save the goat. That was all you."

"No, you stood there watching me struggle for like, twenty minutes, and then you just bent down and got him free on your first try."

He squints as the memories come back to him. "Oh yeah... But I only tried because you were so persistent. Anyway, nobody was annoyed. They were all rooting for you, remember?"

"At first," I say. "Everyone cared at first."

"Until they realized it wasn't going to be easy. That's when everyone gave up. Except you."

I can still see the disgust on Christy's face as she watched me take the goat by the horns and try to push his head back through the hole. If it had been a puppy or a kitten, I think everyone would have moved Heaven and Earth to save it, but because it was a stinky farm animal with big horns, they thought it would be best just to let the farmer know so he could take care of it. And they were probably right. Aisha, always the voice of reason, was the one who pointed out the farmhouse farther down the road and suggested we just stop and leave a message there on our way to the concert. But I, in all my young-girl dramatics, insisted that we couldn't leave before the poor animal was free. For all we knew, he could have been stuck like that all day, kneeling on his front legs, getting more and more tired... my tortured imagination made me frantic. *Intense*, I realize wryly. Even back then I was too much, inconveniencing all my friends for the sake of accomplishing some task I'd set my mind on. Finally, anxious not to miss the concert, everyone hopped back into the van and drove to the farmhouse to see if the owner was home. Everyone, that is, except for me and Sky.

"You stayed with me," I remember out loud. It was the first time I'd ever found myself alone with him—with any boy, for that matter, aside from my brother—and I'd felt like such a child. I smile as I recall the way Sky stood there politely while I kneeled in the mud, surveying my fruitless efforts with a thoughtful expression. Then, an embarrassed laugh blows through my lips. "You were like, 'So... do you know what you're doing?'"

Sky laughs, too. "I thought you must have had some experience working with goats or something, the way you just grabbed this strange animal by the horns and started moving its head around like you were driving a dirt bike!"

Now I'm full-belly laughing. "I just felt so bad for him! His skull was bigger than that hole! I couldn't imagine how he'd gotten his head through in the first place."

Sky snaps his fingers. "And that's what you said, too! That's what gave me the idea to push his horns down flush with his neck. I figured, that must have been how he got it through, reaching for some grass on the other side. So really, it was all you. You saved that goat."

"At everyone else's expense," I sigh. "We almost missed the concert because I was being inconsiderate."

Sky shrugs. "Not to the goat. The farmer wasn't home, remember? So if we'd left when everyone else wanted to, that little guy probably would have been stuck there all night. Or even longer. That's when I realized how cool you were."

I scrunch my nose. "Really?"

"Totally. You were the youngest person in the car, and you were this bold little animal rights activist in retro jeans and high-tops. You had this red scarf thing in your hair, and I remember thinking you looked like Rosie the Riveter. And you didn't buckle even for a second under peer pressure. It was... just really cool. Back then, it was easy to forget how young you were, because you always seemed so sure of yourself and what you wanted."

My cheeks warm. I force a laugh. It comes out as little more than a puff of air. I want to tell him I never felt sure of myself, that I don't feel sure of myself now, that I just go along with things because I'm too afraid to admit that I don't know what I'm doing. Instead, all that comes out is, "I can be kind of intense."

Sky considers this, then supplies, "Passionate. It's a good quality."

Compliments have always flowed easily between me and Sky since we were kids, but this feels different—the way his eyes take me in, as if he can see more in me than I see in myself. I feel vulnerable, naked under his gaze. My heart feels like it's trying to escape from my chest like a hot-air balloon. I swallow. "You're pretty cool yourself."

He grins. "Is that your professional assessment?"

"Very professional," I tease back, finding my footing again. "I've conducted extensive research."

"Oh yeah?" He quirks an eyebrow. "What does this research entail?"

"Years of observation. Field studies. Thorough analysis."

"And your conclusion?"

I pretend to consider it seriously. "That you see your own good qualities reflected at you in others. That's why you're so agreeable all the time. It's because you see everyone else as if they were as likable and funny and kind and noble as you are." Now I'm the one slipping into serious compliments.

Sky's mouth twitches. His brow furrows as he searches my face. Maybe he feels the compliment is undeserved, but he doesn't say so. In his silence, the space between us feels charged with electricity. His eyes flick to my lips for just a moment, so briefly I might have imagined it.

This is it. The drop I signed up for when I boarded this ride. Everything in me wants it to happen—to feel the rush of leaving my body behind—to freefall into the unknown and forbidden territory that lies on the other side of friendship. But this is Skylar Townsend: the boy who was friends with everyone. The one who sees the best in others because he's such a nice guy. I can't stop the words that tumble from my mouth. "Most people seem to organize others into boxes, and then they only associate with people within their own box. But you don't do that. You never have. You have this magnetic way of treating everyone like an equal—like a friend."

Maybe it's the word "friend" hanging in the air between us now that makes something shift in his eyes: a flicker of doubt, of caution, and then a decision.

Sky leans back and rests his head against the window. "That's really kind of you, AJ. Thank you."

And just like that, the thrill ride is over. Good sense douses the crackling electricity that filled the cab only moments before, and as the swelling in my chest deflates, my heart returning to a steady, dutiful march, I take a steeling breath and manage a smile. This is for the best. We're not meant for fireworks and flames. We would get burned. "Thank you for picking me up today. And for everything after. I had a really good time with you, Sky Guy."

"Me too, Jay-Jay." He returns my smile.

I pop my door handle and shiver against the instant chill outside. "See you when I see you?"

He nods. "Yeah."

Snowflakes feel like tiny pinpricks on my face as I make my way up the slick driveway to the house. The soft *tick, tick, tick* of them landing on the ground tells me they're turning into freezing rain. When I reach the front door, I turn back. Sky's truck is still there against the curb. He's waiting to make sure I get inside safely. Only once I open the front door and stand in the pool of warm light that spills from inside does he drive away.

I watch his taillights disappear into the swirling snow.

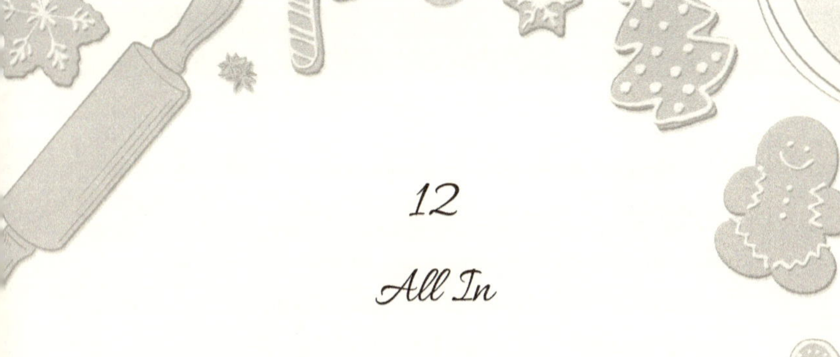

12

All In

I CAN'T SLEEP. EVERY time I close my eyes, I see Skylar's grin, his eyes dancing with laughter. I feel his hand take mine as he pulls me into the snow. Warmth tickles my body like pins and needles, only pleasant.

My eyes fly open. *No.* I can't feed these feelings. I can't think of Skylar this way. I'm leaving soon, and he's staying here, and he's not the type of guy to have a no-strings-attached fling. He's my friend. I don't want to risk that just because we're both in town and I'm distracted. Gritting my teeth, I sit up in bed and give my head a firm shake, as if I could somehow shake thoughts of him out.

After I came home tonight, my mom and dad broke the news to me that Tiffany and her kids won't be coming tomorrow, after all, because of the snowstorm. We watched news reels showing just how bad the roads were in Portland and Eugene, with entire school buses of children stranded for hours and cars abandoned on the side of the road.

Suddenly feeling guilty, I reached out to Benson to see if he'd made it to work on time before the chaos hit, and he was quick to assure me he had before asking if I got home okay.

I'm glad our date didn't keep Benson from his patients at the hospital, but the aftereffects of the storm are just beginning. Who can say how long we'll have to wait before the roads are safe enough for my siblings to make the drive home for the holidays?

The thought of spending another day playing tow-truck heroes with Sky sounds more appealing than it should.

I'm not naive enough to kid myself into thinking there's no chemistry between me and Sky, or that I could only ever see him as a friend. And I'm not meek enough to believe he hasn't thought the same thing. But here's one thing I know for certain: Sky is one in a million. He's always been a safe space for me, someone I could go to for sound advice without fear of judgment. He was my hero as a teenager, and now he's a long-lost treasure I never want to be without again.

I'm not willing to risk losing that for a few weeks of passion. And from the decision I saw in his eyes tonight, I think he's come to the same conclusion.

So friends we are and friends we will stay. I need to focus on the reason I'm here. It isn't to destroy childhood friendships with rebound flings.

Slipping out of bed, I flip on my lamp and retrieve my laptop and field notebook before climbing into bed again and sitting with my back up against the headboard.

This article for the RNN newsletter is just what I need to get me back on track to achieving my dream of working at *Verité*.

I open my laptop. My fingers rest on the keyboard as I try to think of a place to begin.

My mind goes blank.

The feel of Sky's hand on mine caresses my memory. For a moment, I'm back in his truck with the smell of melting chocolate and marshmallows and the musty old heater. His voice rings through my head, warm with laughter: *You've got fists of steel, woman!*

I smile, catch myself, and shake the memories away. *What is wrong with me?*

Roanoke Community Center, I type into my word processor.

The cursor blinks expectantly.

My hands hover over the keyboard.

Stop thinking about Sky.

Don't think about him.

Community center! Why does Roanoke need a community center?

I go to write the question down, just to have something to write, but it's gone before I type a single word, my mind as blank as the snow-covered lawn outside my window. A familiar cold stiffness creeps up my shoulders, gripping my neck. I can't breathe.

With a gasp, I snap my laptop shut and just focus on my breath. *In two, three, four. Out two, three, four, five, six...*

I lean back on my headboard, blowing out as if through a straw, my eyes closed.

Sky's voice seeps back into my mind. *Do we even recognize what we have until it's gone?*

I wonder if he was thinking of his mother or of Africa. Or was he thinking of his relationship with his dad? Maybe it was everything; the way change seems to be overtaking Roanoke like unchecked English Ivy.

Now it's Sharla Marie's voice echoing in my brain: *Have you seen the new police station?*

I remember the sight of the station when I first came home, looking so out of place in the landscape of my childhood memories. For a moment, I feel the sense of loss that Sky and Bea described. Then suddenly, I feel ashamed of the disgruntled feelings I had about my mom's kitchen updates. Here I sit in my childhood bedroom surrounded by memorabilia that's remained practically untouched since I was a teenager, with both my parents alive and healthy and sleeping soundly just down the hall. I haven't lost anything. Not really. Sky can never go back to a space that's been untouched by the loss of his mother. And now Bea is about to lose everything she's ever known. Her family is gone, and before much longer, she'll lose the only house she's ever lived in and her family's legacy as well.

Maybe this is what's wrong with Roanoke these days. Maybe the town has lost the sense of community it once had because the glue that once brought everyone together has been forgotten, just like Bea and her family's house, left to crumble and decay alone in the woods.

It isn't right.

The beginnings of an idea prod me to scroll through Sharla Marie's interview. What did she say about knowing when to hold on to what's old because it's worth keeping?

Before I even realize I've reached for it, my laptop is open again, and the soft clack of my fingertips on the keyboard fills my ears.

I'm vaguely aware that this is the first time I've written in over a month, but I don't pause to celebrate it or give it a second thought, because I'm on a roll and I need to get these words out before the stiff cold steals my breath away again.

The next morning, I feel electrified as I stand at the new buffet counter in my parent's kitchen with my phone pressed to my ear, waiting for Donna Shipley to answer my call.

I bounce on my heels anxiously and review my notes.

There's a click. "Hello?"

My heart leaps. "Mrs. Shipley! Hi, this is AJ Banner. I'm working on that article you requested for the RNN January newsletter, and I was wondering if you had a minute to talk about it?"

There's a pause as Donna orients herself to the rush of information I fed to her far too quickly. "Yep," is all she says.

Now it's my turn to reorient myself. I forgot how blunt and to the point she is. No wonder I was scared of her as a kid. "Thanks. So, I've been interviewing people around town, and there's definitely a recurring theme of loss when people talk about community involvement. They miss a connection to Roanoke's past. And Bea Carston is about to lose the Morley Mansion and her home." I pause. Afraid of losing Donna's interest, I get to the point. "What do you think of using the Morley Mansion for the new community center? It has so much—"

"No," Donna says, cutting me off.

I fumble over my words before trailing off. "Oh. Why not?"

She heaves a heavy sigh. I imagine her the way she used to look behind the Student Resources desk at school, leaning back in her swivel chair with her arms folded and her eyes rolling behind fluttering eyelids as she musters the patience to explain herself. "The idea came up in a board meeting, but it was a unanimous no. It's Bea's family property, and things get sticky when you try to run something like the Neighbors Network on someone else's property. The house is in bad shape, and even if it weren't, it wouldn't accommodate the needs we anticipate for our community center."

"Do you mind if I ask what needs you're referring to?" *What about the needs to connect with the past and help a struggling neighbor?*

Donna rattles off a list of requirements in the same impatient monotone she used to recite school rules while signing a hall pass. "ADA accessibility, spaces big enough to accommodate large groups, public restrooms, sports courts, future possibility for a swimming pool, passes fire safety, up-to-date electrical and plumbing, Wi-Fi... There's a lot to consider, and old houses like the Morley estate have tiny hallways and cramped rooms, and getting it to work for our needs would require more work than just building something new from scratch."

I don't know why I didn't expect that she would have already thought through all of this. Hearing her list the reasons now, I vaguely recall having heard them already at my mom's book club last week. I feel slightly embarrassed, but also frustrated. "But the house already has a history of community involvement. And it would really help Bea out—"

"Bea is getting old. She hasn't been able to keep up with the house for several years now; that's why it's in the state it's in. What she needs is to be relieved of that burden. But that's another story. Once we get our community center underway, we'll be able to do a lot more to help neighbors, like Bea, who are aging out and need more support."

"What about the neighbors who have stated they don't *want* a new building in Roanoke?"

I realize almost as soon as the question shoots from my mouth that I've slipped into my journalist persona and lost the personal connection I meant to have with Donna throughout this conversation.

Donna reacts. "I'm grateful you're taking your interview process so seriously for this article, AJ, but don't make it more than it needs to be. It's just a newsletter. All we need is something to get people excited about the prospect of a community center, not a call for social reform. If that's below your skill set, don't bother with it. You should enjoy your vacation time with your family."

"No," I choke out, "I'm sorry, I didn't mean to... I want to write the article. It's good to do something useful while I'm in town. I just had this idea and got excited. Of course I should have known you would have looked into it already. I'm sorry for butting in. Seriously, thank you for this opportunity."

"That's alright. Is there anything else I can help you with?"

"No... No, thanks for your time, Mrs. Shipley."

Donna's goodbye is as curt as her greeting before she hangs up.

I stand there staring at my phone for a few moments. *It's just a newsletter.*

I know I should feel embarrassed for getting carried away, but this is the first time I've felt like a journalist in months. A fire has been lit inside me, and Donna's rejection only fans the flame. She might see it as *just a newsletter*, but she doesn't realize she's given me a platform. And when there's a message to share and a platform on which to share it, a good journalist can inspire change.

And I'm a good journalist. I'm a dang good journalist. And this is my chance to prove it.

Theodore barks from inside the house a moment before the floorboards groan under Bea Carston's footsteps as she makes her way to answer the door. She looks surprised to see me standing on her porch.

"Hi, Bea." I hold out a plate of my mom's Roanoke-famous banana bread. "I hope I didn't catch you at a bad time?"

She blinks, her dog jumping and yapping at her feet. "Down, Theodore!" she snaps before opening the door wider. "Come on in, hon. We're just watching *Matlock*. Down, Theodore!"

Theodore sniffs cautiously in my direction from a safe distance, with his one good eye on the plate of banana bread in my hands.

"He'll pester you for a bite, but don't give him any," Bea cautions. "He's got diabetes. Vet says no more human treats for him."

"My dog's on a strict diet, too," I say.

"He got diabetes, too?"

"No, just allergies. He gets itchy skin and goopy eyes."

Bea humphs and turns down the TV volume with her remote during a TV Land commercial. "Seems like everybody's got diabetes these days. My brother had it, God rest his soul. And now even the dogs are getting it."

Maybe banana bread was a bad idea. I'm about to say as much when Bea reaches for the plate. "Here, I've got some honey butter that'll go great with that. Does it have chocolate chips?"

"Always."

"Nuts?"

"I think there are some walnuts."

Bea makes a face. "That's alright, hon, I'll pick them out for us. Do you want some cranberry juice? I have cranberry juice."

"I'm alright, thanks—"

But Bea has already disappeared into the kitchen and must not be able to hear me. She calls out, "I'm just going to zap these real quick." The sound of beeping microwave buttons accompanies her voice a moment before the drone of the appliance starts. "You go ahead and have a seat, hon."

I sink into the end of the couch with the least wear, and Theodore sniffs at me again before scampering into the kitchen after the smell of warm banana bread.

Bea returns a minute later with two plates of the warm banana bread lathered in honey butter. "Oh, there he is," she says at the sight of Matlock back on the screen. She takes her place in the worn indent on the other end of the couch, her eyes lighting up. "He's good," she says. "He can solve any case. Do you like *Matlock*?"

I consider lying but then say, "I've seen bits here and there."

Bea explains what's happening in the episode, and I listen and watch with her for a few minutes while we eat our banana bread, and I try to come up with a smooth transition into the reason for my visit. But it quickly becomes apparent that no opening will come up anytime soon as long as Bea is focused on the show. So I dive in.

"Bea, how long do you have before the sale of the Morley Mansion is final?"

Her eyes stay on the TV screen. "There's an inspection at the end of the month. After that, we sign the papers."

"The thirty-first?"

She nods. "Oh, look, he's going to get caught!"

I wait for a commercial break before diving back in. "You know, I've been thinking about you and the house. I think there might be a way to save it so you won't have to give up your home. Have you ever considered registering the Morley Mansion as a historic building?"

"Isn't that what it is?"

I shake my head. "We know its history here in town, and it has historic significance to us, but there's a way to make it officially registered by the government. As a registered historic building, it would be protected from demolition, and you could even get grants to pay for the restoration."

Bea's full attention is on me now. She leans forward in her seat, thoughtful. "You mean they'll give me money to fix the old place up?"

"Not only that, but they can also provide a budget to maintain the house after its restoration. And if the house were a registered historic house, I think you could get the community involved in its care and maintenance so you wouldn't have to do all that upkeep work by yourself."

She folds her arms and leans back in her seat thoughtfully. "How do I apply?"

"The application process will take time. It could be several months before you hear back—"

"That's too long," she says. "I've only got till the thirty-first. When it fails inspection, it'll be condemned, and I'll have to pay a condemnation fee."

"Right," I say, scooting to the edge of my seat. "But I think we could buy you some time if we can do just enough repairs for the house to pass inspection before the end of the month. If the house passes, you won't have to pay the condemnation fee, and it would give you the time you need to go through the application process."

Bea chews on this for a moment. "How we going to do that?" she asks. "I don't have the money to pay for repairs. And who's going to be able to fix things up that fast?"

I smile. "I have an idea where we can get the money. Leave that part to me. As for the repairs, I know a great contractor. What do you say?"

She shrugs, looking skeptical but open. "Well, what have I got to lose? Guess it's worth a try, if you think we can do it."

"I think we can!" I send Sky a text message.

> How fast do you think you could flip a house?

"It's not as bad as I thought it would be," Sky says as he taps a crowbar against his palm. At his feet, a floorboard he pulled up from the hallway in the Morley Mansion reveals the worst of the water damage. "Most of it is just in this corner of the house, so I don't think you'll even need to touch the flooring in the ballroom—which will save a lot of money." He leans against the wall behind him and folds his arms. I don't know if it's that flannel work shirt he's wearing or that he just tore up a plank of wood with a crowbar and his bare hands, but the shape of his chest and the bulk of his arms are distracting. I have to look away to keep my thoughts focused on the conversation at hand.

Bea stands beside me in front of the parlor window, where the daylight streams especially bright from the snow outside. "What about the sewage problem? That was what the city was most concerned about."

"I'll need to get a plumber to do a closer inspection, but from what I can see, it looks like if we just update the plumbing, that should fix the problem."

"What'll that cost, all together?" Bea asks.

Sky scratches his chin with his thumb. "Ballpark estimate? I'd say you're looking at around twenty grand, minimum. More if the mold is bad."

Bea shakes her head. "That's what I thought."

We're standing in the parlor across the hall from the bathroom where the pipe burst. Here, the floors and walls weren't touched, but the bathroom was stripped down to the studs when a repair crew came in to deal with the flood before Bea realized she wouldn't have insurance coverage to pay for it and sent the crew away. There's a pile of torn-out floorboards near the base of the stairs. Aside from this, the rest of the house looks surprisingly immaculate, as if Bea has continued to clean and polish it weekly despite the lack of events.

"Would that be enough for the house to reverse its condemned status?" I ask Skylar.

He tilts his head from side to side as he considers. "There's a lot that still needs work—it's going to need a new roof, for one. But, yeah, fix the water damage in this corner of the house, install new flooring, update the plumbing... I think that should be enough. The city might come back and say it needs a new roof, too, but the rest of the repairs shouldn't be a problem for now."

I always admired Sky's knack for making things when we were teenagers. It wasn't uncommon even back then for him to do minor repairs around our parents' houses when we were hanging out, just because he noticed it needed to be done or because one of our friends' moms would ask if he'd mind taking a look. But seeing him now as a man, I'm still amazed that he's able to tell so much after a quick walk-through in a house.

"I don't have the money," Bea says again.

"I'll work on that part," I remind her. "But let's say we can get the money you need; is this something you want to pursue?"

Bea takes in our surroundings: the faded rug and period furniture, the peeling wallpaper, and the framed photographs of her ancestors. "My brother and I used to play here while my mother got it ready for events. I can't imagine losing it. These walls are all I have left of those memories." She runs her hand along the window frame. Dusty particles glimmer in the air, softening her features and making her look angelic, haloed by the light outside. Finally, her blue eyes meet mine, rimmed with tears. "If you think it's possible, please do whatever you can to save the house."

"I promise." I look to Sky. This plan will only work with his help.

He nods, and a smile flickers on his lips, but I can see the hesitation behind it. "We'll see what we can do."

We follow Bea out of the house, and she locks the front door with a key that looks like it belongs on a book cover. "Thank you both so much," she says as we drop her off back at her house. "You've given me hope."

After she's gone, Sky and I walk to our cars. "Do you really think it's possible?" I ask him.

He blows out a breath. "It'll be tight, I'm not gonna lie. I could do a lot of the labor for free, no problem. The idea is kind of exciting. And they did a lot of the work for us when they tore out the flooring and dried everything out after the flood to prevent black mold. So there, at least, it's mostly going to be a matter of putting things back together, assuming no further damage has occurred while the house sat. But the materials won't be cheap, and getting other contractors this time of year to finish in such a short time...that would be a miracle."

"Well," I say, "Christmas is the time for miracles."

He casts an admiring sidelong glance at me that makes my heart skip a beat. "What do you have up your sleeve, AJ Banner?"

I bite back a smile. "You'll see. So, are you in?"

He looks from me to the house and exhales through puffed cheeks. "I'm all in."

13

Let's Just Say We're Doing It for an Old Friend

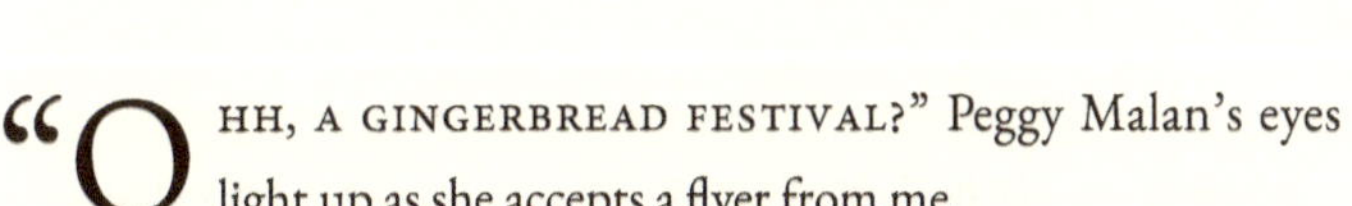

"**O**HH, A GINGERBREAD FESTIVAL?" Peggy Malan's eyes light up as she accepts a flyer from me.

Today, her house smells like nutmeg and cream from her home-made eggnog and gingersnaps on the table in front of her parlor window, which looks like an image from *Better Homes and Gardens*.

"It's a fundraiser," I say, shimmying my shoulders in a way that I hope comes off excited and not weird as I pass out more flyers around the book club circle. I've kept the details fairly sparse, since I don't know for certain if the Morley Mansion will be decent in time to host the event, but on the flyer, there's a cheery image of a gingerbread person and a QR code to the event website I whipped up the day before, where people can buy tickets, sign up to bring a gingerbread house to be auctioned off, and stay abreast of updates.

It's Saturday afternoon on the seventeenth, and the snow has most-ly melted. Aside from a few dirty, slushy remnants that cling to the shadows outside, it's almost impossible to tell any snowstorm hap-pened at all. My siblings and their families still had to delay their trips home until next Wednesday, but it gives me the time I need to focus on throwing together this event to raise enough money to cover the renovation costs on the Morley Mansion. With only a week and a half before Christmas, I'm hoping I can make this happen by the twenty-third. Which means I'm going to need some help.

"What's the cause?" asks Reagan Keys, pushing her large glasses up the bridge of her nose as she peers at her flyer.

Beside her, the blond girl, whose name I still don't know, has already pulled up the website on her phone from the QR code. "Save the Morley Mansion?" she asks.

"It's about to be demolished," I explain. "Bea Carston will lose her home and everything she's ever known—her family's legacy, her livelihood, all gone."

Donna Shipley grunts as I hand her the last flyer. Lest she think I'm going behind her back or trying to undermine her after our conversation, I quickly explain, "Bea wants to have the house registered as a historic building. She can get grants to pay for the restoration and upkeep. She just needs more time. I wrote an article about it—"

"Yes," Donna says over me, "Margot got your article and shared it with the board." The way Donna says it doesn't sound good.

Matilda Hatch jumps in. "It was a lovely article, AJ. So thoughtful and touching..." She looks unsurely at Donna before clasping her hands as she tries to put her next words as delicately as possible. "It just isn't quite what we wanted for the newsletter."

Donna cuts to the chase. "We aren't interested in maintaining a historic house museum in Roanoke that frankly won't bring in any tourists. The RNN's focus is on taking Roanoke into a strong, connected future with a new community center that fits the needs of the rising generation, not on preserving relics from the past. If you want us to publish your article in the newsletter, we'll ask you to revise it to reflect our goals for building a community center."

Thankfully, I had the foresight to publish my article on the event website instead. "I understand," I say. "This event is separate from all of that. I promise, I'm still working on an article for you."

"But we *do* love the idea of this fundraiser," Matilda gushes, looking to Donna to back her up. "We talked about doing some kind of holiday charity event this season, didn't we? But nobody stepped in to spearhead it."

Donna nods. "That's correct. If you're willing to take the lead on this, you'll have the Roanoke Neighbors Network's support. We'd be happy to collaborate on this event."

"I can do a kids' corner," Reagan Keys says. "We could have face painting and graham cracker house decorating... My girls need to earn their community service badges, so this would be a perfect opportunity for them to help."

I hardly say thank you before Matilda is talking again. "Margot Pratt is the head of the RNN Events and Outreach Committee; she can help spread the word and get you some ticket sales. You have her contact info already for the newsletter. But let me also put you in touch with Tonya Rodriguez, who heads the Fundraising and Sponsorship Committee. Between the two of them, you'll have lots of helpful resources at your disposal."

"Has the newsletter gone out yet?" Donna asks.

"I don't think so," Matilda replies.

Donna nods at the flyer in Matilda's lap. "Send Margot a picture of that and see if it's not too late to include it in this month's newsletter. That should give us a good head start."

"Wow, thank you—" I try again, but Sharla Marie speaks up from behind me.

"AJ, do you have any more of these?" She holds up her flyer. "I'll put one in my shop window, and I'm sure I can get the other shop owners downtown to put one up in theirs."

"I can bring you a stack today," I tell her.

"Get me a handful, too," says Reagan. "Breana and I can get them up at the local schools." She nods to the blond girl beside her.

"And I'll post the QR code to our mommy group," Breana adds, thumbs already flying across her phone screen.

"Put me down for refreshments, AJ, dear," says Peggy Malan.

Claire Tan is right on her heels. "I've always wanted to be in charge of an auction. If you don't already have someone in mind for that, I hope you'll consider me, Amelia Jane."

I'm speechless. I hoped I might get people excited, but I didn't expect this overwhelming acceptance. Energy pulses through my veins and thrums in my ears.

We can do this, I think. *We can make this happen. We can save the Morley Mansion!*

And when we do, I'll be on such a high from it all that I'll be able to start my first day at *Verité* with my head held high.

Later that evening, my phone buzzes with a call from Sky as I drive to Sharla Marie's to drop off a stack of flyers. "Hey, Sky Guy."

"Hey Jay-Jay, we're in luck. My dad called in a favor to his old buddy Rod, who's a plumber, and he's got some time tomorrow to check out the Morley Mansion at no charge."

"No way!" I practically squeal. "Sky, I can't *believe* how well people are responding to this fundraiser already. I really think we have a shot at pulling this off."

"Well, let's not get ahead of ourselves," he cautions, but I can hear how big he's smiling. "There's a lot we need to figure out. I can donate my labor for free, but there's still the problem of paying for materials, and…we're gonna need some more hands. I'm a fast worker, but if I try to tackle this on my own, it'll take months, not weeks."

"Right, yes." I try to rein in my enthusiasm, but excitement still bubbles below the surface. "I spoke with Tonya Rodriguez a bit ago—she handles all the fundraising stuff for the RNN, you know—and she said she'd talk to her husband about maybe volunteering some labor."

"That would be incredible. My dad and I have worked with them on lots of projects over the years. They know what they're doing." There's a knocking sound in the background, and Sky grunts.

"Are you at the house right now?" I ask.

Sky said he wanted to do a more thorough inspection this morning so he could create an accurate project plan and budget before shopping around for supplies and submitting labor bids.

"Yeah," he says, "I'm just finishing up."

I look at the clock on the dashboard of my mom's car. It's nearly seven. "Were you there all day?"

"Not *all* day, no. I did a few jobs for my dad around town, then came back to finish up."

A realization hits me then, and I feel like an idiot for not thinking of it sooner. "Are you sure this won't be too much for you right now, Sky? Tackling this huge project and working for your dad?"

Sky huffs a laugh. "Yeah, you don't need to worry about that. Business has been slow for my dad. The only jobs he's been sending me on are warranty runs."

I hesitate, because Sky has always been one to downplay his struggles, and I don't want him to take on more than he can bear because of me.

As if he can read my thoughts, he says, "AJ, I've got this. I wouldn't take it on if I wasn't excited about it, okay?"

"Okay..."

"Okay. So, I'll let you know how the plumbing inspection goes tomorrow, and then we'll really have some fun!"

I laugh, my excitement resurfacing. "I can't wait!"

"Me neither. See you soon?"

"See you soon."

As I hang up, I feel like I'm walking on air. Things are coming together, and Sky...the way he said, "See you soon," makes me wonder if he has another impromptu meetup in mind.

I can't wait to see him again.

The realization sobers me at the same time as I approach a Stop sign. *Yes*, I think, *stop!* I don't know if it was confronting Benson, or if I've finally gotten over my breakup with Adam, but something has changed in the last couple of days. I'm finally feeling like myself again. The writer's block that's plagued me for over a month seems to have melted, and I'm ready to host a community event and write some more promotional articles to make a difference in the world: all things that will prime me to slay this probationary period at *Verité*. The last thing I need is to get into another messy relationship.

No matter what, I can't let Sky's kind gray eyes and his lopsided grin distract me.

14

Change of Plans

T HE AIR IS CRISP when I meet Sky in the horseshoe driveway of the Morley Mansion on Monday morning. He looks especially rugged in his work flannel and Carhartt pants as he takes two hard hats from the back of his truck and hands one to me. "Morning." His breath freezes in a silver mist that wafts my way.

I take the hard hat. "Should I expect falling debris?"

Sky buckles on a tool belt, his face shaded by his hard hat as he shrugs. "It's a construction site. You never know what you're going to get." He grins. His excitement is palpable.

"You look like you're about to go to Disneyland," I laugh.

There's a loud scrape of metal on metal as he yanks a heavy toolbox to the end of the truck bed. "Oh yeah, demo day is my favorite." He spins a hammer into his belt like a cowboy holstering a gun before lifting the toolbox from the truck and holding it at his side. Eyes sparkling with delight, he shoulders a long tile scraper like a lumberjack and nods to me. "Let's go break some stuff."

I turn around to keep from gawking at him like a swoony teenager. "I thought you liked fixing things, not breaking them," I say as we make our way up the porch steps.

"They're both cathartic in their own way."

As I fish in my purse for the key Bea gave me, I'm hyperaware of Sky standing behind me, close enough that the clouds of his breath drift in my peripheral vision in waves with his every exhale. This is why fantasizing about kissing old friends is a bad idea: the images come back at the worst times. My hands fumble through the mess of crumpled receipts and pens in my bag until I finally grasp the ornate head of the brass key. "There it is," I laugh nervously. I purse my lips with concentration, squeezing the key tightly to keep my hand from trembling as I unlock the door. It opens with a whine on its hinges.

I stand aside for Sky, but he motions for me to lead the way. "After you."

As I step into the cold, dark entryway, it feels so different from the lively, warm place I remember on the night of my first Snow Ball. Gone are the twinkling lights and sparkling decor. Gone is the aroma of warm food, the sound of music, the energy of young people laughing and dancing, but there's still that velvety cord blocking access to the stairs. Even when we came here with Bea the other day, she'd already had the lights on, and her presence had made the place feel less like the haunt of ghosts. In the dark, with just the two of us, it feels strangely intimate and forbidden.

Sky finds the light switch, and suddenly, the ghostly shadows vanish. The arched stair railing and original wood floors gleam from Bea's faithful polishing. There are no cobwebs in the crystal chandelier overhead, no dust fogging the surfaces of the antique furniture that was pushed up against the entryway walls and left there after the bathroom flooded. Despite the pile of wood flooring by the stairs and some rolled-up rugs beside the furniture, the house looks remarkably clean and stately.

"Poor Bea," I say, imagining her all alone in this vast house, cleaning it dutifully every week, even with no promise of ever hosting another event.

Sky doesn't ask what I mean. He nods, as if the same thoughts were running through his mind. "It's a good thing she kept up with her cleaning routine, or she might not have caught the flood until it was too late."

Something blooms in my chest—that feeling of wholeness I felt in Sky's truck after Norma's diner. It feels good to not have to explain myself to him. When I look at him, he's watching me with an admiring smile that warms deep in my belly.

He clears his throat, shakes himself. "Let's start in this back hallway. That's what got the worst of the water damage."

I follow him past the parlor where I once sat to massage my feet after Benson snubbed me. Funny, I haven't heard from Benson since he texted to ask if I made it home alright after the snowstorm. I'm sure he's been busy at the hospital. But until now, I haven't thought about him once since that day. Our failed date must have done the trick, because I've been able to write again for the first time since Adam dumped me, and when I think of that night twelve years ago, rubbing my feet in that parlor and nursing my wounded pride, the ache is gone.

Floorboards creak beneath our feet as Sky leads us down the hall toward the bathroom. Heavy drapes cover the window at the end of the hall. Sky throws them open, flooding the hallway with glimmering specks of dust and daylight. Silhouetted against the light, his shoulders look especially broad, his movements smooth and familiar as he runs a hand along the windowsill and clicks his tongue. "I hate to tear out this trim. You don't find woodwork like this in houses today."

I swallow and straighten my hard hat, just to occupy my hands. *Keep it together, AJ!* "Why do we have to take out the windowsill?"

"It's damaged," he says. "They brought in industrial fans and dehumidifiers after the flood, and things were mostly dry when Bea sent the cleanup crew away, but since the house sat so long, whatever moisture was left did a number on these walls." He points to some X marks made with blue painter's tape that he left on the surrounding walls last Saturday. "That one, that one, and this one all need to be repaired. See this?" Crouching on his haunches, he points to some cracks and warping in the walls near the baseboards. "We need to replace the plaster. And if the studs are moldy behind, we'll have to replace the entire wall."

There's a brief temptation to make a stud joke, but it's quickly replaced by a sinking feeling in my gut. "Is that going to be a lot more expensive?" We've had a steady stream of ticket sales come in for the Gingerbread Festival over the weekend—an impressive stream, in fact. But even with that, I'm not sure how much we can realistically expect to make from this last-minute event.

Sky straightens and tilts his head. "It'll add to the cost, for sure, but the most expensive part is going to be replacing these antique floors. I don't even know if we'll be able to find wood like this."

"Is there any way we can salvage it?"

"That's what I'm hoping for. That pile in the entryway got the worst of the damage. I've looked through it and there's probably a lot we can save, but some of it was just ripped out without much care. And these that were left in the hallway... See where they're warped in places?" He bounces lightly on one spot where the wood is especially uneven, and it gives slightly under his weight with a creak. "These boards we can fix with the right treatments. But if there are any that are so damaged that they're rotten and crumbling, those will need to be replaced."

I'm not sure what I expected. When we did our walk-through with Bea the other day, it all felt so encouraging. It seemed like a lot of the work was started for us, with demo done in the bathroom and checks for things like black mold and lead in the walls already out of the way.

I thought all we'd have to do was put things back together. But if we'll have to tear out entire walls and reframe them...

Sky must see the rising panic in my face, because he's quick to supply some positives. "We might get lucky and only have to replace the plaster in the hallway from chair rail height down. That would save time and money. And fortunately, I'm pretty comfortable with plasterwork. It's very similar to materials I used in Ethiopia, so I'm not worried about that at all."

My understanding of construction doesn't go much further than guys breaking stuff with sledgehammers on HGTV before a team of designers comes in and makes the space beautiful again on tight deadlines. We've got the tight deadline, but we don't have a team of designers. We have me and Skylar.

"Okay..." I eye the cracked walls, the warped floors. "Let's say we can salvage all the wood floors, and we only have to repair the plaster from the chair rail down. How long would it take to do everything?"

He has his answers ready. "We can tear out the old plaster in a couple hours easily. Putting it back up is more time consuming, but I think we could do it in a few days. Maybe treat some floorboards with wood bleach where they've got water stains..." Perhaps afraid of losing me, he summarizes quickly. "Assuming there's no black mold, and assuming we can salvage all the wood, if we work overtime without long breaks it's *possible* we could finish it all in twelve days."

My stomach drops. "But...that would mean working on Christmas."

He sucks in a breath before continuing in a rush. "Yeah, but only minor work. I created a construction schedule that accounts for all of that, and it looks doable. In theory." He tilts his head with admittance. "Construction never works out the way it looks like it should on paper." He takes in the disappointment on my face and is quick to clarify, "It's going to be close. Really close, I won't lie. But we can hope for a miracle, right? What have we got to lose? If we rip it all up and can't put it back together in time, it gets demolished anyway."

I take a deep breath. "Right." I need a moment to gather my thoughts, and he gives it to me without my having to ask. I pinch my lips with my fingers as I peer through the bathroom doorway behind Sky. It's dark in there, but I already know from our walk-through with Bea that everything's stripped to the subfloor and studs. There was no black mold when the cleanup crew first came to assess damages three years ago, but who knows what could have been growing in there since then?

One thing at a time, AJ.

I hold my head in my hands, as if it might keep my thoughts from going everywhere. "Okay, let's go over the worst-case scenario."

"There's black mold and we get sick and die," Skylar says too quickly.

Still holding my head, I stare at him. "Wait, are you serious?"

He smiles. "You said worst-case scenario."

How does he always manage to laugh? He can't be serious. "How likely is that scenario?"

"On a scale of one to ten? Point-zero-zero-one. Black mold won't kill us unless we're living in it for an extended period or one of us has a compromised immune system."

I roll my eyes. "Okay, what's the most likely worst-case scenario?"

He's just as quick with this response, but this time he's not laughing. "There's black mold and we have to hire an exterminator, which we can't schedule until January because of the holidays."

My jaw drops, but I snap it shut again. "Okay, I guess that's better than dying."

Now he smiles.

As much as I want to be annoyed by his unshakable good humor, his method worked. Nothing sounds like that big a deal when you compare it to dying. I release my head and take a resigned breath. "Okay, so no matter how we paint it, the worst thing that happens is that we can't finish on time and the house doesn't pass inspection. Bea loses her home and her family legacy, and the town loses this priceless treasure."

"But," Skylar points out, "the buyer will still pay the same price for the land, and Bea will have the support and commiseration of the town, who will all want to make sure she's taken care of after the festival you host draws attention to her, and she still will be better off for your trying."

I meet his eyes. He really means it.

"How do you always know the right thing to say?" The swoon in my voice is enough to make me blush. I try to play it off as teasing with a flutter of my eyelashes and my hand on my heart.

He plays bashful with a shuffled kick of his foot that is too cute to be allowed as he waves off my compliment. "Nah, you're just sayin' that." Then he grins. "But I'm serious. Whatever happens, you're doing something good here, and I think only good can come of it."

"You mean *you're* doing something good here," I say, taking in the X's taped to the wall from the Saturday he already spent here doing a free inspection. "None of this would be possible without you. You're doing all the actual work and I'm just...writing stuff."

He considers this. "Different kinds of work. Both necessary if we're going to pull this off. But don't worry"—he comes to stand in front of me, so close that we're nearly touching, and I hold my breath as I look up into his face before he gives my hard hat a light tap with his knuckle—"you'll have a chance to get your hands dirty. You ready?"

I swallow, grateful he can't hear the thoughts racing through my head. "Where do we start?"

His arm comes up, and for the briefest moment, I think he's about to cup my face. Before I can decide if I'm going to let him, he's already reaching past me to tap the wall behind me. "Right here," he says with a knock.

I'm standing in the way I realize, heat rising behind my neck. Of course he had a perfectly logical, non-romantic reason for coming this way. I stumble quickly to the side and turn to face the wall, clearing my throat. "Okay, right. Let's tear it down." I sound out of breath. How embarrassing.

If Sky notices, he's kind enough not to be awkward about it. "Moment of truth. If there's black mold, this is where we'll find it—and any other issues we need to plan for. Here. Stand back."

I'm about to ask what other issues he means, but as soon as I've stepped aside, Sky raises his tile scraper and swings it at the wall with the ease and brawn of a Greek god. "Just loosening up the plaster," he explains between swings. Then, wedging the edge of the tile scraper into a crack in the plaster, Sky knocks away the biggest chunks. The plaster comes free from the slatted wood lath behind as easily as if it were a crisp meringue.

Once the hole is big enough, Sky leans his tile scraper against the wall and grips a pane of lath. His shoulders strain against the fabric of his shirt as he yanks once, twice, and then pulls the pane free with a grunt. He sets it to the side carefully before pulling a flashlight from his tool belt and shining it into the wall cavity.

I wait with bated breath for his assessment.

He says, "Whew," in a way that could either be a relief or *Whew, this is worse than I thought.*

I brace for the worst.

Sky meets my eyes with a smile. "No black mold."

"No?" I go up on my toes hopefully.

"Not that I can see. Even if that's the only Christmas miracle we get, I'd say it's a pretty good one."

We have twelve days to pull off this impossible scheme. Of those days, one is the Gingerbread Festival, one is Christmas Eve, and one is Christmas Day. As Sky and I spend the next hour removing plaster from the lower half of the walls in the hall, Sky walks me through the game plan he's come up with.

"We need to finish the demolition today," he muffles through his face mask as he smacks the plaster with a sledgehammer—just hard enough to loosen the plaster's grip on the lath backing without breaking it.

I come behind him with the tile scraper and pry the broken plaster free as he showed me. White dust fills the air, fogging our goggles as chunks of broken plaster crumble to the floor. I feel like Wonder Woman wielding a spear in a war zone.

"Days two through six, we'll frame and install new lath and plaster," Sky says between hammer swings, "replace any rotted subfloor, and prep the walls for paint."

I nod. "Okay, and by then, we'll need to block off this portion of the house during the Gingerbread Festival."

Sky reaches the end of the hall and drops the sledgehammer before leaning against the opposite wall to take a break. He raises a gloved hand, and I can only imagine he must be crossing his fingers—it's too hard to see through the cloud of plaster dust and the bulk of his gloves.

"If all goes according to plan, we won't have to work on Christmas. But then, after Christmas, we'll really have to double-down to reinstall the salvageable wood floors, replace any unsalvageable planks—assuming we can find wood to match in time—finish sanding and staining the floors, install baseboards and trim, all that."

Except that I won't be here after Christmas to help finish, I realize. My flight leaves on the twenty-seventh so I can have a week in New York to prepare before starting with *Verité*.

I pause, tile scraper raised. "Do all those things have to be done for the house to pass inspection?" I ask. "The painting and trim work?"

When I look over my shoulder at him, Sky is watching me.

"No," he admits without looking away. "As long as the house is structurally sound, with plumbing and electrical up to code, it doesn't technically need to be finished." He nods at me. "Nice form."

Is that a flirtatious tone I hear through his mask? I look down at myself, covered in plaster dust and sweating through my mom's borrowed paint T-shirt and gardening pants. He must be joking. "Thanks," I say, playing along. "I've been practicing my demolition poses." I pry off another chunk of plaster for good measure.

"It's paying off." He chuckles. "You've got some muscle."

Maybe he's not joking. Warmth floods my body at the compliment. Before I can say something stupid about what I've noticed about his form, I clear my throat. "Okay, so as long as we can get the big stuff done in time, we'll be alright."

Sky straightens. "Yeah, I think so. Hang on, let me grab some garbage bags from the truck."

He leaves me alone, chipping away at the wall and making an even bigger mess of Bea's house. An unsettling feeling prods at me. Am I starting something here that I can't finish? The thought of leaving Bea with an unfinished house isn't the way I want to go. And leaving Sky to finish it all himself doesn't sit well with me, either.

I pull away the last chunks of plaster as Sky returns with the garbage bags, and we shovel armfuls of debris into them.

When we get to the walls in the bathroom, Sky shakes his head at the exposed studs. "These need to be replaced." He taps the soft wood with his hammer, and pieces crumble from it like cornbread.

"How much will that put us back?" I ask.

He rubs his chin, then turns to the wall on the opposite side of the bathroom and inspects the studs there. "Both of these walls need to be reframed. Probably all of them. That means the subfloor is definitely going to need to be replaced in here, too. And replacing this exterior wall is going to be a bear in the winter. This is going to be our biggest time and money suck."

The bathroom is small. I remember the line that formed outside it on the night we all got food poisoning at the Snow Ball, and an idea plays in my mind. "What's on the other side of these walls?" I ask, stepping over chunks of discarded plaster as I make my way back out into the hallway to check.

Sky calls after me, "There's a broom closet on the right, and a second parlor on the other side."

I walk into the broom closet and run my hand along the wall that separates it from the bathroom. "Could we just leave one or two of the walls down to make room for a bigger bathroom?" I call out. "Maybe add a toilet or two?"

He follows me to the closet and leans against the doorframe with a laugh through his nose. "If we had more time and a team of plumbers, why not?"

"Well, yeah, I guess I don't mean we install the toilets yet. But maybe we could just not reframe these walls and make the bathroom bigger for now? Then when Bea gets the funding she needs to restore the house, she'll have the option to add some more toilets and bathroom stalls."

"That wouldn't really fit with the whole historical house restoration, though, would it?"

"No, I guess it wouldn't."

"But," Sky says, "it would make for a better public restroom. May I?" He motions to the wall behind me before squeezing into the closet to inspect it.

In this tight space, I press my back against the wall to make room for him. He pulls off a glove to run his bare hand along the back wall of the closet. He smiles and shakes his head. "Even in the closets, the craftsmanship in this house is incredible."

I'm mesmerized by his hand, strong and calloused from years of construction work, yet gentle as his fingertips brush against the smooth plaster. The admiration in his voice is enchanting. He loves this work.

Standing so close to him, my heart beats faster by the second. It takes all my concentration to slow my breathing, to keep my chest from accidentally bumping against his arm.

"This wall will probably need to come out, too," he muses, seemingly oblivious to my palpitating heart. "If they aren't load-bearing, we could just leave the walls out for now, frame out the exterior wall, and let Bea decide what she wants to do with it after that." He turns to face me, so close that I have to crane my neck to look up into his face.

My mind buzzes frantically. What did he just say? "Right, okay," I say breathlessly, nodding as if I'm considering his words.

His ungloved hand comes up and gently plucks a piece of plaster from my shoulder. I hold my breath.

"Worst case," he says, his voice softer, "she'll just have a huge bathroom and one less parlor."

"Worst case," I echo. Thank goodness for the clunky goggles and face masks we're wearing, or I don't think I could trust myself this close to him for another second. I clear my throat and step out of the closet. I'm already starting something I might not be able to finish with Bea's house—I can't do that with Sky, too. Only one demolition at a time.

My pulse slows once we're out of that small space, my head clearing.

Sky follows me back to the bathroom. "Either way," he says, "this exterior wall and the subfloor are going to up the cost quite a bit."

I bite my lip. This project is getting bigger. "We're going to need more money," I think out loud.

People may be excited about the Gingerbread Festival, but with Christmas in a week, I don't know how deep anyone's pockets will realistically be for the fundraiser part of the event.

"What are you thinking?" Sky asks. He's watching my face closely.

"I have an idea," I say hesitantly. "Not a good one, but an idea. It might be terrible, actually." I can't even bring myself to say it. That's how dumb I'm afraid it will sound. But it won't even be worth mentioning if I won't be in town long enough to carry it out. I pull off a glove and stick it under my arm before reaching for my phone. "Hang on. Give me a minute."

I leave Sky in the rubble with white dust swirling in the air around him and make my way to the clean air outside before removing my mask and goggles and opening my email. There have been more ticket sales for the festival since I last checked this morning. Feeling encouraged by this, I thumb open my airline app and look up my flight number.

Then I call the airline.

My hair is still wet from my shower when I plop into bed that night with a roll of dental floss and call Jody to fill her in on my change of plans.

"Is this bad news?" my roommate intones.

I huff a laugh. "What? I can't call my favorite roommate to check in without there being bad news?"

"Girl, it's one in the morning!"

Crap. "I'm sorry, I totally forgot to consider the time difference. I'll call you tomorrow."

"No, it's fine, I'm still up."

"Is Devón there?"

"Duh."

I roll my eyes. "Is he going to move in or what?"

"Maybe. What's the emergency?"

I comb my fingers through my wet hair and give it a good tousle to help it dry with some volume before unwinding a strand of floss. "No emergency. I just wanted to let you know that my flight plans have changed to January second, so I won't be there for your New Year's Eve party, after all."

Jody guffaws. "And you couldn't just text me?"

"Well, I promised I'd be there and now I won't. I thought a broken promise deserved a phone call."

"What happened to your flight?" she asks. "Oregonians can't handle a little snow?"

"We can't," I confirm. I could just leave it at that, but I feel that uncomfortable itch as if I'm lying by not telling her. "But my flight wasn't canceled. I just pushed back my return date. I've got some things I need to do here."

"Boo," she jeers. "You're such a party pooper! Are you seriously working? You're supposed to be on vacation."

"Well, it just so happens that I am *hosting* a party, thank you very much." With my phone wedged between my cheek and shoulder, I start flossing my teeth.

"Is that supposed to make me feel better? Because what I'm hearing is, you're ditching my party to throw one of your own on the other side of the country."

I freeze mid-floss. "Okay, never mind, you got me. It's a work thing. I'm organizing this fundraising event to help me brush up on my writing and events-planning skills before I start at *Verité*. But we need to raise more money, so I'm also organizing a New Year's Ball kind of thing to see if we can convince this tiny town to drain their pockets even more for a good cause and buy tickets."

It's quiet as Jody muffles the sound of herself filling Devón in on the conversation. "Workaholic," she says when she comes back.

"I love you, too."

"What happened with that guy you went out with?"

"Nothing. The snow cut our date short." In fact, I still haven't heard from him since our quick check-in with one another that night. His mother is doing some volunteer work for the festival, but she hasn't acted like she even has any idea that her son took me on a date.

"Pathetic. I'm using your room as a second paint studio. Your sheets are going to smell like solvent when you get back."

"As long as that's all they smell like," I mumble.

"What was that?"

"I said I'm glad you're keeping my room company."

"Just come hoooome," she groans. "The fridge looks like a frat house shrine without your nasty hippy food to balance it out and make me feel like I'm a responsible adult."

"Aw, you do care."

"Whatever. You need me. I can't believe you're working when you should be on vacation. Actually, no, I can totally believe it, and that's what's so sad. You've got to let loose, woman! You're going to wind yourself up into the tightest little knotty knot and start your new job, like, all wound up."

"Are you drunk?"

She laughs. "Not like *drunk* drunk. But don't change the subject. You need to relax. Have fun. You know? Treat yourself. Hook up with someone."

"Okay, I'm hanging up now. I'll see you on the second, okay?"

"Find yourself a hottie!" Jody yells before I hang up.

15

Gingerbread

S TANDING IN PEGGY MALAN'S kitchen the next day, I feel like I'm in Santa's bakery. The smell of warm gingerbread is intoxicating. I can taste the cinnamon and nutmeg with every breath as I pull sheet after sheet of golden-brown rectangles from her double ovens before replacing them with more dough ready to be baked. The countertops are bursting with cookie towers on silver trays, half-constructed gingerbread houses laced with glossy royal icing, bouquets of candy canes, and tall glass jars of sparkling sugarplums.

Peggy is in full-on pastry chef mode in her flour-dusted Christmas apron with red-and-white-striped ties. "Chocolate goes with the fondue set and fountain in the breakfast nook," she says, directing her husband and adult kids, who unload entire boxes of chocolate melts from the car. "Aaron, watch that caramel! We can't afford to burn another batch. Melanie, those pastries can go in the freezer out in the garage. Top shelf on the right, under the blue number two tag."

I spent the morning raiding the local repurposed lumber yard with Sky in search of affordable materials for the new subfloor and stud replacements at the Morley Mansion. Ticket sales have exploded over the last twenty-four hours since the RNN newsletter went out, and I know I have Reagan Keys and Breana Funk and their mommy group to thank for most of those sales. At ten dollars a ticket, we already have enough to pay for most of the framing materials out of pocket, with the rest purchased on credit until more money comes in after the festival. I'll be in a world of pain if those funds don't come through, but I can't allow myself to think about it.

Tim Rodriguez agreed to volunteer some framing labor with his sons, Tony, Josh, and Lucas. Tony was married in the Morley Mansion, and Andrea Rodriquez had her Quinceañera there, so Tim said that helping for the next week would be their way of thanking Bea. That will save us a ton of money on framing labor costs, and it's freed me up to help with festival prep. For the moment, things are coming together at a pace I wouldn't have thought possible only a few days ago.

The RNN offered to pay most of the festival expenses from their events budget, since they'd been planning to do some kind of holiday event, anyway. That's been a lifesaver, for sure. But I'm on my own for the New Year's dance. I remember that they used the same decor every year for the Snow Ball, so someone must have it stored somewhere. If I can set it up in the ballroom of the Morley Mansion, that would be venue and decorations at no cost, which would leave catering and music as the main expenses. Of course, none of that will matter if the house doesn't pass inspection in time, or if the bathroom is unusable.

Just as I'm wondering if I can add those preparations on top of everything else I'm doing for the festival, and the actual renovation, Peggy asks me a question.

"Sorry," I say, "I was lost in my thoughts. What was that?"

"I said, how is your gingerbread house coming along?"

"It's still early, but I think we can pull it off. Sky and the Rodriguez boys are hopefully working on framing out some walls today. I'm heading over there after this to see how it's coming along."

Peggy looks confused for a second, then laughs. "I meant your *gingerbread house*, dear! Not the Morley Mansion."

Now it's my turn to be confused. I force a laugh with her. "Oh, right. Sorry, I've got renovations on the brain."

"So," Peggy asks, "how about your gingerbread house?"

Peggy is supplying several gingerbread houses for the festival, which will be auctioned off to the highest bidder. So far, she's one of five artistic bakers who have volunteered to do so. But as she waits for me to answer her question, I realize she's right to expect that I would provide a gingerbread house as well. "Oh, um, yeah... Sky and I are going to start working on it tonight."

"What's your theme?" she wants to know. Her spread is ambitious, ranging from Disney castles and beloved nursery rhymes to popular TV show settings.

I say the first thing that comes to my mind. "The Morley Mansion."

"You're making a gingerbread replica?" She looks delighted.

"Um, yeah... We're gonna try?"

Curse me and my big mouth. The only gingerbread house I've ever built was a simple boxy one made of graham crackers and frosting. And why did I rope Sky into this with me? He's doing so much already. But then, if he knows how to frame a real house, maybe doing it on a small scale with cookies will be easy for him?

I touch the sheets of gingerbread walls and roof pieces in front of me to check if they're cool yet. How hard could it be to make these? Just roll out the dough and cut it to the right dimensions... It's the turret of the Morley Mansion that will be the real challenge.

"Could I borrow your recipe?" I ask Peggy.

"Well, now, I don't use my cookie recipe for these," Peggy explains. "I like a soft gingerbread cookie. But for these I just use a generic construction-grade gingerbread recipe. Just leave out any leavening agents so the biscuit will be nice and firm. You want to make sure it cools completely before you pick it up, too. I'm going to leave these ones overnight. Otherwise, they can break before you even start constructing. You'd better get a move on if you want to finish your house in time. Only three more days till the festival!"

"It shouldn't be too complicated," Sky muses that night as we stand in my parents' kitchen. He's freshly showered after a long day of framing and treating floorboards with wood bleach, and I can smell the balsam and sandalwood from his soap as he leans against the counter next to me with folded arms. "Bea gave me the original blueprints for the house. We could just go off of those and scale down the dimensions to make a tiny version."

"You have the blueprints?"

"Yeah, they're out in my truck, actually. Let me run and get them."

I feel bad as I watch him go. Even with his smiles and the pleasant light in his eyes, he can't hide how physically drained he is from the day. Why did I drag him into this? He's doing more than enough on this crazy project I somehow convinced him to help with, and now, am I really going to make him spend the next three evenings building a cookie house when he could be resting?

As soon as Sky returns with a roll of large papers, I sigh guiltily. "Thank you so much for helping me with this. Once we have the dimensions figured out, I'm sure I can take it from there so you can go home and get some sleep."

His brow furrows. "And when are you going to get some sleep? You're the one doing all the running around and pulling all-nighters to write articles to inspire people to pay for this venture."

"That's different. The work I'm doing energizes me."

"And this stuff energizes *me*." He rolls out the blueprints on the dining room table. "I'd feel left out if I found out you were building a little gingerbread replica of the mansion without me. You know I used to build a gingerbread house with my mom every year growing up? I was getting pretty good at it." He doesn't look at me when he says this last part. Instead, his eyes comb over the blueprints as if his memories are only an afterthought to the project at hand.

I don't argue with him after that.

"Wow, I didn't realize I was working with a professional." I lean over the table beside him to see the blueprints for myself. For how old they are, there's hardly any wear on them. They must have been well preserved in storage for most of their lives.

Sky runs a finger along the faintly drawn lines of the house to point out the numbers written at each point. "These are the measurements we're going to need. Do you have a notebook?"

I'm quick to retrieve the notebook I left on the kitchen counter, and I click my pen to let him know I'm ready before he reads off specs for me to copy out. "Let's start with the front-facing walls," he says.

Thirty minutes later, my head hurts just from watching him do all the calculations in his head to give us the dimensions of each wall at 4.8 percent of the original.

"You know..." I tap my pen against the notebook as I take in all Sky's calculations. "They have placement tests at PCC—you might remember more calculus than you realize."

He shrugs. "Maybe." It looks like he's chewing on this idea for a moment, but then he straightens. "For the turret, we *could* just use something like a Pringles can covered in icing and candy to make it look like gingerbread. Or is that cheating? Who's judging this thing?"

"The guests," I reply. "There will be voting cards at the entrance with a number for every gingerbread house, and people will rank the houses for different categories. No one would know if we fake the turret for that part. But whoever buys the house in the auction might feel duped when they take it home and realize there's a Pringles can instead of gingerbread."

Sky hesitates. "You're going to auction off the gingerbread houses? Will people actually buy them?"

I lift a shoulder. "We'll find out, I guess. I've seen this kind of thing done before, when I lived in Boulder. But then it was a bunch of bougie rich people who could use the gingerbread houses as decor for their lavish holiday parties. I'm honestly not sure how it will go over in a place like Roanoke, where we're all a bunch of cheapskates."

Sky raises his eyebrows. "You might be surprised. People here can be pretty generous when it's a cause they care about. The article you wrote about Bea and preserving Roanoke's past was really effective. Look how people have responded already."

That's true. I still can hardly believe how quickly ticket sales have been flying in, and the way people have leaped to help every time I've asked. "You must have seen a lot more of this side of the town when you helped your mom with events," I muse.

He nods, eyes returning to the blueprints. "Yeah, for sure. Those were good times." He taps his fingers against the table before sucking in a breath and smiling as if I hadn't just brought up his dead mother a second ago. "We're going to need a lot of dough for this."

"I've got several batches chilling in the fridge right now. I wasn't sure how much we'd need, but I can make more tonight if we don't have enough."

He claps his hands and rubs them together. "Let's get baking!"

After Sky leaves, my mom sidles into the kitchen with a knowing sparkle in her eyes. "You two are adorable together, AJ!"

I look up from the sink, where I'm scraping gingerbread dough and flour from a wooden spoon with my thumb under the running water. "We're just friends."

She takes a wet mixing bowl I've already washed and starts drying it beside me. "Looks to me like you could be more, if you let yourself. You're here, he's here, and you clearly have chemistry."

I scoff. "I'm not going to risk my friendship with Sky for a brief romantic fling."

"Who said anything about a fling?"

"That's all a romance between me and Sky could ever be."

"Why?"

"Because"—I tap the wooden spoon against the sink with more force than I mean to—"I'm leaving in a few weeks. I live across the country, remember? And goodness knows, I'm not about to gamble my career for a guy."

I wish I felt as nonchalant as I sound.

Mom holds out her hand for the wooden spoon. "Not even for true love?"

I give her a look as I pass the spoon. "Mom, come on. A few weeks ago, I thought I was bringing Adam home to meet the family, and look how that turned out." I turn off the faucet and pull a dishcloth from the ring on the wall to dry the sink. "I have a track record for being a bad judge of men, and of relationship longevity. I've been working too hard for too long to get this job at *Verité*, and I'm not going to just throw that away because I like a boy."

"But you went on a date with that Miller boy."

"Well, that's different."

"Why? Because you're not attracted to him?"

I laugh at the absurdity of such an idea, replacing the dish towel before leaning my back against the counter to face my mom. "No, it's because physical attraction is all there is between us."

She pulls in her chin. "And that's desirable?"

"For a brief fling, yeah. When things are strictly physical, there's no hard feelings when it ends, you know? You have fun, then move on with your life, and no one gets hurt. Win-win." I'm not even sure if I believe what I'm saying, since I've never tried a no-strings-attached fling in my life, but it sounds appealing at the moment.

Mom raises her eyebrows and sighs through her nose as she puts the wooden spoon away. "If you say so. No wonder your generation is turning out to be the lonely one."

I almost say something about her generation being the one stuck in loveless marriages, but I hold my tongue. What do I know about loveless marriages? I'm one of the lucky ones whose parents adore each other. If anything, I should be taking notes from her. She and my dad did something right to have the marriage they have. I've always wanted what they have. I just don't see how it could happen with Skylar when his life is here and mine is on the other side of the continent.

The next day, Peggy and Donna meet me at the Morley Mansion in the afternoon to go over final plans for setting up the festival. The Rodriguezes and Sky are hard at work putting up the new lath and plaster, and the whir of an electric saw and the *puff-thump* of a nail gun punch through the air.

Donna waves at the dust particles in the air as we make our way through the busy entryway toward the ballroom.

I hurry ahead to pull back the dusty drapes in the ballroom to let in some daylight before Donna and Peggy step inside. "The power is off while we make sure all the electrical is up to code," I say, apologizing. "But by Friday, it should be back on, so we can use these gorgeous chandeliers."

"Should be," Donna repeats with a frown. "What if it isn't?"

"Then we use Sky's backup generator and go by twinkle lights."

"How cozy," Peggy says politely.

I move right along. "I was thinking we could set up tables here and here. The kids' corner over there. And then maybe arrange all the gingerbread houses in the center."

"I'll need easy access to the kitchen," Peggy points out. "I'd like to transfer as much of the food over on Thursday as possible. Will the power be on by then so I can utilize the fridge and freezer?"

"It should be up and running by then. I'll let you know."

"Is the kitchen even in good working order?" Donna asks.

In truth, I've been spending so much time on the portion of the house we're trying to repair that I haven't given the kitchen much thought. "Let's go check it out," I say, and lead the way.

"Bea says this house was built for entertaining," I say as we go, more to cover my nerves about the kitchen possibly being in a poor state than anything else. "So, the kitchen has easy access to the grand dining room and the ballroom."

"I remember," says Peggy.

That's right. She's helped with more events in this house over the years than I even know about. I let her enter the kitchen first, and she immediately begins checking things. It's clear she knows her way around.

Donna asks about the water damage. "None of it reached the kitchen?"

"No, it was all contained in the corner around the bathroom."

Donna furrows her brow and grunts. "So, the bathroom is also under construction, I take it? What do you intend to use during the festival? We have to have a working bathroom."

This is the part I'm the most nervous about, but I do my best to stay optimistic. "We have a plumber coming in later today to help us get the bathroom in working order in time. It won't look pretty, but it will be usable."

"People will have to walk through a construction zone to use the toilet?" Donna doesn't even try to keep the disapproval from her voice.

I take a deep breath, force a smile. "What better way to show our progress to the benefactors who are making all of this possible for Bea? Would you like to see how it's going so far?"

Donna nods before looking to Peggy. "Well? What do you think?"

Peggy has her head all the way in the large gas oven. She straightens up at Donna's question. "It all looks good to me. A little dusty, but otherwise in good shape. I want to make sure we bring a backup tank of gas for this oven, though, just in case. Can we get some towels in here to put around the freezer, AJ? You don't want all that ice buildup in there to melt while the power is off and get water all over the floor."

"Good call," I say. "I'll get on that as soon as we're done."

"It might not be an issue," Peggy says, "being the dead of winter and all. I just don't know how long the power has been off or how long it will be off. Better to be safe than sorry."

"Of course."

Next, I walk them through the construction. "We'll block this off with plastic for the festival," I explain as we go. "I'm having a big banner made to hang in front of the plastic so the entryway will look a little more festive. But of course, we'll make sure the path to the bathroom is open and clearly marked. Maybe line it with twinkle lights and trees to make it more inviting."

Cold air rushes toward us down the hallway from the bathroom as we approach. Donna and Peggy pull their coats around them more tightly. I shiver, but I already know what to expect. We enter the bathroom to an open view of the frosty, overgrown lawn and sparkling fir trees on the right side of the house where the wall is being reconstructed.

Sky balances on a ladder, supporting a wooden beam over his head while one of the Rodriguez brothers nails the joiners into place. Despite what I told my mother last night, I feel a familiar thrill in my chest at the sight of him.

As soon as Sky releases the beam and climbs down the ladder, he removes his goggles and wipes his brow with the back of his forearm. Beneath his hard hat, his sandy locks look more unruly than ever. "Hi ladies, came to watch the show?"

"They wanted to see the bathroom," I explain. "Is that alright?"

"Be my guest." He holds out his hand to the middle of what is now a spacious room. The toilet and sink are gone, leaving only plumbing hookups in the floor where they used to be. Admittedly, it's not the most encouraging sight.

Donna's eyebrows fly up, and I fully expect her to ask where the toilet is. But she says, "This is so much bigger than I remember."

"We took out some walls," I explain. "That used to be a broom closet over there. And all that space back there was a second small parlor." I explain our plans to leave it this size for now and not worry about reframing the other walls so that there's potential to add in some more toilets and bathroom stalls. I wait for Donna's disapproval to resurface, but she merely takes it all in with furrowed brows.

Finally, she nods. "Well, as long as there's a functioning toilet and sink by Friday. And a *wall*"—she eyes Sky, silhouetted by daylight where the wall has yet to be framed behind him—"it could work. You're cutting it close, though. It might be wise to rent a portable outhouse just in case. One toilet never was enough for this place. We struggled with it at every event. Adding some stalls would be a good investment for Bea, if she manages to keep up with the place."

We thank Sky, and I walk Peggy and Donna back out to the front door. We stop on the porch to wrap up our meeting and finalize what all needs to be done by Friday. Then Donna looks at the house behind us. For the first time, there's a hint of approval in her eyes. "It's a nice thing you're doing here, AJ. I only hope it won't go to waste."

"It won't be a waste if Bea can see how hard we tried."

She nods, considering. "She couldn't keep up with this house before it fell into disrepair. My concern is that you'll get it all fixed up, and then she'll have to sell it anyway because it's too much for her to look after."

"She won't be able to live on her own for much longer," Peggy agrees.

"Well, that's for her to decide," I say.

The women share a look. Then Peggy squeezes my arm in a way that's meant to be encouraging, but that feels more like a mother smiling at a child who just doesn't understand.

When they leave, doubts creep into my gut. Is this a fool's errand? Am I wasting my time and Sky's? Jody's accusation comes to mind about working when I should enjoy my vacation.

Tomorrow, Tara and Tiffany are coming into town with their families. Will I miss out on quality time with them trying to chase this pointless project?

No, I tell myself. *This is a good thing.* Skylar thinks so, and so do I. I'll enjoy the time I have with my family, and it will be even better working for a good cause together.

16

New Traditions

TIFFANY AND TARA HAVE seven kids between them, all under the age of thirteen. I've heard they're very well behaved wherever they go, but I only get to see them at Grandma and Grandpa's house, and here they may run amuck like wild animals, because everything they do is adorable to my mother. My sisters have been here for all of ten minutes before the living room is a battlefield of fallen Nerf pellets, half-naked Barbies, and discarded dress-up clothes.

The adults take refuge in the kitchen while I practice detailed icing work on Skylar's and my gingerbread house.

"So"—Tiffany plops onto a bistro stool beside me and pops a chocolate rock into her mouth from my bowl of decorating candies—"you and Skylar Townsend are getting pretty cozy, I hear." She waggles her eyebrows suggestively.

My shoulders drop as I give my mom a look. "Seriously?"

She throws her hands up defensively. "I didn't say anything! Your sister hears whatever she wants to hear."

"I wonder where she gets it from." I roll my eyes good-naturedly.

"Little Skylar Townsend?" says Tara. "I thought he married your friend."

"They broke up, like, ten years ago, Tar," Tiffany half shouts. "Keep up!"

I've been told all my life that my sisters and I look almost identical, but Tara got our dad's tall genes and a willowy build, while Tiffany and I are both built like our mom, though Tiff is slightly taller and more athletic than I. Tara keeps her hair short in a classy pixie cut with subtle highlights, and Tiffany's dark hair has been in a perpetual sporty ponytail for as long as I can remember.

Tara's two-year-old Lilly shuffles into the kitchen in a pair of my mom's old high heels from the eighties with a stuffed dinosaur in a doll's dress wedged under her arm as she sucks her thumb.

Delighted by this new excuse to change the subject, I set down my piping bag and kneel with arms open wide. "Lilly girl! What pretty shoes you have on!"

For a moment, it looks like Lilly might accept my invitation and rush into my arms, but then she rushes to her mother's side instead and peers at me shyly from behind.

"That's your Auntie AJ," Tara says to her. "Remember how we talk to her on the phone sometimes?"

"Lilly"—my mom drops into a crouch beside the little girl and takes her hand out of her mouth—"I thought you stopped sucking your thumb?"

"She did," Tara sighs. "But whenever we travel, she starts back up again. It's the long car ride. I almost wonder if I should just give her a binky so I can take it away again once we're out of the car."

"That's what we did with Milo," says Tiffany. "I'd rather deal with taking away a binky than fighting the thumb-sucking every time."

It always makes me sad when the younger kids don't remember me, but Lilly's never actually seen me in person because I've been in New York since she was born. This is my chance to butter her up while I can so she can't forget who I am! While my sisters and Mom talk mommy stuff, I wrap up my piping bag so the icing won't dry out and put it away. I'll work on the gingerbread house later tonight with Sky, once he's done at the Morley Mansion. For now, it's time to work my auntie wiles on this little girl.

A handful of blueberries and a few flower clips later, Lilly sits in my lap on the kitchen floor and lets me braid her fine auburn hair while she clips flowers onto the stuffed dinosaur's dress.

Tara's and Tiffany's other daughters, Violet and Tatiana, are most likely playing dress-up upstairs, which is how Lilly got my mom's shoes. No doubt Lincoln, Tara's youngest, is up there with them. The older boys try to dash through the kitchen a couple times with their Nerf guns, but after being chased out a third time, Tara gives her husband a look, and he jumps up from the dining room table, where he's been playing a game of chess with Tiffany's husband, and claps his hands loudly. "Okay, boys, downstairs! No guns up here."

Uncle Mike is scary when he's trying to focus on a chess game, so the kids are usually quick to obey him, but this time twelve-year-old Conner, his oldest, hesitates. "Grandpa's blowing up air mattresses down there," he whines. "He told us to play up here."

"Why don't you play in the backyard?" Mom suggests.

"It's too cold." Tiffany's ten-year-old Eli pouts, his Nerf gun swinging uselessly at his side.

"Then play something quiet up here until Grandpa's done," says Tiffany.

Conner says, "Can we have the—"

"No tablets," Tara says. "You got so much screen time in the car it's a miracle your brain hasn't melted into your shoes. Go look in the game closet."

"Those games are sooo boooring," Eli groans.

"What?" I laugh. "You don't even know what's in there."

Conner taps his palm with the butt of his Nerf gun as he says, "Yeah, we do. It's just a bunch of old boxes that fall apart when you try to pick them up, and they're all missing pieces and stuff."

I can't help but laugh. "I'm sure they aren't *all* missing pieces. What about a card game, like Uno or Bluff?"

"What's Bluff?" Milo says from behind his big brother Eli. They both have their dad's textured black hair, but Milo inherited the darker skin and big brown eyes. It's crazy for me to hear him talking in complete sentences now since he was Lilly's age the last time I saw him.

"Oh, that one's fun," Conner says.

"What is it?" Milo repeats.

"Go get the box of playing cards and I'll teach you," I say.

The boys scramble down the hall to the games closet, and we hear boxes tumbling a few moments later.

"I told you they fall apart when you try to pick them up," Conner calls out.

My mom rushes to help them, leaving just me, my sisters, and Lilly in the kitchen.

"So, AJ," Tiffany says, "does Sky look sexy in a hard hat?"

I cough and cover Lilly's ears. "Don't listen to your Aunt Tiffany. She's full of wild ideas."

"Aren't you going back to New York after Christmas?" Tara says seriously with the same thoughtful tone and expression I've seen her use with her kids when they ask to do something she doesn't think is a good idea. "How's that going to work?"

"We aren't dating!" I force a laugh. "Sheesh, you two. He's just an old friend who happens to have helpful construction experience."

"And gingerbread construction experience," Tiffany says. "Good with tools and good in the kitchen. I bet he's good at lots of things."

"He is," I agree innocently, ignoring her suggestive tone. "Sadly, graphic design isn't one of them. Do you think you could help me make a poster for the New Year's Ball? I need to start advertising that ASAP so it won't feel like it's coming out of nowhere when we start selling tickets at the Gingerbread Festival."

Tiffany waves off my attempt at a subject change as if it were a fruit fly. "Yeah, yeah, I can put something together for you. So, have you planted your tulips next to his tulips yet?"

"It's not the season for tulips," I say, and clip a sprig of holly into Lilly's finished braid.

"That's right, it's the season for mistletoe," says Tiffany.

"It's the season of giving," Tara says pointedly. "I think it's admirable the way you're spending your vacation doing this nice thing, AJ. I'm sure Miss Carston really appreciates it. She's been alone for so long. Maybe we should invite her over for Christmas?"

I don't know why I didn't think of that. "Yeah, actually, we should. I'll mention it to her when I go over tomorrow."

Before Tiffany can bring the conversation back to Skylar, I peer around the cabinets to where her husband, Brett, sits at the dining room table with Tara's husband, Mike. "Hey, Brett, did you bring all your music equipment?"

"Yeah, I got you, AJ." He juts his chin in a cool guy nod before making his next move on the chessboard.

Brett used to be a DJ when he and Tiffany first met, but now he's a full-time dad while Tiffany brings home the bacon with her graphic design business. I know he still does gigs occasionally when the opportunity presents itself, and Tiffany assured me it's something he enjoys; otherwise, I wouldn't have asked him to bring all his stuff to help us out at the festival and the ball.

"We had to bring a second car just to fit all that stuff," Tiffany says. "Hope you're ready for some quality sound at your events, because Brett brought the whole kit and caboodle."

"Only the best for my girl AJ," Brett calls out.

"You're the best, Bro!" We give each other an air high five across the distance that separates us.

"Speaking of 'Bro,'" Tiffany says, "when the heck is Luke coming?"

Mom returns to the kitchen then with the kids on her heels, carrying a clear plastic container of playing cards. "He has a big event tonight in LA, but he and Kesha fly in tomorrow."

"You sure?" Tara says with a hint of laughing doubt.

Mom raises her shoulders. "He sent me their flight details, so I can only assume that means they bought tickets."

Luke's work as an audio-visual technician in California often gives him the chance to be a fly on the wall at some crazy fancy parties. It won't surprise me if he comes to Christmas full of new stories about the celebrities he's seen.

"Okay, so Luke's coming tomorrow," Tiffany says. "And Sky's coming tonight, right? I need to make sure he's good brother material."

"Okay!" I struggle to my feet with Lilly and wave for the other kids to follow me into the dining room. "Who wants to learn how to play Bluff?"

After several rounds of Bluff (the Banner family version of BS), Tiffany gets too competitive to tease me anymore.

By the end of the day, I have to move the gingerbread house into the dining room to make room for dinner prep in the kitchen, and it quickly becomes apparent that the kiddos can't be trusted with all that candy and icing. For a while I'm able to fend them off, but when I look over my shoulder and see that Milo and Lilly have slipped past my notice just long enough to drive their toy cars over the aluminum foil base and up to the front door of the house, I know I'm fighting a losing battle here.

I text Sky.

> Hey, do you think it would be ok if I brought the gingerbread house to your place? It's going to be devoured by wild children over here.

He replies a moment later.

> Bring it on over! I was just about to head your way.

I can practically already smell the balsam and sandalwood on his skin as I read his text. His hair is probably still wet from his shower. Good thing Tiffany won't get to see him like that. I'd never hear the end of it! A handyman who bakes *and* cleans up well to boot!

Sky comes out to meet me in the driveway so he can help me carry in the gingerbread house. The moment he appears, I'm grateful that I came. The last thing I need is for Tiffany to see him looking that good, bent over a gingerbread house in those jeans, delicately piping icing with those hands that are capable of tearing down walls and raising heavy beams over his head.

"Hey, thanks for letting me bring this over." Why do I sound breathless? I clear my throat and look at the gingerbread house in the trunk of my mom's car instead of at Sky's face.

"I should have offered sooner. We've got plenty of room here." There's a hint of humor in his voice that I don't understand until we walk through the front door, each carrying one side of the plywood and aluminum foil platform.

There are Christmas lights glowing from the rooftop outside, but inside, the house looks sad and bare. The only hint of Christmas is an undecorated tree standing in a dark corner of the living room. We set the gingerbread house down on the kitchen table.

"You haven't decorated your tree yet?" I ask as I unwind my purple scarf from around my neck.

Christmas is next week.

Sky shrugs with one shoulder, then brightens as he bends down to get a better look at the gingerbread house. "Hey, this looks good! Nice piping work on the porch. Very Queen Anne."

"Do you know what that detailed work is called?" I say with a hand on my hip. "That fancy spokey woodwork around the Morley Mansion's porch? Gingerbread detailing! I just learned that today."

"I did know that, actually. Pretty fitting, huh? And I'm sure you've caught the name of the street the house is on."

"Nutcracker Circle. It's too perfect. If this isn't the place to host a gingerbread festival, I don't know what is."

Doug Townsend walks in then from the garage and removes his work boots. "Hi, Son," he says without looking up.

Sky clears his throat. "Hey, Dad, we have company."

Doug looks up and freezes for the briefest moment at the sight of me. He looks older and thinner than the last time I saw him, his skin hanging around his jaw like a deflated balloon, with dark circles under his eyes. Grief has etched deep lines into his face that break my heart.

Then he smiles. It's only a flicker, but I see the old warmth I remember. I see Sky's kindness and handsome jawline. "Hi, AJ. You look so grown up."

"Thanks, I've been eating my vegetables." The words spill out awkwardly, because I can't come up with anything clever to say. I'm turning into my dad!

Fortunately, dad humor must be what's called for, because Doug laughs. "Good girl." Then his eyes land on the gingerbread house behind me, and a strange look crosses his face, somewhere between fear and hope, as if he isn't sure if he's just seen a ghost or an angel. But the look is gone almost as quickly as it appeared, replaced by soft thoughtfulness. "House looks smaller than I remember."

It takes a moment for me to catch on to his joke; I'm still shaken by that expression I saw on his face. That must be where Sky gets his ability to recover and slide into humor so quickly.

Sky quips back without missing a beat, "All those industrial heaters and fans made it shrink. I don't know how we'll get it to pass inspection now."

"Looks like you've got your work cut out for you."

"Yes, sir."

"I'll leave you to it, then. Never mind me." Doug hangs up his coat on a hook beside the garage door and heads past us into the living room, where he flips on the TV before settling into an old armchair. At an angle, he's still partially facing us, with the glow of the TV screen flashing different colors across his face in the dark. It's a sad sight when I think this is how he likely spent most evenings alone when Sky was away.

Why haven't they decorated their tree?

Sky claps his hands and rubs them together, bringing my attention back to the task at hand. "Okay," he says, "what's next?"

"We still have a lot of piping work to do around the sides. But the roof also needs some shingles. I've got Frosted Mini-Wheats or Necco

Wafers we could use for that, depending on how whimsical we want to go."

Sky leans against the counter on his elbow and holds his chin as he considers. "Hmm. It looks so elegant with just the piping. I almost hate to spoil it with shingles. I mean, if we're going for a realistic look, it should be missing half the shingles on the east side, anyway."

I kind of hoped he'd say that. "We could also just pipe the shingles on."

He nods and stands straight. "Yeah, I like that idea. I think it could look wicked classy."

"Wicked classy?"

"Yeah, you know?" He grins. "Simple elegance. Not a lot of clutter. Let the architecture speak for itself. I mean, the house is a work of art, just as gingerbread!"

"Thanks to you," I nudge him with my elbow, then notice his dad is watching us. I step away. Too flirty.

Sky eyes my sidestep but says nothing. "You're doing so well on the sides. Do you want me to start on the roof?"

"Sure." I pull the Tupperware of royal icing from my bag, along with some piping bags and tips, and Skylar handles them with a familiarity that makes me wonder as he practices his piping on a plate to get the flow right. "Have you worked in a bakery or something?"

He doesn't look up from his focused piping. "I used to do this with my mom, remember?"

Suddenly, I understand the look on his dad's face when he saw the house. Maybe for a second he did think he was looking at a ghost, seeing a gingerbread house on his kitchen counter again for the first time since Kate died.

Is this the first time?

I look at Doug sitting in the dark with the undecorated tree hidden in the shadows. When Sky's mom was alive, she would have had not just the tree decorated by the week of Thanksgiving but the entire house. I never saw the inside of their house during the holidays, but Kate had a reputation for her style and arrangements. Surely there must be a box of her Christmas decorations around here somewhere.

"Sky, why haven't you guys decorated the tree yet?" I ask again as we both begin piping on opposite sides of the house.

Sky glances toward the living room, where his dad certainly can't hear us over the sound of the TV. "Decorating for holidays was my mom's thing. My dad and I always put up the lights and got the tree, but then my mom did the rest."

"You never helped decorate the tree?"

"No, I did. It's just...the bin with all the ornaments is with her other stuff." He hesitates, holding his piping bag up so it won't drip as he considers his next words. Then he looks at me sheepishly. "It sounds kind of ridiculous to say it out loud." He shakes his head and resumes piping. "We just haven't been able to bring ourselves to bring down those bins, I guess."

"Not once?"

He shakes his head no. "Kinda silly, huh?"

"No, not silly at all." I can't imagine how it must feel for them. Kate was such a force when she was alive, Doug and Sky were probably used to doing whatever she asked. Without her there, which of them would step up in her place and initiate all the tasks she used to head? "Do you feel like that's your dad's place?" I venture. It's just a hunch, but I can tell I'm right when Sky glances back at his father.

His shoulders drop. "Maybe. Yeah. It feels like the respectful thing to do—to let him decide when he's ready..."

He doesn't say it, but I hear it in his silence: *Ready to be the parent again.*

I think of the look I saw on Doug's face when he saw our gingerbread house. There was fear and pain, and hope and longing all wrapped together. Does he miss this? Seeing his son and his wife bringing the magic of Christmas into his home? "Maybe he's waiting for you," I say. "If you were usually the one to do these kinds of things with your mother..."

For a second, I think Sky is annoyed by my prying, but as quickly as the expression tightens his jaw, it releases again. He considers my words, then sadness softens his eyes. "Yeah. Maybe."

I want to say that Kate wouldn't want them to live like this, that she would want them to celebrate as if she were still alive, that she would want them to look after each other. But I don't need to say it. I know Sky's already thinking it. It's probably been torturing him for years. And who am I to come in and tell him how he should grieve? I've never lost anyone so close to me. How could I possibly understand?

"I'm sorry," I say. "I shouldn't have... I have no idea what I'm talking about."

He doesn't say anything.

We pipe in silence. Maybe it's only a few moments, but it feels like ages. Have I offended him? Have I finally crossed the line into that previously undiscovered territory where Sky can't laugh off his feelings?

Sky sets down his piping bag and flexes his hand to relieve a cramp. "Excuse me for a minute."

There's a sinking feeling in my gut when he walks away. He rounds the corner, and the sound of his footsteps creaks its way upstairs.

Doug and I make eye contact. I can't face the question in his eyes. What the heck did I do to his son?

Why couldn't I just keep my big mouth shut? I feel like an awkward intruder standing in their kitchen, making delicate swirls and loops of royal icing on this confectionary structure.

As the minutes pass, my discomfort edges into nausea. Maybe I should leave.

Just as I finish my last flourish, determined to go home, the stairs groan again under Sky's weight and he reappears with a large green plastic bin in his hands and a garland draped around his neck like a boa. He plops the bin on the floor beside his dad's chair.

Doug looks surprised. I can't hear what Sky says to him, but Doug looks reluctantly at the bin. He rubs the back of his neck, nods, then waves a hand toward the stairs.

Sky goes back upstairs.

Doug stares at the bin beside him like it's a bomb he needs to deactivate. His eyes flick up to me.

I quickly resume piping—or at least, I try to, only to realize I've just finished my section. Heat pulses in my face under Mr. Townsend's gaze. I'm not even sure if he's still looking at me, but if he is, I need to stop looking like such a snoop! I don't want to start piping another wall if I can't finish it in one go. I consider working on the roof, but Sky's scallop work there is so tidy, I don't want to ruin it with my clumsy hand. I settle for outlining the horseshoe driveway instead. We haven't decided yet what we're going to use for that, but tracing it with a little royal icing shouldn't hurt.

What feels like an eternity later, Sky returns with two more bins stacked one on top of the other.

This time, I barely catch Sky's words as he faces his dad, hands on his hips. "Are you ready?"

Doug nods in a way that looks like surrender, and Sky opens the first bin.

The task in front of me is a blur in my vision.

I shouldn't be here.

Quietly, I gather my supplies.

In the living room, Doug turns off the TV as Sky turns on the floor lamp. Now I can hear the low rumble of their voices as they pull items one at a time from the bin.

"Oh, wow," says Sky, "I forgot about this."

"We got that our first Christmas together, before you were born," says Doug.

I resist the urge to look, determined to give them privacy.

"Mom always put this on the mantel," Sky says. From the corner of my eye, I see him move to the fireplace and place something small above it.

"You made this one," his dad says of another piece.

"That's terrifying. We should hang it on the front door to scare off bandits."

Doug chuckles, and the sound tugs at my heartstrings. There's an ache behind the levity.

"Uh-oh," says Sky. "Your singing fish!"

"Your mom hated that."

Sky laughs in that same longing way. "She was so embarrassed whenever people saw it."

"We can get rid of it."

Sky pushes the button on the wooden mount and a warped, slow-motion robotic version of "Jingle Bell Rock" plays, making all of us grimace.

"Needs batteries," Sky says.

"Nah, just throw it away."

The sound of rushing water drowns out Sky's reply as I rinse my piping tip in the sink. With my back to the living room, I don't hear him come into the kitchen, so it makes me jump to turn around and find him standing beside me.

"Are you leaving?" he asks.

"Oh, yeah, I don't want to intrude. The south-facing wall is done. I can come back and finish tomorrow." I move to grab my purse, but he catches my hand.

"Please stay," he says.

The longing in his voice makes my breath catch. I meet his eyes, surprised at the warmth in them. It's enough to melt me, but I don't understand why, after I butted into his personal life and then looked on awkwardly while he and his dad shared such a vulnerable moment with one another.

"I don't want to intrude," I repeat quietly.

"It's a comfort to have you here," he says just as quietly. "We're not really...good at this kind of thing."

By "this kind of thing," I can only assume he means feeling things without making light of them.

"I don't think Dad's seen a woman in the house since... You don't know how different it feels to have you here. Please stay."

He's still holding my hand. I feel rooted to the spot. Even if I wanted to leave, my legs are a useless jelly, my chest frozen, suspended in place. But I don't want to leave. I want to stay with Sky. I always want to stay with him. With the warmth of his hand swallowing mine, and the sincerity in his eyes striking me dumb, I feel myself nod. "Okay," I manage.

He nods his gratitude, gives my hand a light squeeze, and releases me. Our fingers graze slowly apart, making my fingertips tingle.

It takes a moment for me to collect myself after Sky returns to the living room. *He's a good friend*, I remind myself. *I'm here for him as his friend.*

For the next several minutes, I focus on the gingerbread house, refilling my piping bag and starting on the next wall. The low sounds of Sky and his dad reminiscing in the next room become an easy background rhythm. It feels like I'm propped in front of a window to the most personal and tender scene this house has seen in a long time, and instead of feeling like an imposter now, I feel humbled by Skylar's invitation to witness this.

Why is my presence a comfort? Is it merely because I'm a woman? Or because having a third party present somehow eases the pressure of how personal this experience is for them?

From time to time, I allow myself a glance at the scene in the living room. There is pain and love and tenderness and humor and tension and relief all unfolding at once. And suddenly I realize they just need permission to do this—to get into the bins they've always thought of as Kate's, to let Christmas be a time of family and celebration again.

It feels forced without the right mood.

So I pull out my phone, open up a playlist of classic Christmas hits, and let the music play just loudly enough that they can hear it. I sing along softly to "The Christmas Song" and watch for any sign the music might not be appreciated. But it seems to have the right effect. Slowly, tension in the next room eases and laughter increases. Sky made me that thermos of hot cocoa the other day, so I know there must be some cocoa mix around here somewhere. I find it in the open pantry—a half-empty tin of some off-brand chocolate drink—and make a few mugs of hot chocolate. I prop a candy cane in each from my gingerbread decorating stash, and when I enter the living room with a mug in each hand, I see that they've turned on *Home Alone 2*.

Doug smiles gratefully as he accepts a mug from me. "Have a seat," he says. "Join us."

Sky makes room beside him on the couch, and I sink into the lived-in brown leather.

Sitting there with the Townsends, laughing at Sky's Tim Curry impression as he says, "You are mistaken, Sir," and drinking hot cocoa while I watch Sky and his dad discover old treasures in the plastic bins at their own pace, I realize something: treasuring past traditions is good, but creating new ones to embrace the way one's family has changed is even more important.

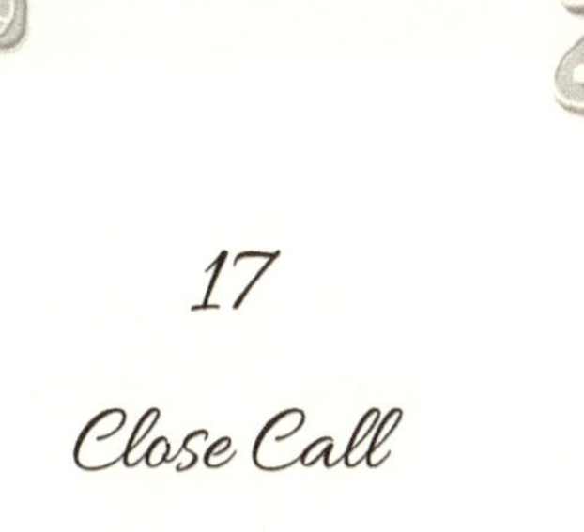

17

Close Call

"**O**KAY, STOP LAUGHING FOR a sec," Sky says through a poorly concealed snicker. "You're shaking the vinyl."

"I'm not laughing," I say. "My muscles are just giving out."

The Gingerbread Festival is tomorrow, and for the past fifteen minutes, Sky and I have been fighting to hang a massive vinyl banner across the plastic that's blocking off the construction corner of the Morley Mansion. We've already dropped it a dozen times. At ten feet long and six feet tall, it's heavy, and keeps trying to roll in on itself. Half the time, we've dropped it just from laughing. My abs are sore from that, and from all the times I've had to climb down my ladder, retrieve the fallen banner, climb back up, and hold the slick, heavy corner up over my head again.

Behind us, the mansion is alive with last-minute preparations. With framing work completed, the Rodriguez crew packed up their equipment to clear the way for Peggy Malan's army of kitchen helpers to unload tray after tray of prepared foods and ingredients from Aaron Malan's van, and Reagan and Breana are setting up the kids' corner in the ballroom with the help of Reagan's daughters.

Peggy's daughter, Melanie, whoops at the sight of the banner as she makes her way to the kitchen with her hands full. "Roanoke Gingerbread Festival," she cheers. "That looks fantastic, AJ."

"Don't jinx us!" Sky says.

"We've got it this time," I say, determined, though my grip is getting weaker with every attempt to hold the vinyl edge in place over my head long enough for Sky to secure his side before hurrying over to secure mine, all while balancing on adjacent ladders.

There's a *puff-thump* from his nail gun before Sky clambers down his ladder, folds it up, and races to me with it under his arm.

This is the part where we keep running into problems. By the time he gets his ladder set up next to mine, his side of the banner either falls down, or I lose my grip on mine and the weight brings his down with it. Staples weren't strong enough, so this time we're trying a nail gun.

"Why don't you just climb up her ladder?" asks one of Peggy's grandkids, who's been watching the whole thing from a settee in the entryway.

Sky tries to explain. "Because it isn't safe for two of us to be on the same—"

"Hurry! It's slipping! It's slipping!" I yell.

There's a clatter as Sky drops his ladder, and I feel mine wobble as he begins climbing below me.

"What about safety?" I yell as his hand grips the rung my feet are on.

"Just hold still."

With my arms pinned to either side of my face, holding the banner in place above me, I can't see what's happening, but I feel Sky's every movement through the metal that's now supporting us both. His arms come around my legs as he grips the sides of the ladder and hoists himself until he's right behind me, his feet staggering my feet on the same rung, his chest pressed to my back, his arms brushing against my ribs.

Heat floods my body from my toes to the crown of my head.

"Hold still," he says again, his face beside mine. My skin tingles at his voice in my ear.

I hold my breath as he reaches overhead to press his nail gun against the banner's corner, the stubble on his jaw brushing against my cheek.

Puff-thump.

I feel the power of each nail being released as Sky's body tenses against mine.

"Okay," he says, "let go."

I lower my arms slowly. With Skylar gripping the ladder on either side of me, I have to hold my elbows close to my chest.

We both wait on bated breath—Sky, to make sure the banner will hold, and me, to keep my heart from racing clear out of my chest at the feel of his body enveloping mine.

"I think we did it," Sky says cautiously before climbing down.

I wait until I feel him step off the ladder before climbing down myself.

The nails seem to do the trick. I'm glad the Rodriguez brothers built a custom frame to hang the plastic on so we wouldn't damage any of the original woodwork in the house.

Skylar and I stand back to look at my banner.

I'm proud of how it came out. There's a cartoonish gingerbread man with classic gumdrop buttons tipping a gingerbread top hat beside the words *Roanoke Gingerbread Festival* in magical calligraphy, with swirling flurries of snowflakes. My graphic design skills are clumsy compared to Tiffany's, but I do alright. It's a skill I'm grateful I had the chance to brush up on before I start working for a major magazine.

Behind us, Peggy's grandson applauds our success. Sky takes my hand, turns so we're both facing the kid, and leads me in a stage bow.

After sitting on the couch together last night in Sky's living room, drinking hot cocoa and watching Christmas movies with his dad, any barrier that might have existed to physical touch between us seems to have melted. Maybe it was the innocence of the circumstances under which we spent the evening leaning into one another as we sank into the leather sofa, the depth of the couch necessitating Sky's hand braced against my knee every time he hoisted himself from the cushions to pull another memento from the bin. Maybe Sky is seeking that same comfort now, because his hand seems to find me for little things like this: bowing to make a kid laugh, to make me laugh.

I know I shouldn't indulge myself in these touches, but it's getting harder to find reasons not to. Easier just to keep focusing on the work at hand.

"Okay," I say. "Now we've got to figure out what to do about the bathroom floor."

"Alright, let's get to it." Sky puts his hand on the small of my back, guiding me toward the bathroom.

As of now, there's only the new subfloor in there, which isn't safe for the public to walk on, but I want to avoid having to use the construction porta-potty. That means we need to install the sink and toilet in there today and figure out some kind of temporary flooring solution.

Sky follows me through the opening in the plastic and down the hallway. "The plaster should be dry and ready for sanding tomorrow, but we can wait until after the festival to do that."

I nod and lean against the doorframe as I peer into the bathroom. "Okay, so temporary flooring ideas. Go!"

"We could make a boardwalk with particle board."

I scrunch my nose. "With kids around? Doesn't seem safe." I imagine my nephews trying to climb under the house through the openings in the subfloor. The last thing we need is someone's kid falling and getting hurt.

"What about remnant sheet vinyl as a temporary solution?" someone says from the end of the hallway.

We both look up to find Doug Townsend standing there in his work clothes, buckling on a tool belt.

Sky looks surprised to see his dad, but he recovers quickly. "Do you think we could get enough to cover this space?"

His dad walks past us into the bathroom, surveying the space. "Maybe." He pulls measuring tape from his pocket and checks the length.

Sky follows him. "It's twelve by twenty. I've only ever installed remnant sheet vinyl in half baths."

"I can call around." There's a *shhhpt* as Doug lets his tape measure roll back into its case. "Check a few different home improvements stores, warehouses. My buddy Pete might be able to get us some for under fifty bucks."

"That sounds amazing," I say.

Sky thumbs his chin. "Would we glue it down?"

"Don't have to," his dad shrugs. "You could just trim and tack the edges. That would give it a finished look and protect the subfloor without making too much work later down the road when you want to replace it with something permanent."

Sky nods. "If you can track down enough for the space, I think it's a great idea." He looks at me for my thoughts, and I can only throw my hands up.

"I trust you guys! You're the experts."

Doug eyes the plumbing hookups. "Could you use a hand today?"

Again, Sky looks surprised. "Yeah, actually, we really could. Thanks, Dad."

Doug nods. "Alright. Let me make a few calls, see if I can track down some remnant sheet vinyl. Then I'll help you get it put in."

When Doug steps out, Sky stares after him, looking bewildered.

"You look like you've seen the Ghost of Christmas Past," I tease.

Sky shakes his head. "I think I might have. Was my dad in here a second ago? Making suggestions? Offering to help?"

I smile. "That's what I saw."

When he meets my eye, I can see the conflicting feelings of hope and caution in his face.

I want to ask Sky how things went last night after I left. But I know it's none of my business. It was an honor to be included for as long as I was, watching Christmas movies and drinking hot cocoa while they pulled beloved and painful memories from a box. I left after helping decorate the tree, but there was still an entire bin of ornaments and memorabilia that they hadn't touched. I wonder if they went through it together after I left, or if it's still there in the living room waiting to be opened.

Sky clears his throat. "Well, if that works out, all we've got left is moving in the toilet and vanity. Can't do that until the flooring is in, so...what's next, boss?"

I chew on my cheek as I run through my mental to-do list. Today, Luke and Kesha fly in from California, and I'd like to be home when they arrive, so the quicker we can finish up here, the better. "Let's see if Reagan and Breana need any help setting up."

It doesn't take long before Doug finds us building a candy cane forest in the ballroom. "Pete's got a couple sheets large enough for the space," he says. "I'll drive over there now."

"Thanks, Dad."

After Doug leaves, Sky sneaks a glimpse over his shoulder at where his dad had been standing. I think I catch the hint of a smile on his face a moment before he gets serious and focuses on the task at hand again. Clearly, something changed for them last night. I'm sure they still have a ways to go in healing their relationship, but at least the process has begun.

Skylar picks me up the next morning with our gingerbread house sitting in the truck's bed, protected in a Styrofoam case Doug built, along with some last-minute decor from the RNN storage unit. We drive together to the Morley Mansion.

"Are you ready?" Sky asks.

I have to squeeze my hands together to keep them from ringing with anticipation. "I hope so. Gosh, there's so much to throw together today. But as long as there's a working bathroom, food to eat, and things to auction off, the rest is just fluff. We can make it work without fluff."

"Fun fluff," he says.

"I hope so."

My stomach is in knots. I've never done anything like this before. What if it's a disaster? What if no one shows up? Or what if they do, but no one wants to participate in the auction and we just threw all this together for nothing? What if we didn't install the new plumbing correctly and we ruin all our hard work with another flood?

Sky reaches over and wraps my clasped hands in one of his, which practically swallows them in reassuring warmth. "It's going to be great," he says. "Just one thing at a time."

"I'm sure your mom didn't get nervous like this before an event."

"Oh yeah," Sky says. "It was always chaos the morning of an event. 'Sky, did you remember to grab the box of ribbons?' 'Sky, why isn't this in the truck yet?'"

"Really?"

"Every time. She would spend months putting these things together and then be just as nervous to make it all come together on the day of no matter how many times she did it."

"Hers is a hard act to follow."

"And you only had a week to prepare. She would tip her hat to you for all you've accomplished in so little time."

"Well, I had a *ton* of help."

"She always did, too. She used to say, 'It's all about delegating, Sky. Break up the work and let other people make it their own, and magic happens.'"

"She was a wise woman."

He nods, his eyes seeming to see beyond the road into some golden land of soft-focus memories. "Yeah, she was. And stubborn. Once she caught a vision, there was no stopping her from making it happen. You kind of remind me of her in that way." He pulls himself back to the truck. "I hope that's not weird to say."

I melt. "It's the best compliment I've ever received."

The corner of his mouth pulls up in my favorite half-grin of his.

We pull up the horseshoe driveway to the front of the house. Peggy will be here soon with her swarm of helpers to bring over the last food items and finish setting up her gingerbread houses, but I'm glad we got here first. In the chaos of renovations and festival preparations, this is the first time it will be just me and Sky in the house since demo day. I know I need to guard my thoughts, but I have so little time left before I go back to New York, and I want to enjoy as much time with my friend as I can get before then.

The first items out of the truck bed are a pair of life-size nutcracker sentinels that are somehow even heavier than I imagined they would be.

"Where'd you find these guys?" Sky grunts under the weight of one.

"They're Reagan Keys's," I grunt back.

I get my guy out of the truck but then can't get it up the stairs. It takes two of us to get one up, then the other, and stand them on either side of the double-door entrance. We're out of breath by the end, but as we stand back to look at our work, the effect is brilliant.

"My mom would have been obsessed," Sky says, panting.

"*I'm* obsessed," I say. Admittedly, I thought the chances were fifty-fifty that those statues might be too cheesy, but... "They're the perfect combination of regal and whimsical."

"And terrifying," Sky adds.

"Like we could legit be entering Santa's magical realm and no naughty-listers are allowed."

"Yeah!"

"I hope we'll have time to get the Christmas lights up," I realize out loud. "If it's too dark, we might lose the magical and whimsical and just be left with terrifying guards barring the entrance..."

"Noted." Sky points both hands back toward his truck. "Let's get this stuff inside!"

He helps me carry everything into the ballroom, where we leave it in a pile that I can go through on my own while he gets started on the lights outside. "My dad will come by in a couple hours to help with the lights," he says.

"I'm not worried. I've seen how quickly you two can transform a space into a holiday miracle."

We're carrying the gingerbread house when I say it, so I can only see the top of Sky's knit hat over the frosted roof. But once we set the house down on the center table in the ballroom, Sky looks at me with such tenderness that it roots me.

"You did that, you know," he says gently. His voice is warm and deep, like mulled cider sliding down my throat and warming me from the inside out. His gray eyes gaze softly into mine, seeing something in me I both fear and long to know. "If you hadn't said what you said...we'd still be in that cold rut we've been stuck in."

I swallow. *Friends. Friends. We're just friends.* "You were ready to get out. I think you just wanted permission. You would have found it one way or another."

"But we didn't. Not until you came along. All of this"—he motions around the ballroom, around the house we've been slaving over for the past week—"it's... I really needed this, AJ." His eyes return to mine. "Thank you."

I don't know what to do with my hands. They wander nervously under his gaze, touching my hair and my coat pockets before I finally grasp my elbow to make them hold still. "I want to thank you, too. None of this would have been possible without you. I needed this as much as you."

He steps around the table with his arm extended for a friendly side hug, and I lean in to it, resting my head on his shoulder as he squeezes me to his side.

We're facing the little Morley Mansion replica we built together, and looking at it, it feels natural to stay that way, with Sky's arm around me, my head on his shoulder.

"We make a good team," he says. His hand softens on my arm and rubs gently up and down.

"Yeah." It comes out as a sigh, tinged with longing I didn't intend.

I feel the weight of his cheek come to rest on the top of my head. If I just tilt my head up ever so slightly...

Would it be so terrible? A harmless kiss after all we've done together. How bad could that be?

I move to face him, and he's already doing the same. We stand forehead to forehead, Sky holding my shoulders. He's the perfect height for me. All I need to do is angle my face up and his lips would be there waiting to meet mine. I want to do it. The desire pulls its way up from my toes, through my legs, to my heart, but stops at my head with a dissonant energy that makes me tremble, like holding matching magnet ends millimeters apart.

I don't want to lose him.

But if he wants this too...

The ballroom door opens, and Sky and I jump apart.

"Oh good, you're setting it up!" Peggy's voice echoes across the dance floor as she backs into the room, holding one side of a large gingerbread house platform. Her daughter Melanie follows holding the other side.

"Wow, Peggy!" I sound breathless in my forced attempt at a smooth recovery. "That looks stunning!" Actually, it's all a blur in my frazzled vision, but I know that anything made by Peggy will look stunning.

Sky clears his throat, then jumps into action. "Allow me." He takes Peggy's end and allows her to direct him and Melanie to the table where it belongs.

My heart feels like a mouse scurrying and scratching against the bars of my rib cage. I run my hands through my hair before busying myself with the folded paper plaque that goes in front of the Morley gingerbread house. It takes all of a second to straighten it out. Then I'm left with useless trembling hands again.

"I'd better get started on the lights outside," Sky says from a table away.

I glance up at him and our eyes meet. There's no regret in his face. There's only a kind reassurance as his eyes seem to dance with laughter at the situation. That's all it takes for my nerves to settle.

When he disappears out the door, I realize I'm smiling.

I shake it off. Time to focus! We've got ten hours before the festival begins, and there's still plenty of work to be done.

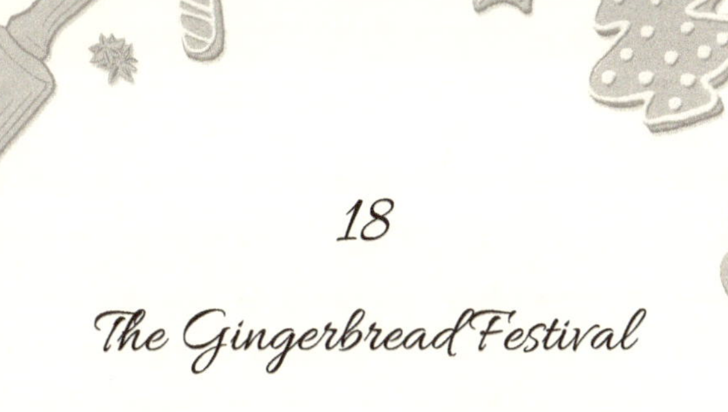

18

The Gingerbread Festival

T HE BALLROOM IS PACKED to capacity with Roanoke's families. Some kids dash from the face painting station to the hot cocoa bar with fresh masks of sparkling butterfly wings, striped tiger cheeks, and bright superhero designs, while others build houses of graham crackers and candy at the low table under a cardboard awning decorated with white balloons and crepe paper that make it look like the roof of a life-size gingerbread house. "The Nutcracker Suite" plays through Brett's professional sound system from its hidden location behind a candy cane forest in the corner while people mill about with voting cards to rate the gingerbread houses on display before the silent auction begins.

Matilda Hatch had the brilliant idea of placing refreshment tables at every corner of the room with something different on each one to encourage guests to move about and get a taste of everything. It's working like a dream. The only challenge is keeping each table well stocked. I feel like a bustling hen running circles around the room to note what needs to be filled where, then to the kitchen and back with fresh trays of charcuterie meats and cheeses, mini pies, cupcakes, and bread wreaths, vases of chocolate peppermint pretzel rods, bowls of cream puffs to fill in what's been picked off the Styrofoam cones that look like Christmas trees, and hot pots of steaming meatballs in a sticky sweet and savory sauce. Peggy's chocolate fountain is a real hit, and keeping the trays of fruit and various bites of cheesecake, crispy rice, brownie, and sugar cookie filled on that table is especially taxing.

I've seen glimpses of Sky throughout the evening, but we haven't had a chance to talk since this morning. Tiffany came to help Brett set up the music equipment just as I was wrapping up my work, and I ended up getting a ride home with them to shower and get dressed before the festival.

The lights on the mansion look perfect. Sky and his dad made the outside look every bit as festive and magical as the inside. Even with the missing shingles and peeling paint and overgrown landscaping. I want to tell him so, but every time he and I make eye contact across the room and I head his way, someone else calls out to me.

"AJ!"

Like that.

I turn to find the guest of honor. "Hi, Bea!"

Bea Carston looks more put together than I've seen her since I was a kid, in slacks and a classy Christmas sweater with earrings. Her face is bright with a smile. "I haven't seen so many people in this place in ten years," she says, squeezing my arm.

I'm carrying a tray of salami and assorted cheeses and crackers. I offer her a bite, but she declines. "I'm on my way to the chocolate fountain," she says with a wink. "Got to satisfy my sweet tooth. You did good here, kid. It looks like everyone is having a good time. If this is the house's last hurrah, it's better than I could have hoped for."

"Let's think of it as the *first* hurrah of many in the house's new era."

"Well, let's hope so."

I'm surprised at the lack of hope in her voice, after all we've accomplished in such a short time. "Have faith, Bea, it's Christmas! Miracles happen this time of year."

She laughs and pats my head before walking over to the chocolate fountain.

Now I've lost sight of Sky again. He's been a popular one tonight as well, with people wanting to hear about the plan for the house, and how construction is coming along, and what other tricks he has up his sleeve. He's a man of many talents. I swell with pride that people get to see what he's capable of, though I know I have no right. He isn't mine, and I can't take credit for any of his brilliant skills.

I barely finish replenishing the charcuterie table when a gentle hand takes my elbow. I know Claire Tan's touch before I turn to face her.

"Amelia Jane, the ballot box is full. We're just waiting on the last few stragglers to submit their votes, and then we can start the auction."

I check my watch. Almost eight o'clock. "Right on schedule! Thank you, Mrs. Tan. I'm on it!"

Peggy's daughter Melanie overhears as she comes to check on the charcuterie table, and she reaches for my empty tray. "I can take that back to the kitchen if you need."

"Thank you," I tell her. "The kids' corner could use some more graham crackers for the houses. And we've got some empty Styrofoam trees around the chocolate fountain. I think we're out of cream puffs now, so could you just take those away?"

"Got it." Melanie is on the move before she gives her answer, waving down her brother on the other side of the ballroom and pointing his attention to the empty Styrofoam cones.

I scan the crowd once more for Skylar, but he must have been pulled away to give another tour of the construction site. Good. We need people to feel as invested in this project as possible before the auction begins.

There's a low stage along the front wall of the ballroom near the candy cane corner, made up of six heavy platform boxes the RNN had in storage. Tiffany's husband set up a microphone for me there, with big speakers behind. He can see me from his place behind the candy cane wall when I step onto the stage, take my place behind the microphone stand, and give him the thumbs-up.

Brett turns down the music just enough that I won't have to compete with it. The microphone groans and squeaks as I adjust the height of the stand, drawing the eyes of the people closest to the stage as I pull a stack of cue cards from my back pocket.

"Good evening," I say into the microphone, then draw back a bit at the boom of my voice. The microphone picks up my breath with a loud puff that hurts my ears. "Good evening," I try again from a better distance. "Welcome to our very first Roanoke Gingerbread Festival!"

Aside from the kids' corner and a few scattered conversations, most people in the crowd turn their attention to the stage and applaud.

"Thank you all so much for coming out tonight. Our ballots will close in five minutes before the auction begins, so if you haven't had a chance to vote for your favorite gingerbread houses, please do! Our gingerbread architects have done some amazing work, haven't they?"

Another round of applause gives me a chance to switch to the next cue card.

"We've got some amazing talent here in Roanoke. This event would not have been possible without the generous contributions of our volunteers. Let's give a big hand to Peggy Malan and her minions for the fabulous food!"

Hoots and hollers erupt throughout the ballroom as Peggy's kids drag her from the kitchen to the ballroom entrance, where she waves and smiles with polite modesty.

I thank the Roanoke Neighborhood Network for funding tonight's activities, Reagan and Breana for organizing the kids' corner, and Mrs. Tan for heading up the auction. Then I come to the important part.

"I'm touched by the hard work and dedication that our selfless volunteers have put in every day to put this event together in under a week. It is amazing what our community can do together when we set our minds to it. All of you are part of that, too. Thank you for making this night of service a part of your holiday season. We've come together tonight not only to meet our friends and neighbors and share the bounty of Peggy's culinary magic, but to help a neighbor in need. Now, Bea is too shy to come up here, but most of you know her from all the years she spent offering this house as a place for events that brought us together over the years. From weddings and Bar Mitzvahs, to school proms and annual Snow Balls, anyone who grew up in Roanoke has shared in the legacy of Bea Carston's family through the Morley Mansion."

There's gentle applause, the audience visibly softening as their own memories fill their faces with fondness. Some even laugh over shared remembrances. I spot Benson Miller in the crowd beside his parents. I didn't expect him to come. But then, his mother did help with the event. And maybe he's home for the weekend to spend Christmas with them. I pull my eyes back to the cards in my hands to keep from getting distracted.

"Now, that legacy is in danger of being lost forever. After a flood damaged the foundation in the east corner, the Morley Mansion faces the threat of condemnation and demolition. When we learned Bea has until the end of this month to reverse the condemnation order and save her house to be registered as a historic landmark, we knew we needed to help. The Townsend and Rodriguez families have generously donated hours of their time and skill this holiday season to put in the necessary repairs for the Morley Mansion to pass inspection. If you've used the bathroom tonight, you've seen their fine handiwork in progress."

Some scattered laughter and a few woops.

"The volunteer hours and labor have been an incredible gift of sacrifice and love from our community. But the cost of materials is still an obstacle to completing this work in time. That's where you come in, our dear friends and neighbors. Tonight's auction is not only a chance to provide stunning works of holiday art for your homes, but a chance to raise the money to save the Morley Mansion, Bea Carston's home, her family legacy, and Roanoke's own historic landmark."

I wait for the applause to subside before making the announcement I'm the most nervous and the most excited about. Time to find out how well it will be received.

"As a last-minute surprise to celebrate when the house passes inspection on the thirty-first, there will be a New Year's Eve House-warming Ball here in the newly restored Gingerbread House!" There are some whoops of excitement or surprise, and some other sounds that I am too nervous to stop and identify before plowing on in a breathless rush. "Tickets are going for twenty-five dollars each. One hundred percent of the proceeds will go directly to the cost for repairs on the house and Bea's expenses to apply to the National Register of Historic Places. You can find more information about the ball and purchase tickets online at the same website as you followed for the Gingerbread Festival. You can also buy tickets in person tonight at the ticket booth in the foyer, and a few lucky couples will earn free tickets in Claire Tan's raffle before the night is through."

With the rumble of applause, I invite Claire Tan up to start the raffle before the auction closes and results are tallied.

I'll need to help collect auction tickets pretty soon, but before that, I make one last sweep of the festival to make sure refreshments are well stocked, volunteers are not getting burned out, and everything is running smoothly.

"AJ."

I recognize Benson Miller's voice before I turn to find him making his way to me from the gingerbread house tables. "Benson," I smile. "I didn't expect to see you here." It sounds like a dig, but I didn't mean it that way. "I mean, I'm glad you came! More people really help the cause. Not—not that I only care about getting your money—I mean, it *is* a fundraiser, yes, but—" *Why can't I shut up already?* "It's nice you came. That's what I mean."

He chuckles. "I promise I'll make a big donation. It's the least I can do, after the way I left you last week. I haven't been able to stop thinking about it."

I try to wave off his apology. "Don't worry about it. I got home just fine."

"No," he insists with a shake of his head. "It was a jerk move. The cherry on top of many that day."

"You had patients to get to. Really, I understand. There's nothing to apologize for. In fact, if you hadn't dropped me off when you did, this event probably wouldn't be happening right now." I didn't realize it until this moment, but it's true. If Sky hadn't come to pick me up, we wouldn't have stopped to help Bea, and none of this would have come about.

Benson doesn't ask to hear the story. "That's kind of you to look on the bright side. But I still feel like a jerk. Let me make it up to you. I'll buy the first two tickets to that New Year's Ball if you'll be my date."

"Oh. Oh gee, I don't know..."

"I'll pick you up," he presses. "No Ubers or meeting halfway this time."

"It isn't that. It's just, I'll be hosting that event, so I'm probably going to be running around like crazy the whole time. I probably wouldn't make a very good date."

"Then that would make us even." He smiles his dreamiest smile, tilting his head down bashfully and looking up at me through his lashes. "Please. Give me a chance to make it up to you."

I don't know if he means make it up to me for the way our last date went or for his snub all those years ago, but either way, under the expectant shine in those rich brown eyes, I can't think of a reason to say no before Donna Shipley approaches.

"AJ, it's time."

I nod to her. Then to Benson, I say, "I have to go do the auction thing." I motion behind him to where the gingerbread houses are so he knows I'm headed that way before I step around him.

He moves aside. "Do we have a date?"

"Okay," I hear myself say.

"New Year's Eve, then. I'll pick you up at seven?"

"Make it six. I have to be here early." I catch Donna's look of impatience and hurry after her before Benson can say another word.

My chest feels tight as I collect auction cards from the boxes in front of each gingerbread house, my head buzzing with hot energy. It doesn't feel like excitement. It feels like guilt.

But why should I feel guilty? I haven't done anything wrong. Why *not* give Benson a chance to redeem himself? Why not finally get that dance I dreamed of all those years ago? The one that he denied me? He's right; he does owe me, and I deserve this.

Don't I?

My face feels hot. My hands fumble with the growing stack of cards. I clutch them to my stomach as I make my way across the ballroom to the foyer so I can review the results with Donna and Matilda. Just as I reach the doorway to the ballroom, Sky is on his way in with a well-dressed silver-haired man in tow.

"Speaking of the one who started it all," Sky says, sidestepping so I'm facing the man behind him, "here she is! This is AJ Banner."

"Miss Banner." The man extends his hand. "Mayor Clark."

I fumble to hold all the cards with one hand so I can shake the mayor's. "Oh, hi."

"Such a delightful event you've put together. And what a project! Sky was showing me the work you've done on the house together. I must say, it's an impressive feat in so short a time. If only our city construction crews worked half so quickly on improving our roads." He chuckles at his own joke.

I try to laugh through the sudden anxious rumbling in my gut. "I wish I could take credit for that, but it was all Sky's doing. He's been working on it nonstop since Saturday."

I meet Sky's eyes, and the admiration in his face fans the heat of guilt inside me. I look away.

"It's been a team effort," says Sky. "We would have been like fleas trying to move a log without Tim Rodriguez and his guys."

I catch sight of Donna listening in and nod in her direction. "The Roanoke Neighbors Network is responsible for most of the festival's success. I'm sure you know Donna Shipley?"

"Of course," says the mayor, turning to include Donna in the circle. "Donna and I have worked together many times over the years. Don't worry, we'll get that community center in no time."

Sky stands close to me, and I suddenly know why I feel guilty. We are a team, he and I. Standing together, it feels like we are one unit, and Donna Shipley is another, and the mayor yet another. We've been together on this from day one, and the New Year's Ball should be *our* celebration. Our night to toast to our success. Our last hurrah before I fly to New York, and we don't see each other again until…who knows when?

Donna and the mayor are already launching into another conversation about the community center, but I can't bear to stand here next to Sky, with him looking at me with such trust and admiration. I clear my throat. "We actually need to tally the auction results." I hold up the cards in my hands for them to see, and the mayor quickly steps aside.

"Of course, of course! Don't let us get in your way. I'm hoping to bring home that big one in the middle there myself. A stunning replica of the Morley Mansion. Skylar tells me the two of you are responsible for that one?"

It's like twisting a knife.

"I think we're calling it the Gingerbread House now," says Donna. She looks at me with an expression that looks foreign on her. Teasing?

"What?" I ask.

"That's what you called it up there a few minutes ago when you announced your New Year's Ball. You said Gingerbread House instead of Morley Mansion."

"Did I?" I should laugh at the mistake, but the mounting guilt in my stomach makes everything feel like it's happening faster than I can process it.

"Well, that's charming, isn't it?" says the mayor, chuckling. "It does look like a gingerbread house, doesn't it? Who knows? Maybe the new name will stick." He winks at me.

Sky must sense my unease, because he's quick to invite the mayor on to get something to eat. Maybe he thinks I'm just in a hurry to find out how much people have bid on the various houses. Either way, his sensitivity to my needs makes me feel worse than ever.

What will he think when he finds out I just agreed to go to the New Year's Ball with Benson Miller?

19

In the Dark

MORE QUICKLY THAN THE festival was set up, it's taken down in a sweep of helpful hands and willing arms. Peggy's kitchen crew made quick work of packing any leftovers into easy to-go containers for volunteers to take home, and the Malan van is loaded up and gone before the last guest makes it out to their car. The gingerbread houses are carefully transported to the vehicles of their new owners, and a group of willing teenagers jumps in to help take down the tables and load them up into the furniture rental trailer, along with any fold-up chairs. Reagan's kids sweep sprinkles and cracker crumbs from the kids' corner while she and Breana dismantle the candy cane forest. My family helps Tiffany and Brett take down all of his music equipment, the mic, and the stage, and Sky and I round up the rest of the decor.

"We can leave the twinkle lights up," I call out when Reagan's husband Scott goes to unplug a strand. "We'll use them again for the New Year's dance."

"What about all these posts?" Scott points to a candy-striped pole on the floor a few feet from me. There are three others just like it throughout the room.

"Those belong to Breana," Reagan answers for me. Then she calls out to Sky, "Sky, do you think you could bring those nutcrackers to my house in your truck? Our van is full to the brim."

"I was already planning on it."

Minutes later, it seems everyone leaves in one last wave, and it's just me and Sky walking around the ballroom to turn off lights and do one final sweep to make sure we didn't forget anything.

As our footsteps echo in the empty ballroom, I realize how strange it is that my family left without even asking if I needed a ride.

"Do you like how my family just assumed I'd be getting a ride home with you?"

"I do." Sky turns off the overhead lights. "I don't want to drive home all by myself in the dark."

I wait for him at the ballroom entrance, and as he makes his way across the floor to me with only the glow of the twinkle lights along the walls, I remember with a thrill when we were last alone.

Would he have kissed me if Peggy hadn't showed up right then?

Suddenly I feel nervous.

The closer he gets, the more intimate this setting feels. Just the two of us in this glowing ballroom, with a key to the front door in my pocket. We've been alone in this house before, but never like this. Never at night, with the smell of baked goods lingering in the air, and the recent absence of music and crowds leaving a still quiet that makes every footstep and every breath sound loud enough to make it feel like we're touching even from across the room.

Sky's walk is a thing of beauty. I've only seen it in short glimpses before now, but as he covers the distance of the ballroom, I can admire the way he carries himself with ease and strength. He looks like an athlete. Or maybe it's just the way his clothes fit him so well; the way his shirt falls over his broad shoulders.

"You knocked that party out of the park," he says.

"We did it."

"One down." He steps into the doorway and reaches behind himself to unplug the string lights. "One more to go."

Now we're standing in the dark facing each other. Only moonlight pouring in from the windows illuminates his shape. As my eyes adjust, his face reflects the faint silvery glow.

That's when I register what he just said. One more to go. He's talking about the dance. *If he kisses me now*, I think, *I'll call Benson tonight and tell him the date is off.*

But Skylar doesn't kiss me. He nudges his head toward the exit. "Ready to get out of here?"

I fall into place beside him as we make our way out the front door.

When we get into the car, I suck in a breath. "So, Benson asked me to be his date at the New Year's Ball."

Bing Crosby croons softly on the radio, filling Sky's silence.

"Oh?" Sky asks.

I nod. "Yeah."

"Did you...say yes?"

"Yeah."

He nods.

"Should I have turned him down?"

"Do you want to go with him?"

No. "I think so."

"Don't you know?"

"It's not that simple."

"Seems pretty straightforward. Do you want to or not?"

"Yeah. Sure. I want to go with him."

"Then it's a good thing you said yes."

I wait for him to say more, but we drive in silence for what feels like an eternity. Just as I'm about to crack and tell him I'd rather go with him, Sky changes the subject.

"The mayor was impressed with my work on the house. He wants to connect me with an opportunity building lower-income housing."

"Oh. Sky, that's awesome! You'll do it, right?"

He hesitates, then shrugs. "Maybe."

I purse my lips. Things seem to be getting better with Sky's dad. Why wouldn't he jump at an opportunity like this? "Is it far away?" I ask.

"Not too far. Just..." He shakes his head. "I don't know. We'll see how things pan out." He turns up the volume on the radio, and Judy Garland's "Have Yourself a Merry Little Christmas" ends the conversation.

When I get out of the car at my parents' house, things feel not quite right. But Sky gives me a half smile. "Good night, AJ."

20

Bea's Secret

THE NEXT MORNING, MY family enjoys breakfast together. My parents have the day off for Christmas Eve, and Sky and I agreed we could take a break from working on the house, too. But I know he's going to be there prepping the plaster for paint. After our awkward parting last night, I want to see him. I want to work beside him and hear him laugh and know that I haven't ruined our friendship.

So I ask to borrow my mom's car.

"You're working again?" Tiffany exclaims.

"I thought you decided to take the day off," says my mom.

"I won't be there long," I say. "It's just a little sanding so we can paint the walls after Christmas. Two hours tops. Then I'll be home the rest of the day."

"Boo," says Tiffany as my mom hands over her car keys to me. "Just admit you're going to make out with Skylar."

Tara scolds her. "Tiff!"

I don't linger to hear more. "Okay, byeee!"

On the way over, I try to come up with what to say. I have a cinnamon roll and a thermos of Tiffany's famous hot cocoa blend, with a secret ingredient none of us have been able to guess to this day, as a peace offering. Should I apologize right away for getting a date to celebrate something that was between me and Sky? Or should I play it smooth and just let him know nothing will change between us by acting like last night never happened?

After all, why *would* anything change between us, just because I have a date? It isn't as if Skylar and I are dating. We never talked about going to the dance together. And if he wanted to go with me, he should have asked.

Anyway, I'm leaving in eight days, so none of this really matters. Does it?

Sure, I want to spend as much time with Sky as possible before I leave. For friendship. But that doesn't mean I have to spend time with him exclusively. I have other friends, too. Benson is my friend. Sure. We've connected over the last few weeks, shared some laughs, some memories. That makes us friends. Why should I turn down a chance to spend time with him when I've spent nearly every day of my holiday vacation with Sky?

The more I think about it, the sillier I feel for fretting over this all night long. Sky is a down-to-earth kind of guy. Surely, he understands all of this without my having to explain it to him. Come to think of it, maybe I just imagined the awkwardness between us last night. Maybe it was quiet because we were both tired after such a big busy day.

By the time I reach the Tchaikovsky streets, I feel easy about everything. It's been a great holiday vacation—better than I could have imagined. Reconnecting with Sky has put me in touch with my inner child, while getting a long overdue apology from Benson has finally put to rest my old childhood anxieties. I've gotten over my writer's block, saved a historic treasure in my hometown from demolition, and I feel more confident in my abilities than ever before. No matter how the New Year's Ball goes, I've already succeeded, haven't I? I feel confident about starting with *Verité* in fifteen days. That was all I wanted from this trip to begin with. So, mission accomplished.

Right?

The forest thins as I pass Swan Lake Drive. Flashes of the Morley Mansion become visible between trees the closer I get. I hope to see Sky's truck when I pull onto Nutcracker Circle.

But his truck is not the only one there.

Similar trucks line the horseshoe driveway. At first, I wonder if the Rodriguez brothers are here. Did we burst a pipe from people using the bathroom last night? Dread grips me at the thought. No, no, no, we can't afford a setback like that this late in the game! But then I see the bulldozer and my dread ices over into something worse.

"What on earth—"

I park behind Sky's truck. He's on the porch, talking to a man in a reflective orange vest and a hard hat. That's not Tony or Josh or Lucas. With my heart in my throat, I fight to throw off my seat belt, fling open the car door, and dash up the porch steps.

"What's going on here?"

Sky doesn't turn to look at me, but goes right on talking to the guy in the orange vest. "No, that's not possible. You've got to have the wrong house. The development company doesn't even own this place yet."

The man checks a clipboard propped against his belly, "There another house on Nutcracker Circle? 'Cause that's what I've got on my schedule today."

"That can't be." I stand beside Skylar. "The inspection isn't until the thirty-first. Bea Carston still owns this house. You can't tear it down."

He throws his free hand in the air. "All I know is, we got the green light. Job came open, weather held, so we bumped this one up. We can have it all finished before the holiday."

I want to scream, but Sky is already speaking with impressive authority. "You need to leave. Now. You don't have the right to tear this house down. Not yet. You need to double-check your legal clearance before you bump up a project like this on your schedule."

The man sizes Sky up. "What are you, some kind of lawyer? You own the house?"

"Bea Carston is the owner." I pull out my phone and thumb to her name on my contact list. "She lives just down the dirt path there, on this property. She can be up here in a minute." The phone is already ringing when I press it to my ear.

"Look, I'm just doing my job. Got the paperwork, got the address. Talk to the bank if you've got a problem."

"The bank," Sky says. "Is that who scheduled this? They had no right to hire you before they own the property."

"Like I said, take it up with them. Now, if you'll excuse us, me and my guys would like to spend Christmas with our families." He motions for us to leave the porch just as Bea answers the phone.

"Bea! Could you come up to the Morley Mansion? There's a demolition crew here who says the bank scheduled them to tear it down today."

Sky and the man continue to argue. I plant myself in front of the double doors beside Sky as Bea shuffles through papers in the background. "That can't be right. They must have the wrong house."

"That's what we told them, but they won't leave."

"Well now, hold on, sweetie. I'll be right up."

When I hang up, the demolition foreman is in the middle of telling Sky that if we ain't the owners, and we ain't the bank, then he doesn't have to listen to us. "Now, you get one, or both, of them to tell me I can't do my job, then we'll have something to talk about."

"She's on her way up," I say. "The owner. She'll be here in a few minutes."

He heaves a disgruntled sigh before calling over his shoulder to his men, "Take five, boys. Let me get this issue sorted out and we'll have you home in time for dinner."

"Why wait?" Sky scoffs. "They're not tearing down this house. If your schedule freed up, just go home. Spend the day with your families."

"I promised them work," the foreman replies. "Been a rough year for everybody. We don't want any trouble, we just want to do the job we were hired for and be on our way."

"I understand. I work in construction myself." Sky nods at the house behind us. "We've been working overtime to get the repairs done on this building so it can pass inspection in time."

He doesn't mention that we've been working for free. He looks more handsome than ever standing there and defending Bea's family home with confidence and authority and kindness. Leave it to Sky to turn a confrontation into a friendly commiseration on work life.

By the time Bea makes it up the dirt road, the foreman has softened slightly. Maybe it was Skylar's relatable shop talk, or maybe it's the way Bea walks with a slight limp and is as winded as if she'd run a marathon to get here.

"What's all this about tearing down my house?" Her voice is soft, sad, confused.

The man's shoulders drop. "Sorry, ma'am. Are you the owner? Do you have proof?"

Bea pulls a manilla envelope from under her arm and extracts a single piece of paper with a shaking hand. "This is the deed to the Morley Mansion. I'm Bea Carston." As he takes the paper and looks it over, she takes out another. "And this is the cash-for-keys offer from Willamette Valley Bank. My eyes aren't too good, but if I'm not mistaken, my signature isn't on there. In January, the bank can seize the house with or without my signature, but until then, the house is still mine."

"Sorry, ma'am. Maybe there's been a mistake. Let me call our scheduling office and see what's the deal." The man steps off the porch and leans against the bed of his truck as he makes the call.

But I'm looking at Bea. She never told me that the bank could take her house in the new year whether she chose to sell it to them or not. How is that possible?

"Bea." Sky's voice is careful. "Did you take out a reverse mortgage on the house?"

Bea tucks her papers back into their envelope. She doesn't meet his eye, just nods her head once.

"You took out a loan on your family home?" It hurts my heart to realize she was so desperate, so alone. I don't mean to sound accusatory, but as soon as the words leave my mouth, I realize it sounds like I'm scolding her.

"I thought I'd have time to fix things before the bank came knocking," she sighs. "But time got away from me. 'Fore I knew it, I get this notice that says I've got till the end of the year to get the house to pass inspection or it goes into foreclosure."

"Why didn't you tell us?" I ask.

Sky saves Bea from having to answer. "It's alright. We know now what we're dealing with. Let's see if we can buy you a few more days."

The foreman returns, looking sheepish. "Sorry about all this, folks. Looks like there was a string of misunderstandings. The bank scheduled us to come out first week of January, but when today's appointment canceled, a new kid in the office bumped up this job without checking the permissions."

Sky shakes his hand. "No harm done. We know you boys were just doing your job. I hope you can still get some extra hours in today somewhere."

As the demolition crew packs up, I watch Bea's face. She can't meet my eye. I don't know much about how a reverse mortgages work, but there's got to be something we can do to save this house.

"Did you send in the application to the National Register of Historic Places? Maybe if we can get the house registered in time, that will protect it from whatever the bank had planned for this property.

Bea sits on one of the porch chairs with a heavy sigh, wincing at the effort. "It's a long process. Lots of paperwork. Lots of proof of this and proof of that."

"That's alright," I say in a rush. "I can help you with that."

She doesn't answer, just watches as the construction crew drives away, leaving only my mom's Subaru and Skylar's truck in the driveway. "I shouldn't have dragged you two into this," Bea sighs. "You've put in so much work. Been so sweet to me. I shouldn't have let you get your hopes up. It was just such a nice dream. I didn't want it to end."

"It doesn't have to end." I look at Sky to back me up, but he just stands there deep in thought. "The house will pass inspection. I know it will. The bank can't seize it then, can they?"

"But the house will go into foreclosure," Sky replies. "Because you owe money on it?"

"Because I've been living in the pool house," Bea corrects him. "That's one of the three conditions where the loan has to get paid in full: I die, I sell the house, or I stop living in it."

"Well, that's easy," I say. "Just move in. The kitchen works great, and the downstairs bathroom is functioning. We could help move you in to one of the guest rooms on the main level..."

It seems like the obvious plan to me, but why aren't Sky or Bea jumping on it?

All Bea says after several moments of silence is "Maybe." Then, after another moment, "I'm tired. Maybe it wouldn't be so bad to take the money they offered to go quietly. It breaks my heart to lose this place. I've lived a good life here. But the fight's taken more out of me than I have left to give."

"Don't give up," I plead, taking her hand. "We'll get this figured out. I promise." I squeeze her hand until she looks at me. She gives me a weak smile, then nods.

"Alright, if you say so. Guess there's nothing to lose by trying."

She walks home after that, leaving me and Sky standing alone on the porch.

"So, if we make it obvious when the inspection happens that Bea has been living in the house," I say, "the bank won't foreclose on it?"

"Maybe." Sky doesn't sound convinced. That isn't like him.

"Hey," I say, "where's that optimism of yours?"

He shakes his head. "Sorry. It's just...maybe we should stop pushing her. Sounds like she wants to take the cash offer and go in peace."

"She's only talking like that because she's tired. She *wants* to keep her home. Remember the way she spoke the other day during the snowstorm? Her heart is here. Her whole life is here. It's all she's ever known."

"But she can't keep up with it anymore. She said so. And even if we could keep the house from going into foreclosure, how long will that last? Until the roof caves in because she can't afford to repair it?"

"She'll get a loan from the National Register of Historic Places."

"Maybe she will. Or maybe the house won't qualify, and she'll be right back where she started, but without a cash-for-keys offer to make sure she walks away with some money before the bank takes her home out from under her."

"She didn't say that."

"Because she's scared. Once she loses this house—and she *will* lose it, sooner or later—she'll be left with nothing. That's what she's afraid of. Right now, she has a chance to at least walk away with some money. Who are we to tell her not to take it?"

"I'm not telling her not to take it! I'm just saying, we can't give up before we've tried everything. We still have six days before the house inspection."

Sky doesn't meet my eye. "This isn't like helping a goat. Bea's a person. We have to respect her decisions."

His words sting. "I know." My voice wavers. "I just... We promised we would help her pass. She has the whole town behind her now, Sky. If she can keep the house, everyone will be here to support her."

He softens, but it looks more like surrender than agreement. "We'll stick to the plan," he says. "I'm just saying maybe we should be prepared for this to go another way."

21

Christmas

I WAKE TO THE sound of whispering voices and little feet creaking their way up the stairs from the basement. I'm not usually a light sleeper, but Christmas Eve has always been the exception. Maybe all those years of determination to catch a glimpse of Santa Claus trained my brain to develop the keen senses of an outdoor tracker only on one night out of the year. Or maybe it's just because I spent all night sifting through everything I could find about reverse mortgages and foreclosures and cash-for-keys deals and what it takes to get a house on the historical registry.

I roll over to check the time. Five in the morning.

Mom and Dad had a rule when I was growing up, where we could wake up and see the tree and enjoy our stockings at whatever ungodly hour we chose, but we were not, under any circumstances, allowed to rouse them from their slumber until seven o'clock.

I wonder if my siblings have a similar rule. Or does anything go now that it's Grandma and Grandpa's house?

My laptop is open before I even realize I reached for it. I snap it shut. *No. Not on Christmas.* I promised my family, and myself, that I would take a break from all things Morley Mansion until tomorrow.

There's no chance of going back to sleep now, with the sounds of excited whispers and poorly suppressed squeals from the living room, so I slip out of bed and down the hall.

The glow of the Christmas tree fills the otherwise dark room. Santa has left a few toys unwrapped for dramatic effect: Scooters with blinking lights, a Victorian dollhouse, a set of laser tag packs. Lilly's older sister Violet tries to get the toddler excited about a baby doll that Santa left in a toy stroller just for her, but Lilly is more interested in pulling everything out of her stocking.

Twelve-year-old Conner looks like he's about to test out a scooter when he notices my presence and promptly puts the scooter back beside the tree. When I was a kid, we had a rule about not touching the gifts until the whole family was present. It looks like that one is still enforced by my siblings.

"Oooh," I whisper, so they know I'm not going to tattle. "Those look awesome! Who did Santa leave those for?"

"There's one for all of us!" Milo cheers, jumping up and down.

Eli claps a hand over his brother's mouth. "Shh! Everyone's sleeping!"

"Aunt AJ, Santa left a stocking for you, too!" Violet retrieves my old childhood stocking, filled to the brim with goodies, and bounds over to deliver it to me.

I settle on the floor with the rest of the kids, legs crossed, and rub my hands together with an eager, goofy chuckle before diving in. The kids laugh as they watch me. This was always my favorite part about Christmas as a kid—the quiet early morning, whispering in the light of the Christmas tree as my siblings and I unpacked our stockings and talked while we ate candy for breakfast.

I'm surprised that Tiffany is still asleep. She used to be the first one to wake up on Christmas mornings, and the rest of us would wake to her jumping on us or throwing candy at us from her stocking or holding chocolate under our noses until we stirred. Has motherhood changed this habit of hers?

Just as I think this, my older sister ambles up the stairs in a flannel robe. She stifles a yawn, plops down beside me, and shakes my shoulders with a feeble "It's Christmas!" At least she tries to shake my shoulders, but the effort seems too much in her sleepy state and all she manages to do is rock me slightly.

"I can't believe these things are still around." I show her a Life Savers Storybook from my stocking. "If that isn't a throwback, I don't know what is."

"Santa's old school." Tiffany yawns. "If it ain't broke, don't change it."

"You mean 'don't fix it.'"

"Same difference." She lays down, using my lap as a pillow.

I adjust my stocking to make room for her.

"Here's yours, Mommy." Seven-year-old Tatiana brings a stocking to my sister.

"Aw, thanks, baby." Then she whisper-yells at the ceiling, "Thanks, Santa! Glad I've been such a good mom all year." She digs through her stocking with one hand until she finds what she's looking for: a Keurig cup. "Eli, baby, will you start some coffee for Mommy?" She tosses the cup to her firstborn.

Eli catches it one-handed with the ease of a seasoned baseball player before dashing off to the kitchen.

I wonder how Sky's Christmas morning will go. No doubt he's still sound asleep. Will he and his dad open presents together? Will they share a kingly breakfast and reminisce over steaming mugs of their morning brew of choice? They'll be joining us for dinner tonight, and I know I should leave Sky alone until then so he can enjoy Christmas with his dad however they choose. But I can't resist sending a single text message.

Merry Christmas, ya filthy animal.

"No work," Tiffany groans, swatting at my phone with a floppy hand.

"It's a Christmas text!" But I put the phone away.

It isn't until the first rays of Christmas morning light shine through the windows and all the adults wander like zombies into the living room with sleep-tousled hair that I feel my phone buzz under my leg. I smile at Sky's reply.

And a happy new year.

I feel strangely nervous that evening as I place a platter of spiral-cut honey ham on the dining room table. We spent the day like Whos in Whoville, in our pajamas, playing with our new toys (or, in my case, curled up on the couch with the new book Tara gave me), tooting horns, crashing drones into light fixtures, and watching favorite Christmas movies while the youngest kids fell asleep on their respective piles of presents with a favorite new toy clutched in their chocolate-sticky hands. Now the house is a whirlwind of kids and parents rushing around to clean up while I help Mom and Dad and Luke and his wife, Kesha, put dinner on the table before our guests arrive. Crinkling wrapping paper competes with the noise of kids as it's crammed into large garbage bags. Milo and Lilly are both cranky from the sugar overload and the lack of sleep, and occasionally their cries ring through the chaos.

Tara's voice rises above the noise. "Violet, will you help your sister get dressed? Boys—*boys!* Put the drone away, for Pete's sake! Go get dressed now! Don't make me ask again."

My brother, Luke, scoffs as he puts the finishing touches on his au gratin potatoes. "Dang, Tara, you've got the mom voice down."

Kesha cocks an eyebrow at him. "Careful, she might turn on you next, Mr. PJ's." She slaps his flannel-clad behind.

"Babe, you know I can be ready in like, fifteen seconds." He places a sprig of rosemary on the potatoes.

I'm impressed. "Wow, Bro, you've come a long way from cereal and nachos."

He quirks a cocky grin as he looks over his masterpiece.

"He's been watching a lot of Gordon Ramsay," says Kesha, turning soft eyes on him. "He's gotten pretty good."

"Sky's a good cook, too." The words slide from my lips like drool from a numbed mouth at the dentist. I backpedal, desperate to give my slipup context that doesn't insinuate I've been thinking about Sky all day. "Cooking must be the cool thing for guys to do these days."

I catch my mom's knowing smile. No one's fooled by my excuses. Not even me.

At least Tiffany wasn't here to hear that.

Grabbing a bowl of brussels sprouts from the counter, I duck out of the kitchen and away from all the teasing smiles.

Maybe this is why I'm nervous about Sky and his dad joining us for dinner. My family is going to make this so awkward; I just know it. Even if they're too polite to say anything out loud, Tiffany's going to be elbowing me at every opportunity, Luke will send me sly winks, and my mom is going to beam and shower Sky with so much fondness that she might as well serve me up to him on a silver chair in a foofy white dress and veil with the wedding march playing from the kitchen speaker.

Good thing Bea is coming, too. Maybe her presence will make my family behave. Or at least give them someone else to focus on.

There's a knock on the front door.

Char barks.

Several kids yell at once, "They're here!"

Luke darts upstairs to get dressed.

I adjust my red V-neck blouse and wonder if it's too formal. Should I have gone with a more casual look? Jeans and a T-shirt instead of slacks?

Weaving through a sea of excited kids while Tara holds Char at bay, I make my way to the front door and resist fussing with my hair before throwing it open.

Doug looks uncomfortable on my parents' front porch as he waits for Sky to help Bea up the stairs. "Merry Christmas!" I gush, hoping to ease his discomfort. "Come in. We're so happy you could join us!"

Sky looks incredible in a sage button-down shirt and maroon scarf under his suede jacket, his sandy locks tamed attractively. My heart soars at the sight of him with Bea on his arm, supporting her up the last step. But he only glances at me briefly with a fleeting polite smile.

I take Bea from him as they enter the house and lead her to a chair in the living room. "Is Theodore alone at the house?"

She points a thumb back out the door. "No, he's out in their truck, on his little bed."

"You don't have to leave him out there in the cold. Our dog is big, but he's a good boy. We can put him in my parents' room so he doesn't scare Theodore."

Bea hesitates, unsure how her little dog will handle all these noisy kids, but ultimately agrees to bring him in and let him lay on his bed in my room during dinner so he can have some peace and quiet without having to wait in a cold truck.

When I walk with Bea from my bedroom back to the dining room after getting her dog all set up, I notice Sky has fast become the center of attention among the kids. He's on the floor with them, helping put together some mechanical kit that my mom got for them. He's explaining how something works to conduct electricity, predicting that a little light will turn on when he touches this to that. A collective expression of awe bursts from the kids as the light turns on, just as Sky said it would.

"Cool," says Conner.

"But it's not plugged in to anything?" Tara's eight-year-old, Lincoln, scrunches his face in confusion.

Sky explains how it works.

Someone ribs me and I look up to find Tiffany, bouncing her eyebrows suggestively as she walks by with a basket of warm rolls fresh from the oven. I realize I've been leaning against the wall, watching Sky in what must look like a pathetically wistful way. Quickly, I straighten and look for Bea, who has already been shown a seat at the table by Tara. The two of them are talking about something, while my parents have Doug in the kitchen, showing him how the countertops he installed are holding up.

My brother saunters down the stairs in a nice pair of gray chinos and a deep red sweater. "Hey, buddy." He grins at the sight of Sky. "Good to see you, man."

Sky stands to greet him, and they grip hands arm-wrestling style and pull in for a bro hug, complete with a hearty slap on each other's backs before separating.

"What's up, man? It's been a minute!" Sky takes my brother in and laughs. "You look like a movie star."

My brother waves this off with an easy grin. "Meh, that's just my wife making a refined man outta me. You haven't met her, have you? I think she's still in the kitchen."

"Not yet, but I've heard good things. She's the personal trainer, right? She keeping you in shape?"

"Yeah, she kicks my butt, man. But how about you? We heard you were out there wrestling lions in Africa or something."

It's easy to forget that Sky and my brother were in the same year at school, because they didn't often hang out with the same crowd. Sky was definitely a lot more outgoing and involved in sports and clubs, while my brother tended to fly under the radar with the gamers and the skaters. But then, it wouldn't surprise me to learn that Sky probably took part in his share of gaming hangouts when invited. It seemed like he knew most people in high school.

I don't know why I feel strange standing there watching them. Suddenly I feel like my brother's little sister again, fourteen years old, an insecure little freshman wondering how I made it into a friends group that included a popular senior like Skylar Townsend. Sky has hardly looked at me since he arrived. Will reconnecting with my brother make him see me as that little girl again?

"How does this one work?" Conner interrupts my brother, holding up a piece to Sky.

"In a minute, dude," my brother tells Conner. "We're having a conversation."

"Try it on the blue nob," Sky says, then winks at him mid-conversation when the piece emits a blinking light, followed by an "Awesome!" from Conner.

I need something to do. I can't just keep standing here watching Sky, wondering why he hasn't looked my way yet. So I circle the dining room table and straighten out place settings, creasing the folds in the dinner napkins to make them look crisper.

Kesha emerges from the kitchen in search of her husband. "Oh good, you're dressed."

Luke holds out an arm for her, and she goes to sidle under it. "Sky, meet my wife, Kesha. Kesh, this guy was a buddy of mine in high school. He just got back from digging wells and stuff in Africa. Kesh loves humanitarian work. She's always volunteering at pet shelters and stuff. Brought home a three-legged dog once, and we're trying to get him one of those robot legs. Hey, you're an engineer, aren't you? Maybe you can build one for him."

Sky laughs. "That sounds like a sweet project, but I don't have any experience in robotics, unfortunately. If you ever need someone to build him a doghouse, though, give me a call."

I know Sky's embarrassed that he never finished college. Just as I'm about to step in and save him from the direction the conversation with my brother is going, Dad emerges with the turkey on a platter. "Dinner's ready!"

Violet tugs on Skylar's hand. "Sit with me!"

"You're sitting at the kids' table," Tara says, cutting in. "We're going to let Skylar sit with the grown-ups."

"Aw man," Sky pretends to be put out. "They never let me sit at the fun table."

As we all take our seats, Tiffany positions herself across from me with a look of approval. "So, Sky," she says, "how is it you're so good with kids?"

"Am I?" He chuckles. "That's nice of you to say. It's probably because I still am one myself."

Then come all the questions about Africa, which Sky answers with just the right details to satisfy curiosity before he tactfully shifts the conversation to Luke. "I've heard you rub shoulders with the upper crust of society these days."

Luke laughs boisterously. "Well, when I get a big job, I guess."

Kesha jumps in proudly. "He put together the most amazing spectacle for this billionaire's party in LA on Tuesday. Show them your kaleidoscope thing, babe."

Luke dabs his chin with his napkin before pulling out his phone to show the video he's shown the rest of us already. "It's hard to tell on the phone," he explains. "You have to be there to get the full experience, but you can kinda see how it works. It's called a kaleidoscopic projection map. Basically, you project colors or images onto something that refracts the light, and you get this dope effect where it looks like the image is in pieces all over the walls and the floor."

Bea squints at Luke's phone. "I don't know what I'm looking at."

Luke turns the screen so it's facing him and he shrugs, a little deflated. "Yeah, it's hard to tell in a video. Like I said, you'd just have to be there."

"It sounds awesome," says Sky.

"Well"—my mom swallows her food—"Doug and Sky, I think it's wonderful what you're doing to help Bea and AJ."

For some reason, Sky's smile looks pained for just a moment, and then his eyes turn to the ham on his fork and the look is gone. "Bea has been a priceless member of the community since before I was born. We all owe her more than I think we know how to give."

Bea says a dismissive "Oh" at that, but my mom rushes to back Sky up.

"It's true! I don't think there's a soul in Roanoke who hasn't made treasured memories in the Morley Mansion. You're the one who opened it up for public use. You grew up in that home, didn't you?"

Bea nods. "I was born in the master bedroom. My brother and me used to play in the woods."

"It must have been strange," Tara says, "to open your home for strangers to host parties in."

"Not really. The house was built for entertaining. My great-grand-father's parties are legendary. My parents were always hosting big parties, too. What felt strange was when the house was quiet and empty. I didn't really inherit my mother's entertaining talent. I'm shy, like my dad. So it seemed like the natural thing to do to let people who like to throw parties do it in the house. Katie Townsend did the house proud every time." Bea's eyes twinkle when she looks at Doug. "I liked your wife a lot. She reminded me of my mother."

Doug nods his appreciation. "Guess I'm more like you. Rather let someone else throw the parties."

"But you always helped," Bea says. "You built any gosh-darn contraption she came up with. I remember trying to get that arch you built through the front door for a Snow Ball one year. I said, 'That ain't gonna work,' and Katie said, 'Well, let's see,' and she asked you to take it apart and rebuild it inside, and by golly, you did it!" She laughs a full-bellied laugh, head thrown back at the memory.

Doug can't help smiling, too. "Yeah, guess it feels good to be useful. Kate knew that about me."

"And me," Bea sighs. "I don't know how to throw a party, but I could always provide the house. I always had that..." The laughter fades from her eyes, and she surrenders it with an *oh well* kind of shrug.

"You'll still have the house," I say.

Why won't Sky look at me?

"How much did you raise at the Gingerbread Festival?" Kesha asks, maybe just to feel like a part of this conversation.

It's not a question I'm fully prepared to answer. "We did well." My voice sounds too high on "well." I spear a bite of delicate scalloped potatoes. "The New Year's Ball should cover what's left once ticket sales start rolling in."

"Did you sell many at the festival?" she wonders.

I shift in my seat. "Well, most people were pretty focused on the festival. We sold a few. I expect we'll get more sales after Christmas, once the holiday rush dies down and people are ready for the next thing."

Truth be told, I'm praying this will be the case. We sold all of ten tickets at the festival, which wouldn't be a big deal if the festival had made enough money to cover material and construction expenses. I'm not the only one who will be in the hole if we don't raise enough money to pay it off. We're still over three thousand short of our goal, and the only way we'll make that up is if half the adults in Roanoke buy dance tickets.

Bea merely repeats the same shrug and smiles the smile of a defeated woman.

"Will the construction be done in time for the dance?" Mike asks.

I realize that we never did the sanding work yesterday as we intended. Sky must be thinking about this, too, because his eyes look faraway when he says, "We're starting the finish work tomorrow."

When the Townsends and Bea leave after dinner, I have the feeling that Sky will head over to the Morley Mansion to finish sanding before the work begins. So I ask to borrow my mom's car, change into my work clothes, and slip away before Tiffany or anyone else can give me a hard time about it.

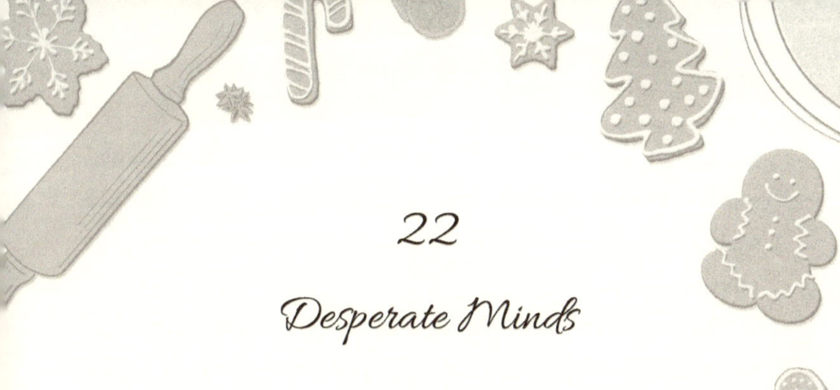

22

Desperate Minds

THE LIGHTS ARE ON in the Morley Mansion when I park behind Sky's truck in the driveway. I follow the *shh, shh, shh* of a sanding block on drywall into the oversized bathroom, with its single toilet and vanity standing out in the middle of the floorless space like a car parked in a shopping center with a contest box beside it.

Sky has changed into his Carhartts and a T-shirt, his mask and safety glasses in place against the white dust that fills the air. With his back to me, I can see the shape of his shoulders through the thin fabric of his shirt as he works the sanding block in smooth, circular motions against the wall. Following his example, I pick up a mask, some goggles, and a sander from the tools corner on my way into the bathroom.

He looks over his shoulder at the sound of my shoes against the concrete floor.

"Hey." I wave my sanding block in greeting. "Great minds, huh?"

He gives a short laugh through his nose. "Desperate minds, more like."

That doesn't sound like the Sky I've been working with.

"How far have you gotten?"

"That wall's done. It's just these three, and then out in the hallway."

I move to the wall opposite him and start sanding any imperfections in the plaster. White dust falls to the floor under my hand like snow.

Shh, shh, shh.

I try to think what I should say. Is Sky distant from me because I told him I'll be going to the dance with Benson? Or is it because Bea seems to be giving up already? Sky doesn't seem the jealous type, so it must be the latter.

"We'll be able to finish in time," I say, trying to reassure him. "The finish work doesn't *have* to be complete in order for the house to pass inspection, right?"

He doesn't answer right away, but when he does, I'm surprised at the edge in his voice. "So, then what? We leave Bea with an unfinished house and tell her 'good luck'?"

I want to tell him, *Of course not*, but what else can I realistically do if the house isn't finished before I have to fly back to New York? "We'll finish it, then."

He laughs coldly. "Do you have a team of contractors hidden away somewhere that I don't know about? Because last I checked, there are only two of us."

"Okay, so we'll do what we can. You're the one who said that would be enough; that even if we failed, at least Bea will know that we tried."

"That was before we found out about her reverse mortgage." His sanding becomes faster, more intense, then stops. He turns around to face me, pulling his mask down to rest under his chin. "Don't you see, AJ? She's going to lose everything no matter what we do. Her best chance is to take the money and find a new place to live. The longer we drag this out, we risk her losing the cash-for-keys offer and walking away with nothing. If you really want to help her, maybe it would be better to spend this time looking for a place for her to live, getting her on the waitlist for low-income housing instead of a historic house registry."

I can't believe what I'm hearing. "That's not what Bea wants."

"She doesn't have much of a choice."

I pull down my mask. "Then why would she go along with this, if she didn't hold out some hope that it might work? Why not ask us to raise money for her to live on instead of putting it into repairing the house?"

"Because she's embarrassed!" Sky's voice is sharp. It catches me by surprise. He softens his tone slightly, but there's still passion behind his words. "Can't you see that? She's embarrassed that she's in this mess, that she's getting older and poorer and she doesn't have anything set aside to take care of herself as she ages. She has no retirement savings, and the one thing her family left to her has been slipping through her fingers for years so she could live off the money from the reverse mortgage. She was hoping she would die before she had to see the house leave her hands completely, but the bell tolled early because she couldn't keep up with maintaining the one thing she had left. That's embarrassing to her. And now we've gone and gotten the whole town involved in this 'save the house' venture, so when it falls through, Bea won't have the option to say it was just time to sell the house. We've robbed her of that dignity. Now, when things don't work out, the whole town will find out she was on a sinking ship and their donations went down with it."

The passion in his voice shakes me to my core. My hand trembles on the sanding block, and I realize I've stopped moving. A deep heaviness settles in my stomach. Swallowing, I turn to face him. "You mean *I've* gone and gotten the whole town involved."

He shakes his head, but doesn't meet my eye. "I didn't say that."

"But that's what you meant, isn't it? I'm the one who wrote the article. I'm the one who organized the festival and lobbied for the fundraiser and drew as much attention to Bea as I could."

"You didn't know. *We* didn't know. We thought we were doing the right thing."

"I still think we are. You heard Bea tonight. She thinks this house is the only thing she has to offer the community. If she loses it, she'll think she has nothing to contribute anymore. She'll think she's lost her worth."

"But that isn't true. Don't you see? She has so much more to offer. Maybe it would be better for us to show her that. Show her she's done more for Roanoke than just let people host events in her family home. Let her know that her quiet generosity and friendly nature have done more good for the community than these crumbling walls."

I know he has a good point, and I want Bea to know that, too. But I'm not ready to give up on this mission we started. "But if she loses this house, she'll lose Roanoke, too. There's no lower-income housing around here. She'd have to move to Salem or farther—somewhere no one will know who she is or what she's lost or what she has to offer. And we promised her, Sky! We promised her we'd do everything we could to help her keep her house."

"*You* promised," he says. "You've got to stop making promises you can't keep on your own. It's just giving her false hope."

"I don't think it is. I don't think anyone has hope anymore. I think I'm the only one who still thinks we stand a chance. But look what we've accomplished so far! We've done so much in such a short time, I just *know* there's got to be more we can do. We at least have to try. Please, Sky, just help me get this place ready in time for the New Year's Ball. You'll see. People will come through. We'll get the money we need, and the house will pass inspection, and Bea will have time to get it registered."

"Maybe consider looking for another venue for the dance. Just in case the inspection fails."

"It won't fail."

"In case it does."

"No, the ball has to happen here."

"Why?"

"It just does. This is the reason we're having the ball to begin with. It has to happen here."

"What difference does it make where it happens, as long as it raises the money we need? You've pulled a lot of last-second miracles in the past week. I'm sure you'll be able to find somewhere else to host the ball."

"It can't be anywhere else. It has to be here. That's the whole point!"

His eyes widen, then narrow. "Is that really what this is about? You recreating the night Benson Miller snubbed you at a dance so you can make it go the way you wanted?"

"What? No! Of course not."

"Then why does it *have* to be *here*?" he says. "Why can't your date to a dance with Benson happen anywhere else?"

I'm so thrown off by his accusation I can't even speak. "It can. It...it just—"

He rakes both hands through his hair with an explosive exhale that fails to be a laugh. "I don't believe this."

"This has nothing to do with my date with Benson. You're missing the point."

"You think getting that dance with him is going to solve all your problems? That you'll somehow overcome all your insecurities and go back to New York on top of the world, ready to tackle anything that comes your way?"

I want to tell him no, that he's way off, but my jaw clamps shut, because he's struck a nerve.

Taking my silence to be a confirmation that he's right, Sky shakes his head in disbelief. "You got us all on board to help you recreate this fantasy. Did you ever once stop to question if someone might get hurt along the way?"

"What about you?" I snap. "What about, 'I really needed this, AJ'? That's what you said after the Gingerbread Festival."

"Because I thought we were doing something meaningful! Helping someone in need, bringing the community together—not fulfilling some personal teenage fantasy of yours."

"I was trying to do something meaningful, too! You're not the only one who cares about helping people, Sky. We just can't all drop our responsibilities for five years and disappear to a foreign country like some benevolent saint! And when you did that, did you ever think of who you might have left behind? And how that might hurt *him*?" I've gone too far, and I know it, but I can't stop. I want to strike him as directly as he struck me. "I might not be this perfect...perfect"—my hands grasp uselessly at an imagined force field that surrounds Sky, as if I could somehow shake the word that describes him from that frustratingly golden aura—"dream person! But at least when I attempt to do something meaningful, I don't abandon my family in the process."

I wait for him to hit back, to come at me with more hurtful words, to point out what a hypocrite I am, since I just sneaked away from my family on Christmas to work on this project with him. But he just stands there, the fire draining from him. Then, face blank, he removes his mask and safety glasses and drops them on the floor.

"Merry Christmas, AJ."

He leaves me standing alone in the cold unfinished bathroom with a cloud of white dust settling to the floor in his wake.

23

This Little Piggy Cried

ROANOKE FEELS SURPRISINGLY COLD after Christmas. It isn't just the ice, which makes driving hazardous, or the frost that gives a gray cast to everything outside, but the people.

I spent the morning of December 26 making phone calls to anyone and everyone I could think of who'd so much as smiled at the idea of a New Year's Eve Ball to encourage them to get their tickets before they were all gone. Most people didn't even answer the phone. Those who did all had some excuse why they probably wouldn't be going after all. "I'm just kind of tired after all the holiday madness," one woman sighed. "You know? Just wanna spend a quiet New Year's at home with my family."

By that afternoon, my frustration bordered on anger. Unreliable, flaky people! How could they all smile to my face at the Gingerbread Festival and say, "Great idea, AJ!" and "Count me in!" and "That sounds just like what this town needs!" and pretend to care about helping Bea, only to turn around now and say they'd rather lie around at home like a bunch of couch potatoes instead?

But my anger didn't last. I knew I had no right to be mad at anyone but myself. I'd asked so much of my friends and neighbors already, and they'd given more than I had any right to expect. The donations given at the festival were beyond generous, with nearly three thousand dollars raised. Considering that most people had already spent their

Christmas charity budget before invitations for the festival even went out, that anyone donated money at all spoke to the spirit of generosity and sacrifice in this humble little town.

Now, it seems, I've maxed out that spirit, leaving Roanoke depleted. People need time to recover and refill their coffers. With the joy of Christmas in the past, a strange melancholy settles over Roanoke and its residents. Maybe this is the melancholy that has gripped Bea and Sky.

Sky.

I haven't heard from him since our fight last night. I'm haunted by the words I said to him, even if I still feel hurt by the accusations he flung at me. Two peace-loving people; how could we have said such hurtful things to each other? How had we let our frustrations escalate to that?

I miss Sky. I ache to hear his laugh and see his easy grin and joke with him about how silly it was to fight. But the wounds are still too fresh. And part of me wonders, maybe I don't know Sky as well as I thought I did. Of course he couldn't always be so quick to laugh things off all the time. Of course he couldn't always let things run off his shoulders like rain. He's a human being with feelings and frustrations, just as capable of anger and hurt as anyone. It was only a matter of time before all that evasion built up into a hot mess of feelings that could only come out in a steamy burst.

I want to tell myself he's unreliable, unstable; that he seems like Mr. Calm and Perfect on the outside, but that he's a loose cannon on the inside. I want to tell myself this as I scroll through potential alternative venues for the New Year's Eve Ball online, and I want to believe it as I drive to the only available space just outside of town: a rundown old barn with reviews complaining of a strong manure smell.

But the truth is, Sky was right.

My reasons for helping Bea were selfish, even if not for the reasons that Sky thinks. I wanted to help her, not to recreate my date with Benson—though I didn't turn down the opportunity when it presented itself—but because I thought it would help me get the permanent position I want at *Verité*. I wanted to know I could pull off the impossible; move people to action with my writing; put together an event that would make me look good. I wanted the confidence that comes with success. I wanted to leave home feeling like the person my parents' friends think I am.

The smell of manure reaches my nostrils before I see the cows grazing in a frosty gray field as I approach the barn. It's quaint from a distance—the classic red barn with white trim, complete with bales of hay and a few stray chickens that scatter when I pull up the muddy driveway. But the closer I get, the more clearly I can see peeling paint and patches of rotting wood.

The owner, a squat woman in black galoshes and muddy coveralls, comes out to meet me when I step out of the car. She has a rooster under her arm.

My feet sink to my ankles in mud. There's a sucking sound with every step I take toward the woman. "Hi, are you Sylvie?"

"That's me. AJ Banner?" When she shakes my hand, I notice there are piglets in her pockets. Real, live, pink, squirming piglets looking up at me with beady little eyes from four pockets in various places on her coveralls. "Don't mind them," she says as if the sight were as common as a dribble of spilled coffee on her shirt. "It's vaccinatin' time. You wanna come take a look inside?" She nudges her head toward the barn behind her before turning to lead the way.

"Thank you for doing this on such short notice." *Suck, shlump, suck, shlump.* "I hope I won't put you too behind on your vaccination schedule."

"It's no biggie. Animals are easier to work with in the cold. They hunker down and draw into themselves a bit, like people. Sorry about the muck. Gets pretty soft out here in the winter. We don't normally get people wantin' to rent the barn after October."

I understand why. There's a whistle inside from several places where the wind blows through cracks in the siding. The barn isn't insulated at all, and it's in full winterized fashion, storing dirty farm equipment and heaps of outdoor furniture piled up like a French barricade. A pigeon flaps loudly in the loft, and a flock of geese peers at us from one corner, honking curiously as they size me up to determine if they need to chase me off their property or not.

"We got a few propane heaters you could use to warm the place up," Sylvie says. "I could throw those in for another fifty dollars an hour, if you'd like. Fifty dollars each."

I already know I can't use this venue. It will cost more to make it pleasant in the dead of winter than I can afford, considering my current budget is zero. But it feels rude to just turn around and leave without at least pretending to consider it.

Moisture seeps through my shoes to my socks. I shiver. What am I doing out here? Is this dance even worth hosting? Maybe Sky is right. Maybe I should just give up now and let Bea take whatever money the bank will give her to hand over the house quietly. Maybe I should spend the rest of the time I have in Roanoke with my family, like I planned to do from the beginning, before I got myself tangled up in this whole mess.

"Is there a bathroom anywhere?" I ask, just for something to say.

"Folks usually rent a Honey Bucket or two when they host events here."

I try to find a reason for that to be the deal breaker, but I'm deflated. "This must be lovely in the summer. Maybe it would be better to save it for an event then."

Sylvie shrugs. "Like I said, folks don't usually want to rent the barn any time after October. July is our peak season. Wintertime, it ain't much to look at."

"Thank you for taking the time to show it to me."

As we walk back to my car, Sylvie asks, "What is this thing you're hosting? A wedding?"

"A New Year's Eve Ball. It's a fundraiser, actually. To save the Morley Mansion from being demolished."

"That old place still standing? I thought Bea gave it up years ago."

"She still lives there. Once it's gone, she'll have to find somewhere else to live."

"Aw, that's too bad. But I guess nothing lasts forever. Gotta know when it's time to let old things go so we can have our hands free to receive something better, my dad used to say."

I nod to be polite. It's a nice sentiment. But I don't see what there could possibly be better awaiting Bea if she loses her family home. Sky's prediction was pessimistic, but it's probably accurate. No retirement savings, no family, no plan. Who's going to catch her when she falls?

"You have any plans for New Year's?" I ask half-heartedly. "We've still got a few tickets available." A few fewer than all of them.

Her laugh sounds like a bark. "Do I look like I belong at a fancy ball?" She hoists the rooster under her arm for effect.

"Everyone deserves a night of magic and music and dancing at the end of a hard year," I say. "Especially hardworking farmers."

She allows this with a shrug. "Maybe so. You got a brochure or something?"

"Just look up 'Roanoke Gingerbread Festival' online. All the information's there."

"Gingerbread Festival, huh? Now that sounds like fun. That gonna happen at the ball?"

My hopes weren't high to begin with, but I realize they were there as soon as they putter out. "It already happened, I'm afraid. Just the dance left."

As I drive away with mucky shoes and the musty smell of goose poop filling the car, it feels official: the Gingerbread Festival was the only thing anyone wanted or cared about, and now it's over.

It's all over.

Back in my bedroom, I re-count the money from the Gingerbread Festival. We're still three thousand dollars short, and no new ticket sales for the ball have come in all day.

My laptop is open beside me, the glaring white of a blank page bearing down on me like a hot interrogation light. But it isn't heat I feel in my skin every time I look at the screen; it's ice. Cold, creeping, clawing its way up my back, gripping my chest, squeezing my throat...

I slam the laptop shut and hug my knees to my chest, rocking as I bury my face.

So much for getting over my writer's block.

This whole trip home has been nothing but a waste of time and resources. I thought I could do something meaningful while I was here—prepare to start my new career with confidence, get over my childhood insecurities, and help out a friend while I was at it. But nothing I've done has changed a thing. I was still a bumbling blockhead when I ran into Benson at the Gingerbread Festival, Bea is still losing her house, and my writer's block is worse than ever. Only now, on top of everything else, I'm three thousand dollars in debt, my flight home is pushed back to the day before I start with the magazine, I've wasted all this time I could have spent with my family, and I've lost Sky.

Why is it the last part that stings the most? Before coming home, Sky hadn't been a part of my life for years. Why should I feel his loss so keenly?

The answer prods at the back of my mind like a hot iron, but I turn away from the heat, falling onto my side before rolling out of bed.

It turns out, Sky was wrong about me. He thought my passion was a good trait, but really it's just stubborn pigheadedness—an inability to see past my own ambitions and know when to let go. It's what chased Adam away. I can't keep living in denial about that anymore. I knew my fixation on the *Verité* application process last fall was driving him away, but I kept telling myself it was only temporary—that I'd make time for him once I got the job, and that he'd be so proud of me he'd forgive me for all the cancelled dates and lack of attention.

Adam was right about me. I'm too intense. Uncompromising. Selfish.

And now Skylar knows it, too.

Maybe it's not too late to change my flight so I'll at least have a few days to get settled back into my life in New York before starting with *Verité*.

Until then, I should spend as much time with my family as I can.

I wander down to the living room, where Tara is reading from her tablet on the couch, and plop onto my back on the living room floor at her feet with a heavy sigh. Downstairs, all the kids laugh as they play with their new laser tag set in the dark with the dads, the sound rumbling through the floor.

Tara slides off the couch so she's sitting on the floor beside my head. She strokes my hair with one hand while still holding her tablet with the other. "You work so hard, AJ. I'm proud of you, little sister."

"For what?" I ask. "For wasting everyone's time and money? For dragging Sky into it and embarrassing Bea in front of the whole town?" I bury my face in my hands. "Jody was right. I should have just enjoyed my holiday with you guys instead of chasing this impossible dream."

"Jody-shmody," Tiffany says as she plops onto the couch behind Tara with a plate of leftover apple pie. "I said that first."

I throw my hands up in surrender. "And you were right! Why don't I listen to you people?"

"Because you're a visionary," Tara says firmly. "You see what could be when others see what is. That's what we love about you. That's what makes you such a good journalist and an even better person."

"You have to say that because you're my sister."

Tiffany speaks through a mouthful of pie. "I'm your sister, and I didn't say that."

"Tara's the oldest sister. That's practically like mom status."

Tara's tongue clicks. "I'm going to ignore that you just called me old. As the most *mature* sister, I have the most life experience, and thus the most reliable opinion."

"Here's what I think," says Tiffany. "I think you would have gotten bored just sitting around the house with Char for two weeks with nothing to do. You thought we were going to be here on the fifteenth. So did we. But then Snowpocalypse hit and plans changed, and you made the most of it."

I crack an eye open to look at her. That sounded suspiciously like a compliment. "But...?" I say.

"But what? *I* can't say something nice and encouraging, too?"

"Tiffany's right," Tara says. "You took a disappointing turn of events and made it into an opportunity to do something productive. And festive. That Gingerbread Festival was more fun than any holiday activity my kids attended all season. And you threw it together in under a week! That's amazing."

"It felt like the old days," Tiffany agrees. "You haven't been home the last few years, so maybe you haven't seen, but Roanoke has gotten kinda boring. There hasn't been anything fun for the kids to do around here when we come home for the holidays. We tried to take them to see the lights at Randolph Farms last year, remember Tara? And there was nothing there. Totally dark. Just a flimsy strand of white lights around the roof on the house. I guess the Randolphs up and sold the farm a few years back, and the new owners didn't carry on the tradition."

"That was disappointing," Tara sighs. "At least there's still Silver Bells. We took the kids there instead."

"Yeah, but that's just a gift shop and free hot cocoa. I spent the whole time trying to keep Milo from pulling everything off the shelves." Tiffany makes a flatulent sound with her tongue. "No, thank you."

I try to let their words sink in. At least the Gingerbread Festival was a hit. Even if I've given Bea false hopes and ruined my relationship with Sky forever, at least people had fun.

"Remember how there used to be some big event to look forward to every season around here?" Tiffany counts them off on her fingers with her fork. "There was the Easter egg hunt on Main Street downtown in the spring, carnivals and fireworks and that one traveling petting zoo thing in the summer, the corn maze in the fall, and there were always neighborhood spook alleys around Halloween..."

"The Festival of Trees in the winter," Tara adds.

"And the Christmas lights at Randolph Farms," Tiffany says. "And those were just the regular events you could always count on. Then there were the activities in between."

"Those were different times." We all look up to find our mom standing in the kitchen entrance hand-drying a casserole dish. "When I was a kid, it seemed like there was even more to do. We were always outside. Every generation seems to become more and more withdrawn."

Tara sighs. "It's sad. I was a chaperone on Conner's field trip in October, and you wouldn't believe how quiet that school bus was. At first, I thought, wow, this is great, these kids are so well behaved. But then I realized it was because they all had headphones in or were just on their phones."

"That's crazy," Tiffany says. "Back in our day, we went nuts on the bus! Belting out NSYNC and dancing and playing games."

As my sisters reminisce about their glory days, I think back to a similar conversation that happened at my mom's book club when I first came into town. When they had bemoaned the loss of community events for young people. That's why Donna Shipley and the RNN were so determined to get a community center up and running. Because they wanted to turn things around in Roanoke.

Suddenly, something clicks in my mind. All this time, I've been pushing for the wrong thing: trying to convince the town to care about preserving a past that they are clearly ready to let go of. All the while, I closed my ears to what the town has been saying they actually need and want: to build a better future based on the needs of the rising generation.

Sky's words come back to me, about learning when to let go of things from the past that no longer serve us.

Then Donna Shipley's words: "We don't need a historic house museum. What we need is a place where the community can come together for activities."

What was it that lady with the rooster and the pockets full of piglets said today? *Gotta know when it's time to let old things go so we can have our hands free to receive something better.*

I've been so caught up in my vision for what I thought needed to happen that I've completely missed what's been right in front of me all along.

An idea strikes me like lightning. I shoot up to sitting, nearly yanking my hair from Tara's hands mid-braid. The sudden movement startles Char, who barks and runs to the window to see what's going on.

"The pool house," I gasp.

It's quiet for a beat as my mom and sisters recover from my jolt. "What house?" Tara asks.

"The pool house," I repeat, more to myself than to her as I calculate. "Bea said she moved into the pool house after she opened the Morley Mansion for public events. But why would there be a pool house unless there was a..."

We want a pool, Donna Shipley had said.

I'm on my feet in an instant and running for the door. "Mom, may I borrow your car?"

Bea doesn't look surprised to see me on her porch. I realize with a twinge of guilt that she must assume that Sky and I have been working at the Morley Mansion all day. I don't tell her that Sky's given up. Instead, I get straight to the point. "Bea, why did you call this the pool house?"

"Because that's what it is."

"Do you mean there's a pool on this property?"

"Used to be. We had it filled in years ago to make a bigger lawn for events. The pool was too expensive to maintain, and my brother didn't want to deal with the liability if someone drowned in it."

"It's filled in, but is it still…there?"

"You mean the cast? Yeah, it's under the ground somewhere." She waves her arm vaguely to the side of the pool house. "I was sad to lose it. Had a lot of good childhood memories swimming in it. But we had a lotta weddings and things on that lawn, so it was the safer way to make money with the space."

I'm already pulling out my phone to run some calculations. "Bea, I think I know a way we can save your house and get you a better offer than the cash-for-keys the bank made you. Do you know how much equity you still own in the house?"

"At least half," she says. "Why? You think you can get the bank to pay me all that?"

"Better." I shoot off a text message to Donna Shipley to see if she's available for a chat before smiling at Bea. "I think you can sell it."

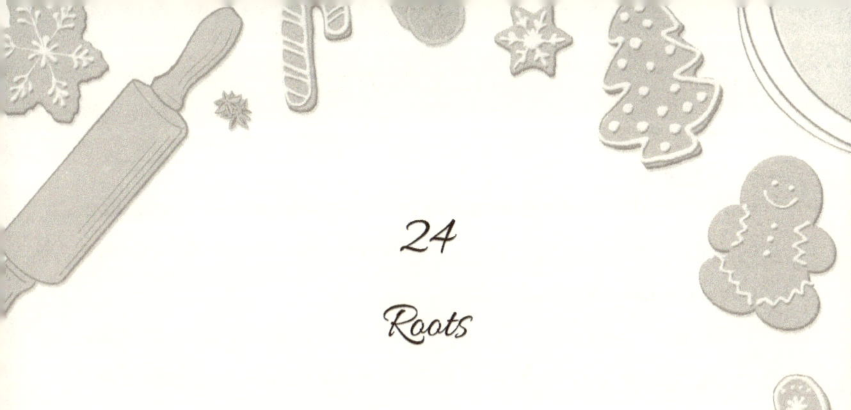

24

Roots

T HAT NIGHT, I SIT on my old bedroom floor surrounded by photographs from a box Bea kept under her bed. She let me borrow it for the night, just in case I might find something helpful in it. And, boy, have I ever! The photographs range from dusty sepia tintypes of men and women in Victorian-era garb standing in front of the Morley Mansion to black-and-white wedding photos in the 1930s to 1950s, from soft pastel polaroids at the swimming pool that's now underground to earthy russet photos of boys with long flipped-out hair and girls in bell-bottoms on the porch steps, from girls with blown out curls and blue eyeshadow posing with their dates at the winter Snow Ball to blurry glossy pictures from disposable cameras in the 1990s of lively Bar Mitzvahs, glamorous Quinceañeras, and sweaty Sweet Sixteens.

It's a stunning tribute to the people of Roanoke through the decades and to the sense of community that has long found a home on the Morley Mansion property. The most surprising part is that not all the faces spread around me are strangers. Several of the faces I associate with Roanoke's aging generation make multiple appearances as their younger selves in this collection, with notes of appreciation scribbled on the back of the photographs in handwriting that various as widely in style and neatness as do the faces of the people pictured.

I recognize a young Donna Shipley in one, with frizzy hair and a burrito-sized corsage pinned to her prairie-style formal dress, standing beside a gawky boy who looks suspiciously like my old AP History teacher at Roanoke High School.

There's a polaroid of a young redheaded girl with deep dimples sitting with her feet in the pool and squinting against the splash of her brother doing a cannonball. That has to be Bea and her brother.

But it's the slightly more recent pictures that tug at me in a way I can't describe. There's a glossy Kodak print from Andrea Rodriguez's Quinceañera, where I can barely make myself out in the blurry background with raccoon eyes from mascara mingled with sweat. The sight is startling. I vaguely remember attending that party in the Morley Mansion ballroom, but I've never seen this picture. And yet, this record of my having been there has existed all these years, stored in a box of other people's distant memories under Bea Carston's bed. I am one of many fluttering leaves on this tree whose branches are about to be cut, whose roots grow deep into Roanoke's soil.

With this imagery in my head, I set the picture on the floor with the others and reach for my laptop. I close my eyes before opening it.

Deep breath in.

Slow, calming exhale.

I visualize putting everything else into boxes in my mind and shelving them: *Verité*, Benson, Sky, ticket sales. They all have a place for later. Now it's just me and these photographs and Roanoke's future.

Maybe no one will care what I have to say. Maybe no one will ever read it. Or maybe they will, and they'll mock me for it, but I don't care. I have to get these words out before I burst.

It's time to write that article for the RNN newsletter that Matilda Hatch asked me to write weeks ago.

Donna Shipley meets me in the driveway of the Morley Mansion. As we walk inside together, the entryway glows with images projected on the wall from Luke's new high-tech projector—a slideshow of Roanoke's residents throughout the years, laughing, crying, smiling, growing. I have practiced my pitch again and again, and I give it with all the conviction I possess.

"In 1890, Friedrich and Pricilla Morley immigrated from England and built this house with the express purpose of it being a gathering place where their friends and family could come stay when they immigrated or came for visits. They had a reputation for hosting lavish parties, and Pricilla insisted on having a grand ballroom that took up most of the main floor. It was Friedrich's idea to build the hallways five percent wider than was common for the era to allow for better viewing of the intricate woodwork and portraits hung in the hallways." I stop at a cabinet beside the kitchen and open it to reveal a dumbwaiter. "The dumbwaiter has been out of commission since the 1940s, but Bea Carston remembers using it as a hiding place and to deliver secret messages with her brother when they were children. As you can see, the well is spacious enough to install an elevator, which would make every floor of the three-story house ADA accessible once a ramp is installed along the front porch."

We make our way carefully up the stairs, and I show Donna the schoolroom where the Morley children were tutored at home for generations, complete with a chalkboard along one wall, a countertop, and cabinets, an antique globe, and several kinds of microscopes. There's a balcony off this room where the Morley children used to observe the night sky through their telescope. I leave Donna's imagination to fill her mind with all the ideas of ways this room could be used in a community center.

"The bedrooms are nothing special," I say as we walk down the halls, barely glancing through a few open doors at the old beds and furniture within. No one has slept in these rooms for at least two decades, though Bea said there was a time when she used to allow guests to stay in them whenever the venue was booked for a wedding. The master bedroom on the first floor was even converted into a bridal suite. Donna won't care about any of that, so I get to the point I think will interest her most: "But there are fifteen of them in all, which makes for twenty separate indoor spaces—when you count the kitchen, the ballroom, the library, the schoolroom, and the parlor—that could be utilized for various types of gatherings."

"But no toilets on the upper floors," Donna says.

"Actually, there are two bathrooms on the second floor and another on the third. In the 1960s, Felicia and Jameson Carston had plumbing connected to the upstairs and installed toilets and a single-sink vanity in each." I push open the door behind me to reveal a tiny, quirky little bathroom of awkward dimensions with a toilet the color of split-pea soup and retro floor tiles. It's the one spot in the house where a Morley descendant really showed their era rather than keeping with the otherwise Victorian aesthetic, but the clawfoot tub looks original. "They're not much to look at," I confess, "but they're working toilets."

A corner of Donna's mouth twitches at the sight. But she keeps her thoughts to herself.

It makes me nervous that she hasn't spoken a word, other than her one question. But then, maybe her speechlessness is a good sign. Pushing away the feelings of self-doubt that threaten to crowd my mind, I keep talking as I lead the way back down to the main level. "Skylar and Doug Townsend estimate that the main bathroom could comfortably hold up to five or six stalls, depending on how many handicapped stalls are desired."

I try not to hold my breath as I catch Donna taking in the pictures projected along the wall. "Where did you find these?" she asks.

"Bea Carston has quite the archive."

Last, I take us through the ballroom to the covered terrace out back, where we have a view of the Morley property. Before us stretches a vast, overgrown lawn sloping down to Bea's current home in the old pool house. Beyond that, the property is ringed with tall pine trees and deep green ferns. I point toward Bea's place. "In the 1950s, Felicia Morley's father, Porter Morley, had a swimming pool installed during the post-war economic boom, shortly before Felicia and Jameson inherited the house upon his death." I pull the photo of young Bea and her brother by the pool from a manila folder I've been hugging to my chest and hand it to Donna. "Bea and Thomas used to spend their summers in the pool house when Felicia and Jameson began renting out the main house for public events. By the 1970s, the family fortune had dwindled to nothing, and renting out the house became necessary for keeping up with the expense of maintaining the property. By the mid-seventies, Bea and her brother agreed to have the pool filled in to make way for a larger lawn area that could support outdoor activities. The pool is still out there, just filled in with dirt and sodded over."

Donna raises her eyebrows at this information. "Huh," she says thoughtfully. She looks between the polaroid in her hand and the stretch of tall grass around Bea's home.

This is as far as I got in my planned presentation. I was hoping she might have something to say by now so I wouldn't have to close the sale, but no such luck. I take a deep breath.

"I wrote the article Matilda Hatch asked for, to go in next month's newsletter. I sent the first draft to you and Matilda this morning. I don't know if you've seen it yet…"

She shakes her head no without looking away from the photograph in her hand.

I forge on. "You asked me to write about the need for a community center in Roanoke. What I've found is that we already have one. It's here, right under our feet. This property isn't just a museum to the wealthiest family in Roanoke's history; it's a well-worn path traveled by all of Roanoke's residents over the past century. Here, memories were made. Here, we've held our weddings and funerals, our summer picnics and winter festivals. Here, we experienced our first heartbreaks, first kisses, final goodbyes, passed from childhood to adulthood, and welded families together through marriage vows. The Morley Mansion has been the central meeting place of our community for as long as we can remember. Maybe it's time to officially make it our community center."

During my monologue, Donna Shipley's eyes come up to my face. She stares at me now for what feels like an eternity, the weight of my words suspended in the air between us as if someone has pressed Pause on this moment, and I dare not move, barely breathe.

Finally, her chin juts forward. Her eyes scan the property again, releasing me from my frozen state, and she says, "Huh."

That's it? I wait on bated breath for her to say more. This is the trick to closing a sale: whoever speaks first loses.

"Impressive," she finally admits. "You've certainly done your research. I forgot there used to be a pool back here."

I wait for the "but" that must be coming.

Donna returns the polaroid to me. "I'll think about it. And I'll need to talk to the board, of course. But you've given me a lot to consider.

The article you wrote, it says all of this? About the Morley Mansion being the center of our community?"

"Not...in those exact words." Will she be angry that I didn't drop the house completely after her last warning?

"Shame," she says, taking me by surprise. "That was a good line. Very effective. Even so, it doesn't change the fact that Bea Carston owns this property, and we want to own our community center outright, to avoid the complications of dealing with a landowner."

"Bea Carston is looking to sell," I blurt. "As quickly as possible. Like you said, she realized she can't keep up with the place, and she has no heirs to pass it down to. For her, the community is like her posterity. The closest thing she ever had to being a mother was watching the kids of Roanoke grow from one event in this house to the next. Selling to the community would be her first choice. Which is why she asked me to speak to you on her behalf."

Donna takes this in with furrowed brows. Once more, she merely says, "Huh," before turning on her heel and heading back the way we came.

I follow her back through the house and out the front door.

"I'll talk to the board," she says once we reach the front porch. "And we'll review your article. I can't make you any promises, but I do appreciate the efforts you've gone through to ensure we leave no stone unturned in our search." Her eyes flit to the dirt path leading to Bea's home. "Do you know if Bea is in?"

"Yes. She said she'll be expecting you if you'd like to talk to her directly."

Donna nods. "I would, thank you. Did you want to join us?"

I shake my head. "No. Thank you for the invitation, but there's someone else I need to speak with before it gets too late."

The whole way over to Sky's house, I run through what I want to say. I've practiced a dozen times, but unlike my pitch for Donna, it comes out differently every time. Disjointed. Desperate.

I know there's no chance of ever restoring myself to Rosie the Riveter status in his eyes, but this isn't about me, or about what he thinks of me. I owe Sky an apology.

When I park against the curb, my stomach feels heavy.

I wish I could unsay what I said about him abandoning his dad. It was a low blow, especially because he'd already expressed remorse for that to me in a moment of trusting vulnerability. Maybe it's too much to hope that he'll forgive me, or that we can go back to being friends the way we were before, but he didn't deserve what I said to him, and I can't leave Roanoke without telling him so.

Sitting in my mom's car, I squeeze the steering wheel as I try to muster the courage to get out. What if Sky doesn't want to see me? What if he doesn't want to hear what I have to say? What if he thinks I'm only here because I need something from him? Maybe I should just leave him in peace...

I shake the thoughts away, reach for the printed copy of my newsletter article on the passenger seat, and throw open the car door before another thought can crowd my resolve.

On the porch, I take a deep breath before knocking.

No one answers.

Just as I raise my hand to knock again, the rumble of a truck makes me turn around in time to see Sky pull into the driveway. Our eyes meet through the windshield. I cross one arm over my chest and hold my elbow awkwardly as I wait for him.

There's a glare on the windshield when Sky parks, so I can't see his face. Is he annoyed at seeing me here? My heart feels like it's in my throat when he opens the door and steps out.

It's the first time I've seen him since our fight two days ago. He's wearing a red flannel work shirt, with the beginnings of a beard darkening the lower half of his face.

"Hi, AJ," he says. There's a heaviness in his voice I can't decipher.

"Hi, Sky." My voice sounds weak.

For a moment, we just stand there. Then Sky closes the truck door and makes his way up the porch steps, passing me as he finds the house key on his keychain. "Want to come in?" he asks without looking at me. "I think we've got some cold pizza."

I shake my head. "No, I don't want to bother you, I just... Sky, I'm so sorry."

He unlocks the front door and holds it open for me. "Come in, AJ. It's freezing out here."

I hesitate before stepping inside, careful not to brush against him as I squeeze past his chest.

The house is fully decorated now. I don't know what it looked like back when Kate used to do it, but Sky and his dad have done her proud. There's a garland wrapped around the stair railing with twinkling lights, and a rustic wood-carved nativity set on the table in the entryway. In the corner of the living room, the tree's lights are off, but it's loaded with ornaments.

"It looks great in here," I say softly.

Sky goes to plug in the tree lights. "Thanks. Yeah, we...found our own place for things. Got rid of some stuff... I think my mom would be okay with it." He sticks his hands in his pockets, looking around the room instead of at me.

"I think she'd be proud of you."

He shrugs. "Hope so." Then his eyes make their way to my face. I can see he's looking for the right thing to say, but that's not his responsibility right now. It's mine.

"Sky, what I said the other night—"

"You don't need to—"

I hold up a hand to stop him. "Please, let me apologize."

He waits.

I take a deep breath. "It was so stupid, what I said to you. I was hurt, and I lashed out like a child. You didn't deserve it. The truth is, I think you're the best man I've ever met."

He cringes and shakes his head. "AJ—"

"It's true! Watching you rush to rescue people who were stuck in the snow, and the way you worked all those long days for free to help a cause you believed in, never once seeking any recognition. You are the most selfless person I've ever met. You give without asking anything in return, and it seems to energize you!" I'm talking too fast, but I can see that he wants to interrupt me, and I need to get this out before I lose my momentum. "You were right about me, Sky. I've been selfish. Thoughtless. I've been making everything about me instead of making it about the things I care about. The people I care about."

Sky holds up his hands to stop me. "AJ, please. Slow down a sec. Can we just...sit?"

My heart is pounding as if I've just run a race, the sound of it filling my ears as I watch Sky move to the sofa.

He sinks onto one side and pats the cushion beside him.

Hesitantly, I sit.

Sky rubs the stubble on his jaw with his hand as he hisses out a sigh. "You don't have to do this. There's nothing you said that I didn't deserve. Frankly, it was what I needed to hear. I've got an annoying habit of thinking I know best. Making myself a saint, as you put it.

I did it to you that first night you were home, after Norma's, and I was confused when you called me out on it, but after the other day...I think I get it."

"No, Sky, no..." I groan, running my hands down my temples before angling to face him. "I shouldn't have snapped at you that time, either. You were just trying to be a supportive friend, and I nearly bit your head off. I was fresh out of a breakup, and I didn't realize how sensitive I still was until I lashed out."

"I was being a know-it-all."

This is not going the way I planned at all. My hands flap at the air in front of me, as if they could somehow rewind time and start this whole conversation over. "No, that's not—this isn't about that. Sky..." I sigh, trying to think where to begin.

Sky purses his lips, waiting.

"Ever since I got hired at *Verité*, I've been struggling to write. At first, I told myself it was just because I was nervous, but really I think it was more than that—something that's been a long time coming. My confidence was fragile, and when my boyfriend broke up with me last month, it shattered. I thought if I could surround myself with people who believed in me, it would make me believe in myself. So, I quit my job early and came home to be with my family... only, it didn't work. It was like, the more people believed in me, the less I believed in myself. So then, I thought that if I could just do something well enough, then maybe I'd be able to get over my writer's block."

The way Sky is watching me, as if trying to read in my face whatever I'm not saying, makes me nervous. I grip the article I brought in from the car. "You asked me once if you could read something of mine. At the time, I was afraid I might never be able to write again, but..." What? Then I had a breakthrough and thought all was well, and then the writer's block came back with a vengeance, but now it's all better? He doesn't need to hear it. *Get to the point!* "I wrote this article. It's for the RNN's January newsletter, but I wanted to give you a copy, because I couldn't have written it without you." I hold out the paper for him.

He looks at it but doesn't move. "Will you read it to me?"

The anxious turning in my gut flares. I pull the paper back to myself and swallow as I scan the text. He doesn't need to hear all of this. "This is just a part," I say. "It's about the town..."

Clearing my throat, I begin: "The strongest trees don't uproot themselves to grow taller; they build upon what came before. Our community has grown from people who asked not what they could get out of it but what they could contribute to it. In the last two weeks, I've watched neighbors selflessly offer their time, talents, and substance to help a fellow member of the community. The Gingerbread Festival was Roanoke at its best. There, we saw the Roanoke spirit of teamwork and creativity in action, from Bea Carston providing the venue to the Rodriguez and Townsend families offering their construction expertise to make it work, from Peggy Malan's famous cooking to Reagan Keys's brilliant activities organization, and all the donated skills and talents in between. I saw an event thrown together in under a week on a shoestring budget that would rival any holiday party in New York City. People may come and go, like leaves that fall and leaves that grow, but the tree remains. Its roots ground our community in the values that have shaped us. Like you, I am one of the leaves on this wonderful tree. I've been shaped by you."

When I finish, I force myself to look at Sky. "You were right the other night. About so many things. I was being selfish. I wanted to prove that I could do it, that I could start a movement with my writing and put together a successful event. But I didn't think about how others might get hurt along the way. After what you said, I did some soul searching, and I realized it wasn't getting others to believe in me that helped me to start writing again. It was writing for a cause I believed in. I don't think I would have realized that without you."

My hands are trembling now. I set the article down on the couch beside me to stop the paper from shaking as I meet Sky's eyes. "I care about you, Sky. And I hurt you. I could never forgive myself if I didn't tell you how sorry I am—"

He takes my hand earnestly and holds it against his chest. "No, AJ, I was wrong. I'm the one who's sorry." His thumb strokes my knuckles, sending a buzz up my arm. "You were trying to do a good thing, using your vacation time to help someone in need. I feel so ashamed."

"You have nothing to be ashamed of."

"I was being an idiot. When I got home that night..." he releases my hand to wave his arm around the living room. "I saw all of this—all the decorations that haven't come out since before my mom died... Gosh, I felt like the biggest jerk. None of this would have happened without you." He rakes a hand through his hair. "I should have reached out to you that night when I realized, but I was embarrassed. I'm still embarrassed." He can't bring himself to look at me when he says it, his knuckles white from how hard he's gripping his knees.

"Why are you embarrassed? All you did was call me out on my crap, and it needed to be said."

He hesitates. "That you took something constructive away from that conversation says a lot more about you than it does about me. I was jealous, I acted in a petty way." He huffs a laugh and pinches his temples with a mirthful grimace. "I threw down my mask like a bratty little kid and stormed off, all butt-hurt."

I can't help the laugh that escapes me, but I shake my head. "That's not how I saw it."

"The image is burned into my brain."

Even though he's trying to slip into the humor that comforts him, his words reignite the flame of guilt I felt in my gut on the night of the Gingerbread Festival. "This was never about Benson. You know that, don't you? I would have said yes to you if you'd asked."

Sky is silent for a moment, rubbing the back of his neck. Finally, he takes my hand. "I know."

A pleasant tingle runs up my arm at his touch. Feeling emboldened, I admit softly, "You're the one I wanted to go with."

His thumb strokes my palm, and for just a moment, I melt. Why have we been fighting this? It feels so natural to be close to him, to hold hands and laugh about our foibles and be vulnerable. I'm on the brink of surrender when Sky forces a smile.

"I should thank you for calling me out at the mansion."

I grimace. "No, don't remind me what I said. I was being reactionary. I didn't mean it."

"No, you were completely right. I've been using good deeds as an excuse to hide from my responsibilities. I knew it was true, but I needed someone to say it. I can't keep running from life under the pretense of being a good Samaritan. After what you said, I did some serious soul-searching, too." He looks at our joined hands, squeezes mine as he braces himself, then releases with an exhale. "Long story short, I applied for winter semester at Oregon State University." His eyes dance with nervous excitement. "I'm going to finish my degree."

I choke out a gasp, then recover quickly and throw my arms around him. "Sky, that's wonderful!"

"Thanks," he grunts as he catches me and holds me tight, laughing. "It's about time."

I sink into his embrace, breathing in the familiar scent of him. Being in his arms feels like coming home. The piece I feared I'd lost again settles back into place.

"I don't think I would have found the courage to do it without you," he murmurs into my hair.

His heartbeat quickens against my cheek.

A thrill rises from my belly. It sweeps through my chest, then catches in my ribs, flapping uselessly, painfully, like a bird against the bars of a cage. Because there is nowhere for these feelings to go. There is no sunset for me and Sky to ride off into together. We're on different paths.

"You would have found your way here eventually," say. "I'm so happy for you, Sky."

Sky's arms slacken.

When we pull apart, I resist the urge to track my cheek along his, to find his lips and lose myself in them.

Sky takes my hand, and we both sit back against the couch.

For a few moments, we take in the glow of the Christmas tree, lost in our thoughts.

"I like you, AJ," Sky says.

"But I'm leaving," I finish for him. "I know."

He looks down at our joined hands, weaves his fingers through mine. "If things were different…"

"Yeah." I squeeze his hand.

He squeezes back. "I'm glad you came home for Christmas. I'm glad we got to spend this time together."

"Even though I roped you into a crazy scheme to make myself look good?"

He chuckles. "Especially because you roped me into your crazy schemes! I wouldn't change a thing."

I melt into the couch, resting my cheek on the cushion as I meet the sincerity in Sky's eyes. "Me neither."

"Stupid fights and all."

I grin. "Stupid fights and all."

He raises our joined hands and plants a swift kiss against my knuckles before withdrawing his.

This is right, I tell myself. *This is the way it's meant to be.* But I can't help the ache that forms in my chest.

A teasing smile plays at the corners of Sky's mouth. "Do you really think I'm a 'perfect, perfect dreamboat'?"

I choke on a laugh. "Dream *person*! I said dream person." I can feel the heat in my face and wonder if he can see it. "But yeah. You are irritatingly good at everything you touch. Good with people, good at building things, and you can pipe royal icing like Mary freaking Berry. I mean, seriously? Mess up every once in a while, will you? You're making the rest of us look bad."

Our arms brush, but neither of us pulls away. He leans into it, then I do. We sit like that, shoulders pressed together, looking at the Christmas tree.

After a moment, he asks, "Who's Mary freaking Berry?"

That's right. He spent the last five years living in a mud hut. "Next time I'm in town, remind me to introduce you to *The Great British Bake Off*."

The part that hangs between us are my words "next time I'm in town." I meant for them to sound hopeful: a promise that we would see each other again and pick up our friendship as it is now without missing a beat. But what fills the silence are the words implied but unspoken: *I'm leaving in a few days. We will have to part, and there's no guarantee that we will ever find this with each other again.* How long before I make it out here again? And when I do, will Sky still be around, or will he have moved on?

Sky clears his throat. "So, are you ready to start with *Verité*?"

I exhale through puffed cheeks. "I think so. I catch a red-eye on the first, and then I'll have about twenty hours to get settled back into my apartment before my first day of work."

"Woof. That's tight. Doesn't that stress you out?"

"Normally it would, but I've gotten used to operating on a tight schedule over the last few weeks." We share a knowing smirk. "In fact, I think it'll be a good thing. I can keep up the momentum I started here and just carry it straight into work without having too much time to fret and overthink things."

"Ooo, look out, Verité! AJ Banner's coming in hot. They won't even know what hit 'em."

"Like a wrecking ball."

"Like a shooting star. They'll wonder how they ever got along without you."

"Aww," I nudge him playfully with my shoulder.

"You've still got a few days to go," Sky points out. "How are you going to keep up your momentum from now until then?"

A mischievous smile threatens to split my face in two. I bite it back. "Well, actually..."

"Uh-oh." Sky sits up straight. "I know that look. What are you hatching, AJ Banner?"

I sit up too, mirroring him. "Ok, hear me out. I know you said we should respect Bea's decision. And yes, I know she's a person, not a goat. But I think I found a way to leave her better off than just taking the cash-for-keys offer from the bank."

I quickly fill him in on the alternative plan I came up with to help Bea.

Sky looks skeptical. "It sounds nice, but there's no way she'll find a buyer in time. January is three days away."

I suck in a breath, trying not to sound too hopeful when I say, "I already have a potential buyer. They haven't made any promises. And maybe it will amount to nothing. But as long as there's a chance…"

"We should try." He isn't just completing my sentence. He's telling me he's back in.

"Really?"

"Of course! We've gotten this far, haven't we?" He checks his watch, then leaps to his feet. "We'd better get going!"

"Going where?"

"The Morley Mansion! We've missed two whole days of work." He holds out a hand to me. "We're going to have to kick it into high gear to get that place ready for your dance on Friday."

With a smile, I take his hand and let him hoist me to my feet.

25

Three Days

THE SMELLS OF PLASTER and lumber greet us like old friends as Sky and I slip past the plastic wall that divides the rest of the house from the construction zone. White dust coats everything like a thin layer of snow. We leave footprints in it as we make our way to the bathroom.

"Still need to finish sanding before we can prime the walls and paint them," Sky notes. "That'll take a day, because of the dry time."

I pull out my phone and start thumbing down notes for our revised renovation plan. "Okay, a day for sanding and painting."

"If we had more people, we could have one team tackle the interior while the other team handles the exterior. We still need to do the siding and painting on the new exterior walls."

"Does that have to be done for the house to pass inspection?"

He weighs his answer with a side-to-side tilt of his head. "Technically, no. But without siding, the walls are more susceptible to water damage, and if the inspector finds any active mold or water leaks, the house will fail."

"How long would that take to do ourselves?"

He rubs the back of his neck. "Maybe a day or two, if we're fast..."

We have three days. Three days to finish everything the house needs to pass inspection. And there are only the two of us now. "Why don't we start by figuring out what all needs to be done, and then we can figure out what's absolutely necessary, and then what's possible."

As if he's been waiting for this permission from me, Sky begins rattling off tasks without another moment's hesitation. "Exterior siding and paint. Prime and paint walls. Sand and stain the floors. If we use a quick-drying polyurethane, it can cut down on dry time. Install tile floors in the bathroom. Replace all electrical fixtures and outlet covers. Install baseboards and trim... That's everything."

Looking at the list on my phone, it seems so doable. But if I've learned anything in the last two weeks about construction, it's that every task takes at least twice as long as I imagine it will. And that's without running into unforeseen setbacks. We haven't even purchased tile flooring to install in the bathroom yet. "We don't have the budget for bathroom flooring. Is that going to make us fail inspection?" When Sky shakes his head no, I cross that item off the list. One task fewer to worry about.

Sky starts tallying items on his fingers. "Things that *must* be done for the house to pass inspection: structural integrity, no active mold or leaks, functioning toilet and sink, functioning electrical and plumbing... I think that's it. We've already taken care of most of those things, which is why I think we should prioritize fixing the siding with what little time we have left so we don't run the risk of new water damage."

From there, Sky calculates how long it would take for the two of us to complete each item on our own. I really hoped we could at least have the floors sanded and stained in time for the dance so people could walk to the bathroom on nice restored wood floors. But Sky is more concerned about protecting the exterior with siding.

"Let's just do the siding," I say. "We've only sold a dozen dance tickets, anyway. It'll be a small party, if it happens at all." It's going to take both of us working nonstop on the house to finish on time, so

I won't have time to plan a fancy dance. Maybe just some music and a few boxes of Costco treats is all I can expect to pull off for that. It won't be the big bang I'd hoped to go out on before starting my next adventure, but at least it will be done.

We spend the rest of the afternoon outside in the cold, Sky showing me how to put the siding on. We laugh and grunt and work up a sweat. I feel strong and capable when I place my first panel on my own with some satisfying *puff-thumps* from the power nail gun. Working side by side with Sky, it feels like we can build anything together. By the time it gets too dark to see what we're doing, and Sky says we'll have to finish tomorrow, I'm not even worried about finishing in time for the inspection.

Maybe the house won't pass. Maybe the RNN won't buy the house. Maybe the New Year's Ball will be a hot mess. But standing there with Sky, breathing heavily and looking at what we've done together, I feel complete.

The next morning, when Tiffany drops me off at the house, the sight of three trucks out front makes my heart stop. Has the demolition crew returned?

"Not this again," I groan.

"What is it?" Tiffany asks.

"They said they'd give us until the first of January!" Without further explanation, I throw of my seat belt and fly up the porch steps. This time, there is no foreman standing around with a clipboard. I follow the sound of men's voices into the house and find Sky laughing with his dad and a handful of other men I've never seen before.

When Sky's eyes fall on me and I see the brightness sparkling in them, in his smile, I relax. Surely, he wouldn't look so happy if this was the demolition crew from before.

"You ordered a Christmas miracle," he says, "and Santa delivered!"

"What's going on?"

Doug Townsend, in his soft-spoken way, introduces the men standing around me. "AJ, I'd like you to meet some buddies of mine: Pete, Jason, Chad, and Joe."

The one called Jason is the first to come and shake my hand. "Hey, little miss, we can't thank you enough for getting this old bear to crawl out of his cave."

"You did what we couldn't," another agrees. Maybe Pete.

"Dad called in a favor," Sky explains, stepping to my side as the men laugh over some inside joke. "Some of these guys came from as far away as Eugene to answer his call."

"I owe him," says one of the guys, a big man with an impressive mustache and a lazy eye. "Was starting to think he was never gonna call in a favor, and I'd be in his debt till I died."

"They're going to help with the finish work for the next three days," says Sky.

Someone comes in behind me, and I don't even have to turn around to know it's Tiffany. She would have parked and then followed me in to find out what's going on. "Does this mean I don't have to plan the ball by myself anymore?" she asks.

I hesitate to answer her. I'm still processing this new information.

Sky smiles encouragingly at me. "We've got this covered. Do whatever you need to do for the ball."

"Are you sure?" I ask.

"Not that you aren't helpful," Sky says quickly.

I stop him before he can put his foot in his mouth. "Say no more. I know where my skills will be put to better use."

Sky puts on his game face. "Get us that money, AJ."

"I'm on it!"

I grab Tiffany by the hand and pull her out of the house with me. We might only have ten guests, but we're going to make this a party that none of them will forget.

The Roanoke Neighborhood Network's storage unit is near the high school. We spook a group of teens who jumped the fence into the facility to catch Pokémon on their phones when we open the gate with the code Donna gave me. As the kids scramble to leave through the open gate like raccoons caught in the trash bin the night before garbage pickup, Tiffany half jokes, "Maybe you should include on the ball invitations that there are some rare Pokémon hiding out at the Morley Mansion."

"That wouldn't sell tickets. It would just encourage party crashers."

She grins. "Exactly."

When I lift the garage door to the storage unit, a cloud of dust kicks up, and Tiffany and I have to wave our hands in front of our faces to see what we're working with. Donna gave me the code for this unit so I could use whatever decor I wanted for the Gingerbread Festival. But since so many people came out of the woodwork to help decorate that event, I never bothered to see what was in here. Now I pray there will be enough in here to cover all our decorating needs for the New Year's Ball.

Tiffany coughs. "Yeesh, if this isn't a sign that Roanoke is overdue for some community events, I don't know what is. How long has it been since anyone opened this thing?"

It can't have been that long, I think when I spy the stage boxes we used at the Gingerbread Festival stacked at the front of the dusty heap. Matilda Hatch brought those.

We split up. Tiffany takes the left side and I take the right as we rummage through decades' worth of craft supplies, decorations, and dusty equipment. There are boxes of costumes from community theater stints that came and went, and stacks of choir music from all the times Christy's mom attempted to start a community choir over my lifetime. I trip over the cord to an old dinosaur of a projector, and an idea buds. "Hey, Tiff, do you think this thing would fit in your car?"

My sister's head appears over the top of a mound of cauldrons and broomsticks from bygone Witchfests. She snorts. "Why bother? Luke can probably hook you up with his phone projector."

A sparkle catches my eye behind Tiffany and I squint. "Oooh, I think that's it!" I make my way past her and, sure enough, here in the far left corner are stashed all the sparkly, dangling snowflakes and fake trees and boxes of twinkle lights and sheer white curtains I remember from my first ever Snow Ball.

Tiffany pries open a plastic bin of silver and gold ornaments. "Jackpot."

"How much do you think will fit in your car? Maybe I should have asked to borrow Skylar's truck."

"We can make a few trips if we need to." Tiffany picks up the bin by its handles and starts waddling back to her minivan.

With all the seats down in back, we manage to fit almost everything except for the Christmas trees.

On our way back to the Morley Mansion, I get a call from Peggy Malan.

"AJ, hon, do you need any help with food for the ball?"

Last I checked, Peggy and her family hadn't bought tickets to the ball. "Oh, are you planning on coming?"

"Of course! We wouldn't miss it. Are you having it catered?"

She knows that's not in my budget. "So far, I've got a box of Costco muffins and a few bottles of sparkling apple cider—"

"Oh, bless your heart. I'll take it from here, cute girl. You just do whatever you need to do to get everything else ready."

"I don't have much of a budget for food—"

"Don't worry about that."

"As in, I have no budget."

"AJ, hon, I've got it. You don't have to do this all by yourself. Some of us want to play the generous saint every now and then, too."

"Peggy, you're a lifesaver!"

"Don't I know it?" She laughs and hangs up without a goodbye, already calling out orders to her kids in full-on pastry chef mode.

I shake my head in wonder as I put my phone away.

"What was that about?" Tiffany asks.

"Peggy Malan just insisted on providing food for the ball."

"God bless that pastry goddess!"

When we get back to the Morley Mansion, it looks like a Banner family reunion in the front yard. The grandkids run up to surround Tiffany's car like puppies crowding their mother. My mom and Tara try to organize them into some kind of useful workforce as my dad, Luke, and Brett and Mike begin unloading the heaviest boxes.

I shake my mom by her shoulders. "I thought you were all going to see the zoo lights!"

She waves me off. "Those don't come on until four o'clock. We'll get there in time if we leave by three."

She makes it sound like no big deal, but that drive into Portland from Roanoke is no joke with cars full of kids who are hopped up on Christmas candy. I know the original plan was to spend the whole day at the zoo to make it worth the drive.

With Doug Townsend and his construction buddies hard at work on the stairs and the whole east corner of the house, and my family moving in boxes of decor, the Morley Mansion feels like a busy beehive when I enter to start setting up.

Once their car is emptied, Tiffany and her husband head back to the storage unit for the trees, while my mom, Tara, and I get to work on the ballroom. My dad figures out how to string the lights along the walls the way I remember it from my first Snow Ball, with the lights running vertically from ceiling to floor all the way around the room. Tara and my mom follow behind him to hang the sheer curtains, creating that romantic soft glow effect. My brother and Tara's husband help the kids hang sparkling snowflakes from the ceiling, and I unload the rest of the boxes to take inventory of what else we have to work with.

There are more tablecloths than we'll have tables for, and sil-ver-and-white sashes to go on chair backs. As I lift an armful of folded tablecloths from one box to see if there are any table runners, I feel the shape of something heavy and angular beneath the fabric. I kneel. It isn't a stack of tablecloths, after all, but a single cloth wrapped around a dark box that resembles an old VCR. As I turn the thing over in my hands, little white flakes fall into my lap.

It can't be…

Leaping to my feet, I run the contraption over to the construction zone and find Sky operating a large floor sander with a face mask on and dust filling the air. I consider waving to get his attention but decide against it. We're all racing against the clock now. Hopefully later I'll get a chance to show him what I think must be the snow machine he made as a teenager.

By two o'clock, the ballroom is mostly decorated. All that remains is hanging the ornaments on the trees that stand in every corner of the room and setting up some kind of entry display. I still have the trailer of rental chairs and tables from the Gingerbread Festival parked out back, but I'm not sure how many to set up. Since Peggy bought her tickets late, I wonder if anyone else might have had the same idea. I'm about to check the ticket sale on my phone when an entire wall of lights goes out.

"Oops." My dad's voice echoes from the other side of the ballroom. He unplugs the strand of lights in his hand and the rest of the lights come back on. Dad catches my eye and holds up the bad string of lights for me to see. "We're one set of three hundred short."

Since he and the rest of my family have to go then so they can make it to the zoo lights on time, Mom leaves me her car so I can run into town and pick up another box of lights.

While I'm at the Ace Hardware on Main Street, I notice how busy it looks across the way at Buttons and Beaus Consignment Boutique. Then I get a text message from Peggy asking for a head count so she knows how much food to prepare.

With a box of three hundred Christmas lights propped under my arm, I check my ticket sales and stare at the phone screen without comprehending for a moment. I refresh the page to make sure there isn't some glitch. But, no, there it is: 105 tickets sold. As I watch, the number updates to 108.

"What on earth...?"

There must be some mistake. Panic grips me for a moment at the thought that maybe the program I used to sell tickets is doing that thing where the page freezes on the last step of someone buying a ticket. What if some poor soul keeps refreshing the page without realizing that every time they do, they're purchasing another ticket?

With my heart in my throat, I sink to sit on a wrought iron bench in the garden section of the store and open the guest list to see if one person's name appears more than once. I'm fully prepared to see Peggy Malan's name filling the page. Instead, the reality is even more staggering: 108 individual names in alphabetical order fill the guest list. As I scroll through, another one appears and then another.

I thumb a message to Peggy.

> Peggy, what did you do? How did you get all these people to buy tickets?

Then, realizing I'm going to need to set up some more tables at the house, I leap to my feet and hurry to the pay counter of Ace Hardware. While I wait in line, I watch groups of teenage girls leaving Buttons and Beaus with bags of merchandise. Some have their mothers with them; some are alone. My phone buzzes.

It's from Peggy.

> Don't look at me. It's all that mushy stuff you posted on the Gingerbread Festival page. That's where I saw it.

I knew when I posted my article to the Gingerbread Festival page, along with a nostalgic slideshow from Bea's collection, that anyone who'd been to the festival would get an update sent to their email. But I didn't expect people to actually look at it.

A quick glance at my social media post reveals that this is likely where most of my new ticket sales came from. There are five hundred likes on the slideshow set to music, and scrolling through the comments, I tear up at the memories people have posted. Several comments say they're so glad the ball has been updated to be a family event, and not just for grown-ups.

"Cashier number three's open," says an Ace employee trying to get my attention and pointing.

I jump forward, apologizing for holding up the line. As I pay for this last box of lights, a new thought dawns on me: How many of these ticket sales are for kids?

We're going to need to put together a kids' room.

Reagan answers her phone on the third ring and yells over the sound of a crowd. "Well, that took you long enough!"

For a second I'm confused. Does she think I'm someone else? "Reagan, its AJ Banner."

"Yeah, I know, you're calling about the New Year's dance, right? You want me to help put together something for the kids?"

"Do you want to?"

"Not by myself, I don't. There's got to be some kind of rotation so no one has to spend the night babysitting. I want to enjoy the ball, too. Scott and I are due for a romantic evening out."

"Of course, yes! You don't need to worry about that. My family and I will take care of everything the night of. It's just the preparation that could use your brilliant ideas. We were thinking a mini movie theater kind of thing in the front parlor with a projector and popcorn and—"

"AJ, I can't hear you very well. We're at the zoo lights. I'll call you tomorrow, okay?"

"Right. Of course. Thanks, Reagan—"

She's already hung up.

Sitting in my car, the nervous excitement buzzes through my body from my toes to my fingertips. This is happening. I consider going back to the Morley Mansion to set up tables and chairs, but I know that will go much faster tomorrow with my family's help, so the best thing I can do tonight is go back to my parents' house and plan the details. We're going to need music and something for every age group.

The next two days are a whirlwind of dance preparations and paint fumes. I don't see Sky except in passing, and I can only pray that his part of this crazy plan is coming together as well as mine, because if the house fails inspection tomorrow, it will all be for nothing. On Friday, the reality that I'm gambling not just my time and money on the hope that the house will pass inspection but so many others' as well makes me sick to my stomach.

Tara finds me breathing into a paper bag on the back deck behind the ballroom and talks me down with soothing back rubs that she's perfected as a mother. "The worst that could happen is the inspection fails and we cancel the party."

"But all these people bought tickets, and if we refund them, we won't have enough to pay for the materials for the renovation. And who knows how much Peggy has spent on food?"

"Okay, so we move the party to Mom and Dad's house."

I groan into my hands. There's no way we'll be able to fit nearly two hundred people into my parents' house! The guest list has been growing every day.

"Or, you know what," Tara says, pulling out her phone, "I bet we could use one of the local churches as a backup venue. Let me call around and see what I can find."

While she does that, I pull myself together. Worst-case scenario: the whole house catches on fire and everyone dies. Skylar's dark method does the trick. Calling the whole thing off doesn't sound as bad as that. So I get back to work, helping Brett set up his music equipment and adjusting table centerpieces.

On the way home that night, Tara fills me in on what she was able to find as an emergency backup venue. The Roanoke Community of Grace Church will let us use their gym, as long as they can approve our music selection ahead of time. The only problem is that they've got an event there all day Saturday, so we would only have about an hour to set up for the dance if we need to move it there. I'm grateful to have a backup plan, but only an hour of setup time would mean ditching most of our decorations in favor of a minimalistic ambience. I doubt we'd be able to get the kids' theater room arranged in time. And with the all-day event at the church, I won't get a chance to assess the layout to come up with an alternative plan until right before we open.

"Hasn't this whole thing been a last-minute miracle to begin with?" Tara says.

She has a point. "Yeah... I'm sure we could pull off something nice." I try to sound more optimistic than I feel.

For the rest of the drive home, I try to reframe the situation, temper my expectations. So, what if we need to have a humbler gathering at a local church instead? *It would be fitting for the season*, I tell myself. Like Mary and Joseph finding a place in the stable instead of the crowded inn. Maybe it would bring the community closer together. Maybe we would all learn that we don't need a fancy party; we just need each other.

But as hard as I try to be the better person, to fill my mind with warm, fuzzy images of my friends and neighbors embracing the chaos with laughter and comradery, I can't stop imagining a night spent wrangling bored children while their parents, dressed to the nines, awkwardly look for a place to set their drinks and plates of food in an empty gym while music plays, wondering why they paid twenty-five dollars per ticket for this experience.

I shake the image from my mind with a shutter. There's no need to worry about it now. Tomorrow morning, the inspection on the Morley Mansion is scheduled to happen. By noon, we'll know if the dance is happening there or if we need to move everything out. I'll worry about it then.

We pull up to the curb of my parents' house. The front door flings open, and several of the kids fly down the porch steps to meet us with a big mint-green box wrapped with a tulle bow.

"A lady brought this for AJ!" several of them cry at once.

I take the box. It's about the size of a box of donuts but feels heavier.

"What's in it? What's in it?" Lincoln wants to know.

Tara claps her hands to hurry the kids along. "Let's let her open it in the house! It's freezing out here."

The kids gather around me eagerly when I settle onto the living room couch and open the box. Inside, I find a handwritten card on top of a layer of white crepe paper with silver flecks. In swoopy letters it reads:

Business has been booming, thanks to your dance! I'm all cleaned out on gowns, but I saved this one for you. Thought I saw you eyeing it when you came in the other day. Let me know if it fits!   —Sharla Marie

I pull away the crepe paper and smile at the sight of sparkling ice-blue fabric. I've been so busy with preparations, I never even thought about what I was going to wear to the dance.

"What is it?" Violet goes up on her knees for a better look.

I pull the gown from its box and hold it up for everyone to see.

"Ooooh," the little girls sigh at the same time Conner says, "That's it? An old dress?"

Milo's confused grimace makes me laugh.

"Go try it on!" Tara cheers.

On closer inspection, the evening gown is vintage-inspired but can't be a true vintage piece. There's too little wear on the satin-like fabric, and the sparkles in the sheer overlay have the luster of a newer garment. The gown slides over my skin like water, falling into place as if it were made for me. The plunging neckline pulls into a blouson waist with a crystal-encrusted embellishment that makes the fabric hug my curves in just the right places before falling in a flattering line to the floor. It was made for someone taller than I am, but if I wear heels, I think it will work. I raise my arms and smile at the way the sheer butterfly sleeves shimmer under the bathroom vanity lights. The pale blue brings out the red in my chestnut-brown hair.

It's a very different dress from the one I wore to my first Snow Ball, but the color and sparkle throw me back. For a moment, I feel like I'm fourteen years old again with butterflies in my stomach and glitter in my hair, brimming with hope that Benson Miller will ask me to dance. Only this time, it isn't Benson's face that comes to my mind.

I see a teenage Sky taking me into his arms with his warm smile and his spiked hair, leaving a fold-up metal chair behind us as he twirls me away.

For the first time, I realize something. If I'd gotten the dance I'd wanted from Benson all those years ago, I never would have danced with Sky.

Stop trying to fix something that was never meant to be fixed.

There in the bathroom, wearing that sparkly formal gown, I dig my phone out of the pocket of my jeans on the floor and call Benson Miller.

The next morning, Sky is at the Morley Mansion with Bea during the inspection, but I'm at Reagan Keys's helping stuff little white-and-red-striped paper bags with popcorn that I pray we'll get the chance to serve tonight to the kids in the parlor-turned-theater room.

There are four of us standing around the kitchen preparing various goodies for the kids. Reagan pops more popcorn both at the stove and with a popcorn machine, while her daughters Prue and Beatrice organize jumbo bags of candies and bowls for the concessions bar.

"Any word yet?" Reagan asks.

I shake my head no. I've been checking my phone every five minutes since twelve o'clock. The inspection started at ten. It's almost one thirty now.

"Maybe no news is good news?" Prue says with a hopeful shrug.

Sky wouldn't keep me waiting like that. He knows I'm biting my fingernails to nothing until I hear the results. Whether the news is good or bad, he'd text me the minute he knows.

Wouldn't he?

"I wish we had parties like this when *I* was a kid," Beatrice says. She's sitting cross-legged on the kitchen floor, pouring M&M's into a tall glass jar that looks like something out of Willy Wonka's chocolate factory.

"You would have spent them just wishing you were old enough to go to the dance with the adults anyway," says Reagan. "That's always how I felt."

Prue flips her long straight hair over her shoulder. "I'm glad we get to go to the dance. I think it will be better than school dances, since it's not just a bunch of teenagers being stupid."

Beatrice sighs dreamily. "I wish we could have gotten dates."

Reagan meets my eyes and rolls hers before scooting her glasses up the bridge of her nose. "Thank heaven for last-minute dances. The last thing we need to worry about at the end of this year is boys."

Right on cue, my phone rings. I nearly drop a full bag of popcorn in my haste to answer it. "Hey, Sky," I say into my shoulder, where my phone is wedged under my cheek as I use both hands to catch the popcorn bag sideways before it hits the floor. Only a few puffed kernels fall out.

"Hey."

His voice sounds disappointed, hesitant.

I straighten, set the popcorn bag on the counter, and press my phone to my ear as I step out of the kitchen for some privacy. "Tell me," I say solemnly.

He sighs. "So, the inspector didn't like the look of the roof on the north side. Said it needs to be replaced."

My shoulders drop. I exhale in a slow burst. "The roof."

"There were some other things, too. The side porch is rotting. Fire escape needs an upgrade. Things like that."

I nod with resignation, though he can't see me. If I leave now and rent a moving van, maybe we can move everything from the Morley Mansion into that and just park the van outside the church so it's all ready to go the moment we're cleared to start setting up there. Maybe we can pull off another miracle...

I'm so busy running through a party-transfer drill in my head, I almost don't catch Sky's next words, spoken through a heavy exhale.

"So, the Roanoke Neighborhood Network will have their work cut out for them after they sign the sales agreement tonight."

My thoughts screech to a halt amid packing imaginary string lights into an imaginary box. "Wait, what?"

"Oh, didn't you hear? The RNN's gonna buy the place to use as a new community center. Imagine that." He's trying not to laugh. I can hear it in his voice.

"Sky." I clutch my phone with both hands to keep them from shaking. "Are you messing with me? How can you tease me at a time like this? I'm losing my mind over here!"

He chuckles, and I'm teetering between relaxing and throwing my phone with frustration. "They made the deal yesterday, but Donna wanted to know what they'd be getting themselves into first, so she came by today and asked the guy for a more thorough buyer's inspection."

My whole body trembles. "But the roof—the fire escape—"

"Yeah, all that still needs to be done. The inspector wrote out a whole list of things the house needs to be in better shape. But it passed!"

"It passed?"

"It passed, AJ!"

I scream. "Sky, oh my gosh! We did it!"

"We did it!"

Shouting with joy, I bounce into the kitchen, waving my phone over my head like a war banner. "It passed! It passed! We did it!"

Prue and Beatrice both punch the air. Reagan does the best mom victory dance I've ever seen, and I throw a handful of popcorn into the air, cheering as it falls around us like confetti.

26

The New Year's Ball

"**C**LOSE YOUR EYES," TIFFANY warns before dousing me with a cloud of hairspray.

I cough. "You have got to warn me sooner!"

We're in one of the upstairs bedrooms of the Morley Mansion, stepping over our own clothes in our haste to get ready for the ball as guests arrive downstairs. Tara and my mom got ready first so they could be down there taking tickets and showing the twelve-and-unders to the movie theater room. Tiffany and I were putting up finishing touches until the last minute, so now we're in a mad dash to get ourselves and her kids ready.

"I can't find my shoes," one of them whines.

"They're in the duffle bag," Tiffany repeats for what must be the fifth time in ten minutes. "Everything is in the duffle bag!" Then she leans over the vanity beside me to apply her lipstick while I do my mascara. "So, no Benson, after all?" she asks through puckered lips.

I twist the cap back on my mascara tube. "No Benson."

"Is he still coming?"

I shrug. "I wouldn't blame him if he asks for a refund."

Actually, Benson was really nice about it when I called to tell him the date was off. He said he was on call this weekend anyway, so it was probably for the best. Part of me wondered if he ever would have told me that if I hadn't called. What would have happened if I'd been counting on him for a ride and he'd gotten called in to work? But I didn't dwell on it for long. Mostly, I'm just relieved I won't have to worry about managing a date tonight.

"Eli, help your brother with his shoes, will you?" Tiffany gives herself a final once-over. "Okay, time to knock Brett's socks off." She winks at me in the mirror before going to usher her kids out of the room. Before disappearing herself, she sticks her head back into the room. "You look hot, AJ Banner! Sky's gonna poop his pants when he sees you in that dress."

And then she's gone.

I stare at my reflection. The dress really does look incredible. With my hair pulled up into a loose curly updo that leaves a few soft locks falling around my face, I feel like I'm ready for the red carpet. Tiffany always was good with hair. I don't have any jewelry, but the sparkles on my gown spit more than enough fire to make up for that. I shift from side to side and watch the way the glittering pinstripes on the sheer fabric catch the light.

As much as I try not to think about it, I hope Sky does stop for a second look at me tonight.

I haven't seen him since yesterday, and we haven't really had a chance to talk since three days ago. Even though I know I'm leaving the day after tomorrow and he's staying here, there's nothing I want more than to spend this my last night in Roanoke with my friend.

I unplug Tiffany's hair iron before slipping on some strappy heels I borrowed from my mom. They don't really go with this dress, but the sheer overlay fabric is long enough to hide them. At least they'll keep me from tripping over the dress all night.

As I make my way down the stairs, the entryway is already crowded with people. I scan the crowd for Sky.

My heart leaps at the sight of him standing near the entrance to the ballroom and looking like he's been waiting for me. Our eyes meet. His run from my head to my feet and back up again with a look of wonder that makes me feel like I'm floating on a warm cloud. He mouths the word *Wow*.

I play bashful with an *Oh, go on kind* of wave, but the heat of a real blush floods my face as I continue down the stairs. Has he seen the snow machine yet? Does he recognize that it's his? There are so many things I want to say to him, all jumbling eagerly over one another in my head the closer I get to him.

I've barely left the staircase when someone steps in front of Sky, blocking him from my view. I try to squeeze through the crowd to him when someone takes my arm to stop me.

"AJ, sweetheart, that gown looks gorgeous on you!"

Sharla Marie looks like she's stepped straight out of a 1940s musical in a truly vintage gold wrap dress with impressive shoulder pads and narrow hips. Her hair swooped into a dramatic victory roll, her lipstick bright red, and her large, jingling earrings resemble something from the black-and-white Cleopatra movie. She clasps my hand and spins me around to see me from every angle.

"Thank you *so much*, Sharla Marie," I gush. "I honestly didn't even think about what I was going to wear tonight. You are a lifesaver. I promise to return this to you without any food stains on it."

I glance quickly back at Sky in time to see him get pulled away by the person who'd stepped in front of him. Someone wanting to see his handiwork on the restored part of the house, no doubt.

"Don't you dare," Sharla Marie is saying. "This is a gift. My thanks for giving my business a much-needed boost. I've never seen the boutique as busy as it's been the last couple of days. Collecting formal wear is a bit of an obsession of mine, even though it doesn't usually sell well.

Young girls usually want the experience of driving to the nearest mall to pick out something new. But the short notice of this event really worked in my favor. There's hardly anything left in my stash."

"Does that make you sad? Since you've been collecting them all this time?"

She chuckles. "It's bittersweet. Sad to see so many old friends go at once, but they weren't made to be left hanging in some old batty shopkeeper's storage. They were made to be worn. And now I get to see them all at once in their full glory." She sweeps her arm around the entryway, where several of her treasured gowns adorn teenage girls and older women alike. Still holding my hand, Sharla Marie gives it a final squeeze before releasing me. "It's the best gift you could have given me. And now I have plenty of space to collect more. But don't let me keep you. I'm sure there are many people who want a chance to talk to you tonight."

I thank Sharla Marie once more before continuing to the ballroom.

Fake snow drifts from the arch over the entrance from the snow machine Sky built all those years ago. As I cross the threshold, the sight of the ballroom fully decorated and filled with guests in suits and gowns makes my breath catch for a moment. Luke's kaleidoscopic projection map is more stunning than I could have imagined. Bea's photographs glow in soft, whimsical projections along the floor and walls, with fragments of the images dancing across the room in shimmering prisms of multicolored light. The effect is dreamy and nostalgic and magical. As I move through the room, the images change, so it feels as though I'm moving through time. One moment it's sepia faces and the next it's pastel picnics on the lawn in summertime. I'm not the only one twirling in wonder to take it all in. All around me, I hear the exclamations of awe as faces are recognized in the images. To my right, a woman grabs her date's arm and gasps, pointing at an image that is out of my range of sight. "That's my grandma and grandpa's wedding!"

Reagan Keys rushes to my side in a strappy sheath dress that looks like one she might have worn to her high school prom in the late nineties, dragging her husband Scott behind her. She releases his hand to grasp my shoulders and blink with disbelief into my face behind her large spectacles. "What is this *magic*? How in the world did you pull this off? Look at this!" She practically shoves me away in her excitement as she throws her arms out wide. Fragments of old photographs dance along her skin in shards of soft multicolored light.

A giddy laugh escapes my chest. "Luke did it! My brother is a genius."

"Genius," Reagan agrees, wide-eyed. She points at me as she backs away, pulling her husband with her. "Genius."

At every corner of the room, tables overflowing with a bounty of Peggy's confections, pastries, and savory delights create a natural flow of bodies as guests move around the perimeter to try a little of everything. It's just as I hoped it would be. As the guests move from one table to the next, they discover each other and socializing happens naturally. Making my way around the room, no one appears to be standing awkwardly with nothing to do. Even so, it's time to officially begin the evening.

I crane my neck for any hint of Sky as I make my way to the stage beside Brett's music setup. Unlike at the Gingerbread Festival, tonight Brett's equipment is on full display for the adults and teens who will appreciate it.

Brett offers me a microphone and leans in to hear my question.

"Have you seen Skylar anywhere?"

He shakes his head, frowning thoughtfully as he scans the room. "Nope."

The stage isn't much higher than a foot, but it still gives me a decent view of the ballroom. Sky's sandy waves don't appear to be present. I flick on the microphone, smooth down my dress, and clear my throat. Brett eases down the volume of the music.

"Good evening, Roanoke." My voice fills the room from Brett's speakers. "Thank you so much for coming out tonight to celebrate the end of this year and the beginning of a brand-new 2017!"

As applause fill my ears, Sky steps through the snowy entrance on the opposite end of the ballroom. He shakes the white specks from his hair like a dog and catches my eye with a grin. Pointing at the machine, he mouths what looks like *You found it!*

I shrug, smiling. The sight of him fills me. I am complete, and the joy of our achievement makes me stand taller. It pulses through my veins, radiates off my skin, and spills from my mouth into the microphone in a laugh. The rest of my welcome speech is a blur of excited energy. I thank all the volunteers who have worked tirelessly to make this night possible. The applause for Peggy's contribution is especially exuberant. But for me, the highlight is when I get to announce the crowning achievement of this season.

"We are thrilled, humbled, inspired, and just...all-around ecstatic to announce that your generosity and support have paid off. This beautiful historic gingerbread house officially passed its inspection this morning and will continue to serve our community for years to come!"

Donna Shipley moves to the stage as I speak, as if recognizing that this is her cue. She holds out her hand to me, and I help her step up. When she takes the microphone, it feels like I'm passing the baton of this crazy, hectic, last-moment project into her capable hands. She must feel it, too, because she gives me a quick hug and presses her mouth close to my ear. "You've done very well, AJ Banner. Very well."

I nod my thanks, then step down.

Donna's voice booms behind me as I make my way to the other side of the ballroom, announcing that the Roanoke Neighborhood Network will be signing the paperwork tonight to purchase this land and this house to be Roanoke's first ever community center. I hear the announcement, feel the rumble of the applause, but my sight is fixed on Sky. I squeeze through congratulations and pats on the back with murmured thanks to each one without taking my eyes from his. And then I hear his name spoken through the speakers.

"Skylar Townsend has agreed to take on the monumental task of continuing to oversee renovations on this project, to bring this beautiful building up to code, and to make it fully wheelchair accessible."

Sky glances at Donna, breaking our gaze. It's only for a moment—long enough for him to nod his assent to her—but in that moment, my steps falter. I may have passed my baton and stepped down from this project, but he has not. It isn't a shocking realization by any stretch, and yet I wasn't prepared for how it would make me feel.

Sky's eyes return to mine. I manage to smile for him, because I am proud, even if it's another reason why he must stay here when I must leave.

I press forward, but I'm too late. The announcement of Sky's new role as foreman of construction of the community center draws the attention of every Bill, Todd, and Chad in the neighborhood who wants to get a foot in the door of that project. No sooner does Sky's gaze return to me, then some guy grips his hand and wants to introduce him to someone else.

This doesn't stop me from trying to reach him, but a hand on my shoulder does.

I look up into the face of Mike. "AJ, how long does Tara need to be playing babysitter?"

"Oh, uh"—I check my watch—"I'll relieve her right now."

By the time I make it to the ballroom entrance, Sky is gone and the fake snow has run out. The snow machine whirs uselessly overhead. I pull a chair from along the wall and stand on it to turn the machine off before using a broom I stashed behind the sheer curtains along the wall to sweep up the fallen fake snow. I never decided whether or not to keep sweeping and refilling the machine all night to keep the snow falling. I consider just letting it be done, but through the doorway, I can see that guests are still arriving. So I climb back onto the chair, empty my dustpan of snowflakes back into the machine, and flip it on again before going to relieve my mom and Tara.

For the next hour, I'm on kid duty with Tiffany in the sitting parlor. The room works well for this purpose, because it's located to the right of the entryway, so parents can drop their kids off first thing when they arrive and check in on them throughout the night if they wish, and we can close the large double pocket doors to make it a separate space from the ball. All the antique furniture has been removed and stored in an upstairs bedroom so that we don't have to worry about it getting damaged. As a result, the parlor feels more spacious and open. Along the left wall stands the popcorn bar on a long table, with paper bags filled with popcorn, and bowls and jars of sweet and savory toppings for kids to experiment with. On the far back wall, a large white sheet is held taught with bungee cords to make it serve as a large screen while Disney's *Zootopia* plays from the projector Luke got for Christmas.

The image is impressively crisp. His wife definitely did her homework on that purchase. A few borrowed bean bags are the coveted spots just in front of the screen, while a few rows of fold-up rental chairs behind them don't stay empty for long between kids going back for more popcorn and pigs in a blanket.

For the kids who aren't into the movie, there are little tables set up on the opposite side of the room with games, and a corn hole setup we found in the RNN storage unit from past autumn festivities.

When Reagan and Breana come to relieve me and Tiffany, I'm determined to find Sky. It's ten p.m. and I want to get my dance with him before midnight.

But I've hardly stepped into the ballroom before I hear the useless whir of the snow machine overhead, all out of flakes. My eyes scan the dance floor in search of Sky as I sweep, but he's nowhere to be found.

A voice speaks up behind me. "I think I owe you a dance."

For a split second, a thrill rises in my stomach. I whirl around, but it isn't Sky standing behind me. It's Benson, dressed in a crisp tux and carrying two drinks in his hands.

He must see the disappointment on my face, because his smile turns penitent, almost pained.

I recover quickly. "You made it!"

"Yeah, one of the other residents offered to take my place." His eyes dart to something behind me, then back to my face.

There's an awkward moment when he notices me noticing the drinks in his hands, while my own are occupied with a broom and a dustpan full of fake snow. But before either of us has a chance to speak, a woman in a silky red dress passes me from behind and takes Benson's arm. "There you are," she says. "You blended in with these picture light things."

Benson hands her one of the drinks he's been holding as he waves the other in my direction. "Jess, this is AJ Banner, one of my old friends from back in the day. She organized this thing." Then to me, "AJ, this is Jessica. She's uh, a nurse at Doernbecher."

As Jessica and I exchange awkward greetings, I'm surprisingly relieved to see her. She's pretty, with wavy strawberry-blond hair, and the way she looks at Benson reminds me of the way I used to see him when I was thirteen.

Benson's next words pull me from my thoughts. "Jess, I kind of owe AJ a dance. Is that...?"

"Oh no," I say quickly. "Really."

"Are you sure?" he asks.

"Positive. I mean," I indicate the broom and dustpan, "I've got my hands full. You two go on and have fun. Enjoy your night off!"

They both look relieved, but Benson hesitates. "Do you need some help, or...?"

"Nope. I've got it. Happy New Year!"

Benson raises his drink to that. "Happy New Year!" He gives me an appreciative nod before sliding his free hand to the small of Jessica's back and leading her away into the crowd.

As I watch them go, I feel at peace. Maybe I could have gotten that dance I wanted so long ago, but it feels good to realize that I don't need it anymore. That chapter of my life has finally come to a close.

There's only one person I want to dance with tonight. If I ever find him.

After refilling the snow machine, I catch sight of Peggy refilling food trays in the corner, wearing an apron over her fancy cocktail dress, and I rush to take a tray of crackers from her hands.

"My turn," I command. "You go dance with your husband. I'll take it from here."

Peggy doesn't argue. She slips her apron over her head and hands it to me with a grateful smile. "Everything is ready to go. It's just a matter of keeping the tables stocked."

As I bustle for the next hour, I catch glimpses of Sky every now and then. Once, he actually excuses himself from someone who wants to talk to him and starts heading my way, but one of the projectors shuts off, leaving a corner of the room dark. With a frustrated sigh, I hold up a finger to Sky and mouth, *One second!*

By the time I make it to the dark corner, Luke is already there, fiddling with the projector. "Old piece of crap," he mutters as he manipulates the cord. For his projection map to work, we had to borrow a lot of projectors from people in town who owned them. This one is an older one my parents had from before the days when Luke told them what to buy. Light flickers from the machine every time the cord is held at just the right angle. Luke glances at me. "AJ, there's some electrical tape upstairs in my bag in the changing room."

"I'm on it."

Luke's messenger bag isn't hard to find. It's the nicest one. Rather than rummage through it and risk bringing back the wrong thing, I just take the whole bag with me.

My brother manages to fix the connection easily enough with the electrical tape, but now I've lost sight of Sky again, and the chocolate fountain table is in desperate need of restocking.

By eleven thirty, my feet ache from running around in these strappy heels. I still haven't had a chance to talk with Sky, and it's almost time to get ready for the midnight kickoff.

Slam!

To my right, a teenage boy sits in a crumbled heap on top of a collapsed fold-up chair on the floor. His friends are quick to make sure he's okay before they're all laughing. I go to see to the broken chair.

"I'm sorry." The kid retrieves the collapsed chair and hands it to me. "I don't know what happened. It just...fell."

"I'll take care of it." I smile so he knows he's not in trouble.

Rather than mess with it, I make my way out the back door to put the chair in the trailer with the other rentals we haven't used. When I step onto the balcony, something catches my eye in the glow of the white lights along the roofline. Was it a snowflake? I pause in my tracks, waiting to see if it will happen again.

"Mind if I cut in?"

The sound of Sky's voice makes my heart skip a beat. I look over my shoulder and smile at the sight of him standing behind me. He reaches for the chair, and only then do I realize that I was hugging it to my chest. It must have looked like I was out here dancing with it.

I laugh softly as he takes the chair, just like he did all those years ago, and props it against the side of the house. "Thank you, sir," he says to it with a casual salute. Then he turns to me, palm out.

My hand slides easily into his. He spins me once before pulling me into his arms, and we sway to the tune of "Moonlight Serenade" drifting from the open doorway.

Sky's chin rests against my forehead. "You're a difficult woman to track down," he says.

"You're one to talk, Mr. Popular," I murmur back, savoring the warmth of him wrapped around me in the cold night air. I smile at the feel of his chest moving against me as he chuckles. "Congrats on the new job, Foreman."

"Thanks." He sighs. "It's going to be a busy semester. I start classes next week at OSU."

I pull away just enough to look up into his face. "How are you going to manage both?"

He nods at the house with a shrug. "We pulled this off, didn't we?"

"This was nothing short of a Christmas miracle."

"It was also nonstop effort. You worked me like a dog, woman."

His playful grin makes me want to close the distance between us, but I settle for a gentle laugh instead. "I've never seen a dog work as hard as you do."

"You trained me well. I think I can handle eleven credits if I'm only working regular hours. And three of the four classes are remote, so I'll only need to go on campus once a week."

"If anyone can do it, you can."

"And you are beyond ready to knock this probationary period out of the park. *Verité* will wonder where you've been all their lives."

A week ago, I might have shaken my head and said he had no idea how competitive the fashion magazine industry is. But tonight, I take the compliment.

Sky pulls back to see my face. "What's this? No negative comeback?"

Now it's my turn to look back at the house and shrug. "We pulled this off, didn't we? Maybe it's better to dream big than to be practical. We had our share of obstacles with the Gingerbread House, but things worked out. I've decided I like this method better than the one where I fret and try to be realistic."

I wait for Sky to say he's proud of me, or compliment me on how much I've grown. But a glance at his face reveals that he's trying not to laugh through his smile. Was what I said really that cheesy? I pull back. "What?"

"You called it the Gingerbread House again."

"Did I?"

"You did it during your welcome speech tonight, too."

"Stop! I did not!"

"You did!"

I clamp a hand over my mouth, embarrassed. In front of all those people. So much for being an advocate for the Morley Mansion. It must look to everyone like I can't even remember its name!

"It's not a bad thing," Sky says quickly. "It's just cute. In fact, Matilda Hatch liked it so much, she's been trying to convince Donna to make that the official name of the community center. It fits. The address is Nutcracker Circle, the architecture has gingerbread detailing..."

I take in the swirling woodwork along the roofline around the balcony. "The Gingerbread House," I say, trying the name out on my tongue again. It feels right.

"This house has a future because of you, you know." Sky's voice is surprisingly tender. "The rest of us would have given up on it, but you pushed through. That's why I know you've got a real shot at that permanent position with *Verité*. Because you don't give up. It's one of the things I love most about you."

He said "love."

My chest swells and shrinks in quick succession. I'm elated and tortured at once, because I'm so happy for him and so happy for me and so proud of us...but I'm leaving tomorrow, and he's staying here, and there's no way around it, and the thought of being separated from him is more painful than I was prepared for.

But, no, I can't think about that. Not yet. He's here now, and I'm here, and we have this moment, this dance. I rest my cheek against his chest and close my eyes. "You care about people and give everything you can to help them. That's what I love about you."

For a few moments, we sway in silence. I listen to the beat of his heart, feel his warmth.

The music fades into a new song, a lively one that has people jumping and cheering inside, but out on the balcony, the stillness of the surrounding forest and the whisper of wind through the gingerbread detailing softens the effect of the loud music just enough that it falls into the background. Sky doesn't release me. I don't step away.

"I should have asked you to the dance," he murmurs into my hair.

I shake my head, try to tell him there's nothing to apologize for, but he won't hear it.

"No, AJ, I should have asked you. I should have stood by your side after the demolition crew came. I should have kissed you at the Gingerbread Festival and drunk you in every day after."

He pulls back so we're facing each other, and my heart is beating so fast that I don't trust myself to stay practical for much longer if he keeps talking like this.

"I've done a lot of stupid things in my life," Sky says. His eyes burn earnestly into mine. "But one of my greatest regrets is that I didn't make the most of every second we could have spent together. If I let you get on that plane tomorrow without telling you how I feel, I'll be making the biggest mistake of my life."

His face is inches from mine. His breath is warm on my skin. The weight of his strong calloused hands on my arms seems to be the only thing keeping me from floating away like a hot air balloon.

I swallow. "Sky..."

"I want you to go to New York tomorrow." His fingers gently brush the side of my face as he tucks a loose curl behind my ear. I lean into the touch. "I want you to pursue this dream you've worked so hard for. I want to see you succeed and grow in all the ways that fulfill you. I would never take that from you. You deserve it. Gosh, you deserve *everything*." He leans his forehead against mine and cups my face in both his hands as if I'm the most precious and delicate treasure he's ever held.

How can he do this to me? Doesn't he realize how much harder he's making this than it needs to be? Yet I can't bring myself to pull away, because I want this, too. I want to drink in the feel of him and the taste of him for every moment we have left. "I want that for you, too," I breathe.

"I also know that no matter what, I want to be in your life, and I want you in mine."

"But we can't have both."

"Can't we?" He pulls back so our foreheads are no longer touching and turns my face up to his with a gentle finger under my chin. His eyes roam over my face, taking me in with such wonder and affection. "I'll be finished with this community center project in a few months, and I can go to school anywhere."

"You mean a long-distance relationship?"

"Only temporarily. My first semester at OSU will end around the same time as your probationary period. When that happens, I'll come to you in New York. We can celebrate you getting the permanent position, and we can plan our future from there."

I hesitate. Could it work? "What if it ruins us? I like us so much. I don't want anything to change."

"Things are meant to change. We decide how they change for us."

He's right. No matter what, we have to say goodbye tomorrow. But whether or not it's goodbye for good is in our hands.

"We make a good team." His voice is soft. "You were out of my life for six years, and I didn't feel whole again until I sat with you in the diner on your first night home. I don't want to lose you again."

The puzzle piece. He felt it, too.

Looking into his eyes, I see that he really means it. He believes we can make this work, even with an entire continent between us. My fears are still there, whispering it's a risk, telling me it isn't practical, it isn't productive. But the belief in his eyes fills me with a warm, reassuring confidence. So what if it's a risk? There's a risk either way, and there's one thing I know for certain: the risk of losing him is the one I'm not willing to take.

"Yes," I say. Then again, through a smile that threatens to split my face and a giggle that escapes of its own accord, "Yes! Let's do it!"

"You're in?"

I rock onto my tiptoes, closing that obnoxious little gap between us at last in a soft kiss. "I'm all in."

Sky's arms surround me, pulling me into him. We fit together perfectly. He kisses me deeply, making up for all the lost almost kisses and years of distance.

We are meant to be together. We were made for this moment, this kiss.

Whatever happens, I know that Sky and I can face it together. We've beat the odds once and we'll do it again.

Somewhere in the distance, I'm aware of the ballroom full of guests counting down to midnight, but Sky and I don't pull apart. As "Auld Lang Syne" drifts on the chilly breeze to our ears, Sky bends me into a romantic dip.

"Happy New Year." He smiles against my lips.

In the glow of the twinkling lights along the roof, little white flakes begin to fall.

Epilogue
Skylar

January 1, 2017

The schoolroom upstairs feels different from the rest of the Morley Mansion. Less grand, more lived-in. I've never spent much time here until tonight. In the dark, the shapes of old desks and lamps and a globe surround us like ghosts of bygone days. Tall windows open onto a balcony built for stargazing, revealing a few stars still glimmering in the last moments before dawn.

AJ is curled against me on the settee that we pushed in front of the balcony window. Her shoes are on the floor, tipped over each other the way she dropped them, her feet tucked beneath her. She sighs in sleep, and the blanket that covers us both slides down her shoulder, revealing the sheer sleeve of her blue dress.

She smells like apples. Not intense like the fruity perfumes some girls wear, but subtle, grounding, like walking through an orchard on a warm September day after rain. I noticed it the first night when I held her in my truck after Norma's diner, and ever since I've wondered if she might taste like apples, too.

She does. And I want to lose myself in her. To breathe her in and taste her skin and feel the heat of her lips on mine. But I settle for the weight of her head against my chest, rising and falling gently with every breath I take, and let her sleep.

She's been on her feet since dawn yesterday, making sure the New Year's Ball went off without a hitch. And after the last guests finally went home at one in the morning, she didn't take a break. She was determined to get everything taken down before she boards her flight for New York later today. By the time we finished cleaning up, it was almost four in the morning, so we figured we might as well stay and watch the sun rise on our last day together.

A loose curl the color of cinnamon rests against her shoulder. When I stroke it, it coils around my finger as if welcoming my touch.

Outside, a faint glow appears behind the snowcapped trees, but I don't want to wake AJ yet. She looks so peaceful. Holding her like this, I feel like a king, and I'm not ready for it to end. The thought of parting now that we've finally come together makes my chest feel like it's being squeezed in a vise.

But I can't keep her here. I have nothing to offer her.

I marvel at the woman sleeping in my arms. I've admired her for as long as I've known her—the way she dreams big and then doesn't let anything stand in her way. She's more driven than I've ever been, and she's worked hard to get to where she is in life. She's successful. Grown up. Going places.

Me? I'm starting from scratch. No degree. No career. Living with my dad. While AJ has spent the last decade chasing her dreams, building a solid future for herself, tackling her responsibilities with unyielding resolve, I hid away from mine in Ethiopia. I had no real plans.

Until now.

Listening to AJ's gentle breathing, watching the way her lips part slightly with every exhale, feeling the way she trusts me enough to fall asleep in my arms, I know what I want for my future.

It's hard to imagine spending the next three months without her, but the last thing AJ needs on the brink of her success is a deadbeat, freeloading boyfriend riding her coattails. I'm going to need these next three months to become the man she deserves.

I take in the room around us. These walls and I are going to get to know each other very well. I've never been supervisor of such a big project. My meager experience in Ethiopia hardly feels like it qualifies me to take this on, but I'm excited for the challenge. Even the thought of going back to school feels less daunting than it used to. After pulling off this Christmas miracle with AJ, I feel like I can tackle anything if it will make me the man she sees in me.

In a lot of ways, I feel like this old house. AJ saw something in both of us, gave us purpose, a new life. And we're not the only ones who will be better off for AJ's believing in us.

Selling the mansion to the RNN was the best possible outcome for Bea Carston. She'll get to stay in the pool house and serve as custodian of the new community center once it's finished. It'll be steady work for her, respect, and the security she deserves. I don't know yet what the RNN has in mind for this renovation, but I know one thing: this house is going to matter again. AJ made sure of that. She's leaving Roanoke, and Bea, and even me, better than she found us.

The first rays of sunlight spill over the horizon, catching the sparkles on AJ's dress in dazzling multicolored prisms. She scintillates in my arms, and for a moment I think about never waking her. But I promised.

"Hey," I whisper, brushing her temple with a kiss.

Her eyes flutter open, still soft with sleep, and she smiles at me like I'm worth something. "Sorry," she yawns, "I didn't mean to fall asleep."

"You needed it." But now that she's awake, I can't resist another taste of those pillow-soft lips of hers.

She responds with a pleasant sigh that nearly breaks me, leaning into the kiss.

My hands want to explore her. I want to trail kisses down her neck and smell the bite of cinnamon in her orchard skin and see what other sounds she might make. But the sensible part of me finds its way through the steam of my desire, telling me to slow down. Steady wins the race, and this is a race I don't want to lose. When our lips part, I settle for a chaste kiss on her forehead that makes AJ smile before she nestles back against my chest to take in the view of the rising sun.

"You know," she says, "several generations of Morley children used this room as a kind of homeschool. Can't you just see them in their little breeches and aprons, crowding around a telescope to look at the stars from the balcony? I wonder if they ever slept out there to watch the sunrise. I would."

I rest my cheek against the top of her head, loving the way she draws stories and characters from the beams of this old house. "Hmm... I'll ask Bea if they ever did."

Our hands find one another, our fingers weaving together. She strokes my wrist with her thumb, sending a pleasant shiver through me. Together we watch the sunrise crest over the fir trees, gilding the snowcapped limbs in fire. It feels like more than just the dawn of a new day. It's the beginning of something bigger for the two of us.

As if thinking the same thing, AJ raises our intertwined hands and kisses my knuckles. "Good morning, boyfriend."

The word sounds so juvenile. Comical, even. I want to be more than that to her, but I smile and hug her to my side. "Yo, AJ," I say in my best Sylvester Stallone impression, "'I think we make a real sharp couple o' coconuts—I'm dumb, you're shy, whaddaya think, huh?'"

She laughs and pulls back with a puzzled furrow of her brow. "What?"

"From *Rocky*, you know? I thought you were a movie buff."

Her mouth forms an "oh" as understanding dawns. Then she admits, "I've never actually seen that one. But hey, I thought you couldn't sit through a movie! How'd you get through an old one like that?"

"Are you kidding me? *Rocky* is a classic! I can make time for the good ones."

"It's that good, huh?" She settles back against me. "I guess we'll have to add that one to our 'watch-together' list."

"Yeah, that should be a good follow-up to the Bakers of Great Britain."

She giggles. "It's *The Great British Bake Off!*"

I arch away from her as she tries to poke my side, then hug her more tightly so she can't.

We settle back into appreciating the spectacle from the balcony in silence. After a moment, she says, "You're not dumb."

I smile. "And you're not shy. It was just the first boyfriend line I could think of."

"What does that even mean, 'a couple of coconuts?'"

I shrug. "I think he's talking about being two imperfect people who find each other and 'fill each other's gaps.' There's another good line about that somewhere, but I don't wanna spoil it. You're just going to have to watch the movie."

Her thumb strokes my wrist again. "I like how your Sylvester Stallone voice came out again when you said 'fill each other's gaps.' That must be a direct quote."

The tingling sensation on my wrist makes its way like fire up my arm, threatening to drive me mad and clouding my judgement. I hardly think before suggesting, "Maybe that can be our first date when you get back to New York."

Her thumb stops.

The fire eases from my arm, and as my mind clears, I realize I've just brought our inevitable parting into this beautiful moment. I'm scrambling for something to say to undo the damage, but AJ speaks first.

"Like a long-distance movie night?" she asks. She sounds more intrigued than upset.

I relax. "Yeah. Have you ever heard of tandem watching?"

"I have. I'm surprised you have. Do they do that in Ethiopia?"

"Oh, come on, it's a different country, not a different century." I roll my head back in exasperation, but in all honesty, I only learned about "tandem watching" a day ago when I was googling long-distance date ideas.

"I'm sorry!" AJ laughs. "You're just catching me off guard with all these movie references and stuff! I had no idea you were so film-fluent."

"I'm learning."

Bells chime then, startling us both. AJ pats herself before her eyes land on the little purse she left on the floor beside her shoes. She dives for it, and the bells sound louder as she extracts her cell phone. "Sorry, that's my alarm. Gosh, I can't believe it's six already."

"You set your alarm on New Year's Day? It's a holiday, woman!"

She scrunches her nose in an adorable way as her shoulders rise and fall. "I know, kind of uptight, isn't it? But my family leaves today. Tara and Tiffany are probably loading up their cars right now. I really wanted to see them off."

I sit up. "What time are they leaving? Can we still catch them?"

"Yeah, I'm sure they're still dragging kids out of bed. Everyone's probably exhausted from last night."

We both cast one more wistful gaze at our perfect view from the balcony before rising. I fold the blanket while AJ puts her shoes back on with a wince. "I wish Tiff hadn't taken my change of clothes home with her last night," she laments for the dozenth time.

Those shoes look uncomfortable, but I can't look away. The way her dress falls over her figure as she bends to buckle the strap of her heel makes me weak at the knees. I've always thought she was pretty, but right now she's stunning. Elegant, sophisticated, more woman than the spunky girl in high-top sneakers and a red bandanna who took a goat by the horns all those years ago. And yet, knowing that girl is still in there is what makes her even more radiant.

"Don't worry about the furniture," I say when she moves to slide the settee back to where we found it. "It's all going to have to come out anyway for the renovation. I'll take care of it. Let's get you home."

As we make our way through the hall and down the arched stair-case, morning light chases away the shadows of the night before, mak-ing the mansion look more like a charming bed and breakfast than the haunt of ghosts. AJ checks the ballroom one last time to make sure we didn't leave anything, then joins me in the foyer.

Crisp winter air bites our skin when I open the front door for her. "After you."

As AJ passes me, she pauses on the threshold and looks back toward the newly renovated corner of the house.

I follow her gaze, thinking of all the work we've done here together, and all the work waiting for me. It'll take time, sweat, patience. But like the rest of my life, it's ready to be rebuilt.

"Promise me we'll come back here," AJ says, her voice quiet.

I squeeze her hand. "We'll watch the sunrise from the balcony. Together. I promise."

She kisses me—steady, certain, enough to carry me through the months ahead. Then her fingers slip into mine, and we turn to face the dawn.

Together, we cross the threshold and close the door of the Gingerbread House behind us.

Acknowledgements

Dearest reader, thank you for stepping into Roanoke with me. These characters have been trapped in my head for so long, it's an honor to finally share them with you. I've been writing since I was eight, and I've always dreamed of the day when I could share my stories with readers like you in a published book. Thank you for making my dream a reality.

This book would not exist without the love and support and encouragement of so many people. First, I want to thank my parents for encouraging my passion for books and writing, and for providing the kind of loving home where pleasant stories could sprout in my imagination.

To Denise Nuttall, who refused to put up with my six-year-old antics during one-on-one reading lessons and urged me to stop guessing the words and sound them out: thank you for giving me the power of literacy.

To Rachel, Reana, Rebecca, and Risa: thank you for being the best sisters anyone could ask for, and for inspiring my imagination with your own. Thank you, Rachel, for inviting me into your room to hear the stories of *Watership Down*, *The Hobbit*, and *The Chronicles of Narnia*. Thank you, Reana, for teaching me how to keep a compelling journal that reads like a juicy novel. Thank you, Rebecca, for illustrating my earliest novel and making me feel like a legit writer at the age of eight.

To Ryan, my favorite and only brother, thank you for drawing my business logo.

Elise, thank you for being the best friend and critique partner a person could ask for from the time we were children. This book would be a hot mess without you!

Renee, I don't know if I would have kept up with my writing dreams if it weren't for you. Thank you for loving my stories on Fictionpress, despite my clumsy teenage writing, and for being my devoted pen pal all these years. Your book is next!

To my beta readers, Abby, AmyJae, Genevieve, Elise, Rebecca, Sarah, and Patrick: your feedback and enthusiasm are worth piles of gold and rubies and diamonds!

Thank you to Will Tyler for editing this manuscript and making it shine. I've never worked with a more pleasant editor!

And finally, a hugs-and-kisses-filled thank you to Bonnie, my sweet little trooper, for patiently waiting while Mommy worked on her book, and to Patrick, the love of my life, for believing I could do it and encouraging me to keep going. I am blessed beyond measure.

The Gingerbread House
Official Playlist

1. All I Want for Christmas is You - Mariah Carey
2. Swing Swing - The All-American Rejects
3. The Lady in Red - Chris de Burgh
4. The Middle - Jimmy Eat World
5. I Hope You Dance - Lee Ann Womack
6. Mr. Roboto - Styx
7. Silent Night - Franz Deuber String Quartet
8. Christmas Don't Be Late - Alvin & the Chipmunks
9. Jingle Bell Rock - Bobby Helms
10. Nothin' For Christmas - Eartha Kitt
11. Sgt. Pepper's Lonely Hearts Club Band - The Beatles
12. I Want a Hippopotamus for Christmas - Gayla Peevey
13. A Marshmallow World - Dean Martin
14. The Christmas Song - Nat King Cole
15. The Nutcracler Suite - The Brian Setzer Orchestra
16. It's Beginning to Look Like Christmas - Bing Crosby
17. Have Yourself a Merry Little Christmas - Judy Garland
18. Moonlight Serenade - Glen Miller
19. Auld Lang Syne - Ingrid Michaelson

Listen now on Spotify!

R.M. Whitaker grew up in the Pacific Northwest, where her imagination bloomed in blanket forts and pillow palaces as she and her sisters crafted stories to keep themselves entertained on rainy days.

When she's not writing, you'll usually find her gardening, experimenting with sourdough starter and other cultured foods, tackling some DIY project that's way beyond her capability, or wrestling goats on her mom's hobby farm.

She lives in Portland, Oregon with her husband Patrick, daughter Bonnie, a feisty Boston Terrier named Jasper, and an exceptionally long gray tabby cat named Simon.

This is her debut novel.

Connect Online

raileebradshaw.com

@RaileeWrites